DarkSide of the Planet

by
David Lee Jones

Published by Salvatore Publishing
Copyright 2009

ISBN 978-0-9561552-1-4

This Book is dedicated to a circle of extremely talented and creative people I was fortunate enough to meet on MyWritersCircle.com and OnceWritten.com.

I am most grateful for Christopher Silva in Germany. He convinced me to keep writing when I was ready to give up.

Others I cannot leave out:

Dr. Daniel Norris, Guy Cousins, Mary Angus, and all the great folks at Salvatore Publishing.

But most important of all, my family and my kids.

All of you have enriched my life and made this experience one to remember for a lifetime. I hope this resulting volume of short stories reflects my appreciation for all those mentioned above.

BARTENDER GUY

EPISODE ONE

My name is Dave. I am a purveyor of adult beverages in a dive right off of Main Street.

It is all I know but I know it well.

See, I live on the other side of the world to most folks, and I don't mean China. What I mean is my day starts when most respectable people end theirs. I am the one who administers the medicine that keeps you sane and from blowing your bosses head off the next day. Also, the mornings after, I keep most pain pill pharmaceuticals in business.

I serve alcohol.

ALCOHOL.

Life's laxative I like to call it. It helps you slide through this world just a little bit easier.

In my line of work you see the dark soul of life rear its ugly head.

You know that successful neighbor with the beautiful wife who you sit next to in church? Well I see him sitting next to a bar room whore, disappearing every half hour to go snort in the bathroom.

I see the dark underbelly of society. It's the nature of the business.

The crazies love to come out in force and invade my world on a nightly basis.

And instant idiots? Oh just add the alcohol and watch them fizz like a glass of Alka-Seltzer.

On this particular night it was extra gory. It was Halloween. You think you see crazies on a normal night? You get an extra side dish of crazy with your main course of nut jobs on All Hallows Eve.

The room was full of masked insanity exploiting itself in drunken ecstasy when she walked in. It was 11:28pm. I knew because I had just checked the old clock on the wall and last call would be in just over fifteen minutes. The Witch, yeah she paid. The Horny Devil still owed for the last round of shots. I was scanning the room ready to collect final tabs when the front door blew open and almost snapped from its hinges.

Her supple form materialized out of the moonless night as the jukebox performed a perfectly timed pause as if to announce her heavenly entrance. Every soul in the room held their tongues as she gracefully glided into the room.

The men undressed her with lustful eyes and the women gazed upon her jealously.

Time seemed to stop. The pause was deafening in its stillness. It was as if she enjoyed basking in the mixed attention she received as a fang filled smile slowly crossed her face.

She was tall and sleek, dressed in black leather with wings that framed her pale but beautiful face from behind. Jet black hair flowed from her horn topped head undisturbed by the wind from the open doorway. Her leather top strained as her well endowed milky breasts threatened to burst from their garment bondage. Her pale skin was thrown into stark contrast by her crimson stained lips and the shiny black ill-fitting dress.

The heavy smoke in the room seemed to part as if she were Moses parting the Red Sea. Her eyes leisurely scanned the bar until they rested on yours truly.

The juke box's seemingly endless pause ended with the sullen tones of "Witchy Woman" by the Eagles.

How fitting.

The murmur of conversation slowly bled back into the room. Most eyes remained fixed on her as she glided across the floor. Many of the men were broken from their trance by sharp jabs delivered by angry mates.

She stepped up to my bar and tapped one of the old regular drunks on the shoulder who was fittingly dressed as a hobo. He promptly responded by passing out and hitting the floor with a loud thud. She nonchalantly stepped over the unconscious man and slid into his seat, her eyes never dropping their gaze from mine.

"Guess he had too much," I said trying to sound suave. It didn't work. Trying to recover my cool I added, "Let me guess...Bloody Mary?"

"Very good bartender," her angelic voice came to my ears and her mouth broke into a sly half grin, "you read my mind."

Well to make a long story short, and cut out the most mundane and boring details, last call went down with only the usual snags. Call a cab for the Hobo, have the bouncer threaten the Horny Devil to pay his tab and watch the Witch slip out back with the nice church going neighbor. By half past midnight the rest of the bar staff finished mopping up and filtered out of the building until it was just her and I left to our idle conversation.

Inevitably we ended up naked on the bar doing our best to fulfil what a human beings only purpose is: procreation. Or getting some good practice in anyhow.

It was as if heaven sang as we performed our love making dance and I didn't even mind the hard surface of the bar at my back as I finished in an explosion of ecstasy. It was the best sexual experience of my life, and no I'm not a virgin. Not even close.

I lay in a sweaty exhausted heap, trying to catch my breath. She lovingly stroked my hair and smiled as she looked down into my heavy sleepy eyes.

"It's a shame I have to kill you," She said in a soft voice. Being used to dealing with the dark side of human society, and knowing a bit about dark history, I knew that she was dressed as a Sucubus.

"That's right," I said with a tired chuckle, "you are dressed as a Demoness. Once you have mated you must kill your lover. "

She smiled as one would at a child who has just said its first word.

"I dress as I always do," she said as the leathery wings flexed behind her and she lifted her body off of mine in flight. She hovered over me still looking into my eyes.

As I drifted into a deep sleep my last thought was the epiphany of the fact she had never taken off her costume during our love making. Only her dress.

The next morning I awoke to the bewildered face of one of the clean-up crew looking down into mine. He was surprised to find my naked form lying on the bar next to a discarded black leather dress. I groggily sat up and felt the piece of parchment under my right hand. Scrawled in elegant handwriting the message read:

DAVE, I COULD NEVER KILL YOU. YOU ARE TOO VALUABLE TO OUR CAUSE. THANKS FOR THE BABY.

"Not again." I mumbled as I struggled off the bar and my socked feet hit the hard wood floor with a painful thud.

Learning from past experience I knew the gestation and growth rate of the modern demon child. I knew that in about six months my demon spawn offspring would be in here trying to purchase adult alcoholic beverages.

"God I hope that he or she has proper legal ID," I said to myself as I pulled my pants back on.

PARADISE ALPHA

Paradise Alpha was a sprawling complex of buildings that soared high above the 'shoreline' of the Sea of Tranquility, a facility engineered to cater for one concept - the namesake of the very rock it stood above.

Tranquility.

The focus of every employee was to pamper you from the moment you stepped off the cruise shuttle. Soft music floated on the air and beams of constantly changing mood lighting caused the landing port atrium to glow. The atrium was a spectacle to behold after the cramped three hour cruise from Cape Canaveral on Earth. This, unbeknownst to the customers, was deliberate. The cabins on the cruise shuttles were made drab and small to intensify this effect.

The landing atrium was a thick glass dome that rose hundreds of feet above the floor of the Sea of Tranquility. From within you could see the blackness of the moon's atmosphere ribbed with the soft pastel colors of the huge steal bands that held the dome aloft.

Customers were also treated to something else: Zero Gravity. Humans were subjected to gravity when travelling through space by shuttle but once they stepped into the landing atrium they were overwhelmed with the ability to fly. Many customers would linger within the dome too long and then have to pay a penalty for missing their reservations.

The concept of Paradise Alpha was the vision of one man. He was present when the lunar terrain was first levelled to build the landing atrium. Now he sat in the facility's control tower sipping a hot cup of Earl Gray calmly watching a computer screen as one of the huge cruise shuttles slowly made its final approach to the landing zone.

"Cruise shuttle Paradise Four," a red haired woman seated at a control terminal in front of him said, through her INPUT, "you are two degrees and drifting off landing target beacon... please compensate."

He sipped on his tea nonchalantly and activated his INPUT.

"Luna," he called the moon's database, "please display the news pages for Earth and Mars for today."

The supercomputer responded in a soft woman's voice within his head, "Yes Mr. Forest, would you like the Moon News page as well."

"That won't be necessary Luna, "he said dryly, "nothing interesting ever happens on the Moon."

"Very good sir."

"Paradise Four," the controller's voice reached Forest's ears with elevated urgency, "you are still drifting...please compensate."

He turned his attention away from the news pages that hung before his eyes and glanced down at the computer screen.

The Controller turned in her seat and looked up. "Mr. Forest sir," the woman said nervously, "Paradise Four is—"

"I see it Controller Lynn," he responded, irritated, "I have a comp monitor too."

"What do we do?" she asked.

"I don't know," Forest answered, "in fifteen years this has never happened. The system is fully automated."

The huge ship lumbered past the first of several safety markers five miles out.

"Luna," he called through his INPUT, "correct Paradise Four's course."

"Sorry sir," the supercomputer responded, "unable to comply."

"What the Hell is that supposed to mean?"

"Cruise shuttle is not responding," Luna said.

Forest jumped from his seat and looked out the thick glass of the control tower as the shuttle approached from the east. The sun glinted off of the metal hull making it appear as a star hugging the moon's surface on the horizon.

"Sir," Controller Lynn shouted, "I see the problem."

Forest bounded off the platform and stood beside Controller Lynn. He looked down at the monitor and followed her pointing finger. A gaping hole was ripped in the shuttle's skin on left side.

"They've been hit - a meteor perhaps."

A fast moving projectile suddenly appeared on the monitor, streaking a trail of fire. It slammed into the side of the cruise shuttle causing the forward half of the ship to explode in a brilliant fireball that was instantly snuffed out by the vacuum surrounding it. The remains of the shuttle crashed down onto the moons surface, shattering into thousands of pieces and sending up a cloud of dust.

Forest stared silently as shuttle debris floated away from the crash site. "Unless meteors have suddenly become rocket propelled, "he said, "I think your theory is full of shit." He spoke to Luna. "Alert Moon Militia and inform them of the situation."

There was no reply from the Moon's database.

"Luna?" he said urgently through his INPUT.

He turned to his controller. "Lynn, is your INPUT working?"

She fixed him with an anxious gaze. "No, I'm getting nothing."

A warning signal bleeped from the control station and three huge ships slowly descended from the blackness toward the landing zone beacon.

"What in God's name?" Forest said, leaning over his Controller. He zoomed in on the lead ship.

The INPUTS within their heads cracked to life and a holographic head slowly materialized in the room as big as they were tall. The head was bald and devoid of ears. Forest and Lynn exchanged a nervous glance. The eyes on the strange figure opened and fixed on the two humans.

"Good Morning Director." As the 'head' spoke its lips parted in a slight grin. "I am here to take over your facility."

"What are you talking about?" Forest asked indignantly, "what gives you the right?"

Outside the lead ship was setting down at the air dock. The tower rumbled as the enormous vessel settled onto the lunar soil.

"Lock the air dock," Forest ordered.

Lynn quickly pressed the buttons on the control panel. "No response sir, I'm locked out."

The head spoke again. "You see Director, I can take whatever I want."

"We'll see about that." Forest leapt behind his comp screen, pressed a button on the side of the monitor and a holographic keyboard materialized on the glass surface in front of him. He knocked his tea cup off the table and sent it shattering to the floor as he attempted to override the lock out command.

Outside the automated gang plank began to extend towards the huge ship's forward airlock. Director Forest looked out at the cockpit of the vessel that was now level with the control tower. He saw several figures milling on the bridge.

A short staccato warning tone sounded from his monitor and the words "access denied" flashed up on the screen.

He slammed his fist down on the glass desk and looked up into the eyes of the holographic head. "Just who in Hell are you?"

A pause before the head responded. "I am the Devil. I am here to take you to Hell."

Maniacal laughter filled the control room as the pressure within the gang plank equalized and the huge ship airlock door slid open. Black uniformed soldiers began pouring through the atrium doorway below them.

"Give it up Director, there is no escape," the head boasted.

Forest looked over and saw the button marked "zero g" on his holographic keyboard.

"Get out of here Controller Lynn," he yelled.

"What about you?"

"I said GO!"

She shot out of her seat and scurried to the exit door looking back over her shoulder as Forest enabled zero gravity within the dome. The atmosphere changed and instantly the intruders began floating into the air.

Forest smiled to himself, but his revelry was cut short. The intruders were wearing gravity boots which they quickly activated. From his vantage point high above them Forest saw the militia methodically working their away around the atrium taking out his staff.

'At least Lynn got away," he thought as he ran across the control room to the set of lockers on the back wall. He tapped in the code on the first locker and the door slid open. He pulled a TazRifle out of the compartment and pressed the charge button, "They're not going to take me without a fight."

He turned towards the exit as the elevator door slid silently open. There in the elevator Lynn stood motionless staring straight ahead with a blank expression.

"I told you to get out of here…" Forest trailed off. He noticed Lynn's right shoulder covered in blood. Her lifeless body fell forward, and she hit the floor face down.

A figure wearing a dark cloak drifted out of the elevator and stepped over the body. The stranger pulled down the hood of his cloak to reveal a bald earless head. Blood ran down the alien's chin and his lips parted in an evil grin revealing red stained fanged teeth.

"You are the Devil!" Forest shouted levelling his TazRifle at the cloaked stranger. He squeezed the trigger and watched the bolt of blue energy strike the dark figure squarely on the chest. The alien jolted but did not fall. His expression barely changed as his body seemed to soak up the energy.

Director Forest stepped back and bumped into his comp monitor. He stood in disbelief as the stranger strode confidently forward.

"How..d-did…" the Director stuttered.

The dark figure grabbed his TazRifle and threw it to the floor. "That really hurt!" He said through clenched teeth and grabbed the Director's right hand, bending it backwards. A loud snap as the bones in Forest's wrist shattered. Forest fell to his knees and cried out in pain.

"What time is your next shuttle due?" the alien said.

"Go fuck yourself!" the Director spat, grimacing.

The cloaked figure placed his forefinger on the Director's left temple and pushed it effortlessly through the bone. Director Forest screamed in agony. The alien fished around behind the man's eyeball until he found what he was looking for. He squeezed the silver capsule between his fingers and pulled it out of Forest's skull, wiped away the blood and held the object up to the light.

"You bastard!" Forest screamed.

"Stop your whining," the alien said nonchalantly," I just need to borrow it."

Forest suddenly felt nauseous. His eyelids flickered and he slumped into unconsciousness.

The alien glanced at the soldier next to him. "Kaldon, discontinue the database disruption."

"Yes Razel," the man answered.

"You want him?" Razel asked.

Kaldon nodded.

"Then take him." Razel watched the soldier bend over and bite into Forest's neck, drinking in his blood. He held the INPUT he had pulled out of the Directors head and telepathically contacted the moon's database.

"We have three hours to get the men and supplies unloaded before the next cruise shuttle gets here."

Kaldon ceased feeding on the Director's blood, stood up and wiped the crimson trickle from his chin. 'How many passengers?' he asked telepathically.

'Six hundred,' Razel answered.

'The men should be well fed,' Kaldon responded.

Razel nodded. 'I will contact Valden on Earth, and let him know the war has begun.'

NIGHTLY RITUAL

She walked the street unaware of my presence, for I was but a ghost flitting through the darkness that longed to reveal its gloomy secrets from beyond the sodium light of the halogen street lamps. Though I moved silently, I playfully shuffled a stone or perceptively moved a branch every so often to darken her soul with an urgent fear of self preservation.

Her pace quickened and her heart raced. I revelled in the dark images that ran through her panicked mind. Excitedly, I fed on their colorful richness trying to fill the dark void within my black soul. The spark within her spirit awakened something deep within me, something I had lost touch with in a life long forgotten. I desperately grasped at the scarcely remembered sensation but it was too fleeting even for my heightened perceptiveness.

She rounded a corner and I cut through an "L" shaped courtyard, thick with overgrown ivy and prickly weeds. My dark gift afforded me such stealth that I managed to overtake a mangy cat without the creature noticing my approach. As my slender fingers curled around the surprised animal's neck, talon like fingernails ripped into the pungent smelling hide bleeding life away in one swift move, breaking skin and bone simultaneously. An exquisite warm stickiness ran in heavenly rivulets over the cold flesh of my hands and arms, but I could only allow a moment's indulgence for my real prey lay just a few feet beyond on the other side of a rusted iron gate.

I peered around the brick wall and up into the beautifulness I had stalked for weeks. I had come to know every contour of her face, from the sprig of auburn hair that jutted over her wrinkle-free forehead, to the elegant curve of her lovely neck that fell away milky below her slender slightly cleft chin.

My carnivore eyesight saw the artery pulsing beneath the thin soft flesh with the excited pace of her racing heart, and my body tensed as she fumbled with the keys to the heavy wooden door. She longed for the desperate refuge from the fear that was beginning to boil away just under her skin, flushing her cheeks and forehead. Her breath came in heavy, uneven gulps as her frightened fingers refused to locate the appropriate key.

Suddenly the haunting long lost feeling energized my aching soul as I grappled with the incarnate urge to feed on the sweet blood coursing through those tender veins only a foot away from my salivating fangs. Over eons my hunting skills had become keen and this moment of attack culminated in the frenzied need to satiate my never-ending hunger. It would be over in the blink of an eye. The moment came upon me, my muscles coiled ready to spring as the atmosphere electrified with anticipation.

Then, as had happened every night since I began stalking her, the faintly familiar feeling disarmed me. As she passed beyond the threshold, my entire body felt strained and spent. I knew I would collapse in exhaustion. Then I would dexterously climb the tree outside her bedroom window and watch as she slept on the other side of the glass convinced she was free from harm. I would linger dangerously close to dawn endangering my own existence, thirstily drinking in the sights, smells and emotions of her dreams. My soul yearned to understand the alien sensations emanating from her slumbering soul.

The chase continued almost every night for several years and the odd sensation always stayed my hand at the point of attack. When dusk came I risked hunting while the sky was still a blazing flame so that later in the evening my hunger would not impede the sensations I felt from her hapless soul. I felt no remorse or guilt, for I was unable.

As is the nature with my kind, we move through ages and countless generations unchanged and primal, as the human world evolves around us. The mystique slowly seeps from each age leaving us as it's only tenants, moving unnoticed amongst humankind – lonely souls distracted by petty concerns and lofty ambitions. We have faded into folklore and legend and are only remembered through romantic tales.

Thus, the inevitable day came when the chase lost it's fascination to me just as the human world lost its own enchantment with my kind. As I crouched in the alleyway looking up into a face that once awed me with its beauty, I saw years of age had passed unnoticed. The sprig of auburn hair had turned gray and the forehead was no longer soft with glowing skin. My eyes moved over her face with indifference until I focused upon her once smooth neck. The wrinkled skin was transparent and the artery underneath glowed red, triggering the carnal impulse to pounce without inhibition.

Sharp fangs pierced her neck and hot sweet blood funneled into my eagerly gulping mouth. Within that moment our souls connected and our hearts beat as one. Memories came rushing back and in that instant before her heart stopped beating, I realized what the alien sensation that kept me from feeding on her was.

Love.

My fascination for her beauty had given away to love upon seeing her soul. The primeval monster I had become could not fathom this feeling. A single tear slid down my flushed cheek as her warm blood flowed and cooled. Her lifeless eyes stared into mine as the tear slid off my chin and splashed onto her face, her blood within my veins suddenly became as cold as my soul.

That night, the last ember of my human soul was burned out with the fading light within her eyes. Now I have become the beast I was born to be, killing without remorse, or discrimination. I am the monster of fairy tales and the fear within nightmares. I am the dark soul that slides through the shadows unheard and unseen, striking when least expected.

I am vampire.

HOME COMING

It was the evening of my thirty-third birthday. My friends had a picnic planned, but like just about every summer day in the southern US, a storm had built up during the early afternoon and washed out our plans. We decided to meet at a bar just outside of the city near the town we all grew up in. I had not visited for several years and was anxious to see my old buddies, reconnect friendships, and maybe even see an old girlfriend or two. Thankfully my old school had started a NING network on the internet and made this event possible.

My recent divorce had left me lonely and stirred an urge to get back in touch with my old core of friends. The fact my home town was nearly a thousand miles from my current residence was a huge bonus – being so far from my recent torment and loneliness made me feel almost 'human' again. Besides, seeing my old haunts brought back memories of a simpler and much more enjoyable time of my life, free from the pressures of adulthood.

I had plenty of time before the party so, being in a nostalgic state of mind, I decided to take a detour and drive by my childhood home. A storm front moved in bringing with it strong wind gusts and frequent lightning as I left the main road.

The house was situated several miles from the highway, nestling in the hills just above town. As I turned into the old back road, memories of waiting for the morning bus, and flying down the steep incline on my HUFFY, rolled through my mind. Now my car struggled up the hill as the rain began to pour, as if cued by a sudden crack of thunder.

The road twisted as it climbed the hill. Up ahead was a clearing in the trees that afforded a spectacular view of the town and valley below. I can never remember a time that I did not sneak a peak through this natural picture frame to admire nature's graceful portrait. I glanced out as I chugged up the hill and took in the stunning scenery. When my eyes returned to the road, I glimpsed a flash of pink and white in the glare of the headlights. Instinctively I hit the brakes.

There, inches in front of my rental car's bumper, a child of around eight years of age stood drenched to the bone, clutching a tattered brown teddy bear.

I leaned across and opened the passenger door. "Sweetheart," I shouted, "hop in before you catch your death."

The little girl reluctantly got into the car, her wet hair matted to her forehead and across her face.

"What are you doing alone on the side of the road?" I asked, a bit too harshly.

"I w-was walking from m-my grandmother's house," she said through chattering teeth, "just down the hill."

"Where are your parents?" My heart began to ache as her bottom lip pouted outward and tears welled in her eyes. "I'm sorry honey, just tell me where you live and I will get you home safely."

"Just over this hill," she said, wiping a tear from her eye with the long sleeve of her dress, "my house is the brick one with the red mailbox on the right."

I was surprised because the description sounded like my old home. I cranked up the heat to help her dry and shoved the car into drive. The engine strained as we climbed the hill we used to call, "planet's edge" when I was a kid. The harsh incline hid a steep drop on the other side. When riding in my parents' car at night and cresting this hill, it looked as if it dropped off the end of the world and into the blackness of space.

"What's your name sweetheart?"

"Angel." She answered hugging her bear tightly, "Angel Donovan."

We reached the top of the hill and the rain began pounding the hood of the car in giant silvery sheets. The frantic pace of the wipers had little effect on the relentless deluge and beyond the windshield the road was obscured by its opaqueness. A deafening clap of thunder accompanied a brilliant bolt of lightning just as the car started downward on the opposite side of "Planet's Edge."

Within the split second of a camera flash I saw the telephone pole slam onto the pavement just ahead, the pole split by the power of the lightning strike. The impact sent up a shower of blue sparks and I slammed the break pedal with both feet.

My effort was in vain, the asphalt was like ice. The vehicle skidded into the pole and I felt my body flying through the air after the violent impact. I landed amongst a nest of live wires which seemed attracted to the exposed flesh on my arms and legs. They delivered several thousand volts into my body, searing my nervous system with white hot agony.

My mind had come to terms with the concept that this was my dying moment, but all I could think of was the little girl in the pink and white dress. Was she safe? As my body convulsed I held onto my sense of sight as long as I could, searching around me until everything went black.

My eyes fluttered open and the world appeared as a blurry harsh white light.

"I'm in heaven," I mumbled to myself with a sigh.

"Oh my goodness no," an Indian voice said, "but it is a miracle you are alive my friend. Although you are going to be hurting like the dickens for some time to come."

Slowly my eyes focused and a dark-skinned doctor materialized, hovering over my hospital bed. The Doctor flashed a set of white capped teeth. "You must have had your guardian angel with you last night. There are many visitors here to see you but you must not overdo it, so I will send in one or two at a time."

The Doctor exited and my old friend Michael entered the room a moment later. As my mind sharpened my thoughts turned to the little girl.

"Is Angel alright?" I asked Michael urgently before he had a chance to speak.

"Angel?" He replied with a dumbfounded look. "Who is Angel?"

"The little girl who was in the car with me?"

"Dude, you must be delirious," Michael said shaking his head, "there was no one with you."

"Of course there was," I tried to sit up but the pain was excruciating, "she was the little girl who lives in my old house."

"Dude," Michael responded, "your house was abandoned ten years ago after the family living there lost their only daughter. She was hit by a drunk driver just down the hill from the house."

"No," my mind tried to cope with this new information, "that cannot be right."

"I am afraid it is my friend," Michael said sympathetically, "your old house was bulldozed nine years ago. I'm sorry."

The pain returned and the nurse rushed in to administer some more of the nerve numbing agent that was within the saline drip at my bedside. Drug induced sleep quickly and mercifully followed.

The next morning my eyes opened to focus upon a tattered brown bear sitting on the bedside table. The label that hung from a pink ribbon wrapped around its neck simply read:

"From your Guardian Angel."

THE CASTLE

Part One

Angela Dodge was an analytical woman. Her belief system was based
on scientific fact and if the intangible was not readily explained she
dismissed it as fantasy. So when her boss at the Beaufort Herald
asked for volunteers for a new expose, she jumped at the opportunity
when everyone else blanched. The assignment was simple: stay
overnight in the abandoned mansion known as "The Castle," down on
Federal Street, and then write about the experience. Angela had
grown up in the old coastal cotton town and had heard all the stories
throughout her youth. But her mind refused the idea that the place
was haunted.

With a sleeping bag tucked under one arm, and her journal
and flashlight wedged under the other, she stood outside the rusted
iron gates and studied the crumbling façade. The name of the wealthy
doctor who had built the mansion escaped her memory and she made
a mental note to do some research when she got home in the
morning. She knew the house had been used as a hospital by Union
soldiers during the Civil War, and now as she stood before the
looming edifice, she felt as though she had stepped back in time.

Behind a moss covered oak tree, the mansion's columned three-
storey front seemed to radiate history as if possessed by a personality
of its own. Shuttered French windows, dusty from decades of neglect,
overlooked the overgrown courtyard.

The setting sun mottled the front of the Greek-style building
through the branches of the oak and palmetto trees in waning blood-
red light. Despite her skepticism, Angela shuddered as she stepped
onto the cobbled walkway leading into the front yard.

On cue a gust of wind blew from the Beaufort River, across the
mansion grounds into her face as if warning her not to approach.
Angela did not know if the sprouting goose pimples on her skin were
from the wind or the growing fear within the pit of her stomach.

"C'mon Angela," she mumbled to herself, "get yourself together girl. Nothing to fear but fear itself." Her words came to her ears without confidence, doing little to dispel her growing anxiety. She admonished herself for being so jittery, and scanned the dark windows as she reached the wide wooden steps leading up to the porch. On the first step, another chill gust carrying the stink of low tide almost knocked her off her feet. She reached for the wooden rail to steady herself. When she looked up, she thought she spied a little girl looking down on her from the third floor balcony. A second glance revealed no one there.

"I must be spooked." She laughed nervously to herself and ascended the stairs carefully avoiding the rotten planks and holes.

The grand oak door stingily held onto a last few flecks of worn paint. The door opened with a creek on its own accord.

"Must be the wind," Angela said to herself as she crossed the weathered threshold. She cautiously stepped inside "The Castle" and began the only night she would spend in the most haunted house in the Southern United States.

PART 2

Angela entered the dusty grand hall and a sound jingled in her ears, reminding her of her pet cat's collar. She dismissed this as a neighbor's pet hanging out somewhere within the house. The musty smell inside the building overwhelmed her, but she quickly became accustomed to it as she began to explore.

The main hallway led to a set of double stairs that started from opposite sides of the foyer and swept elegantly up to meet one another at the top floor. A grimy chandelier, laden with cobwebs hung from the ceiling, missing several pieces of crystal. Numerous spindles were absent from the stair railings, giving the impression of an upside down grin of broken teeth.

On the landing, two large ornate doors stood ajar revealing the master suite. Angela decided this was the room she would stay in and made her way carefully up the stairs to drop off her belongings. She ascended the steps, and once again heard tinkling bells coming from down below. She shrugged it off and entered the bedroom, laid her sleeping bag on the dusty boards and placed her journal and flashlight on top. Her eyes were drawn to a patch of wall where the stained wallpaper had peeled away. Behind the faded paper, a name was scratched into the stucco.

Lewis Hillard Kelly
50th PA. Regiment, CO. G
1864

Angela scrawled the name in her journal. She decided to explore the grounds for the remaining hour of light before settling in for the night. She went downstairs and wandered outside. At the back of the house, she stood below the kitchen window and stared at the ground where a giant "dead" spot appeared within the bushes and tall grass. She wondered why nothing grew here but her thoughts were interrupted by the jingling of small bells once again.

Another gust of chill wind sent hair flying into her face. Angela pulled a rubber band from her pocket and, while tying her hair back, spied an object reflecting sunlight from the lower branch of a gnarled oak tree near the rivers edge.

She waded through the grass towards the tree, squinting at the sun's low angled rays. Angela made out the silhouette of what appeared to be a pocket watch.

"This is an odd place for you," she said as if it could understand her. She had to stand on her tiptoes to get near the watch but, after three attempts, she got a grip on it. The metal was cold to the touch. She yanked on the timepiece. The chain stubbornly held onto the branch for a few seconds until she finally wrenched it free.

"Must be my lucky day," she said, turning it over in her hands.

Suddenly she heard children's laughter coming from one of the arched entrances to the basement behind her. She shoved the watch into her pocket and headed back to the open entrance.

She poked her head inside. "Hello... anyone there?"

The question was answered by the tinkling of bells. The sound frayed on her nerves - probably an annoying wind chime or something of that nature hanging in the basement. Her only impulse was to silence them.

She entered the basement. A single shaft of red sunlight shone on the far wall entering through a broken window. Angela saw drawings on the wall, written in red and blue crayon. She stepped closer. The pictures appeared to have been made by two different people, judging by varying degrees of talent in the artwork. The red drawings were simple but neat, as if made by the hand of a child. The blue crayon was more haphazard as if the artist had born down too hard and there were several smudges. Angela read four lines that were written within the collage of artwork.

WHAT IS YOUR NAME? Written in the pretty child's handwriting.

GRENAUCHE. Was the roughly scrawled reply in blue. **WHAT IS YOURS?**

EMILY. Was the reply in red, accompanied by a smiley face drawn after the "y."

     Angela smiled as she studied the artwork. At the base of the wall she noticed a small doll half buried in the dirt. She uncovered it and brushed it off. It was roughly stitched - two red buttons for eyes, and faded orange yarn for hair. The tattered dress was a flowered fabric, the size of Angela's palm.

     As she gently sat the doll at the base of the wall she noticed a worn green crayon half buried in the sand. She picked it up and wrote:

MY NAME IS ANGELA. She inserted her own smiley face at the end.

     A chill ran down her spine. The air seemed heavy and an acrid smell came to her nostrils. The temperature plummeted and she swore she felt a presence.

     She turned and hurried for the exit as twilight descended outside. She reached the basement door and heard the bells once again. Angela stopped dead and stared back at the wall, barely visible now in the fading light. The artwork was gone. Goose pimples sprouted upon her skin and she shuddered as she read the new writing in blue and red crayon each adorned with a smiley face of its own.

HELLO ANGELA. NICE TO MEET YOU ANGELA

PART 3

Angela sat on the top step of the front balcony and took deep breaths to calm herself. Her heart raced and fear burned in the pit of her stomach. She wanted to run for the car, but her rational mind quickly doused her anxiety.

"C'mon girl," she said to herself, hugging her arms close to her body, "you always had an overactive imagination. You're grasping at ghost stories. Snap out of it."

She steeled her resolve, and got back to thinking scientifically. She wandered back into the house and retrieved her flashlight – one of those heavy long handled types that policeman used. The light was bright and the torch could double as a weapon if she found herself in danger.

A feeling of dread permeated her soul. The jingling echoed from downstairs and this time she followed the sound. She slowly made her way down the steps, pointing the flashlight at anything that moved.

Angela felt invisible eyes watching her. She reached the bottom of the stairs and flashed the light into the darkness. Movement seemed to swarm all around her, but the beam revealed only dust motes floating on the still air. She felt drawn toward the back of the house and crept into the kitchen. She peered out the window into the night and saw the silhouette of the old oak tree, a glowing green orb hovered beneath the lower branches. A chill ran the length of her spine as she reached inside her jacket pocket and her fingers closed around the metal pocket watch. To her surprise it was hot to the touch, yet she did not feel the warmth through the fabric of her jacket.

Beyond the tree, Angela saw slender tendrils of fog reaching across the lazy Beaufort River. A few wisps seemed to defy the breeze as they coalesced and made their way toward the shore. Angela swore the fog was taking on the shape of a woman as it reached the edge of the grassy yard.

Blood rushed inside her ears, her heart raced as she fled back to the front of the house away from the apparition. The flames of her fear reignited as fragments of memories long forgotten flashed across her minds eye. The sound of a child's scream and the crashing of glass echoed from a far off past. She saw blood snaking in tiny rivulets down the walls and draining into the floorboards.

From the front porch came the sound of heavy footsteps. She flipped off the light and slid behind the heavy oak door, flashlight ready to strike.

A soft knock on the wood, and Angela felt her heart jump. The knob began to turn. The hinges creaked and the door opened. Angela peered out and within the soft light of the moon she spied the back of someone's head poke through the entrance. She acted swiftly, bringing the metal flashlight down upon the head of the intruder. A painful thud and the man fell to the floor, sending the bags he was carrying crashing across the boards.

The man groaned and Angela prepared to strike again. She stopped herself.

"What did you do that for?" The man said sheepishly rolling over onto his back and rubbing his head.

Angela turned on the flashlight and shone the beam directly into the astonished eyes of her boss, Richard Thorn.

For the next twenty minutes, and several apologies from Angela, Thorn unloaded the bags onto the kitchen counter. Within the supplies were two gas powered lanterns that burned, to Angela's relief, with an unfaltering cheery light. She did not mind the eerie dancing shadows the beacons threw upon the walls. She was just thankful for the company.

"I thought you might need some supplies," Thorn said, opening a bottle of water and handing it to her. "However, the assignment is still about spending the night here alone."

"I know, I know," she said letting out a sigh and staring off into the darkness, "this house just gives me the creeps."

"Come on," Thorn said with a chuckle, "this doesn't sound like the fearless headstrong woman I saw back at the office an hour and a half ago."

"Richard I..." She bit her lip and thought about her confident bravado before leaving the office. "You know what Mr. Thorn, you're right."

"I am?"

"Yes," she said gathering her resolve, "tell me about the man who built this house."

"Hmmm, I might have to dock this 'background' research out of your overtime," he said playfully. Upon seeing the serious look on Angela's face, he cleared his throat and continued on like a high school history professor. "The house was commissioned by Dr. Joseph Frickling Johnson in 1859. I understand it took a while to build. Building supplies only made it sporadically through the naval blockade imposed on South Carolina at the time and many of the mantle-pieces and bookcases were borrowed from other wealthy Beaufort home owners. When supplies were available the contractors pushed their workers to the limit. Most of them were slaves of course. There was an urgency to finish the house due to the war. Five workers lost their lives building this place."

"What kind of man was this Dr. Johnson?"

Thorn paused and collected his thoughts. "He was wealthy of course. If you read the literature of the time you'd find Dr. Johnson to be an honest, hard working citizen who's only vice was his love for the extravagant. But wealth could only buy the media of the day, not the people. The house was completed shortly after the death of his wife. But then came the strange disappearance of his slave butler's son and stories began spreading throughout colonial Beaufort."

"How do you know all this?" Angela asked, her voice trembling slightly, "and don't tell me it's your business to know."

His gaze scanned the kitchen ceiling as if looking through to the upper floors. "I wrote a report in my senior year at High School. The librarian at the county library gave me boxes of old letters from the 1860's and 1870's written by members of high society and Confederate soldiers. Mr. Daner, the librarian, had spent a lifetime accumulating these documents. I discovered that the Doctor's wife drowned in the river and local gossip suggested it wasn't an accident."

"What about the butler's son?" Angela asked barely above a whisper.

"Dr. Johnson hung the kid from the old oak in the back yard," Thorn said, nodding at the window, "apparently the boy stole his pocket watch."

A lump choked Angela's throat and an uncomfortable tickle grew within her stomach as she reached into her pocket and pulled out the timepiece.

"You mean like this one?" She held it up and opened the watches lid. Inside was a worn black and white picture of a woman. Thorn stared at the picture. "That's the doctor's wife." He stared at Angela anxiously. "That watch was never found."

"Until now," Angela swallowed the painful lump in her throat.

Angela's boss stayed for a couple of hours and helped her settle in. They found a storage room full of firewood in the main hallway and Thorn stoked up a fire in the large fireplace in the master bedroom. Angela hung close to Richard thankful for the company. She felt as though the darkness wanted to grab her and drag her into frightful oblivion.

"This is your last chance Angela," Richard said, pulling on his parka at the front door, "I can see the effect this house has on you and I won't blame you if you choose to back down from this challenge."

"No sir," she said with a regretful sigh, "I'm determined to endure this with a level head. I have a reputation to protect."

"Very well then," he gave her a friendly hug, "good luck."

He turned to leave, but paused in the doorway. He spun around and handed her a pager. "I know this is against the rules of the challenge, but I want you to have it just in case."

She smiled and kissed his cheek. "I expect to be employee of the month after tonight," she said.

He crossed the porch, smiled and waved before passing through the iron gates, leaving her once again alone with the house.

As she made her way back inside, the vast emptiness of the place bore down on her - over a hundred twenty two years of history. Angela heard the bells tinkle from the basement beneath her. Why now? They had ceased while her boss was here. Now the otherworldly feeling of the place came rushing back to her, as if the house knew she was alone again.

She decided to ignore the bells and go upstairs to write up her journal. Back in the bedroom suite, the warmth of the fire comforted her. She sat upon her sleeping bag, pulled the watch from her pocket and opened the lid. The time was frozen at 1:13. Angela looked at her own watch - 11:22. She tried to move the hands on the pocket watch to the current time but the gears would not budge. Shrugging her shoulders she put the watch down beside her.

An icy hand gripped her heart. She heard someone whispering downstairs. She held her breath and strained to listen. Was that a faint scream?

"Just your mind playing tricks old gal," she said as she picked up her pen and opened her journal to the first page.

BEEP BEEP BEEP.

The pager bleeped in her pocket and she dug it out. She expected a message from her boss but as she read the words on the crystal screen, the hairs on her arms stiffened with fear.

COME PLAY WITH US IN THE BASEMENT

The room filled with jingling bells. The pages of her journal began flipping of their own accord and she saw blue and red crayoned art filling every page. The windows burst open and a gust of wind doused the lanterns and extinguished the fire in the hearth, plunging the room into semi-darkness. Only the moon cast any light. Wisps of smoke hung in the air and the acrid smell of spilt lantern fuel tickled Angela's nostrils and burned her eyes.

She wanted to spring to her feet and run for the doors but they suddenly slammed shut, their heaviness quaked the room and sent a shower of stucco and plaster raining to the floor. For a moment all was quiet. Angela got under the sleeping bag and pulled it up to her chin.

"Let Me OUT!" A male voice filled the air, reverberating through her flesh down to her bones. She saw tracks of crimson staining the inside of the doors, as if someone with bleeding fingers were clawing at the wood. Her ears were filled with a chorus of pleading voices but their words indiscernible. Angela's blood turned to ice and she let out a scream of her own.

The uproar was instantly silenced, as if the voices had fled to the far dark corners of the house, vanquished by her cry. All Angela could hear now was her breath coming in quick uneven staccato beats. The temperature plummeted and she felt a crushing sorrow inside her mind. Her eyes widened as the door knob turned. She tried to shout, but the air was now too cold to breathe.

Oh God. She only managed a soft whimper as a solitary tear rolled down her cheek. Please help me God.

The door creaked open, and the tall figure of a gaunt man dressed in a Union soldier's uniform drifted out of the shadows and

30

through the doorway. Angela's heart fluttered as the soldier marched forward, eyes staring straight ahead. His face was grey, his eyes pale and seemingly unseeing. His booted feet stopped at the foot of Angela's sleeping bag, musket in hand. She pulled the sleeping bag up to her nose, her heart beating loudly in her ears.

The soldier stood like a zombie, no expression upon his face. Angela was paralyzed with fear. She stared in horror, peering over the fabric of her sleeping bag, as the soldier stood guard unwavering. It was an age before he finally moved. With a sudden flash, he leveled his rifle and squeezed off a single shot. The blast was deafening.

Angela let out another scream and felt a warm patch spreading under her sleeping bag as her bladder emptied. She stole a glance at the wall three feet above her head and saw a small smoking hole where the projectile had struck.

The soldier turned on his heel and marched over to the far corner of the room where he sat down on an old dusty chair, the only piece of furniture in the entire house. The soldiers gaze stared right through her.

With every fiber of her being she tried to look away, but her eyes were locked with his and waves of terror began flooding her soul.

"Who the Hell are you?" She asked as desperation finally fueled her to act. For the first time the soldiers expressionless face broke into a warm smile and his apparition slowly faded away to nothingness. Angela wasted no time. She threw off the sleeping bag and tried to jump to her feet but something had suddenly grabbed hold of her leg.

She wanted to scream out again but the overwhelming taste of wood suddenly filled her mouth.

"Bite down on this when the pain gets to be too much," the disembodied words floated to her ears as she felt the pressure of someone tying a tourniquet to her upper thigh. Suddenly a sharp pain began searing away at her upper leg but she could not scream as her teeth were clamped down on an unseen stick of wood.

"Angela," she heard a small voice scream out of the darkness outside of the room, "this way!"

The room once again filled with the sound of the jingling bells as the sensation of the grizzly "operation" fell away. Angela stood up. In the open doorway she saw the pale form of a little girl. Her image glowed pale and shimmered in the moonlight and she beckoned Angela to follow.

Desperation prompted Angela forward, as again the chorus of crying pleas echoed through the room.

"Hurry Angela," the little girl's ghostly voice urged, as her form floated through the balcony rail into the open air and slowly floated downward, "Grehauche can only hold him a few moments longer."

Angela sprinted for the door only to have them slam shut in her face. Blood pooled on the floor and red streaks splattered the walls. Her heart sank as the temperature plunged and the bluish moonlight turned a sickening green. She felt her stomach lurch and she began to dry heave as she darted forward and tried to unsuccessfully turn the door knob. Angela turned and slowly sunk to the floor and looked up into a ghastly floating green face hanging within the center of the room. Tears rolled unchecked down her cheeks and terror filled her soul as the face split into an evil grin.

"Her legs are mine."

Angela sat on the floor, her back uncomfortable against the heavy oak doors. The disembodied head that was the green glowing entity floated agonizingly slowly towards her. As hard as she struggled, she was unable to move her arms and legs. Her heart pounded and the flow of adrenaline ached within the muscles of her extremities.

The ghostly form drew closer and the room seemed to change. First, the air became heavy, possessing a humid stickiness uncomfortable on her skin. Moans and screams came to her ears and, through the open windows, distant cannon fire and muskets cut through the thick atmosphere. Moonlight was replaced by lantern light as Angela's eyes fixed on the silky curtains swaying on the breeze.

The acrid smell of lantern fuel was overwhelmed by a myriad of new fragrances. Mingled with the medicinal odor of chloroform, she smelled gunpowder, sweat and decay. The bitter taste of blood mingled with the sharp chalkiness of dust dancing upon her taste buds.

'Death.' Her mind awkwardly contemplated the word. The room cried, echoed, reeked and tasted of it.

As the entity approached, his body materialized from the ethereal until his imposing form stood over her, solidly human. His eyes moved over her body hungrily taking in every inch within dancing lantern light. Even though she was fully clothed, she had never felt so naked, or vulnerable.

The ghost held up a cattle horn and an evil smile spread across his rough, unshaven face. "Before I have your legs," the sinister voice resonated loud within her ears, "I will have you."

She struggled fruitlessly and confusion set in as he placed the cattle horn over her mouth. Chloroform. Even in her frantic state, her mind latched onto the smell from her ninth grade science class. What were they dissecting? Fear permeated her soul as she realized she was already losing rational thought.

The entity's smile grew broader as he removed his coat and his tongue flicked eagerly across his lips. Angela watched impassively. She was becoming detached from this odd reality. "This is not happening!"

Suddenly from the center of the ghost's chest, a shaft of dark metal ripped through his white blood stained shirt. A crimson spray exploded into the air and seemed to hang motionless, defying gravity and reflecting lantern light to Angela's dimming eyes.

"How beautiful," she observed, as she strained to keep her eyes open.

The ghost's body dropped to the floor. Behind him, framed in the moonlit window, stood the ghost of the Union Soldier Angela had seen earlier. He held his musket before him, the bayonet dripping blood.

"He shall never ravage you again Tillie," The ghost said and slowly faded away in the sudden moonlight. The doctor's body faded away a moment later.

Angela slumped onto the dusty floor. She could not hold off the impending sleep any longer, but before her eyes closed, the beeping sound of the pager afforded her a few more moments of wakefulness.

With her last ounce of strength she placed her hand into her pocket. She struggled to pull the device out and it took all of her might to depress the button and light up the crystal screen.

GOOD NIGHT EMPLOYEE OF THE MONTH.

SWEET DREAMS. RICHARD 1:13AM

She heard something slide across the floorboards. To Angela's astonishment she saw the pocket watch moving towards her on its own volition. It stopped in front of her face and began rocking back and forth and stood itself up on its end. The lid popped opened and, in the moonlight, Angela saw the second hand sweeping past the six.

"It's working again," her mind sluggishly formed the thought. The time read 1:13AM.

The rest of the night she slept on the dusty floor. Several times during the night her eyes fluttered open responding to the sensation of someone stroking her hair. She saw the ghost of the little girl sitting before her. Alongside the girl was another ghost. A dark skinned dwarf dressed in a torn and tattered jester's outfit. She heard the soft jingle of bells and for the first time that day or night, it did not bother her.

The sight of the ghosts did not frighten her for she could feel their intention with the immortal part of her being. They were here to guard and protect her while she slept. Content she was safe; Angela closed her eyes and slept. In the morning she found herself snuggled inside her sleeping bag with only the dying embers of wood in the fireplace to greet her.

She sat up and looked around. The walls were covered with shredded wallpaper, no blood. The bare patch where the soldier's name had been scratched had vanished and so had the bullet hole.

She stretched and began gathering her belongings. Sorrow ached in her soul but her mind could not figure out why. The overall creepiness of the house was replaced by an empty loneliness and she found herself unable to hold back a torrent of tears.

"Was it all just a dream?"

Angela scoured the room for evidence of last nights experience when her eyes fixed on the journal.

"The drawings!"

But when she checked the pages she found they were blank. Already the memories of last night seemed to be slipping away into obscurity. She frantically searched for the one item that would solidify within her mind that the events of last evening had occurred. The watch.

Sadly, it was no where to be found. She packed up her gear and made her way to her car. As she reached the outside of the gate she looked back at the abandoned house behind the ancient moss covered oak. It no longer looked imposingly creepy to her, but seemed stripped of its personality, its identity.

She breathed in a lung full of salty coastal air, got into her car and started the engine. The pager went off as she put the car into gear. She checked the screen.

WAKEY WAKEY, EGGS AND BACY! DO YOU BELIEVE IN GHOSTS NOW? RICHARD. 8:45AM

Angela looked back at the house and asked herself the question over again. 'Do you believe in ghosts?'

BEEP BEEP BEEP. She looked at the pager and received the answer.

WE LOVE YOU ANGELA, COME BACK AND PLAY WITH US AGAIN. EMILY AND GRENAUCHE.

Angela checked her rear-view mirror and, there on the dash underneath the back window, sat the small roughly sewn doll with the red button eyes, and faded orange yarn hair. As she drove away a smile parted her lips as a single solitary tear rolled down her cheek.

CHATTING CAN KILL YA

Connie sat at her computer desk and began the nightly ritual of checking her email. It had been a long day - two hours overtime and her muscles ached like hell. She logged onto MySpace and entered her password. Her mouth watered as she caught the heavenly scent of Italian cuisine wafting from her neighbor's house.

"Mrs. Antonucci must be making her famous spaghetti again," she murmured to herself. A faint smile crossed her face. She knew the doorbell would ring shortly and the old bat would have her talking for hours. Thankfully Mrs. Antonucci hadn't figured out how to use the computer her daughter had bought her for Christmas. There would be no peace for Connie If the old lady learned how to use it. She chuckled at the thought.

Mrs. Antonucci was widowed four years ago when her husband of forty years passed away. Now she spent her time cooking Italian dishes which she distributed throughout the community every evening. Connie was "lucky" enough to be her last stop. Not that she minded. Connie was also alone after her divorce three years ago and she endured the old lady's company, as monotonous as it was. She felt lonely. Besides, she could not cook and Mrs. Antonucci's pasta was to die for.

Three new emails flagged up on the screen and she clicked the link. As she waited for the next page to load she checked her reflection in the window between the slats. Night had fallen, and her desk lamp provided a nice reflection for her to examine her disheveled look. She sighed and glanced back at the screen.

Two of the emails were spam, the first an online "dating" site and the other was giving away free cell phone ring tones.

The third was from her ex-husband.

"Oh God, what excuse does he have for not having the alimony this month?"

She gloomily clicked the link and the page popped up.

Her husband had once been a doctor with a thriving practice on the good side of town, but since the divorce the business had folded through neglect. He had become unpredictable and slightly crazed. Connie had to go through the courts to obtain her alimony payments after two and a half years of not seeing a penny. The past half year he had gotten a nighttime job. She did not know where he was working but things had improved between them until two weeks ago when he began acting strange again.

Connie's eyes scrolled across the screen. "Need two more weeks to get your money, having problems paying my bills."

It came as no surprise. She sighed, and noticed she had a new friend request on the screen. She clicked on the link.

"Anything to get my mind off him," she said, as if a bad taste were in her mouth. She read the new profile as it flashed up on her monitor.

"DoctorD."

"No picture," she murmured, strumming her fingers on the desk, "never a good sign." She clicked on the default image bringing up the profile and noticed the person's hometown was the same as her own. The profile showed this person had only one friend...TOM, everyone's friend.

"Tom's friends," she chuckled, "two hundred million strong and growing." She stared a moment at the "no picture" default image and idly clicked the back button to the friend request page. "Screw it!" she said, and against her better judgement accepted a friend request from someone she did not know. The melodic tone of her 'chat chime' made her jump.

DoctorD: Thank you for accepting my friend request.

'Wow,' she thought, 'it was as if he were waiting on me.'
She responded.

ConnieWAS: Saw you are from my hometown.
DoctorD: Small town people have to stick together, right?

Connie sat back and scratched her chin. She wanted to say something clever but decided to keep it short and simple. She responded with the first question that popped into her head.

ConnieWAS: Are you really a Doctor?

DoctorD: That is what I like to call myself.

"Very elusive," she said to herself, "not a good sign. Probably married." Connie had picked up the habit of talking to herself when she was alone. It helped her feel less isolated from the outside world.

ConnieWAS: You did not really answer my question.

DoctorD: Nor have you answered mine.

She began losing patience.

ConnieWAS: Do I know you?

DoctorD: BRB.

"Great," she sat back in her chair and sighed, "the greatest evolution in communication and I still get put on hold." She waited a moment, picked up a pen and twirled it on her desk. She began to doodle on a piece of paper. "Fuck this!"

She moved her pointer over the chat box and had it poised over the 'close' button when her doorbell rang.

"Mrs. Antonucci to the rescue!" She jumped to her feet and hurried down the hallway to the front door, her empty belly growling with anticipation. Her mouth watered as she turned the knob. She opened the door and the humid night air pushed against the cool air-conditioned foyer catching her in the middle. There was no one at the door.

Puzzled, she checked the front porch and front yard but saw nothing in the darkness beyond. In the distance she heard kids laughing and wrote it off as a childish prank. She closed the door and locked it behind her, went to the kitchen for a glass of water, and a cookie to tie her over until Mrs. Antonucci came calling. Connie sat in front of her TV with every intention of avoiding her computer room, and her new friend DR. D. She was about to turn the television on when curiosity drove her back to her computer desk.

The chat box was still in the foreground but the BRB message DoctorD wrote still hung there. She munched on the cookie and stared blankly at the screen. She grabbed the mouse and was about to close the chat box when the chime almost made her choke on her cookie.

DoctorD: Ah, you are back!

DoctorD: You look very tired tonight.

She swallowed hard. Cookie stuck in her throat and she snatched for her glass of water. Her eyes watered as she thirstily washed down the dough, coughing at the tickling in her throat. Electricity crackled in the air, causing chills to run down her spine.

ConnieWAS: How did you know I was back?

DoctorD: Because there was no one at the door.

Suddenly the temperature seemed to drop and her skin turned to goose flesh, hairs stood erect on her arms and neck. Her heart beat wildly in her chest and she forced herself to calm down.

Her head began to ache with her heightened blood pressure as she typed the next words with thoughtful deliberation.

ConnieWAS: How did you know that?

DoctorD: Because I was at the door.

Connie stared at the words on the screen as the breath momentarily left her lungs. She pounded away on the keyboard the clicking of the keys and the beating of her heart loud in her ears.

ConnieWAS: Are you some psycho?

DoctorD: I will let you be the judge. Why not come next door and discuss it over dinner with me and Mrs. Antonucci.

Connie's eyes shot to the window, and her startled reflection gazed back at her. She jumped to her feet and yanked the cord on the blinds. The blinds came crashing down on her head with a loud bang and tumbled to the floor. She peered through the reflection to the window opposite her yard, reached down and turned off the lamp so she could see. It was Mrs. Antonucci's kitchen in the window beyond. The place she spent most of her days making the delicious Italian dishes she loved so much. The visage that greeted Connie threw all of those good feelings into stark contrast. Framed in the window pane was Mrs. Antonucci's body gently swinging from the ceiling. Blood dripped from one orthopedic shoe and ran over her naked shriveled toes of her other foot.

Connie belted out a scream that filled the room. She bolted for the door, focusing on just one thought. "Call the police!"

She reached the hallway and the doorbell rang. She stopped and hunkered down, ducked into the kitchen and grabbed the phone. No dial tone.

Fear grabbed her with icy fingers and clutched at her heart. Connie heard the window shatter as if it were far off in the distance. Time slowed, and her senses were suddenly razor sharp. She heard every sound, saw the inside of her home in vibrant colors. She even smelled the spaghetti wafting through the damaged window and felt the cold sting of the kitchen knife as the blade drove into her chest and pierced her beating heart. Her eyes focused on her attacker and her fear seeped from her body as her life faded from existence.

At the Coroners Office the young orderly wheeled the two bodies into the examining room.

"Two new ones for ya Doc," the orderly said busily chewing on a piece of gum.

"What do we have Charlie?" The coroner asked, as he rounded his desk.

"Two murder victims," Charlie answered nonchalantly. "Females. One in her early seventies and the other in her mid-thirties."

The examiner unzipped the body bag and studied Mrs. Antonucci's face. "Probably stabbed with a kitchen knife," he said blandly.

"How did you know?" Charlie asked, pausing in mid chew.

The coroner answered with a shrug. "After working here as long as I have you can just tell."

Charlie grabbed a clipboard and began his paperwork as the coroner moved to the next body bag. He unzipped it and stared at Connie's face. The woman's eyes stared lifelessly at the ceiling.

"Funny how easy it becomes after the first kill," he said thoughtfully. "almost as if the killer can't stop at just one."

"Crazy bastard," Charlie exclaimed and momentarily looked away from his clipboard at Connie's lifeless face.

"Shame," the examiner responded, "she was beautiful."

"Hey Doc?" Charlie said placing his clipboard on the desk. He walked over to the other man and put his hand on his shoulder. "You're not getting sentimental on me are ya?"

"Naw," he responded snapping out of his revelry, "It's just that this woman looks a bit like my ex-wife."

"Hey speaking of," Charlie grabbed his clipboard and resumed his paperwork, "Are we still going to get to go to that Panthers game? Did you get to talk to her today about your 'situation'?"

"No," he answered, zipping up Connie's body bag, "when I got there she wasn't home. The old lady next door let me use her computer to send her an email because I couldn't get through to her on the phone."

"That was nice of her." Charlie commented chomping away on his gum.

"Yea... funny thing. The old lady didn't even know how to turn her computer on. Said she got it for Christmas."

"Old people and computers," Charlie chuckled.

"Hey Charlie," the examiner asked, "Are you hungry?"

"Sure. My shift finishes in ten minutes."

"Good," the coroner said, smiling, "I got some leftover spaghetti someone made me for dinner. It's to die for."

TOOTHIE

Part One

Greg struggled against the straps that bound him to the bed. "Suicide watch!" He screamed at the cell door, "Damn you fools!"

He thought of the creature he was trying to save these people from. He had named it 'Toothie,' a creature born from the dark sticky place in his soul, a creature that in recent weeks had ravaged his mind.

Now the wall between his imagination and reality was wearing thin. It was only a matter of time before Toothie broke through into reality. The creature had become stronger in recent days and Greg would be damned if he was going to be responsible for the death of innocent people. He had come to know the depths of evil this beast possessed and shuddered at the thought.

"You cannot stop me!" The chorus of voices said, as the ghastly visage of the creature's fanged face filled Greg's mind. A shiver ran down his spine. Saliva dripped from hundreds of sharp glistening teeth. The monster's face had no eyes, and black oily flesh dripped from its grinning skull.

"That's what you think!" Greg screamed at the snarling face within his mind. He steeled himself and reached for the shard of glass he had earlier hidden under his mattress. His fingers closed around the sharp edges and the pain pushed back against his imagination.

Toothie screamed.

Greg closed his hand tighter around the broken glass and reveled in the pain. He felt warm sticky blood run over his fingers, and he smiled at Toothie.

"You don't have the guts!" Toothie jeered, "I know you can't do it!"

"Fuck you Toothie," Greg replied, working the piece of glass back and forth over one of the straps, shredding material and skin.

The strap gave way and he sat up. He grabbed the glass with his other hand and held it over his wrist.

"Damn you to Hell Toothie!" Greg sliced through the soft skin. Blood spurted from the wound and he lay back down on his bed with a sigh of satisfaction.

As the vision of the creature dimmed, Greg heard Toothie's laughter and realization gripped his soul. These past few days Toothie had been goading him to do just what he had done. Greg cursed himself and he knew that he had just let the creature free into the world.

"I will make you proud," Toothie said, as Greg slipped into death.

Later that day, as the maintenance man scrubbed at the blood stains on the bed he idly stared and wondered where the black inky substance came from that covered the cell room floor.

Part 2

The Puppet

Donovan Thomas opened the door to the "operating room" and paused in the doorway shivering. It was just after midnight in the sub floors of the Royal London Hospital and he cursed the late August cold that seeped through the buildings old stucco walls. The basement floor was freezing and the dark room held the cadaver more so.

He lit the lantern and its feeble light pushed against the oppressive darkness. Donovan felt as if he were in a spotlight about to operate on a stage. He had recently watched 'The Strange Case of Dr. Jekyll and Mr. Hyde' in a London theater and the flashback sent an involuntary shiver down his spine.

He stared at the pale body lying before him and remembered two weeks ago when he accepted the offer from the city Coroner Dr. Maxie to help out. It was a violent time in London with anti-Semitic feelings and roving gangs, no wonder there were so many bodies turning up. Donovan was glad to take a job to help out the city coroner. He was a promising student at University and having a body before him instead of a text book was invaluable experience. It was taboo to use dead bodies for study.

"Hello Donovan." The sudden interruption made him to jump out of his skin.

"Christ Willy," Donovan snapped, "I nearly dropped my lantern!"

"That's okay Donny boy," Willy answered with a jovial smile, "I have my own."

"Quiet down," Donovan whispered, "you know we aren't supposed to be here."

"Ah Donny," the young scribe chuckled as he walked to the desk and lit another lantern, "you know this part of the hospital has been deserted for years."

Donovan was relieved that the second lantern added brightness to the ambience of the room. He sighed and turned his attention back to the body.

"How did this one die?" Willy asked, unrolling a piece of parchment.

"Suicide." Donovan answered dryly, studying the gaping wound across the right wrist.

"Right," Willy answered, ink quill at the ready. He paused a moment before he wrote, "what's the date again?"

"Party too much at the Ten Bells earlier did we?" Donovan asked with a knowing smile. "August 31st."

"Victims name?"

"Gregory something, not that it matters. The man was insane and had no next of kin."

Donovan readied his instruments for the autopsy. He pulled a scalpel from a drawer. "Ready?" He looked over at Willy who nodded back quill freshly dipped in ink. "Making first incision now." Donovan paused before making the first cut. He glimpsed dark liquid on the victims arm. He thought it was blood at first, but this was black as ink, and it was beginning to pour out of the wound.

"Something isn't right," Donovan said panic ruling his tone, "something weird is happening."

"Stop goofing." Willy responded.

Donovan looked to the victim's face and gasped as the eyes fluttered open to reveal the same black inky substance dripping from the sockets.

"What the..." was all Donovan managed to get out before the body before him seized the knife and neatly cut his throat. Donovan dropped to his knees desperately clawing at the gaping wound with trembling hands.

Willy jumped over his desk with a bloodcurdling scream only to meet the same fate less than a minute later.

Greg's mind tried to grasp what was going on. It was as if he were in a dark dream. His mind was sluggish and he fumbled to grasp onto his last memory.

"Where was I?" The question slowly solidified itself in his mind, "What just happened?"

"I have given you life Father." Greg heard within his head and his last moments in the hospital above came rushing back as the dark dripping face appeared within his mind's eye."

"Toothie!"

Part 3

The Puppeteer

Greg's mind was disconnected and listless.

Cold. Dark. Confusion.

"Your body is dead," Toothie's voice gurgled in his throat like one whose lungs were filled with mucus, "your synaptic fire is weak."

The words took a moment to register. Greg felt emotionally detached, his body cold and uncomfortable, like his soul was wearing a poorly tailored suit. The adjective finally came to him stubbornly. His body felt saggy. His soul was crying for escape.

"I discovered I have a use for you," Toothie continued. "When you gave me life, you failed to give me sight."

It was only then that Greg felt the cold liquid oozing down his face. He touched his cheek with his fingertips and they came away covered in the black inky substance. He felt the thrust of Toothie inside his dead body, the icy touch on his soul. A touch that was purely simple minded in its purpose to perform evil, as if every sinister feeling and dark emotion he had ever experienced had manifested into this foul inky creature.

He felt something else that rattled him to the core, where his soul feebly burned with the last embers of life. The raw power that Toothie possessed. Suddenly the creature was present within his mind as if someone turned on a light. His brain sharpened and his mind cleared.

"Now Father we are one," Toothie said. As the demon spoke, Greg felt a breath of cold air fill his lungs. It tasted foul and he wretched black ink.

"Father and Son together again."

Greg struggled against Toothie's hold but knew it was futile. He knew it because Toothie knew it. He could feel the creature's mind within his. The evil blackness that coursed through his cold body was powerful and hungry. Hungry to do evil. And Greg was absolutely powerless.

He cursed himself as 'they' walked over to the two bodies that lay on the floor. Toothie controlled Greg's body like a puppeteer might pull the strings on a marionette. The movements were lethargic at first but gradually became more dexterous and purposeful.

Soon they were dressed and stepping into the dark Victorian London night. Greg felt Toothie's excitement, Toothie's contempt. And he watched as the creature he had manifested began a reign of terror that would be talked about around the world. He had to watch as the foul deeds were done with his own hands.

Greg cursed his existence.

Part 4

Polly

The rain abated as she stumbled on the wet cobblestones onto Buck's Row. Her head swam from the effect of the gin but she was thankful for the warm feeling that glowed inside her. The chill dampness stuck to her skin, and she was ready to find sleep after this long miserable day. It was getting late and she knew she had to ply her trade once more to come up with the doss money to get back to the warmth of her bed at the workhouse. Buck's Row was the best place to turn a trick. One of her "repeat" customers lived nearby, past the Essex Warehouse and the cap factory. She only knew his first name - Jack.

The narrow street was flanked by a row of two-storey houses on one side and a cluster of dingy warehouses on the other. The gloomy light from a gas powered lamp on one end of the street reflected off of the wet cobblestones beneath her and water ran in rivulets down the gutters. A gust of wind blew stinging cold rain into her face and she pulled the collar of her coat up around her ears. She squinted up at the sky and marveled at the red glow illuminating the clouds. The light emanated from the wharf fire she had just discussed moments before with a friend. A shiver ran down her spine and despite her inebriation the street felt inexplicably evil. She was used to the mean streets of East End London and the sleaze of Whitechapel, it was all she had ever known. And yet she had never felt so unnerved.

A figure walked towards her silhouetted by the gas lamp. She thought she recognized him.

"Jack," she breathed. "Thank God."

She would do her business and collect her money. Then she would dispatch this uneasiness in her warm bed back at the Lambeth Workhouse.

She called out again. "Jack is that you?"

The man's face was obscured by the gas lamp illuminating his form from behind. She halted in her tracks as the man quickened his pace towards her. She stumbled backwards but the heel of her boot caught on a stone and sent her reeling to the wet street with a thud.

She tried to cry out but the man was upon her. A cold hand grasped her throat and cut off her air supply.

"I'm not Jack my love," the gurgling voice came to her ears, "our name is Toothie."

Her eyes widened with fear as she spied the long sharp knife silhouetted against the red tinged sky. Sharp explosions of pain bloomed about her abdomen and she sensed the frantic jab of the weapon. Her vision dimmed and she glimpsed the stranger's eyes. 'So odd,' she thought to herself as death detached her from her pain and her soul began to float from her body.

So black.

Dripping ink.

Then with one final slash of the knife Toothie cut through her throat and dispatched Mary Ann "Polly" Nichols from this world.

Part 5

Dead Vision

When Greg was alive he would have made the walk home from Buck's Row in twenty minutes. This night it took two and a half hours. He sat at the end of his bed and looked into the mirror in his small apartment just off Hope Street, east London.

The grey morning light touched his face. Toothie had now gone. Greg watched thick ink drip from his sockets and dry up leaving behind the dead eyes that stared back at him. The urge to blink was overwhelming but his dead nerve endings and facial muscles did not allow him. All he was left with was dull bleary vision. From the haze he could make out in the mirror he was almost thankful the lifeless lids could not respond.

He was also thankful that his mind remained sharp. Toothie's power seemed to have left a residual energy. But his gratitude was short lived. He was beginning to experience the same lethargy in his mind that he had experienced the night before.

The ghastly knife caked with blood was still in his hand.

With all his might he lifted the blade to his left eye. The knife seemed so heavy but Greg was determined that Toothie would not use him as an instrument of death any longer.

He was shocked when the dead hand that gripped the knife suddenly turned to gooey ink and dropped onto the soiled mattress. He watched in awe as his hand reformed back into its former grey skinned dead self.

Toothie would not let him go.

Greg's mind shut down and his lifeless body slumped onto the bed. He was now hovering above his cadaver. His soul felt a glimmer of hope and tried the slip its earthly bounds. Greg winced in pain and saw the black inky chain cutting into his soul. He was the property of Toothie and would not be freed. He cursed as his soul settled back down into his corpse and into a bizarre dream-laden sleep.

In the dream, Greg saw himself one year earlier, when he was still considered sane. His winter trip to Egypt. He saw the Pyramid of Khufu as if he were a fly on the wall. He saw himself enter one of the freshly opened chambers of the Pyramid. His mind no longer remembered these events and he watched as if he were observing them for the first time. His vision slewed and suddenly he was riding atop a giant spore. To his horror, the spore drifted right into his own mouth. Suddenly he awoke. It was night once again, and Toothie was back within his mind.

"Good evening Father," Toothie's voice gurgled.

Part 6

Dead Dream

Greg began to think the demon was poisoning his soul. He found delight in the moments the monster returned to his body and woke his soul from the dead dreams. The dead dreams had told him a lot about Toothie's past, but the invigorating return to his body and the break it provided his soul from straining at the monsters chain eased his pain.

The second kill was exciting to Greg. Toothie was getting better at controlling his dead body and Greg was enjoying the rush the monster got from his kills. He found it exciting, even fun.

Greg watched through the dripping inky eyes as they snuck up on an unsuspecting woman and dragged her struggling into a narrow side street. He reveled in the thrill they may wake someone and get caught as they ushered their fraught victim into a dilapidated yard off Hanbury Street not far from the Ten Belles. He still tasted the brandy and felt its warmth in his dead stomach as they pushed the girl towards the back corner of the yard and pinned her on her under a doorway.

Greg swore he heard someone in the shadows before Toothie managed to get a hand over their prey's mouth. The woman mumbled a stifled, 'no' but she was confused and drunk. Greg began to realize that his role was to act as lookout for the monster, for Toothie knew nothing of controlling his human body's senses. Greg also begrudgingly knew this was the only reason Toothie allowed his soul to live on.

He felt a rush when Toothie cut the first artery in the woman's neck. On the other side of the fence was an adjoining yard. Anyone could walk through at any moment and Greg swore he felt his heart beat for the first time since his 'death.'

What made it more exciting was that the East End sky was afire with pre dawn light. The sun would rise in less than half an hour. These early hours were bitterly cold but his dead body no longer felt the chill. Only warmth. The first splash of the woman's hot blood on his icy dead skin was ecstasy to Greg. He felt black ink rush through his veins as Toothie began sawing at the woman's neck. Greg spied her eyes wide with pain and terror. Then an unexpected feeling came over him. He watched in the soft light as the life slowly left her terrified eyes. Her soul was free. His soul belonged to Toothie. He watched in horror as Toothie began ripping open the woman's stomach and pulling out the contents.

The demon knew the inside of a human mind, but he now wanted to see the internal organs of a body. The rage that had previously been purged from Greg's soul when he gave birth to this creature suddenly returned. The feeling glowed furiously like a black hot flame. Greg's earlier revelry melted away with the ever brightening sky on their way back to Hope Street.

As Toothie left Greg's body and the sun peeked over the skyline, his synaptic fire began to dim. His frightened mind grasped at the waning power that Toothie left behind but to no avail.

"I have to send Toothie to his own dead dream," was his last sluggish thought as his soul yanked on the black inky chain and he slowly drifted back into a dead dream of his own.

Part 7

Fiery Dawn

Greg became confused within the dead dream. He saw himself in an unfamiliar environment atop a great temple, high above the world looking down on a canopy of lush trees. The sky to the east was flame red indicating the morning sun was ready to burst forth and bring dawn's fiery brilliance.

Greg had a sense of vertigo as he looked down the steep steps leading to the jungle floor. Crimson red painted the side of the monument that possessed the steep stairway. He looked at his hand and noticed he was holding a heart still dripping with exquisite warmth in fingers. Behind him a giant pyre burned fiercely and the heat on his back was almost unbearable, but it was warmth nonetheless. His deceased body craved and missed it.

Greg felt Toothie stir deep within this mind. The familiar hatred and darkness washed over him. He heard a strange language within his head but he understood the peculiar dialect - Toothie's gurgling voice. The creature repeated the same words over and over again.

"The Day has Come, the Day of Dead."

What surprised Greg was how powerful Toothie had become. He could feel the dense blackness of the creature's blood course through his body. His heart began to beat furiously, pumping dark inky blood painfully through open wounds all over his body. Black blood oozed from every orifice. Toothie's face was in his mind's eye, the fang filled mouth hungrily tearing at human souls.

"The Day has Come, the Day of Dead."

Greg watched a line of half-naked natives climb the steps towards him atop this ancient temple. They chanted the same phrase with hypnotic reverence. Greg threw down the heart as the woman leading the line of natives approached.

"The Day has Come, the Day of Dead."

Greg felt a hopeless sense of desperation and in that very instant he knew Toothie did not have long. A lump grew in his throat as the woman dutifully walked up and knelt before him averting her eyes to the smooth grey stones at her feet. Her skin was dark olive, her face framed by her long black hair that stirred in the morning breeze. Greg thought she was the most beautiful creature he had ever seen. Then he felt Toothie's contempt bubble to the surface. The demon abhorred anything precious, and to a human what is more precious than beauty.

The woman was prompted to rise and Greg noticed another emotion stirring within his soul. Love. He felt a different kind of hatred that he believed did not emanate from the monster's dark soul. Confusion was overcome by realization. This woman was Toothie's host's mate.

"NO!" he heard the blood curdling scream within his soul. Then there was the unmistakable laughter that was Toothie's response.

The woman grabbed her breasts and dutifully pulled them aside to allow easier extraction of her heart. Greg was taken back as he noticed that within her dark brown eyes he saw love and absolute devotion. And something else…godlike reverence.

"She didn't know," Greg thought within the dead dream, "about the monster within her loved one."

"The Day has Come, the Day of Dead." She repeated the words as she stepped closer. A smile parted her lips as she closed her eyes and threw her head back waiting for the knife's steely bite.

A sickening feeling overcame Greg as the scream of Toothie's host permeated this soul once again. Futile. The creature was just too powerful. The monster's hand would not be stayed. Greg watched, a helpless bystander, as the curved knife raised into the air, hungry to part skin and bone and remove its prize. The moment was electric with love, venomous fury and blind hate. Greg felt the host's body wretch black ink.

Then something wonderful happened. The floodgates of the horizon broke and dawn burst forth. Toothie staggered backward as if the blazing light that flowed over earths lip was a hurricane blast. Everywhere black ink touched dead grey flesh and burned with an acidic smoke. Searing heat burned every nerve ending as dead flesh boiled in black burning ink.

Toothie's power died away and months of decay restrained by the evil monster ravaged the host body in seconds. Nature furiously dried up the tissue leaving behind ashes and burnt bone.

The woman ran over and dropped to her knees, digging at the dead ash, sobbing.

Greg's perspective changed and suddenly he was afloat on the morning breeze. He could not help but look back to catch one more glimpse of the beautiful olive complexion as he rode straddling a strand of dark drippy DNA encased in a hard protein shell, drifting on the breeze.

Part 8

Black Blood, Red Ink

After the second killing, Toothie began to wake Greg almost nightly. Instead of spontaneous mutilations, the monster started planning his ghastly murders. They would spend long dark nights wandering the shadowy places and tucked away corners of Whitechapel.

Greg was surprised how many of these seedy spots there were in the neighborhood he had called home. When he was alive he had walked past many of them oblivious to their existence. He had also noticed that Toothie was getting to know the thrill of stalking his victim. Sometimes he would follow a victim for several nights, before making a kill. The creature's powers had grown significantly and he had become adept at camouflage. They could easily hang out with the unclean inhabitants of east London without anyone noticing the dripping inky eyes and rotting flesh that was now beginning to peel off of Greg's bones. The monster seemed to have the ability to make Greg's rotting corpse look healthy and whole to those that laid eyes upon him.

Greg also noticed that black blood was starting to seep through some of the more damaged areas of his grey flesh. He remembered the dead dream and knew what was going to happen to him. Despite his condition, he shivered. There was something about himself that rattled his soul. He was beginning to enjoy the kills - the only time he felt close to being alive. Greg felt the turmoil grow within his soul and welcomed the inevitable fires of Hell that would eventually cleanse his existence.

At the end of each night, the monster insisted Greg read the newspaper to him to learn more about their victims. Toothie began a dangerous game with the authorities. The creature marveled at how inept the police were and began taunting them through written word. He forced Greg to write a letter to the local newspaper knowing the police would eventually receive it.

Toothie wanted it written in blood.

Greg flashed back to their last murder and realized why the monster had grabbed an empty bottle and saved some of Annie's blood. At the time he thought the creature was saving it to drink. The evil monster threw a fit of rage when the blood thickened and could not be used to write the letter. The demon settled for red ink instead.

Toothie became inspired and decided to stir things up with the authorities. He told Greg to mention that he was going to send the police a piece of a victim's ear after the next murder. This new taunting technique had given their nightly stalking an exciting edge as the police doubled their efforts. Toothie's excitement was palpable and his black blood surged vigorously through Greg's veins so that Greg had to wipe inky liquid from his nose as it dripped charcoal blood.

The rain-soaked night did not affect the duo as they made their way down Settles Street. This was Toothie's favorite weather. The rain had picked up and came down in sheets that pounded noisily on the cobbled lanes. The monster was ravenous for a kill in the waning hours and became frustrated when they heard shouts from a public house up ahead. A couple emerged from a doorway ten feet away and ran past them – a woman accompanied by a man with the dark mustache, sandy eyebrows and wearing a billycock hat.

"That's Leather Apron!" someone shouted from the pub.

'Leather Apron' was the nickname paper allocated to the murderer by a local newspaper. Toothie decided this woman would provide the perfect victim for a delightful frame up job. The demon would kill her and the murder would be pinned on the man she was with.

Toothie melted into the shadows as the couple turned onto Berner Street and ducked into a doorway. They began hugging and kissing. The duo looked on as the man and woman carried on in a not so discreet manner in the darkness of the doorway. Greg could feel the monster's seething fascination as they watched the couple copulate. The creature reached inside his jacket and closed his dead fingers around the hilt of Donovan Thomas's surgical knife.

After a few moments the couple finished and the man pressed a few coins into the ladies hand. The two parted company in opposite directions. The man returned to the public house and the woman continued down Berner Street. Greg felt the pulse of ink quicken beneath his cold skin. They fell into step behind the woman and he felt the lifeless flesh on his face split open and ooze blackness as Toothie cracked a grin.

The hunt was on.

Part 9

Berner Street

They stuck to the shadows as they followed the woman along Berner Street toward the London School Board building. Greg and Toothie hung back and waited for the perfect moment to move in for the kill. The monster was giddy with anticipation. The woman stopped and began talking to a sailor. The two spoke briefly and then began hugging and kissing.

"You would say anything but your prayers," the sailor said to her as she dragged him into a dark alley.

"She's at it again?" Greg murmured in disbelief.

"The bitch deserves to die," came Toothie's gurgling reply. "And soon she will pay her penance."

This time the plying of her trade took considerably longer. Greg could feel the creature's dismay that their victim was not on the move. Dark blood coursed through his veins, brittle and dry from disuse. Greg felt an inky trickle run down his earlobe and down his neck. There was no time to wipe it away for their prey suddenly re-emerged from the alleyway and adjusted her black crepe bonnet. The man was nowhere to be seen. She pulled a packet of cashews from her pocket and popped one into her mouth before continuing on her way.

As they followed her, Greg heard a ruckus up ahead, emanating from a two-storey building - the International Worker's Club. His pulse quickened and his heart lurched in pain as it beat with unfamiliar exertion. A spill of black molasses ran over his lip and slipped down his chin. He wiped it with his sleeve and edged back into the shadows as a police constable turned the corner and strolled past them.

The woman stopped in front of a large building and began conversing with a young man wearing a black coat and deerstalker. The discussion became heated and the man tried to grab the woman and forcibly drag her away by the arm.

She yanked free and stumbled back into the adjacent alleyway. As she fell to the ground, the man looked up and spotted a police officer loitering further along the street. He turned up his collar, glanced around and disappeared into the crowd milling at the entrance of the pub next door.

Toothie knew the time had come and wasted no time crossing the street. Greg felt his heart race at a frenzied pace and feared it just may explode drenching his insides in black ink.

Their prey pushed herself up against a wall as they stepped into the alley. She held out a rusty pocket knife and waved it defiantly as they approached.

"You will not take me sir, not without a fight," she sneered, flashing her smoke stained teeth. She lunged forward and sunk the knife deep into Greg's chest. Black blood sprayed into her frightened face. She stumbled back, panting for breath, an expression of bewilderment slowly crossing her face and she realized her attacker still stood.

Toothie was now in complete control and Greg heard the rush of blood pumping in his ears above the din from the club next door. Toothie grabbed the hilt of the woman's knife and yanked it from Greg's lifeless chest. Another spray of black blood marked their victim as he lurched forward and grabbed her, pulling her up close. She tried to scream but her voice was muted. Toothie was squeezing the breath from her lungs and she could not be heard.

"May I have this dance?" Toothie whispered and smiled through Greg's mouth. He began swaying with the sobbing lady in a mock dance.

He held up the knife and her eyes rested on the blade. Toothie placed a hand over her mouth and she let out a soft whimper as he shoved her hard against the wall, thrusting his pelvis forward to pin her.

Greg felt the unexpected surge of sexual energy rush to his groin as Toothie began sawing at the woman's neck with her own knife. Warm blood sprayed delightfully across Greg's face and over his hands. As he watched the life fade from her eyes he was appalled that he felt no remorse, for in that moment he was awash with the feeling his dead body craved most. Life.

The monster stepped back and allowed the body to slump to the ground. He readied the knife and prepared to begin the mutilation when the neighing of a donkey echoed off the alley walls. They turned and saw the donkey and cart filling the entrance to the alley.

Toothie melted into the darkness as the driver jumped to the ground and walked slowly up the alley. He stopped when he saw the woman lying on the ground. As the man called out for help, the duo made their escape through the alleyway and into a yard. The fleeting feeling of life seeped away from Greg as they climbed the fence and stumbled onto the cobbles on the other side.

He barely paid attention to Toothie's outrage as he launched into a mumbling tirade within Greg's dead mind. He did not even hear the monsters comments until he finished the last sentence.

"That whore got off lucky!" The creature's gurgling voice trailed off.

Part 10

Red Handkerchief

Greg got the impression that the monster's irate rage hovered around them like some dark barrier, the evil within agonizing to reveal it's self and punch through into the living world. At the same time nature was on the outside with salivating gnashing teeth wanting to break through and devour Greg's dead body. He was caught in between in some kind of dark tug of war, his soul slowly being eaten away.

The rain started again as they made their escape down Commercial Road. It was past one in the morning, but the east end still bustled with activity and the melee provided ideal cover for their escape.

Toothie was furious that he had not fulfilled his promise to come away with a severed ear from their victim. He was determined to get the prize. The pulse within the dead body raced with Toothie's rage and hatred. For the first time since his death, Greg felt his body ache as the monster's pumping blood coursed through his hardened veins. He was hemorrhaging dark sticky liquid from a dozen wounds, mainly around his hands and face. A stifled groan escaped his moisture craved lips.

They turned left onto Aldgate High Steet. Toothie was still livid that his enjoyment had been cut short on the last incident and set his mind to find another victim before the night was over. At that moment, a hapless woman almost bumped into them. She scurried from an adjoining street and continued on in front of them. Unbeknownst to the pair, this lady had just been released from Bishopsgate Police station for drunkenness.

Toothie smelled blood as he focused on the red handkerchief neatly tied around her neck. Through the oozing dead eyes Greg saw what he imagined a predator envisions when focusing on its prey. The bustling activity around him became a dull blur as the red handkerchief jumped forward into stark contrast to the surrounding environment. Greg felt an unfamiliar tingle and realized that Toothie was becoming more powerful with each kill, as if he were feeding his strength from each incident. The demon's rage threatened to drive Greg into fervor, his heart pounding with excitement as the creature prepared to pounce.

Then something unexpected happened; Greg held Toothie back as one would restrain a dog on a leash. Greg's surprise at this action was overwhelmed by the creature's fury as he railed against being restrained.

"The time is not right," Greg whispered, attempting to calm the creature, "we must wait."

He braced himself for retaliation, but Toothie did not react. Within Greg's mind, the creature's mouth turned upward in a dripping inky grin. The duo slowed to let the red handkerchief gain ground as the hunt began for the second time on this dark damp night.

Their opportunity came two blocks later as the red scarf took a right onto Duke Street. A church bell chimed in the distance, unnoticed by the unfortunate woman as the duo closed in. Greg was once again awash with the feeling of being 'alive.' His senses sprang to life and he felt a primeval urge to hunt and kill. He could smell the dampness of the woman's clothes, the stink of cheap perfume and cheap whiskey on her breath.

Stalk silently. Stop. Slow down - slither like a snake.

Greg was completely submersed within the ocean of darkness that was Toothie. Unfamiliar sensations and memories long forgotten permeated his being. None of these feelings were the treasured happiness his soul longed for, but pain, despair, and sorrow.

Rage threatened to overwhelm him. So absolute, so intense. He found it hard to comprehend one soul could feel so much contempt, so much bitter fury.

Three grime-caked workers exited a busy night spot up ahead. The sign above the door said, The Imperial Club. The red handkerchief hurried past the men as their eyes hungrily watched her. Greg and Toothie quickened their stride to make it appear they were accompanying the woman.

She stopped and turned on her heel. Toothie and Greg almost ran into her over for they were still eyeing the trio of blue-collars. They stumbled to a stop. The trio's laughter faded into the rainy night and they were now alone. The auburn haired woman fixed hazel eyes on them.

"Fancy buying a woman a drink?" She asked with a playful smile. "The least you can do fer stalking me so."

Toothie reached inside his jacket and closed his dripping dead fingers around the hilt of the surgical knife.

"My Lady," Toothie slightly bowed from the hip as he spoke through Greg's cracked lips, "I have my flask right here."

She smiled again as he offered her his arm and they continued walking down Duke Street turning into the unlit Mitre Square.

The monster would make up for his earlier disappointment. Toothie worked in mutilation as an artist would in oil paints, or a sculptor in granite, and Greg had looked on through dead eyes as the monster performed his unspeakable acts. In the next fifteen minutes red handkerchief would not only lose her life, but her right ear as well. One of her kidneys and a piece of another organ would become grizzly prizes of the one who had become known to Victorian London as the Ripper. We know him as...

Toothie.

Part 11

Moth to the Flame

Another dead dream and another glimpse into the dark creature's history. This time his victims were oriental and Greg appeared to be the ruler of this foreign country in some ancient time. He saw himself torture and kill people with rage and reckless contempt. He drank the blood of one unfortunate soul and felt the creature stir inside him. Toothie's grinning visage appeared within this minds eye.

"Mothers milk," Toothie gurgled in a foreign dialect. Once again Greg was surprised that he understood.

A shiver shot through what remained of Greg's soul. In life, he and his family had been strict Catholics. Even in adulthood, before his mother died, the two would attend mass at St. Mary's church every Sunday. His mother was now buried in the small cemetery behind that same church. Greg always believed that he would meet her in the afterlife. In Heaven. That word lingered within the dead dream like a fluttering moth drawn to a strange light. His soul would never see his mother's lovely face again. Not after Toothie had used his body, the very temple of his soul. He was surely destined for the fires of the eternal abyss.

The eerie light and fluttering moth distracted his thoughts. The moth grew closer and upon closer inspection Greg realized that it was not a moth at all, but an angel - the most beautiful angel he ever could imagine. It was his mother.

Greg felt a dull pain in his heart and the agony of the prison this evil creature had condemned him to. He strained against the inky chain holding him to his dead body as his mother, aglow with brilliant heavenly light, reached out a loving hand. She smiled at him.

"Mother!" He cried, his voice filled with pain. To his astonishment the voice did not come to him as his own, but Toothie's. Dread threatened to capsize him into the dark waters that Toothie's chain had anchored him in.

"Do not fear my child," his mother's voice filled his head, a voice of tenderness, with eyes full of love. "We will soon be together."

"Mother." Greg started to sob. "You don't understand what has happened to me!"

"No son," She responded with a loving smile, "you do not understand."

Confusion set in as she moved closer. His heart felt as though it could burst with love and pride. She embraced him and the darkness of the monster fled to the unseen corners of his mind. In that moment, hope filled his being but was quickly dashed as he looked into his mothers loving face. He saw a shadow of sadness cross her features and instantly knew she could not free him.

"Son, the creature that possesses you has purged your soul of almost all its darkness. You do not see this for the creature will not let you."

Greg could hardly believe what he was hearing. Hope rushed back in. The gloom deteriorated and he found strength in his soul where once there had been only despair.

"I cannot free you," his mother said, "but there is something I must show you."

Greg was overwhelmed with joy. A stark contrast to the darkness he had recently experienced and it convulsed within his spirit. His soul cried with happiness. Bliss filled the emptiness and he was no longer within the dead dream. He stood on a rocky plain overlooking a valley bathed in fiery red light. Streams of molten rock rolled past, flames licking at the edges. There was no single point of light in the sky, no sun, but the entire sky was ablaze horizon to horizon.

"Is this hell?" Greg asked of his mother.

"Not quite," she said, the smile fading from her face, "it is Toothie's home."

She swept her arm across the valley floor before them and Greg saw they were standing on a small rise in the center of the gorge. His eyesight adjusted against the harsh red light and realization set in. What he thought was a shadow cast by the far lip of the valley was no shadow at all but a sea of black plants. He looked down at the black rivers flowing from the rock beneath them as it drained into the lava that emptied into the valley around them. The plants seemed to be feeding off the lava, soaking up the molten rock as a tree might absorb rainwater.

His mother pointed to the sky. "Watch, but do not fear. This was millions of years ago, long before mankind."

The sky darkened and billions of stars twinkled. The earth glowed as the fiery rivers splashed the dark vegetation in a rust colored light. A wind picked up, sending spores from the plants across the valley floor. The spores caught fire as they hovered inches above the lava and danced on the wind in a shower of red embers. They fluttered into the sky and twirled beside the icy starlight.

A bright blue star shone in a sharp halo of focused light, then exploded in a huge fireball signaling its death in a brilliant supernova. Three minutes later the shock wave reached Toothie's home planet, obliterating the land a chaotic blast of destruction. The planet's death throe was a spray of rock, lava and vegetation splashing into the inky blackness of space.

Nothing of the alien planet survived, except the spores floating on violent solar winds.

"This is where Toothie's journey began, my son. Millions of years passed before Toothie made it to Earth. The story of this foul creature's story ends where you are now. I'm sorry Greg, but you are the monsters current chapter."

He looked into his mother's eyes and was sickened to see them leaking inky tears. Then her face split into a wide fanged smile.

"Wakey, Wakey Greg." Toothie's gurgling voice came to his ears once more. "You've been talking to that bitch of a mother of yours haven't you, naughty boy?"

Part 12

Other Side of the Glass

Toothie's wrath lasted through the early hours of the cold November night. Outside the rain lashed against the windowpane for the third time since the monster had wakened him. Through the frosted glass Greg stared lifelessly, longing to see the sun just one more time on the other side of the glass...

Greg looked around the cramped living quarters, a room devoid of light with shattered furniture, and black stains covering the curtains and bed sheets. The place was as dead as he was.

The creature was desperate for more blood. He finished his latest tirade and they finally hit the East End Streets. On this particular night the rain and cold had driven even the heartiest of drunkards indoors and the streets remained mostly deserted.

The monster forced Greg's dead body through the roughest neighborhoods of Whitechapel, desperate to release his malice upon another victim. Even the lifeless nerve endings within his grim cadaver began to burn under the immense pressure of the ink coursing his brittle veins. Black fluid dripped from lacerations all over his body. Toothie's anger grew and Greg felt as though he was going to burst. His heart pounded painfully as they turned into Thrawl Street, and then an almost angelic sound reached their ears. The duo slowed as the melody slowly rose to a crescendo on the cold breeze. They reached the end of the street and stopped when they turned the corner. Melodious lyrics materialized out of the grey night, a song sung in a woman's haunting somber voice.

> Scenes of my childhood arise before my gaze,
> Bringing recollections of bygone happy days.

Greg felt a skip in his pounding heart. A missed beat caused by the beautiful sound of the voice. Or was it Toothie's anger that caused the altered rhythm?

> When down in the meadow in childhood I would roam,
> No one's left to cheer me now within that good old home,

Greg knew the tune from his childhood. His mother used to sing it to him in her later years. He felt the monster's fury bubble up as the creature reacted to this latest memory.

> Father and Mother, they have pass'd away;
> Sister and brother, now lay beneath the clay,

This last line brought a grin to the beasts face pictured within Greg's Mind's eye.

Was this melody actually soothing this savage beast?

> But while life does remain to cheer me, I'll retain
> This small violet I pluck'd from mother's grave.

They saw the young lady walk towards them and stop momentarily to converse briefly with a bedraggled man, who shook his head - 'no'. She bowed her head and trudged up the street toward them. She began singing her dirge once again.

Well I remember my dear old mother's smile,

As she used to greet me when I returned from toil,

Always knitting in the old arm chair,

Father used to sit and read for all us children there,

But now all is silent around the good old home;

They all have left me in sorrow here to roam...

She was so intent on her song that she bumped into them, and almost slipped on the wet cobbles. They grabbed her gently and steadied her on her feet. She looked up into dripping dark eyes only to see what Toothie told her mind to see.

"Oh kind sir," she said in a Welsh accent, blue eyes full of tears, "I have not the money to pay the boss and I fear he is to turn me out this evening. Could you spare some doss money so I may pay for my room?"

Greg felt sorrow as he studied her delicate features. His mind flashed back to the hacked up face of their last victim and felt the creature's hatred for all that is beauty flooding forward. This one was the most attractive of all of their victims so far, but what tore at his soul most was the resemblance that this woman possessed to his own late mother. He summoned all the remaining strength within his tattered soul and commanded his swollen black saliva-soaked tongue to shout out a warning. A shock resonated through Greg as his soul reeled from a striking blow from the Monster.

"Haven't you done enough today?" Toothie's voice hissed within his mind, "I will do the talking. You just sit back and watch as I tear this bitch's beating heart from her chest."

"My angel," came the beast's sickening sweet reply through Greg's cracked teeth. "For one with such a beautiful voice, you should be dry and warm by a cheerful fire."

She smiled and pushed a blond tuft of hair out of her eyes.

"Where do you live my dear?" Toothie asked using Greg's mouth like a skilful ventriloquist. "We need to get you inside and warm by the fire. I would just kill myself if you were to catch cold and lose that angelic voice of yours."

They walked the block and turned a corner onto Dorset Street, before walking into Miller's Court where the young woman was staying.

"I would like to personally see to your health angel," Toothie said through quickening excited breaths, "You will be all right for what I have told you."

"All right, my dear. Come along. You will be comfortable." she said as rain water ran into her eyes. "I've lost my handkerchief."

Toothie handed her a red handkerchief, a grim prize stolen from his last victim. Greg's soul screamed in pain as the young lady led them into Millers Court.

She pointed. "Mine is that one," she said and wiped water from her face with the red handkerchief. "The first window on the other side of the glass. That is where I live."

Part 13

Drawn Lines

Greg stared in horror through dripping eyes as Toothie made the woman sing while she undressed. She stripped off her damp clothes down to her chemise, neatly folding and stacking her garments upon the bed stand.

Greg felt blood charging through every vein within his possessed body, a reaction to the euphoria Toothie felt at being completely in control and hungry for the kill.

"What is your name, child?" the monster asked with a contempt that only Greg could hear.

"Mary Jane Kelly," she answered, giving away the last possession she had in this world. As she smiled and lay down upon the bed, Greg cried out in anguish for he knew the creature owned her completely.

"You can call me Ginger," she said with a coy smile.

Greg was plunged into a pool of misery for all he could picture was his mother's loving face. This woman was almost identical. He sank deeper when Toothie climbed atop her and flashed the knife. Light from the fire reflected off of the blood-stained metal. An evil grin slowly crossed his dead face and the facade that the monster hid behind dropped away revealing their true form.

Mary Jane's eyes widened with terror and her breath caught in her throat.

"Sing bitch!" Toothie ordered and slashed her cheek with a swipe of the blade. She choked as the creature administered another left handed blow that opened up a gash on her other cheek.

Greg plunged deeper into despair as he struggled against the evil undertow, fighting to reach the surface. Within his mind he saw bubbles flow in every direction but could not find the path upward. He tried desperately to grab and stay Toothie's hands but the monster was just too powerful.

Then Greg saw defiance within the woman's eyes that distracted from his anguish. He felt a sudden admiration for the woman as she decided she was not going to go out a sobbing mess and her voice suddenly carried throughout the room with a commanding resonance.

Toothie hacked away at her lips and face, yet she continued to sing despite the splayed wounds. In a furious torrent of deadly slashes the creature conducted his worst mutilations to date, shredding skin, bone and tissue from Mary Jane's writhing body. The whole time Toothie kept her alive with his dark power so she could pay for her defiance. The gurgling sounds that escaped her tattered mouth were no longer melodious, but to Greg's dead ears, it was the most beautiful music he had ever heard within his wasted lifetime and they sent the dark beast into a violent raging fit.

At that moment, Greg felt the monster's power slip. He pictured his mother's face glowing with a beautiful grin, bathed in angelic light. Upon studying her visage Greg looked to the window and saw the light was gathering rapidly outside.

The monster began to drift from Greg's dead body, but Greg found power within his mother's smile and grabbed onto Toothie with every ounce of strength. Toothie, reeled against Greg's grasp but the demon had spent so much power keeping the girl alive he was too weak to break free from the death grip.

"Look to the window," Greg heard his mothers voice. Above the courtyard the gray clouds parted, letting a single beam of brilliant sunlight shine into the alcove. It glinted off a window across the courtyard and reflected down into Mary Jane's room.

"Hurry," his mother's voice commanded.

A coat hung in front of Mary's window obstructing the sunlight. For the first time since his resurrection Greg controlled his own body. He clumsily tore down the coat and let the sunlight in.

Toothie's scream shattered his mind. Greg felt the chain that held his soul melt away and the dead skin on his corpse began to flake. His soul floated from the body but with all his might Greg held onto the monster to stop him leaving the physical plane. They were thrown back against the fireplace. Black blood boiled and dry skin caught fire. Greg reveled in the excruciating pain, for he and the monster were still in an embrace, feeling it together.

"Why have you done this Father?" Toothie asked sobbing, "I gave you life."

"No," Greg responded, "you gave me Hell."

With the last word Toothie's power faded and nature's vengeance was swift. The dead body collapsed into the fireplace and was engulfed in a brilliant funeral pyre, flames so hot, they melted the spout of the teakettle that sat on the nearby stove.

Greg's soul was free, floating high above the planet when his mother's angelic form appeared in brilliant beauty. Greg was overwhelmed. The feeling of love and peace was unlike anything he could have ever have imagined. He tried to recall the pain and anguish he had felt in the past three months but the feelings were gone.

"Your soul is pure," his mother smiled at him, "the monster has stolen all of your darkness."

"Mother-" Greg was cut short.

"I am no longer your mother Greg," she said tenderly. "We are now but two souls, neither one superior or belonging to the other. We shared a brief moment together down on the battlefield."

"Battlefield?"

"I must show you something." She said softly, and once again their souls merged as they had done in the dead dream before. They were somewhere deep in space when the two souls separated.

"That is our sun," she said, and pointed to a small yellow star. A dark cloud crossed their view of the sun. Greg instinctively knew that this was the cloud of spores that had dispersed from Toothie's dying star system millions of years before.

They were on a collision course for Earth.

"Toothie knows they are heading for Earth," Greg was told by his mother's soul, "he is gaining power so that he may rule them. When you saw the demon as the Mayan priest he had developed a calendar that counts down the arrival date of the spores. That is the day the real war between Heaven and Hell begins Greg. And you having been purged of all evil are to be one of the pure souls to lead the angels into battle...."

The police investigators had done their work and the body had been carted away. The room had been sealed so no one could enter the door and windows were nailed shut. A sudden and unexplained gust of wind blew hard into the courtyard at Miller's Court shattering a pane of glass within the former apartment of the slain Mary Jane Kelly. The wind stirred up the dust in the fireplace into a hazy cloud within the room.

Douglas McFadden was loading luggage onto the boat when he suddenly
gagged and went into a slight fit of coughing. After recovering he was overwhelmed with the feeling he needed to leave London on an adventure. So upon loading the last piece of luggage onto the boat he conveniently stowed away within the boat's baggage compartment headed
for New York City.

TIME SCOPE

More than two hundred men and women filed into the auditorium and took their seats. The announcement had come earlier in the week that all the top scientists in the country should meet in the small deserted town, forty miles south of Vegas. The subject of the gathering was undisclosed. The only accompanying message mentioned 'a matter of extreme urgency.'

Doctor Cofore crossed the stage to the podium and waited until the doors were closed. Once his audience was settled, he began his address.

"Welcome, ladies and gentleman, and thank you for attending this meeting at such short notice. The venerable scientist's voice boomed from the podium's microphone.

A hushed murmur of questioning voices rippled through the room accompanied by the anxious shuffling of feet and the harsh sound of sliding chairs upon the wooden floor.

"Please folks, I know all of you are wondering why you were invited here, but please hold all questions until the end of the assembly so we can get right down to business." Dr. Cofore cleared his throat, and the lights dimmed. "As many of you know, five years ago the government began funding our psychic programs here at SyTech."

A white screen descended behind him and a projected imaged appeared - an odd red plastic helmet sprouting wires and what looked like television tubes protruding from its crest. The image was greeted with a wave of derisory mutterings and even laughter from the back of the room.

"I am proud to present," the Doctor continued, pretending not to notice, "our department's first success. This is what we call, a Dimension Scope."

An Asian scientist jumped to his feet. "Is this some kind of joke? This is what your company has spent billions of American Tax dollars on?"

"Please Dr. Nogasaki," the speaker said, hands clasped in front of him in a disarming manner, "this is a real piece of scientific equipment."

"It looks like a child's toy!" the Asian scientist responded.

"Please sir," Dr. Cofore answered in a measured tone, "if you sit down and observe, one of our young psychics will demonstrate how scientifically valuable this helmet is."

"Who did you get," the question came from an unknown source in the back of the room. " BUCK ROGERS OR FLASH GORDON!?!"

The crowd erupted with laughter and the tension evaporated.

Doctor Cofore calmly scanned the amused faces in the crowd.

An overweight, grey-haired astronomer yelled at him from the front row, "I can't believe I came all the way from Mauna Kea for this!"

Dr. Cofore signaled a nod towards back of the hall and the curtains behind him parted to reveal a young man strapped into a metal chair.

The audience fell silent.

The young man wore the Dimension Scope upon his head. The wires burned with a red hot glow and the "TV tubes" shone with a brightness that made everyone in the room squint and overt their eyes.

Dr. Cofore watched the crowd with smugness as the audience slowly became accustomed to the glare emanating from the stage. In the space approximately one foot above the helmet a blue smoky vortex churned and spun, creating a dull glow. The crowd stared in awe.

"This is Kian," Dr. Cofore said, striding to the side of the stage to allow a better view of the young man. "Kian is our most gifted psychic. After several trials he is now able to create the conduit you see above his head allowing him to see inter-dimensionally."

The Doctor looked upon the sea of awestruck faces focused on the psychic seated behind him. A lump of pride began to swell in his throat. Doctor Cofore now had a captive audience. He continued his speech.

"Until now, our results have yielded glimpses into the past." He paused to revel in the attention of the crowd. "That achievement was attained with the scope at partial power." A smile spread across his lips as astonished gasps circulated the auditorium. There was a nervous shift of chairs but all attention was now fixed upon the elder scientist.

"Tonight for the scientific community," he said with a sweeping gaze, "we hope to see not only the past, but the future."

He paused for dramatic effect but every person in the room already knew what his next words were going to be.

"Tonight the Dimension Scope operates at FULL POW...."

The last words were cut short by a great sucking sound from the back of the stage. The room was plunged into darkness for a second before the lights flickered and came back on. The nervous murmurings returned as Dr. Cofore made his way to the unconscious chair-bound psychic at the back of the stage. As he struggled with the straps the young man's eyes fluttered open and focused on the scientist.

"Dr. Cofore?" Kian asked momentarily confused.

"Yes son," he answered, "tell me what you saw."

Kian pulled the helmet off and rested it in his lap. He looked groggily into the eyes of his boss as comprehension slowly returned.

"Did you see the past?" Cofore asked excitedly.

Kian's brow furrowed and he nodded his head. A shadow of fear crossed his face.

Dr. Cofore exhaled the breath he had been holding in one loud gasp. "And the future?"

Kian's eyes fixed on the elder man with urgency and he shoved the helmet into the scientist hands. "I only saw about two hours into the future Doctor. Sorry, but it's time to go." The young psychic stood up, and pushed past the Doctor, heading for the stage exit.

"Kian!" the Doctor yelled after him, "where are you going?"

"To spend a little time with my family."

Suddenly the auditorium was filled with a cacophony of beepers and cell phones.

Dr. Cofore looked around the room at fearful faces shouting into cell phones and PDAs. His gaze fixed on the white-haired fat astronomer he had heard earlier. The man's face was beet red, his eyes wide frightened disks.

"What in Hell is going on?" Dr. Cofore shouted over the tumultuous din. He did not hear the response but fear gripped his own heart as he cursed his ability to read lips.

HUGE ASTEROID ON COLLISION COURSE WITH EARTH.

"How long until impact?" He mouthed the question back.

TWO HOURS...

THE WORLD MACHINE

You go to work five days a week and toil to eek out a meager existence. The government knows you as a social security number. Their data banks are full of these numbers and their behaviors – not people, just numbers. The numbers are demographics. You are a collection of ones and zeros.

Your bank knows you as an account number. The management at the apartment complex knows you as a unit number. No one knows your name outside the odd collection of people around you looking for their own distraction from the world machine.

The only time your name is put into print is as a result of a computer program matching the numbers you are identified by to an array of information that stores your name - you guessed it, a series of numbers. This is usually the result of you owing money, or some company wanting you to spend money.

The modern world has dehumanized us to the point where we are zombies, working towards a walking death, sleeping our way through a mundane structured life.

Nice, clean and orderly. No mess.

We crave to forget how unimportant we really are. Many of us distract ourselves on the weekend trying to recapture our humanity in this short space of time. The world calls us and puts us back into our place on Monday morning.

Nice, clean and orderly. No mess.

Take the case of Jared Chrism for example - employee number 228716 at the National World Bank over on highway 6. He has worked with numbers as long as he can remember. He has molded and shaped them as if they were clay and worked them into artful reports. The masterpiece symphony he composed exists as twenty-one years of flawlessly filed data, all delivered within their deadlines. At a cost. The numbers have sapped his life energy, stolen its magic for the World Machine. As a result Jerad's number was matched to an array of information within the company's database and was presented with an Employee of the Month certificate for each of the twenty-one years he served the bank.

Employee 228716 was the perfect employee - until today.

Insanity lurked in every corner of Jared's drab life, and today it would pounce upon him. This morning insanity took the form of a malfunctioning alarm clock. The fact he overslept by twenty minutes derailed his whole day.

Upon going to the dryer, insanity met with 228716 once again, this time in the form of wet clothes. Somehow, during the night, the dryer had managed to shut off. So, with wet socks and underwear, Jared grabbed a stale doughnut and headed to the car.

Insanity struck again within Jared's garage when a failed alternator prevented employee 228716 from starting his conservative 2002 Honda sedan. Anger boiled inside his gut and caused his fingers to tingle. The day had not started routinely.

He hurried down the lane, shirt un-tucked, briefcase in hand. The bus-stop was at the end of his road. As he rushed down the sidewalk, he stepped into a pile of insanity and the stench did not take long to reach his nostrils.

"Damn dog owners," he cursed, wiping his shoe on the wet grass. "Haven't they heard of a pooper scooper?"

At that moment he noticed more insanity. His socks. He was wearing two different colors. As black and brown mockingly laughed at him, he heard the city bus rounding the corner. He stepped back onto the sidewalk but his wet shoe skidded beneath him, and he slipped onto the hard cement, ripping a gash of insanity in his damp dress pants.

228716 barely caught the bus but he was relieved that at least something had gone right. Then, Insanity hit him hard, spilling him against the window and cutting open his forehead on the broken glass. A traffic light malfunction allowed a car into the intersection right in front of the transit bus, causing the driver to slam on the breaks.

"Sorry folks," the bus driver called over his shoulder, "we just blew a tire. Everyone off the bus."

As they exited, a sudden thunderstorm lurked above 228716's head. He opened his umbrella, but as he unfolded it, a gust of wind jerked it from his grip and sent it tumbling down the street.

By the time he got to the office on highway 6, he was a soaked, tired, stressed out, bad smelling and bleeding. He was an hour and ten minutes late. 228716 hit the revolving door running, only to have a delivery guy try the door from the other side.

228716 was punched on the nose and the contents of his briefcase spilled out within the confined section of the revolving door.

"Why can't this just be a normal Monday morning?" he cried as he shuffled papers haphazardly into his briefcase. Insanity would answer in the form of employee number 232117 tapping on the glass of the revolving door and pointing to his watch.

232117 was Jared's trainee five years previous. Now this young upstart was trying to take over 228716's position as top employee. A real ass-kisser.

"The Boss wants you in his office pronto mister," ass-kisser said, in a nondescript tone. "I suggest you get those bloody wet buns moving."

228716 returned a mumbled reply as he passed the young upstart.

"Oh, by the way," 232117 said with a sneer, "your report is due in ten minutes."

As Jared entered the elevator, he got stares from the other occupants. Upon smelling the odor, the other passengers promptly departed at the next floor. The door slid closed and Jared stared idly at the buttons. His finger hovered over the twenty first-floor button, his boss's floor. Then, without a thought, he pushed the button labeled 'roof' instead.

Insanity sped the elevator car to the top of the building with unusual speed. Seven minutes later 228716 stood on the precipice staring down at the city below. He saw the traffic moving in perfect tandem, not too fast, not too slow. In the distance a steady stream of airliners took off from the airport and he marveled at how evenly spaced this process was. Like clockwork.

"The World Machine is well oiled indeed." Jared said, as he stepped off the ledge and 12.2 seconds later insanity punched his time card for the final time.

Downstairs, in the basement the boss was talking to the new computer technician going over the details of the company's newly installed super computer database.

"Sir," the young tech continued excitedly after spewing forth over ten minutes of geek talk, "this baby is linked to every database around the globe, every system that might affect the financial stability of the bank and our company. We're talking everything, from weather satellites to the transportation system on and underneath our streets. We can track storms, monitor traffic, and keep tabs on our employees any and every second of the day."

"Good, tell me where 228716 is," the boss said, "I need him to hear this before I give him that promotion."

"No problem sir." The tech began tapping the keyboard at his monitor station, "we can punch him up right here and find out where he is."

The technician punched up 228716 and the program matched the numbers with the information array. An immediate response flashed up on the screen.

The Boss and the Tech stared at the result, dumbfounded.

"228716..................INACTIVE"

"That's funny," the tech mumbled, "that's the message reserved for terminated employees."

"Well if he doesn't get his ass down here right now," the Boss said irately, "he's going to find himself in a world of hurt when I do just that."

"As I was saying," the tech continued, "this new system is tied into everything and can conjure so much information, its mind boggling. God knows what we can achieve with this thing. It can even correct internal bugs that find their way into the software. Its so cool, we came up with a cute nickname for it," the computer geek chuckled.

Mumbling an explicative, the Boss checked his watch once again."Oh, yeah," he responded only partially interested, "and what would that be?"

"We call it INSANITY."

SOULFUL MUSIC

Debbie was a somber and thoughtful young lady. Her circle of college friends would describe her as a "Goth." Dark colors were all her wardrobe possessed, and the color of her hair changed almost daily. But underneath the brooding exterior was a natural beauty that struggled to shine through the harsh exterior of black eye shadow and clothing. No matter what she tried, she could not squander this inner light and despite her outward depression she failed to keep others from wanting to be around her.

It is an undeniable truth that opposites do indeed attract.

That is why Debbie and Steve were best of friends since the day they met at the end of high school. They were immediately attracted to one another, but aside a shared interest in music, they had absolutely nothing in common.

Steve was a light hearted young man with a witty sense of humor. His zeal for life made him a beacon within Debbie's shadowy existence. In truth, Steve was the reason she had not succumbed to slashing her wrists or putting a gun to her head. Her home life caused her misery and no one understood the gothic mask she wore.

But all that became trivial when she answered the door one day to be confronted by Steve's mother. Debbie squinted against the brightness of the spring day as the gray-haired woman relayed the bad news on her doorstep.

Steve had gone missing. He was supposed to pick his mother up at the bus station but had failed to show. That was not like him. Steve was the most reliable person Debbie knew. She felt a lump in her throat. Steve would have called if there was a problem.

"I already tried his cell phone," Steve's mom said urgently, "I even called the police but they said they couldn't do anything until he had been missing for more than forty-eight hours." With a look of disgust she said, "I thought he might be with you."

Debbie was too anxious to notice the woman's barb. She grabbed her cell phone and dialed Steve's number only to get a 'mailbox is full' message.

"Don't worry Mrs. Sweeny," Debbie said, snatching up her car keys, "I'm sure he's okay."

After dropping off Steve's mother at her house, she made her way to the bus station, the last place her best friend was supposed to be. The station was a frenzy of activity and the drone of white noise was deafening to her ears as she frantically searched the faces in the crowd. She picked her way through the bustling hordes, showing people Steve's photo, only to be shunned time and time again.

She wanted to scream in desperation when a haunting melody floated to her ears cutting through the din around her. The music sounded light-hearted and joyful. She found herself confused. The tune reminded her of her friend. She reeled around looking for its source. In a corner opposite a wall of brightly painted lockers sat a long haired man sitting upon a tattered suitcase, strumming a guitar. He wore a dusty wide rimmed hat that covered most of his face. A scraggly long beard peeked out from underneath brim.

A member of ZZTop, Debbie thought. She stopped and stood quietly before the man who continued playing as if he did not notice her. Debbie stood uncomfortably shifting her weight from one foot to the other, not wanting to rudely interrupt the exquisite music that strummed from the beat up guitar. She was startled when the man finally spoke.

"You are a music lover," he said without looking up, "I can see it in your eyes." His fingers continued to strum the melody.

Debbie shrugged and held up Steve's photograph. "Have you seen this man?" she said.

"Steve Sweeny," the musician replied, "he was here this morning standing right where you are now."

Hope lightened her heart. "Do you know where he is now?"

The man continued to play for several moments causing an uncomfortable shift in Debbie's mood.

"He is a delightful young lad," the musician murmured. "You see it do you not?"

"Sir," Debbie replied desperately, "I really must find my friend. It's urgent."

The man played on and Debbie was starting to think the guy was crazy. He said he had seen Steve. He knew his name, and this was her only lead.

"Please sir," she said on the verge of tears, "I'm willing to pay you."

The man stopped playing. For the first time he slowly looked up from beneath the brim of his hat. Debbie felt a shiver run down her spine. The musician's eyes were completely white.

"I will help you," the man said, and began playing the lighthearted tune once again. "Sit down beside me and humor an old man a while longer. Then you shall find your friend."

He played on, but the beauty of the music had gone along with Debbie's patience.

"He inspired this one you know?" The musician said with a shadow of a smile.

"Excuse me?"

"Your friend – he inspired this tune."

Debbie decided to humor the man for Steve's sake. "What key is it in?" She asked, irritation heavy in her tone.

"Oh, I don't know notes," the man smiled, "I just play with souls."

"You mean soul don't you."

"huh?"

"You play with soul." She answered. "You said souls."

"Did I?"

Debbie let out a heavy sigh and instantly the man stopped strumming. He slowly turned his head and stared over with blank eyes then lifted his guitar and offered it to her. "You play," he said, "I know you can."

"Yes, but I don't have time. I must look for my friend."

"You will," the musician said, and as he smiled sunlight reflected from a nearby window caught several gold teeth through his grinning lips, "first you play."

Debbie reluctantly grabbed the guitar and shot the old man a loathing glance. Her fingers plucked the strings and then slowly she began to strum a tune.

"What's your name?" She asked playing the guitar intro to "Stairway to Heaven."

"Billy Lee Zachary Bub."

Upon hearing the name her mind slowly processed the information as she played through the first several bars of the song. A thought of caution entered her mind and she noticed the reality that was the bus station was becoming lucid around her with an almost dreamlike quality.

"Stairway" was no longer the song that met her ears as she played on dreamily. Now a very somber, thoughtful yet familiar melody emanated from the instrument within her hands as the old mans maniacal laughter rose in the back ground. The song sounded almost Gothic.

Her mind slowly formed around her last thought as she unwillingly passed through the portal between planes.

"B. L. Z. BUB."

TRIAL BY JURY

"Is the jury online?" The judge asked, taking her seat.

"Initiating the call now ma'am." The Clerk of Court pulled his Personal Interface Glove onto his right hand and the holographic control screen leapt into life before him. He made several rapid hand motions and the laser emitters embedded within the wall of the small room radiated the holographic image of a twenty first century courtroom.

"Going way back today aren't we Carter seven – two forty seven?" The judge sighed and flashed the man a ghost of a smile.

"My apologies, ma'am," Two Forty Seven answered respectfully, "thought a different venue would be a nice change from the antiseptic feel of the Judicial Omni Forum."

"Nice touch Two Forty Seven." She donned her own Personal Interface Glove, this time allowing him a full smile, "nostalgic and rather romantic. Even for you."

The judge cleared her throat and sat upright. She glanced at the Clerk and gave a nod. Another whirlwind of hand movements from Two Forty Seven and one by one several holographic images flashed into the jury box. A moment later, seven anonymous ghostly human forms sat within the box leaving one chair empty.

"Clerk," the judge called out, slightly annoyed, "where is Juror Six?"

A sudden flash of blue light and the empty chair was filled with a human default image.

"Sorry ma'am," the shimmering image responded, "I had to answer a call of nature."

"Well," the judge said, flashing an admonishing glance at the tardy juror, "Barring anymore distractions let's get this thing started. Send in the prisoner."

A door opened and a man of medium build, jet black hair clipped close to his scalp walked into the room. His features were rugged, and he wore a set of brown coveralls, the attire worn by maximum security prisoners. The man marched into the centre of the room with a posture that indicated military training. He stopped before the judge and stood to attention.

From the ceiling, two laser cannons dropped from the trap doors and trained their muzzles squarely at the prisoner's head. The prisoner showed no emotion, his eyes fixed intently at the judge.

"Jurors," the judge said, shifting her gaze in their direction, "it is my duty to inform you that as per agreement 1705 article 267-2710 of the Terran Statute Tome your identities remain hidden from public and governmental databases and bandwidths. These proceedings are isolated and scrambled, not to be viewed until all parties involved have expired. Also, as per agreement 1705 article 298-2718, none of you will be held accountable for the condemnation of the prisoner. Please indicate your understanding of this proclamation."

One by one, the holographic images of the jurors changed from hazy blue auras to green ones.

The judge swiveled in her chair. "Clerk, begin ghost file 1187-2729 and start Encryption Transcript starting with the unanimous acknowledgment of primary mandate by our jury."

Two Forty Seven pressed a few holobuttons and an empty dialogue field appeared in the space above the judge's head. As she began to speak the words materialized instantly within the box scrolling from left to right.

"Prisoner A113, known by military designation Alpha-Zed 1652a, you are charged with the murder of your wife Mary Ten - Three Seventy Two. How do you plead?"

The soldier's gaze never left the judge's eyes as one corner of his mouth turned upward in a wry smile. He moved his lips to respond but held his tongue. A diagnostic screen appeared over his head. The information box showed the prisoner's brain wave patterns, heart rate and blood pressure readings. Alpha-Zed 1652a knew it would be indicated within a fraction of a second if he were to lie.

"If I may I would like to address the court?" he said.

The judge sighed. "This is highly irregular, but I will allow it. Just be aware that your imminent execution is scheduled in twenty two minutes. Do not waste the court's time."

"Thank you ma'am," AZ 1652a bowed elegantly, "I appreciate your generous kindness."

"Prisoner, do not test my patience, I only allow this because Terran Law entitles you to a closing statement before you proclaim your g-." She paused catching herself and cleared her throat, "-innocence."

"I humbly apologize, ma'am."

"Just make it quick," she responded leaning back in her chair.

"As you wish," he bowed again, enraging the judge even further. The soldier walked over to the railing and faced the default holographic images. As he moved, the two laser cannons kept precisely trained on his skull.

"My removed anonymous ladies and gentleman, our society is now at a cross roads-"

"Objection!" A computerized voice cut through the room after a short staccato beep. "Irrelevent."

The soldier fell to a knee and grabbed at his throat as immense pressure from an unseen source closed off his esophagus.

The judge smiled down upon the prisoner. "It seems the Planetary Prosecution Protocol Program does not like the tone of your little speech, but I find your ramblings amusing, so I will overrule."

A brief silence ensued and the jury turned their attention to the awestruck Clerk as he stared dumbfounded back at the judge. The Encryption Transcript Program struggled with relaying verbiage as the only sound within the room was the guttural choking of prisoner A113.

The judge turned her attention to the Clerk. Two Forty Seven, I suggest you hit the override button on your holoscreen or you're going to have to file a lengthy report on how you prematurely and illegally executed our prisoner."

The Clerk shook his head and enabled the Override Protocol for the first time in his long career.

The prisoner got back on his feet and nodded thanks at Two Forty Seven. "I owe you," he said brushing off his coveralls.

The Clerk answered with a roll of his eyes.

"Please continue A113," the judge said, "you have exactly twenty minutes and sixteen seconds remaining before you die."

"Thank you," AZ 1652a answered with a bow and a lavish sweep of his arm that infuriated the judge. He turned to the jury. "The zeal of our race over the eons has allowed us great jumps in our evolu-"

"Objection!" The computerized voice strangled the man's words once again.

"Clerk!" The judge commanded, "Please disable the Planetary Prosecution Protocol Program immediately!"

The clerk looked up in disbelief. Upon seeing her features twisted into a mask of dark contempt he reluctantly punched the necessary override command into his holoscreen.

"Warning!" The staccato computer voice echoed in the room, "Planetary Prosecution Protocol has been taken off line."

The lighting in the courtroom changed from a soft white to a harsh red.

Two Forty Seven shot the judge a look of disapproval as he punched in a flurry of codes into his holoscreen. Four smaller laser cannons dropped from the ceiling taking aim at the prisoner and a dense force field of blue energy surrounded the man. A metallic thud shook the walls as a heavy iron door slammed shut over the courtroom entrance.

A smile parted the lips of the judge as she relished the power she held over her captive. This quickly changed to a scowl as the soldier looked at her through the force field with a huge grin of his own. He glanced at the jury and felt satisfaction for upon each default image was a look of concern. He could not help the ominous grin that flashed across his face as for the third time, he addressed the virtual gathering.

"Man has reached one of these points in history once again. Our evolution has bounded forward and our seed has spread throughout the solar system. But we have abused the cosmic speed limit due to our fervor, lust for knowledge and personal gain. Our race has upset the natural balance just as it has done before. Now we must do as our forefathers did and pay for these indiscretions."

The judge stood up and shouted. "So you brutally murdered your wife in cold blood with your Tactical Mendleson Suit to serve this ludicrous philosophy?"

Two Forty Seven tried to calm his superior. "Ma'am can you not see that he is trying to goad you? Please get a hold of yourself."

"Can it Carter!" She yelled.

"Ahem!" The prisoner got their attention, "I still have over eighteen minutes."

All eyes in the room, virtual and physical, trained on the judge. She smoothed back the strands of hair that had fallen over her brow and sat back into her chair. "Please continue your enlightening lecture prisoner," she said.

"My wife was not murdered," AZ 1652a responded, "she was sacrificed."

"Oh this I cannot wait to hear," the judge scoffed. She bit her tongue as the prisoner looked over and waggled his finger at her.

The prisoner walked over to the edge of the force field and peered through, "Judge, I'm glad you brought up the Mendleson Suit. Clerk, could you please display a graphic of the military hardware for the jury?"

Two Forty Seven looked up at the judge awaiting her nod of approval. She smiled contemptuously and gave the go ahead. A flurry of depressed holobuttons and a graphic of the Suit slowly spun in virtual space within the center of the room.

"Ah," the prisoner crossed the room accompanied by the whirl of mechanical gears from the laser cannons following his every move, "the Tactical Mendleson Suit. Observe, ladies and gentleman. Created by the Einstein of our time Mendleson Six - Six Two Four."

There was a thoughtful pause before AZ 1652a continued.

"Or maybe he is the Oppenheimer of our time. No matter, just look at it folks. Marvel at its single-minded purpose and destructive power, impervious to any known weapon or environment and totally self sufficient to not only its weapon systems, but the user as well. You could survive six months on the atmosphere deprived moon in one of these things? Six months within the crushing sulfuric acid drenched environment of Venus, or even six months on the oxygen-less baked surface of Mercury."

"Sixteen minutes," the judge stated flatly, "I fail to see any relevance to this case."

The soldier ignored the judge's statement and pointed at the suit behind him without turning, "This military equipment defies the laws of the known universe in its ability to synthesize organic and inorganic material from a holograph."

He paused and took in his captive audience. The diagnostic dialog box above AZ1652a's head indicated a change in his brainwave patterns. Normally this would trigger a warning from the Planetary Prosecution Protocol Program, but it was disabled and only one person observed the shift - the Clerk. He wanted to covertly warn the judge but her attention was squarely on the soldier.

"That is why," the prisoner continued as the courtroom illusion flickered with a surge of energy, "I put it to you ladies and gentleman of the jury that this creation before you was not made by the hands of man." AZ 1652a swiveled on his heal and leveled an intense gaze as he faced the judge, "but was constructed by God himself."

The prisoner paused and a nervous energy circulated the room. No one, physically or virtual dared utter a response.

"And this Saber of Heaven," the prisoner said, raising his arms to the ceiling, "shall be wielded by my preordained soul, for I am the one who is to bring balance back to the nature of our existence. I have been sent to punish man for his ungodly endeavors and unending arrogance. I am the Great Equalizer."

"Enough of this farce!" The judge shouted. "Damn the extra filing Two Forty Seven, I authorize the execution of prisoner A113 immediately!"

"But ma'am-" The Clerk protested.

"I have made my ruling Carter," she spat the words venomously, "do it now! That is an order!"

Suddenly the room shook and chunks of concrete cracked from the ceiling hitting the floor in a chorus of thuds. An immense force clanged against the iron door of the courtroom and a huge dent appeared.

"Two Forty Seven," the judge yelled, fear governing her voice, "re-engage Planetary Prosecution Protocol!"

The holoscreen before the clerk winked out of existence and he looked back at her helplessly raising his hand into the air.

Alpha-Zed 1652a looked up at the judge with an ominous grin as chaos rained down behind him and a second blast of energy buckled the iron door even further. Curtains of sickly green light radiated from the twisted breaches as the huge metallic hand of the Mendleson Suit ripped it from its hinges.

The judge frantically depressed the fire command button upon her personal holloscreen but the laser cannons did not respond.

"Your Honor," the prisoner shouted above the ruckus, "you know what the best thing about the Mendleson Suit is?"

The hinges on the door snapped thrusting a shower of concrete and sparks into the room. The heavy portal groaned and collapsed to the floor with a deafening thud. The impact sent a shock wave across the floor, knocking both the judge and the Clerk to the floor, choking them in a cloud of powdery gray dust.

The Mandleson Suit, this military monstrosity, represented as a virtual image spinning in the middle of the room now stood in all its terrifying glory, solid and imposing, eager to serve its Master Operating Pilot – the prisoner.

Prisoner A113's voice reverberated within the sudden still silence of the room with hollow resonance. "As you can observe, the best thing about the Mandleson Suit is its ability integrate its command programs into any Military or Government control system."

As the last word echoed into the dust laden silence, the judge saw the array of laser cannons slowly turn their aim upon her. Six red beams of light coalesced into a single shining amber dot centered over her heart as she lay on the debris strewn floor behind her desk. The blue force field separating her from the rest of the room faded to nonexistence.

"Oh shit," she exclaimed as the weapons discharged their blue plasma destruction, dispatching her body into all corners of the room. The laser cannons then shifted their red beacons of death upon Two Forty Seven.

"Go ahead!" The Clerk shouted surprised by his own bravado, "do it quickly."

AZ1652a turned and walked towards his war machine as the immense torso of the mechanized monstrosity split and separated revealing a pilot seat within its command cockpit. Before he climbed the access ladder that lowered to the floor before him he paused and turned to Carter Seven dash Two Forty Seven.

"Let it be known sir," he said with odd compassion in his voice, "that I am a man of my word. You saved my life," he paused and looked over at the virtual jury who stared mesmerized through holographic eyes. The prisoner glanced at the dumbfounded Clerk of Court, "Yours is the first life I save."

He paced over to Carter and held out a hand to help him off the floor. The Clerk stared up at the soldier with a look of fear and despair before reluctantly accepting.

"Now go forth into a new world," the prisoner said patting Two Forty Seven on the shoulder, "and live life as nature intended. For today by the Hand of God the Equalizer will commence to cleanse the world of man's unholy technology with the destructive power he has brought upon himself." He turned and strode back to the Mendleson Suit facing the virtual jury as he did so.

"And you the ladies and gentleman of the jury," he said with a smile as he leapt onto the first rung of the access ladder, "tell the world that it will soon be liberated from the evilness that holds all within its grip. God has passed his verdict and all who stand against him shall be dispatched into the eternal fires of Hell!" The soldier bounded up the ladder and the huge torso of the Suit snapped shut around him.

Six months later the Equalizer had returned the balance of the nature that man's technology had almost completely destroyed. A thousand years of peace would reign before God would pass his final judgment upon man with the imploding of the life giving star that had enabled the very existence of humanity. Thus, the balance of the nature of the universe was restored and our race passed into extinction leaving behind but a few meager trinkets speeding through space as a testament to our existence...

THE BARTENDER GUY

Episode Two

DISCLAIMER:

ALL THE FAMOUS NAMES WITHIN THIS STORY HAVE BEEN POORLY IMITATED.

NO FAMOUS PEOPLE WERE HARMED IN THE WRITING OF THIS STORY.

I HAVE ONLY MET ONE FAMOUS PERSON IN PERSON IN MY LIFE AND HE WASN'T REALLY ALL THAT FAMOUS SO JUST FORGET ABOUT THAT GUY.

Excessive neurological activity stemming from inhibitory neurons not functioning properly. These neurons failing to excrete levels of the neurotransmitter that inhibits the transmission of other neurons leads to a high level of activity in the brain responsible for human emotional arousal. The result being? A human individual feels fear.

It is me Dave again, your bartender, remember me?

Well, right now I couldn't care less whether you do or not, because I am scared shitless. Yep, fear.

That same feeling a married man feels when leaving his pregnant girlfriend's house banging all six cylinders of his Japanese import needing a good old gas guzzling two more because he can't get away fast enough.

Life is like that for humans on this planet.

It is what was instilled in us by our poo throwing distant ancestors that saved us from the pea brain behemoths that tried to eat them for dinner. Thus, allowing us to evolve while those ancient monsters were left millions of years ago in the dust with egg on their faces. Well, faeces on their faces is more likely.

So, over eons of life on the planet here I am at our species' pinnacle. And I don't mean I am the perfect specimen of humanity. I am probably one of the farthest from it. Yours truly is but one of billions of her latest model. And right now I wish I had a handful of poo to throw.

See, right now Davie is standing in front of a six foot, seven inch behemoth ex-boyfriend with my pants down around my well evolved ankles, while his former girlfriend lays half naked on the couch behind me.

So, you could say, my neuro inhibitors are a bit low and the emotional arousal part of my brain is banging on all six cylinders. Meanwhile, my sexual parts are banging on nothing. So I grab for the only handful of shit I can find. My power of negotiation.

Being a bartender requires a BA in BS. My well honed negotiation techniques were well oiled and had averted many a bar fight and assured casualties from countless bar room brawls. Unfortunately, it had failed me this night, because it was also well lubricated from many a nights conquest with a bunch of the local young ladies.

Yet here I call on it once more to get me out of the hard spot I was now in. Or was it because of the soft place my hard spot was not in now? Sorry for the stray thought. It just kind of slipped out.

I began negotiating like an OJ Simpson trial lawyer to get me out of the predicament I had wormed my way into. I sized my opponent up and flung my first volley of crap at the lumbering lumberjack like male.

"Can I pull my pants up?" Shear genius, first volley, misdirection. Here I find it hard avoiding any rhymes with erection because I know someone out there was thinking it. I know I was. Ten minutes ago. But now I am fighting for my survival, and sex is not an option.

Then something unexpected happens that affirms my belief that woman are, no doubt, the smarter sex. The, half naked, ex-girlfriend jumps up from the couch and steps in between the half-witted hulk and me.

"Now you boys calm down!" She shouts and shoves her ex boyfriend with one hand while, with the other hand behind her back performs a card trick David Copperfield would have been proud of. She shoves a player card at me. I am momentary ruled by confusion as I deftly grab and look at the sports player. The name on the card is (currently copyrighted popular ex sports star). Now I know I am in a deeper pile of shit I could never wrap my hand around to toss. The picture upon the card is none other than (currently copyrighted popular ex sports star), this bumbling behemoth. I quickly shove the card in my freshly zipped up pants.

"(Currently copyrighted popular ex sports star)," she purrs his name with a quick look over her shoulder and a wink before turning back to (currently copyrighted popular ex sports star), "now it is not like you lost me in a card game!"

With the last word she stomps on my foot with her heal and understanding hits me like a pink frosted bowling ball.

Watch out Johnny Cochran, let the negotiations begin.

"Hey you must be (currently copyrighted popular ex sports star)," I say pulling out the card from my, now freshly, belted trousers and I shout excitedly, "I have your rookie card right here!"

Second handful of poo successfully delivered. Flattery builds the giant's confidence.

(Currently copyrighted popular ex sports star) staggers a moment and involuntarily wipes unseen feces off of his face. His brow furrows and confusion sets his face as the old football days play upon the little silver screen within his pea brained head.

Now for the final dung assault.

"(currently copyrighted popular ex sports star)," I say pulling a pen from behind my ear (yes, bartenders always have one behind their ear), "will you sign my official (currently copyrighted popular ex sports star) rookie card for me?"

Two hours later, after having to play against the big dolt in his officially licensed video game, I am now banging away on all six cylinders of my Japanese import, wishing I had eight. But for the fact my ancestors flung poo a million years ago and (currently copyrighted popular ex sports star's) parents mated with the lumbering behemoths of yesteryear, I evolved to negotiate another day.

Oh and let me not forget to mention here, women are the more intelligent species of the human race. And in closing of this episode, the smartest of their sex is now having make up sex with (currently copyrighted popular ex sports star). It was the best sex I almost ever had. I shall never forget her.

It is not a complete loss though. I now have a (currently copyrighted popular ex sports star)'s freshly signed rookie card. Now I need a fresh pair of underwear so I bid you all a farewell until next time. Now go out there and fling some poo!

THE SILVER POLICY

Part One

Tyler spent his days in the manufacturing plant, building a machine for people more fortunate than he. He worked the insulation line, padding the outer hauls of luxury space suites that would eventually end up in Earth's orbit. Using a dispersion insulation gun, Tyler sprayed an insulation liquid into the gaps within the polymetal skins of the plush Extreme Environment Compartments. The liquid's chemical composition allowed the mixture to expand and dry three seconds after application.

Tyler toiled on the units and dreamt of one day living in one himself. His tastes had always surpassed his station in life. He longed to be among the rich living in space, looking down upon the planet. He saved and skimped every way possible so he could visit the Dream Salon at the weekend. The frugal life he lived during the week was forgotten during his weekend sessions at this expensive salon, living the 'good life' within a virtual existence.

Prior to logging in each workday Tyler attended the morning safety meeting where he was reminded of the dangers the chemicals posed if they came into contact with human skin. Tyler dismissed the notion. He was an old hand, and did this every working day of his life. But today, he wished he had spent a few extra credits on a reinforced safety suit. The gun hose ruptured and insulation liquid sprayed onto his right arm and leg. He watched in horror as the fabric of his sub-standard suit evaporated instantly into a fine orange dust. The excruciating pain that followed forced Tyler to his knees. His arm and leg turned to pools of thick bubbling goo as he writhed on the floor. Safety protocols were activated and company medi-bots were on the scene, sedating him seconds later.

Tyler woke up three hours later on the 378th floor of the Governmental Medical Institute's hospital complex. He felt an uncomfortable pinch on his right shoulder and hip as the seals of the Prosthetics devices chaffed his skin. Looking down he saw the hollow molds containing the pressurized nanomachines weaving the synthetic material cloning the arm. The nanos created skin, bone and muscle from his stored DNA code.

Tyler looked through the plexiglass wall at the technicians working behind the control consoles. Behind them the door slid open and in walked a gaunt looking man with pasty skin and oily black hair. The technicians continued working oblivious to the distraction. The door to Tyler's room slid silently open and the man entered.

"Mr. Suttles," he said with a smile, "I am your Government Insurance Coordinator." The lanky suit scanned Tyler's CompChart at the end of the bed with a microcomputer. A moment later there was a staccato beep and the man grinned. "Ah, very good," he said squinting at the scrolling results on the chart, "excellent news. All of your organs are in perfect working condition."

"My arm and leg are useless," Tyler mumbled.

The Insurance man walked to the edge of the bed. Tyler stared insultingly at the man's hand as the agent prompted a handshake with his wounded hand. The man chuckled, "Sorry, just a little insurance joke."

"When can I expect to get out of here?" Tyler asked with a scowl, "I need to get back to work."

"Normally this is outpatient surgery," the man said, rubbing his chin, "and we can clear you by the days end."

"Good. I still have a few hours left on the shift."

"Mr. Suttles," the Insurance man looked at the chart quizzically, "I see here you have a Silver Policy. Very economical."

"Yeah, so what?"

"Well," the man looked coldly down into Tyler's eyes, "it expires at midnight."

Tyler looked through the plexiglass at atomic clock on the wall behind technicians. It read 11:58PM. Tyler felt his heart sink. The uninsured were taken to the Basement. The hierarchy of society dictated that those without insurance be used as donors. Donors. The word sent a chill down his spine.

The Basement was where organs were removed and sent to be used to prolong the life of Platinum Policy holders. The folks living in Earth's orbit - the rich.

"I...I c-can renew can't I?"

"Of course you can Mr. Suttles," the man said with another big smile presenting the CompChart, "we just need your thumb print signature right here."

Tyler breathed a sigh of relief and pressed his thumb to the chart just as a buzzer sounded and the clock rolled over to midnight. He laid back on the bed and felt slight pressure at the base of his wounded appendages. Confused, Tyler watched as the Surgery Prosthetic Regenerators' seal broke from his skin and rolled off the bed. Both units hit the floor and the patient watched in horror as the nano machines spilled out and rolled in all directions. Seconds later, one by one, they popped in tiny flashes of electrical light as the room's pressure crushed them. Immediately his exposed nerve endings exploded in pain and he felt the warmth of gushing blood down his right side.

"What the Hell?" Tyler exclaimed through the haze of pain.

The insurance man held up the chart close to his face and pointing to a timer counting downward from thirty minutes.

"Mr. Suttles," the man said with a devious glint in his eye, "It will take half an hour to process your new policy."

Tyler fought against the pain and the coming of unconsciousness as hard as he to no avail. As he slowly slipped under the last words chilled his blood.

"Hackers," he saw the insurance man speak into his microcomputer through dimming vision, "We have a bleeder."

Part Two

Tyler saw himself sitting in a big comfy chair in front of a huge oblong oval window. He held a snifter of Brandy with one hand and puffed on a pipe filled with the finest tobacco in the other. The combination tantalized his taste buds.

A fire blazed in a huge fireplace behind him reflecting off the polished tiles of the luxury suite. Tyler looked through the huge polyglass portal down upon the Earth. This was much like one of his programs at the Dream Salon, but more extravagant. Tyler took a long draw from the snifter and puffed on his pipe exhaling the sweet smoke with complete exquisite satisfaction.

He heard a buzzing in his left ear. He turned to see a large metal mosquito hovering a foot away from his face.

"What in God's name?"

The flying insect lunged forward and Tyler felt the sting of its bite stab into his neck. He swatted at the flying menace as it hovered before his face. It darted towards the thick black portal and to his horror, burst through the poly glass. Tyler was sucked out and suddenly he felt himself falling.....

"Aye," he heard a muffled voice, "he's comin' round. Hit him with one more shot of adrenaline."

Another stab at Tyler's neck, and once again he felt the excruciating pain gnawing away at his extremities as he lay in a warm puddle of blood next to gurney.

He looked up at two men wearing blood stained aprons and felt the sensation that he was falling. He realized he was going down in an elevator. And, in modern day society, down was always bad. In this case Tyler knew the destination was the basement.

"Hello Mr. Suttles," one of the men said with a smile seemingly too big for his face, "we are your Hackers today."

"What is the meaning of this?" Tyler blurted, "I renewed my policy!"

"Oh?" The second Hacker said holding up the CompChart, "According to this we still have six more minutes before policy renewal."

The first Hacker held up a surgical saw and pressed a button making the shiny blade whirl. It sounded just like the buzzing mosquito within his dream. Suddenly a morbid realization hit Tyler. These men had awakened him so they could begin "hacking" him while he was fully aware of the experience.

"You can't do this!" He cried out, wincing at the pain the effort caused his wounds.

"Oh we do it all the time," the first Hacker said, "There was this one bloke-"

A PING as the elevator came to an abrupt halt. The doors slid open and there stood the Government Insurance Coordinator.

"What took you so long?!" The pasty faced man asked irately.

"Sorry Mr. Manson," the Hackers said in unison.

They wheeled the pleading Tyler across to a steel 'operating table' and roughly tossed him onto it. He cried out in pain as his wounds exploded in fire.

"For God sake!!" He screamed with the little strength he had left, "don't do this."

The Hackers tied him down and gagged his mouth with a leather strap.

"Just bite down on this strap when the pain gets too excruciating," the Hacker said with a chuckle

The other Hacker wheeled over a table full of menacing instruments. The operating lights glinted ominously off of the shiny tools, perfectly designed to do their purpose.

Tyler screamed through the leather strap as the whirl of the surgical saw revved up once again. Despite the unbearable pain, he tried to move but was bound too tightly. This was it he thought to himself. The end.

A loud beep cut through the room as the clock on the CompChart held within Mr. Manson's hands reached zero. The whirl of the saw ceased and the only sound in the room was the hum of the surgical light above.

Manson studied the chart a moment.

"Congratulation Mr. Suttles," he said in disappointment, "your policy has been approved."

Tyler relaxed and exhaled a sigh of relief. That was cut short when the saw began humming away again eager to bite into his flesh. He felt the blade slice into his skin and sink into the muscle of his right thigh. For the brief moment the pain rivaled the other wounds, until it all became one gnawing tortured hell.

"You see Mr. Suttles," The Insurance Agent shouted over the saw, "because the Silver Policy only covers your lungs, heart, brain and eyes, we can claim the rest." Blood spurted from the artery in Tyler's leg and sprayed the agent in the face. He paused a moment and casually wiped the warm liquid from his cheek.

"That is," Mr. Manson held up a hand and the sawing ceased. "Unless you would like to upgrade to a Gold Policy?"

With tears streaming down his face Tyler emphatically nodded affirmative.

"Your 'good' thumb print signature." Manson said with a chuckle, holding up the chart to Tyler's right hand.

The hapless Tyler pressed his thumb to the pad as hard as he could.

"Very good Mr. Suttles," Manson said looking at the scrolling information on the chart. Tyler's heart leapt to his throat as the saw again whirled away and dug into his flesh. The Government Insurance Coordinator held up the chart in front of Tyler's pain racked face showing him a fresh thirty-minute clock.

"It will take thirty minutes to process your Gold Policy."

Part Three

This time when Tyler returned to consciousness instead of falling, he felt as though he was floating on air. He opened his eyes and tried to breathe but found he could not. His brain was in a panicked frenzy as he stared wildly at his surroundings, tried to draw another breath but his throat muscles contracted in vain.

After several minutes he concluded that death was not coming, nor was his ability to breath. He could not understand why he was still alive. Tyler finally managed to focus on the space around him. His vision cleared and he saw a collection of machines across the other side of the 'operating room'. Within each machine a small window afforded a view inside. Tyler squinted hard to make out the contents. Organs.

One small squat machine possessed a rat's nest of wires on the surface and within he saw a heart pumping. A second machine, this one tall and slender, had rubber tubes feeding into the top, pumping air in and out of a pair of purple glistening lungs.

Again Tyler's throat contracted, grasping for air. His brain railed against the need to breathe and panic spread until his eyes focused on the smiling face of the Government Insurance Coordinator.

"Mr. Suttles," Manson said with a chuckle, "how are you feeling?"

Tyler's mouth struggled to work but all that came out was a clacking of teeth.

"Speechless I see." The agent smiled, "or could it be because you have no vocal cords? I am thinking the latter. Anyway, just sit back and relax and I will fill you in."

Manson pulled up a chair while Tyler tried to scream an obscenity.

"I regret to inform you that your Gold Policy was denied. It seems you did not have enough credits. But, I have good news. Your organs," he said with a sweep of his hand behind him," will enhance the lives of several Platinum Policy holders, which the Government Insurance Company is eternally grateful."

The agent shot a quick glance over his shoulder at the two Hackers busy cleaning up the area around the 'operating table.' Then he leaned in close to Tyler's decapitated head.

"Here is the best part," he whispered with a smile, "you are finally going to experience your dream of living in orbit."

Tyler's mouth worked up and down and his brows shifted.

"You see," Manson continued, "when your Silver Policy expires in a month, due to your absence at work, your brain and eyes are going to Xavier Loftus. The President of the Insurance Company.

"He has this incurable brain disease, I will not bore you with the details, but he will receive your brain and eyes. So, you really are lucky. Look on the bright side. Your eyes will finally get to see one of your finished luxury suites actually in working orbit."

Manson got up from his chair and tugged at his jacket straightening out the wrinkles. He looked down at Tyler's head with a mock frown.

"Too bad your memory is to be erased and imprinted with Mr. Loftus' thought engrams, you might actually get to enjoy the experience."

Tyler watched horrified as the agent packed away his organs for transport. The hopelessness and depression his brain was going through was mercifully ended with another injection, this time into the gum behind his upper lip. Sweet sleep came two minutes later.

Part Four

When Tyler awoke, he immediately knew something was wrong for he still had his thoughts and memory. He sat bolt upright and found himself in a lavish king sized bed adorned with silk sheets. A beautiful woman stirred at his side.

"MMMM," she mumbled snuggling back under the covers he had just pulled from her body, "you were amazing last night. It was like you were someone else."

She turned over and began quietly snoring.

Tyler got up and found a silk robe. He stumbled into the next room and, to his surprise; he recognized the room as the one he had seen in his earlier dream. Next to the comfy chair in front of the large oval window a gentleman stood with a brandy in one hand and a pipe in the other. The man stepped back from the chair and motioned for Tyler to sit. Tyler obeyed. As he sat down the man handed him the items.

"Anything else Mr. Loftus?"

"N-N-no," Tyler stammered.

"Very good sir," the man replied and slowly walked out of the room.

A fire blazed in a huge fireplace behind him reflecting off the polished tiles of the huge luxury suite. Tyler looked through the huge polyglass portal down upon the Earth. He took a long sip of brandy and puffed on the pipe as he pondered what the hell was going on. The combination of tastes tantalized his taste buds as he wondered why he was still Tyler Suttles.

He heard a buzzing in his left ear. Tyler instinctively swatted the air expecting to make contact with another metal mosquito. Instead his butler's voice came to him.

"Sir you have a visitor at the front airlock. Should I send him in?"

"Yes," Tyler said uneasily.

The butler left the room and in walked Mr. Manson carrying a battered and bloodied CompChart in his hands. He walked up and held out his hand prompting a hand shake. Tyler felt the adrenaline infuse his muscles as they tensed ready to knock this man to the floor. Anger stirred his heart as his face set in an ominous scowl.

"Easy now," The Government Insurance Coordinator said with a wink, "I could end this right now with a word into my micro computer."

He pulled up a chair and motioned for Tyler to sit down.

"You see," the man said with a devious grin, "I have placed a microcharge in the base of your brain and if you do not do as I tell you....you will die."

Tyler stared with contempt, but said nothing.

"Good," Manson said, "I'm glad we have an understanding."

He presented the CompChart to Tyler. "Your thumb print signature please."

Tyler obediently pressed his thumb to the pad.

"Thank you Mr. Loftus," Manson said and jumped from his chair. As he strode toward the exit he paused and turned on his heal. "By the way. I took the liberty of renewing your Platinum Policy. Free of charge of course."

The agent's laughter echoed off the walls as a deflated Tyler idly puffed at his pipe and watched the Earth slowly turn below his window.

Meanwhile on the surface…

Tony Upton rode the elevator to his Company Office ready to begin another day at the Insurance company. He had been Vice President for fourteen years and life was good.

The elevator doors opened and two men wearing blood stained aprons stepped inside.

"Hello Mr. Upton," one of the men said, "we are to be your Hackers today."

"What is the meaning of this!" The VP said, outraged.

"It seems your Insurance Policy has expired." The other man said stabbing Mr. Upton in the neck with a syringe...

HEARTBROKEN

Calvin Kinsington looked out over the city from his penthouse office in downtown Atlanta. He had it all. The great job, the flashy car, and a five million dollar home in the suburbs. His every whim was catered for, from the finest chefs to the best prostitutes that money could buy. He was content with everything in his life. It was almost perfect.

The middle aged executive looked down at the ice cubes melting in the scotch and soda he had poured thirty minutes earlier. He had yet to take a sip. His mind was on Joanne, whom he had met a month ago, quite by accident. He had just finished a round of golf when he decided to go back to the office to tie up some loose ends on his latest deal. As he stepped into the elevator, a sickly looking man walked in after him holding a single red rose. The brightness of the petals threw the paleness of the man's skin into stark contrast.

Calvin sidled away from the man in fear of catching whatever sickness was ailing him. The elevator stopped at the thirteenth floor and as the doors slid open and the "ping" of the cars bell slowly faded into silence, his eyes fixed on her.

Time seemed to slow as the woman looked up from behind the reception desk and lit up the room with a smile. Her face was a picture of exquisite beauty framed by flowing dark auburn hair. She stood waiting, as the sick man stepped off the elevator and Calvin's eyes lustily poured over her supple body. He felt his blood pressure jump and arousal peeked his senses as the woman gracefully slid from behind the desk.

"For me?" she asked as the man held out the rose. Her voice came to Calvin's ears as a siren's melody beckoning him to step off the elevator and crash onto the rocks. His heart skipped as the elevator doors began to shut and his eyes focused on her nameplate upon the desk. Joanne Supples. His focus darted back eager to catch one last glimpse of the gorgeous apparition that was Joanne. Calvin's eyes fixed on the dark ruby heart shaped pendant she wore around her neck as the doors slammed shut burning its image into his mind.

As the day wore on he found his mind in a ruby red funk. The unfinished papers spread out on his desk screamed for attention but he ignored them. He was within his office on top of the world, yet his mind was forty two floors below him on the thirteenth. The vision of Joanne the receptionist still haunted his heart. He felt its rhythm quicken within his chest as the woman's face flashed across his mind. He breathed a heavy, forlorn sigh. His eyes darted over the papers atop his desk and his mind picked out random words within their type.

Rose

Beauty

Fire

Love

Supples

Joanne.

He sat up in his chair and pulled out the last page he had read. He skimmed the black ink and honed in on two words that jumped at him from within the obscure bondage of a long paragraph - PROMOTION REQUEST.

He quickly pressed the button on his intercom to his secretary's desk and cleared his throat.

"Mairi?"

"Yes sir?"

"You're fired."

There was a pause as Calvin read over the promotion request excited as a smitten elementary school boy.

"Can you repeat that sir?" came a shaky voice from the intercom, "I didn't catch what you said."

"You're fired. Pack your gear and get the hell out."

"Fuck you!" Mairi's reply cracked through the office, but Calvin did not grasp the tension. He was busy floating amongst the clouds. Nothing could bring him down. Not Mairi, not the sickly rose toting man, not the executive of the rival corporation he had lost to in golf earlier that morning. He was seeing the world through ruby red heart shaped glasses. He would have Joanne Supples and no one would stand in his way. Except Joanne.

In the past month he had done his best to win her over, but she did not budge. She refused his offer to be his personal secretary even after he offered her three times her current pay. Calvin had spent so much time on thirteen, that he had neglected his own work. And still it wasn't getting him anywhere.

Loneliness slowly ate away at his heart, so he soaked it in scotch and soda and wondered what to do. This night, as he watched the sun sink below the Atlanta skyline his heart answered. A sharp pain blossomed in the center of his chest and sent him to his knees. Muscles tightened and his body sunk into a painful unconsciousness.

'Her pendant is now black,' was the only stray thought cut through the pain before all was lost to darkness.

flatline sound effect/////////////////////////

Calvin did not know how much time had passed when the blur of light came to his eyes and the dull itchy ache of stitched up torture gnawed at his chest. He tried to move but every nerve synapses within his body protested at the effort.

"Mr. Kinsington," a dark skinned Indian doctor sharpened into the foreground, "you should not do this. It only aggravates your incision stitches. Lay still my friend."

Calvin tried to speak but his mouth felt full of cotton and his throat ached from the dryness. He felt fire throughout his upper torso like his chest was full of buckshot.

"You are very fortunate Mr. Kinsington that we found a new heart for you after yours failed. Someone two neighborhoods away was not so fortunate and decided to blow his own head off with a shotgun." The Doctors face split in a tooth capped white grin, "Good for you he did not shoot himself in the chest."

The executive felt an initial repulsion at the strange heart beating in his chest.

The doctor checked the morphine drip next to his bed. "Oh my goodness," he mumbled, "My, my, my. Cannot find any good help these days. Your morphine's gone out. You must be hurting like the Dickens. I will go get the nurse." The Doctor turned to leave the room and said over his shoulder, "By the way young man, the widow of the heart donor wanted to see you. I will send her right in."

Calvin could barely stand the intense pain that seem to fill every pore of his being, and into every corner of his soul. There was a strange tingle in his heart moments before the door opened and in walked a sad-eyed, auburn haired angel.

He felt a smile cross his face despite the pain. He did not even see the nurse at his bedside changing his morphine drip. He breathed her name and his eyes fixed on the bright blood red pendant hanging round her neck as he slipped into a warm merciful floating dream. "Joanne."

After his recovery, Joanne and Calvin married. But his bad luck had already begun with the implant of the heart. It wasn't the organ itself, but the rest of his body felt as if it were dying. Life with Joanne was hell; it seemed his new heart was forever broken.

Then, due to his absence, the business was bought out by the rival company and the executive who had beaten Calvin at golf. The new owner moved into Calvin's penthouse office. Joanne kept her job at the firm and remained on the thirteenth floor, while he stayed at home and pined away for her at home, penniless. The only item of value he had left was his gold Rolex.

One day, ten years after the day of the transplant Calvin decided to spend the last few dollars he had on a red rose, and visit Joanne at work. His heart felt sick as he walked up to his old office building and entered the lobby. He climbed into the elevator with a man in khaki pants and a lime green polo, shouldering a bag of golf clubs. He avoided eye contact and pushed the 13 button.

"Calvin Kinsington?" The man said around the eight floor. The man chuckled. "Jesus, you look like hell dude, I suppose you don't play much golf these days from the looks of ya."

"Fuck off Christopher," Calvin turned to his old rival executive clutching the rose in so hard the thorns bit into his flesh and sent warm blood seeping over his white fingers. The ping of the elevator sounded and opened up onto his auburn haired angel. From behind the desk she looked up and his heart sank for she sat amongst a forest of red roses. The exchanged look of guilt that passed between Christopher and Joanne was obvious and Calvin felt the rose in his hand snap, dripping crimson onto the white carpet of the elevator floor.

He dropped the rose, reached inside his battered old dress coat and his bloody fingers curled around the cold steel of the Colt revolver he had traded in his Rolex for one month earlier. He stood with the sliding doors of the elevator preventing them to close and pointed the gun at Christopher's head.

Calvin smiled when the man's eyes widened with fear and a fresh urine stain bloomed on the front of his khakis. The man's eyes filled with pain and he clutched at his heart as he collapsed to the elevator's floor.

"Go, die in peace," Calvin said stepping off the elevator letting the doors slide shut. He turned the gun on Joanne who stared from underneath her brow with a half smirk. Calvin was about to pull the trigger and wipe that smirk off of her face but his eyes focused on her dark ruby red pendant and understanding took root within his mind. He turned the gun at his chest and watched the smirk leave her lips.

"This heart has always been yours," he smiled and pulled the trigger. As the bullet pierced his heart the dark red pendant around Joanne's neck burst and both of them slumped to the floor.

Upon initial inspection the cause of death of Calvin and Christopher were immediately determined by the coroner. The death of Joanne was a bit harder to determine for upon her autopsy, the woman had no heart within her ribcage.

DEATH'S RIGHT HAND

Fire licked his legs and he savored the pain. This was a prelude to what he would spend eternity enduring but he considered it worthwhile for he had sacrificed himself for something beautiful. He had dared to love.

He had known failure throughout his life and the world considered him an outcast. This isolation drove him to make the deal that would forever rule his destiny. He recalled the fleeting sweetness of the initial revenge and cursed himself for the paltriness of the return garnered from his transaction with the Devil.

He had been ready to serve out his penance then, but he learned the cruel lesson that the Great Dark One doesn't deal in absolutes. He was to become an agent of the Grim Reaper delivering death to countless souls unable to realize the one thing his tortured spirit craved. His own demise.

Now, as the acrid smell of burnt flesh met his nostrils, his mouth watered in anticipation for what lay ahead. His soul cried out in agony, but the gut wrenching pain was exactly what he had come to cherish. He looked upon it as the debt he owed to the souls he had robbed from this world cutting short the chance of them finding redemption before moving onto the next.

The Dark One looked upon him with favor for he had won over so many souls that now anguished in the Under World. This growing population would soon become the strong force Lucifer would utilize to encroach upon, and take over the rule of Heaven.

The fire had claimed his legs and the searing purification had moved to his midsection. He looked through the growing flames at the villagers gathered to witness the witch burning. He smiled through his pain knowing those who gazed upon him would soon meet their own fate at the hands of fiery justice, for the innocents they had claimed through their misguided self-righteousness.

As the flames devoured his stomach they turned to taking his heart. As blood boiled within the furiously pumping organ his thoughts turned to Tabitha. She was the purest soul he had ever encountered and the stone that was his heart became human once more upon their first meeting.

When the executioner called her out he could not help taking the blame for the accusations and sparing her life. The village elders wasted little time before tying him to the stake. Little did they know of the lives they were sparing by taking his. But there was only one he cared about. He scanned the mob seeking out her beautiful face for the last time.

The flames caressed his shoulders and neck and he clenched his teeth against the scream that welled within his convulsing throat. He was determined not to show any pain denying these weak souls the satisfaction of him responding to his suffering.

Tabitha's form materialized in front of the crowd and he felt his heart ache. Even though he had lived upon this earth for eons this was his first true love. He was astonished that his venomous soul was able to assimilate the emotion after the lifetime of darkness he had endured.

Now, upon seeing them usher her to the podium next to his, the hatred and scorn rushed back into his being. The executioner shoved her forward causing her to stumble and the crowd erupted in laughter.

He focused all of his anger on the executioner who grinned back at him wickedly.

"I see your word," he said with a contemptuous smile as he effortlessly broke his bonds, "is as weak as these ropes you have bound me with."

An uneasy hush fell upon the crowd as he stepped through the flames. He reached the edge of the podium and the onlookers gasped as burnt flesh and charred bone became whole again before their widened eyes. He looked past his beloved and leveled his gaze at the executioner. He basked in the fear that radiated from the crowd and he drew strength from it. He grasped the crucifix around his neck with one hand and raised the other pointing at the stunned executioner.

"I curse thee."

As the words floated upon the air the executioner screamed in agony. His hands shriveled and his eyes glazed in blindness. The man's legs rotted beneath his black robe and snapped at the knees. He slumped over writhing in anguish and choked upon maggots that suddenly filled his mouth and nostrils.

"As for the rest of you," he looked over the awestruck assembly of villagers, "the plague!"

Screams filled the air as the crowd dispersed in every direction. He smiled as many of them stopped with hands upon knees profusely vomiting.

"That's right my children," he said beaming and arms raised palms upward towards the sky, "go forth and spread my work!"

He looked down into the tear streaked face of his one and only love. Tabatha's beauty was even stunning in her upset state.

"And for you dearest," he said jumping down from the podium and grabbing her up, "a quick and painless death."

He kissed her trembling lips. Upon pulling away he watched the life bleed from her crying eyes. He gently laid her upon the ground.

"See you in Heaven my love."

I DID IT

Tyler awoke with a start and sprang up in his bed. He stared around wild eyed, his breath coming in short quick shallow gasps. His heart raced and his mind was a blur of incoherent thoughts. He tried to grasp onto one but his head was a chaotic jumble. He did not know where he was. He felt the remnants of a dream on the fringes of his consciousness and as it slipped away he desperately tried to grasp onto it. He swung his legs over the side of his bed and dropped his head into his hands.

His skull ached with a fiery pain and his eyesight was tinged red as if he were looking through a scarlet veil.

"I DID IT."

The single thought burst forward through the tumult of randomness and with it his head instantly cleared. He raised his head and looked around him realizing he was in his room. His leg muscles ached with the shock of being jolted awake and he heard the blood rushing in his head with the beating of his heart. With each beat a soft pain accompanied his heart's cadence in his ears.

"I DID IT."

It was more than a thought, more like a soft whisper. With each word a sharp pain raked across his nerves.

"What the hell..." he grabbed his head in pain. It hurt to talk.

What did I do last night? Sarah had come over late and they had watched a movie, but he could not remember crawling into bed. He turned to look behind him. Sarah was not there. The blankets were kicked aside as if someone had left abruptly.

"I DID IT."

This time it was a hack saw on his nerves, uncomfortable warmth tickled his stomach. He pushed himself off the bed and stumbled to the bathroom almost losing his balance. His head began to swim and chaotic thoughts once again filled his brain as he opened the bathroom door. He braced himself against the door jamb as a gust of warm air brushed past his face. The bathroom was steamy and smelled of juniper berry shampoo. He heard running water behind the shower curtain.

"I DID IT!"

This time it was so loud it rattled his skull. He clutched his head and his pyjamas clung to him in an uncomfortable stickiness. He stumbled towards the shower and snatched the shower curtain aside. Behind the curtain a strange man stood under the shower pelted by hot water. He was fully clothed in black; no face just a featureless blur under a dark hood.

The bathroom light glinted off something in the stranger's hand – a machete.

"I DID IT!" The stranger screamed as he raised the machete and thrust it toward Tylers head.

"NO!!" Tyler screamed as he sprang upright in his bed his hands held before him in a defensive manner.

"I DID IT!"

He looked around the room to see the early morning sun shining red against the far wall.

"Thank God it was just a dream." He sighed shaking his head.

"Tyler are you up?" He heard Sarah's sweet voice from the bathroom.

"I am." He answered, pushing himself off the bed.

"Come join me in the shower," she yelled over the gushing water.

He smiled and pushed the door open. The steamy air hit his face and he began to swoon. His vision blurred as he stepped over the threshold. He slipped on the wet tiles and crashed to the floor next to the tub. He closed his eyes and his head exploded in red pain. The sound of running water echoed in his ears as the familiar warmth tickled his stomach. He slowly opened his eyes and his sight focused on a jar of pills that lay in front of his face.

He read the label. Vicodin. His eyes slewed over the floor and he saw several pills scattered across the floor glistening in the oppressive humidity. He noticed a chalky taste in his mouth and felt a sticky warmth on his right hand. Realization gripped his soul as he focused on the blood stained machete clutched in his quivering hand.

He looked up into Sarah's blue lifeless eyes, her head bent at a grotesque angle over the edge of the tub staring straight at him.

Behind and above her Tyler read the words scrawled across the tile in his girlfriend's blood and his handwriting. As he read his own life slipped away as the words were washed from the porcelain tiled wall.

"I DID IT."

BROKEN WEB

The story I tell is not for you. I tell this not for myself, nor for the authorities, who will inevitably drink in these words when all of this is over. It is not a confession. What I have done is justified. Mary took my heart and in the empty space left behind is now only the venom of hate. Now my vengeance is complete and you will never discover the bitch's body, for there is nothing left to find.

Daniel felt the rage boil in his blood while he read the letter in his trembling hands. He cursed at the empty room. "What did that bastard do to her?"

He wandered through Mary's apartment. Overturned furniture and the disheveled state of the place indicated a struggle.

"I'll kill him for hurting her!"

In the kitchen he reached for the phone, intending to call the police. As he dialed he felt a stab of pain and a tickling on his neck accompanied a second later by a piercing pain just below his jaw. A fiery rush ran down the artery in his neck and Daniel's eyesight began to dim.

"Not unless I kill you first." A blurry image stepped from the shadows and stood before him. The stranger calmly plucked the phone receiver from Daniel's hand just as the operator picked up on the other end. Daniel tried to reach out and strangle the man but found his arms were paralyzed, frozen at his sides.

"Nine-one-one, what is your emergency?"

Daniel tried with all his might to hang onto consciousness.

"Quickly, send the police to 1313 Mockingbird Lane," the stranger said excitedly. "There has been a kidnapping!"

Even though his sight left him, Daniel could hear the wry smile in the stranger's tone. Terror filled his soul as the last words faded along with waning awareness.

"And a murder."

ONE WEEK EARLIER...

Their relationship lasted a year and a half. Joe had fallen deeply for Mary, but his feelings were not reciprocated. Within the past few weeks she had started seeing another man and had rapidly fallen in love with him. Mary told Joe it was over, she tried to be honest.

That night, in a deep depression, Joe lay quietly in his bed in the darkness of his room and stared at the ceiling for hours. He had always teetered on the edge of sanity, and this latest episode was the final nudge to send him sprawling into the shallow water of the psycho pool. He gleefully waded in, curious to experience just how deep it got.

He noticed a spider on the wall. It crawled down and crossed the short distance to his bed. He studied the creature's progress with detached amusement. He admired the spider's graceful movements, purposefully focused on arriving at its destination. The spider scurried up the bedspread and stopped on top of the blanket at Joe's chest.

The creature paused in front of his face; dark liquid eyes stared at him, reflecting the dull light from his alarm clock on the bed stand. The spider seemed almost curious as to Joe's depressed state. Joe watched as one long hairy leg cautiously lowered over the edge of the blanket and touched the bare flesh on his chest.

He watched in fascination, but refused to move a muscle. He did not want to frighten the spider away, he was curious to see what the creature had in mind. The spider slowly made its way up Joe's neck and crawled into his left ear canal. Tiny legs tickled his flesh and he gritted his teeth, fighting to keep still.

The creature squirmed for a few moments and then settled as Joe slowly became accustomed to the odd sensation of his ear's new tenant. He began feeling strange emotions as odd alien landscapes rolled across his mind's eye.

Weird screeching and clicks slowly coalesced into human speech.

"Why do you mourn so?"

Joe swallowed and accepted that it was the spider speaking to him.

"My girlfriend, she...she left me."

"Left you where?" The spider asked curiously.

"N-no," he answered resisting the urge to dig in his ear with a finger. "She is seeing someone else."

"Your mate, she has eyes does she not?" Asked the spider confused.

"She chose another mate," Joe explained speaking slowly as he would to a child. "She did not want to mate with me anymore."

"If you were a spider you would not mourn so," the creature said with conviction. "It would be clear what you should do."

"And what would that be?"

"Kill the competing mate. Then take her and forbid her to 'see' another."

As Joe contemplated the spider's words, an evil grin parted his lips. "I like the way you think spider."

ONE MONTH LATER...

Mary came to consciousness and shook her head sluggishly, trying to shake the cobwebs from her waking mind. She felt as though she were awakening from a weekend bender. Every muscle in her body ached, and a sharp pain burned away within her skull.

She became alarmed, realizing her arms and legs were bound in some kind of sticky thick glue that seemed to stiffen against her struggling movements.

Mary felt immense pressure within her stomach. A burning that slowly burst upward into her throat. To her horror she felt thousands of tiny creatures crawling up into her mouth. She tried to breathe and cry out but her lungs filled with wriggling masses and she suffocated as they ate away and burst from her gaping mouth.

The last sight her dying eyes took in was that of Joe, smiling down upon her, a little spider resting upon his shoulder.

BARTENDER GUY

Episode Three

Hey folks,

Once again it's Dave, your buzz specialist.

I serve alcohol.

Alcohol is defined as any of a series of hydroxyl compounds, the simplest of which are derived from saturated hydrocarbons, having the general formula $CnH2n+1OH$, and include ethanol and methanol. The effects are well known to any human who has experienced:

Loss,

Love,

Pain,

Sorority/Fraternity life,

First date anxiety,

First date,

Procreation (successful enabling of)

Political Career,

Bachelorism/Bacheloressism,

Marriage,

Divorce,

Barmitsvah,

Birth of child,

Graduation of child,

Imprisonment of child,

Loss of Job,

Loss of spouse,

Loss of pet...

I could go on for days with excuses for the modern person in our society to ingest this volatile colorless liquid. Just typing the above list made me want to take a stiff shot, but I digress from my point.

I like to look on alcohol as life's little laxative. It helps you slide through this world just a little bit easier easing the pain of the before mentioned experiences. But did you know that this little molecule disguised as a simple sugar to our human physiology has a far greater purpose and affect than our collective consciousness comprehends? There is a war being waged within our planetary society as a common foe is vanquished on a nightly basis all over our planet.

The first line of defense is not the mighty militaries of our superpower countries, or the technological prowess of the world's combined scientific community with their "all seeing" layer of spying satellites pulled snugly around our planet's atmosphere. Nor is it, my fellow planetary inhabitants, a secret society of plasma cannon totting, brain erasing black clad suited men protecting us roaming our city and town streets in anonymity.

Do not fear though my brethren and sleep safe tonight for there is a force far more powerful than all of these entities combined. We tirelessly ward off the continuous onslaught of swarming off planet-ors keeping our mother Earth firmly seeded with our humanity. No conquering alien force will ever take our world as long as there is breath enough in the last of our number to purvey our wares and fend these would be invaders off.

We are known by many names all over the world. Cantinero, barista, barmenis, baarimikko. With every nationality, race, creed, gender and color our task remains true despite our diverse ideologies and political beliefs. To protect our world from alien domination...and to get fellow human beings plastered.

We are the proud,

We are the well versed in Mixology,

We are the world's bartenders.

Our secret weapon is one of disastrous and dastardly destructive power throughout our crowded corner of the universe. We protect the sanctity of our secret weapon hiding its clandestine formula in devious mixtures with odd names like "Screwdrivers", "Royal Flushes" and "Harvey Wallbangers".

There are those amongst us that even tauntingly named offensive recipes "B52's", and "Sidewinder Missiles" endangering the anonymity of our well kept secret weapon. But fear not because we have always managed to keep the molecular mix in the middle muted to the vigilant ears of our off world enemies.

For the tantalizing formula that numbs our brains and keeps our sanity barricaded against the tribulations of our mundane everyday stressful lives has a far more diverse effect on our freakish foes. It renders them entirely brain dead sending them back to their home worlds with fractured minds and drooling babbling tongues. You may have even personally seen an alien life form bested by one of your planetary defenders before your very eyes without even knowing it....think about it.

In closing I would just add this one tidbit. Next time your brain has been professionally numbed by your preferred buzz specialist be sure to thank them personally with a bow or shake of the hand. TIP YOUR BARTENDER WELL for they are not just responsible for that peaceful warm and fun feeling you are leaving with within your belly. They are the reason man still rules this planet unhindered by alien invasion and domination!

THIRTEEN CURVES

Part One

Every town has one. They are rooted in culture and loosely tied to faint wisps of mysterious history. Over years of telling and retelling they become more extraordinary and outlandish. But deep down they romantically tantalize our belief that there is more to this life than just this physical plane we exist within.

They are haunted places.

These locations stir the fear within one's soul and defy reality by playing tricks on the rational mind. I grew up in South Carolina, which has more than its fair share of ghostly places and haunting tales, but the most intriguing spot I discovered was when I moved to upstate New York in the mid 1980's.

To explain my experience I must first tell the tale as it was relayed to me. It has several versions and variations, but we have all heard this urban legend in one form or another. This is how I first heard tell of the ghost of Cedarvale Drive, or more popularly known as, THIRTEEN CURVES.

When the great glaciers of the last ice age receded over what we now call 'New York State' they left behind one of the most awe inspiring spectacles of landscape known as the Finger Lakes. North of the largest lake - Skaneateles Lake - a slender creek not quite large enough to be a river ran through the hills. Over eons this small creek managed to cut a sizable gorge through the higher grounds connecting Lake Skaneateles with Onandaga Lake to the north. Around this northern lake man would eventually settle and the town of Syracuse was born. The Lakes would soon be named and the small creek would become known as Nine Mile Creek.

In the mid 1800's Lake Skaneateles became a popular boating destination and with the eventual invention of the car, roads started snaking across the countryside. Because the beautiful finger lake began attracting such interest a road connecting the growing metropolis of Syracuse to this desirable location was eventually erected. The steep hillsides around this fingerlake were formidable obstacles and it was inevitable that Nine Mile gorge, with its small creek, would become the likely site for a connecting roadway. This would become known as Cedarvale Road.

The steepest part of the gorge cut through rugged terrain and possessed thirteen curves. The hairpin curve in the middle of this treacherous stretch was a ninety-degree turn that claimed more than a few lives as the population exploded and people migrated regularly through the pass.

Our ghost story takes place several years later, centered sometime in the early 1940's. A wealthy Syracuse businessman married his sweetheart and the couple decided to honeymoon on Lake Skeaneateles. Being financially solvent he was able to afford the luxury of a 1940 Packard Super Eight Limousine - the finest automobile of the time.

The happy couple climbed into their brand new black Limousine and headed out to the countryside. Highways did not exist at the time so Cedarvale Road was the only route to reach the bed and breakfast that was their honeymoon destination. By the time they reached Nine Mile Gorge the sun had set and the moon had just begun to rise over the eastern lip of the Onondaga Valley. The lunar disc was magnified by the dusky atmosphere and glowed ominously red as if to warn them not to enter the gorge. The couple took little notice and entered the dark pass beyond.

They reached the first curve. A dense fog hung over the slow moving creek and collected around them in a thick blanket, shrouding the landscape in a stubborn opaqueness. The glare of the head lamps intensified the effect and the businessman slowed the car to a crawl. Each curve became sharper and more treacherous until they passed the infamous seventh curve.

The man smiled as his new bride snuggled up against his arm having dozed off after their exhausting wedding day. He grasped the wheel in his leather driving gloves and sighed contently as the purr of the powerful engine came as a melody to his ears. Everything about this day had been perfect. And yet he felt a growing anxiety as he counted each curve. He had heard the stories of the hairpin curve that was just around the next few bends, and an involuntary chill ran down his spine. Gruesome tales of this stretch of road had been the subject of many fireside ghost stories throughout his childhood. He was determined that these would not put a damper on the happiest day of his life.

He rounded corner six and slowed even further, determined he was in absolute control of the vehicle's considerable horsepower. His muscles tensed and his foot hovered over the break pedal as the road began to taper sharply to the left.

Suddenly the shoulder of the road came into view and to his horror he heard the engine leap to life, a deafening crescendo of powerful pistons pounding under the hood. He slammed the brake pedal with all his strength. The next few moments came as a blur, highlighted by screams of terror, and the steely bite of stinging pain. His body was thrown high into the air as cool air kissed the gaping wounds in his flesh through shredded gashes within the fabric of his clothing. After a dull thud of pain in his head he felt cold water lapping around him, seeping through his garments and onto his skin.

He lingered in his disorientated shock for just a few moments until his mind focused on his bride. He scrambled to his hands and knees and looked about trying to get his bearings. The fog around him was lit in a heavenly light that prompted him to look skyward. In the branches of a huge oak he saw the crumpled car nestling like some macabre Christmas ornament.

Part Two

He scanned the creek bed for his beloved and felt the odd sensation that he was caught in a spotlight, eyes scrutinizing his every move with bated breath. An icy hand gripped his soul as he heard a muted whimper above him within the tree.

"Oh God, no!" He urgently searched the shattered vehicle above him squinting into the beam of the head lamps. Groaning metal and cracking branches sent debris upon him and his worst fear was affirmed as a drop of warm scarlet splashed upon his cheek. It mixed with the creek water that dripped from his wet hair and slipped down to the corner of his mouth. The salty metallic taste played upon his tongue sending a wave of bile from his churning stomach. He tried to scream his wife's name, but the burning lump that hung in his esophagus stole his voice.

Suddenly a loud snapping sound smacked his ears as the huge branch that held the Limo gave way. Instinctively he dove out of the way, clearing the falling wreckage before it slammed into the creek and sent a spray of water over him. He crawled over to the mangled car, tried to open the passenger door but it refused to budge.

The fall had shattered the headlamps and plunged the creek bed into complete darkness. The stillness weighed down on him with a nagging heaviness as his eyes adjusted. On cue, the moon cleared the gorge wall and lit the fog around him in a ghostly green glow.

"Anna!" He shouted into the car. The only sound that came to his ears was his labored breathing and the trickle of water from the stream. He called her name once more and held his breath listening hard for a sound from his beloved wife. A faint rustle caught his attention and he plunged a shaking hand into the blackness, reaching around and cutting himself on shattered glass from the smashed windshield. He ignored the pain and fished around until his fingers brushed against the unmistakable texture of clothing. He was aghast that the fabric was soaked in warm stickiness.

He found her hand and was momentarily relieved when it weakly grasped his. She was alive. He grabbed hard and tried to pull her towards him but immediately let go as a scream pierced the stillness. His heart sank and tears rolled down his cheeks as he scrambled around to the other side of the crumpled heap. This door too was jammed by twisted metal.

Moonlight streamed into the broken vehicle revealing his bride. The blood soaked dress appeared black in the moonlight and threw her pale face into stark contrast as he gazed upon her through blurry tears. Her body was pinned under the engine block. The arm he had grabbed was free from the mangled machinery, but was bent at grotesque angles in two places. A pang of guilt gripped his heart upon realizing he had caused her additional pain by pulling on it. This was nothing compared to the guilt he felt knowing he was the cause of this dreadful accident.

Hopelessness overwhelmed him. There was no chance of pulling her from the wreckage. He needed help. Every fiber of his being tried to push time back ten minutes as he knelt beside the car and his body heaved with heavy sobs. He looked to the heavens and prayed. He could not leave her. He saw the break in the fog closing up. Fearful he may not see his wife alive again he looked back into the car and gazed upon her face.

The facial muscles that had been contorted in agony just moments before were now an expression of calmness. His heart broke as his mind pictured her glowing beauty as it had been at the altar earlier that day. Now her face was a picture of sereneness and the realization she was about to slip away fueled his urgency.

"Stay with me Anna! I'm not going to let you die."

He saw her eyes focus on him and she nodded her head ever so slightly.

"I have to go get help," his eyes welled with fresh tears, "whatever you do, don't let go! I'll be back as fast as I can."

"I-I- I-I-I-ove yo-you," she said between painful gasps, barely above a whisper.

"I love you too," he said through trembling lips. He moved as fast as his legs would carry him back in the direction they had come. His hopes a passing car would discover him on the roadside were never realized. He ran through the pain and exhaustion until, he reached the small hamlet of Cards Corners two miles up the road. Cards Corners was a small collection of houses and a gas station, but it did not take him long to find a handful of helpful men to help him with the rescue.

An hour later the groom returned to the scene with the rescue party. He rushed over to the wreckage to rejoin his wife hoping she was still alive. Confusion turned to shock when he found the car empty. Blood was pooled within the depression her body had made within the car's leather seat, but this was the only evidence that she had even been there. The sheriff arrived shortly after and quickly dispelled suggestions that maybe wild dogs or a bear had gotten to her. He explained there was no way to get her out from under the heavy motor of the car, there would still be traces of her left.

The search continued for three weeks but no clues were found. The groom, never lost hope and for the next five years exhausted his entire fortune searching for his lost bride. He eventually returned to the scene penniless and heartbroken. This night was much different from the fateful night five years previous. There was no fog and the moon was just a fingernail shaped sliver in a brilliant star speckled sky. From under the same oak he had lost his wife the groom hung himself in an effort to rejoin his beloved.

When conditions are right, and the fog is thick, it is said the ghostly apparition of a blood soaked bride can be seen wandering near the stream around the Seventh curve. On clear moonless nights her groom still serves out eternity carrying on his unrewarded search for his lost love Anna...

Part Three

Upon moving to New York State I had to make a fresh start. I had no friends and, because we moved at the beginning of summer, I had to stew for close to two months before beginning school. Within that time I occupied myself with reading. Mostly science fiction and fantasy, with the occasional horror mixed in.

When school began I was in for culture shock being a Southerner in "enemy territory". You would have thought I had moved from an alien country judging from the odd stares I got on a daily basis. My first school year in New York was hell, until people found out that I had a car and a SC driver's license.

See, at that time in upstate NY you had to drive with a daytime permit until you were seventeen. Even then you had to have a parent present. I had the ability to invade the night time roads legally unhindered by adult supervision. Immediate friendships flourished and I found myself with a nifty circle of compadres in just a few weeks. During the weekends and on vacation my circle's favorite pastime was to travel the dark country roads and try to scare each other with ghost stories. This was when I heard first of Cedarvale Road and the Bride of Thirteen Curves.

My first time within the gorge was an anxiety fille trek for I had to pay close attention to the dips and turns so not to lose control of my 1982 silver Honda hatchback Accord. One of my friends droned on in my right ear with the haunting tale but my concentration was squarely fixed on the road ahead. I barely made out the details of the story and had it repeated upon reaching the end of Nine Mile gorge.

When I reached the seventh curve, my car seemed to sputter as if it could feel the ominous history attached to the hairpin hell. I too felt a cold chill run down my spine sending adrenaline into my extremities and making my arms and legs ache with a dull throbbing pain. But, was it pain of over-stimulation or spirits from the past reaching from behind the veil of time and touching my soul?

Whatever the cause all my teenage body registered was shear excitement. I lost count how many times we ran that gorge that year. Although we never caught a glimpse of the tirelessly searching groom or his beloved Anna, the rush never ceased. Thirteen Curves remained our favorite destination.

Randy Thompson was one of my first real close friends. He was a huge guy, built like a college football linebacker. During my junior year my circle of GHOSTRIDERS decided it was time to initiate

Randy into the group. Our routine was simple but brilliant. We would run the curves and feign engine trouble right before the fated seventh curve. I had a nifty trick with my old Accord where I could nudge the key in the ignition and it would kill the engine without having to take it out of gear. I would pop the hood and leave the others in the car with our new initiate. Anyone who has ever pulled a prank knows this one is a classic.

While behind the hood I would let out a yelp, kick the front bumper a few times, and "disappear" behind the brush below the lee-side of creek's hill. One by one the other members would repeat the routine until the "pledge" member was left inside the car. It worked flawlessly every time, scaring the unbeknownst greenhorn senseless. It was all clean fun until this fateful night in early October of 1984.

We had always amended the story's weather details to reflect the current conditions upon the telling. This added to the excite-filled suspense that all was favorable to see the bride, or the groom. This night was different though for the conditions were exactly as the haunting tale foretold. I remember swallowing a lump in my throat upon spying the dull red lunar disk hanging on the limb of the planet as we approached the gorge's entrance.

As we rounded the first curve, it was as if the fog saw us coming. Billowing clouds rolled down both sides of the road and converged on the Honda as we came out of the first curve. An aching fear burned in my gut as I began counting curves just as the hapless groom had done in the original ghost story. I slowed to a crawl as we approached the seventh curve and, despite my frightened mood, I killed the engine just before the bend. To add to the excitement I improvised and killed the headlights as well.

The air within the vehicle was electric with fear, and I felt a giddiness that straightened the hairs on my arms and legs. My breath became shallow and my heartbeat quickened as I reached for the door handle to exit the car.

"Not again," I said with a knowing sidelong glance at my friend in the passenger's seat, "the battery cable must have come loose."

I reached down to pull the hood release and froze as a low guttural voice floated on the fog.

"Get out of the car!" The disembodied voice ordered and my heart leapt into my throat. I exchanged glances with my frightened companions.

"Did you hear that?" I asked with a trembling voice.

The scientific definition of fear goes a bit like this: excessive neurological activity stemming from inhibitory neurons not functioning properly. These neurons failing to excrete levels of the neurotransmitter that inhibits the transmission of other neurons leads to a high level of activity in the brain responsible for human emotional arousal. The result being, a human feels fear...

I for one had never experienced the type of fear I was at that moment and that may have impaired my ability to rationalize. If you asked me after the experience I may have told you I saw the groom standing before the car pointing a gun through the windshield when I flipped the headlights back on.

I restarted the car and slammed into reverse as fast as humanly possible. I did my best to make a three point turn into a one pointer and got the hell out of there as fast as I could. After turning in the opposite direction we heard a gunshot echo around the gorge. I heard the bullet ricochet off of the asphalt just outside the driver side door. The surreal feeling after our 'feigned' fright had turned real fear made my head spin.

It took several hours to wind down after the night's events and sleep never came to me. As I lay awake staring at the patterns the popcorn finish made on my ceiling, I relived the nightmare several times in my head. Morning came and I wandered downstairs where my brother was watching the morning news. The logo behind the desk reporter read "Thirteen Curves". I shoved my brother out of the way and planted myself before the tube.

"The man," the reporter read from the TelePrompTer with emotional indifference, "dressed in a wedding tuxedo, was hit by a car on the infamous seventh curve of Cedarvale Road late last night and was pronounced dead at the scene. The black 1940 Packard Super Eight Limousine that hit the man was left abandoned at the scene. The car had no plates and was in severe disrepair. Police suspect foul play because the only clue to the driver's identity was a bloodied wedding dress found in the back seat of the vehicle."

And that was the closest I have ever come to seeing the Bride of Thirteen Curves...

VIRACOCH'S VENGENCE

"Wait a moment Doctor, I think I see something," Helen, moved towards a statue in the center of the huge underground chamber. She stepped carefully over the ancient bones scattered across the ground, bleached white with the passage of time.

Dr. Hirham followed his assistant; his curiosity peeked by the excitement in her voice. There, in the flickering torchlight he saw them. Four crystal skulls neatly lined up at the base of the strange statue.

"Whoa," he said under his breath. "Unbelievable."

"You know what these are don't you?" Helen asked in a reverent tone.

The Doctor said nothing as he stared at the artifacts on the floor in awe.

She bent over and picked one up. The skull was heavy and solid throughout. She handed it to the Doctor.

He expected the skull to be cold to the touch after sitting in this dank cavern for so long, but to his surprise it felt warm and seemed to vibrate in his hands.

Helen paused for dramatic effect, building suspense before she explained the origins of the artifacts. Over the years Dr. Hirham had learned to counter this annoying trait by pretending not to be interested but the suspense was killing him. "Helen?" He tried to prompt her with a hand gesture, and almost dropped the skull.

"Okay, I'll tell you. These are the four skulls of wisdom," she said excitedly.

"What? The holy relics used by the Incan Sun God?"

"No, the Sun God is Inti." she answered shaking her head. "These were possessed by Viracocha, he that came before Inti. These skulls were said to be the source of his power. Power that could bring enlightenment and death at the same time. It was written that Viracocha used these to bring down fire from the sky vanquishing all the enemies of his people."

"It seems there is still power over fire left in these skulls," the Doctor replied. "Check this out." He moved the skull away from the torch flames and the fire sputtered out plunging the room into blackness. When he moved it back towards the torch, it leapt to life again.

"Unbelievable," she breathed. "Hirham this is the holy grail of pre-Incan beliefs."

"And we are the ones who uncovered it!" Hirham said excitedly. "This is absolutely amazing. These pre-Incans were more advanced then anyone had ever imagined."

"You may be more right than you know Hirham." She bent down and picked up a strange relic tucked behind one of the remaining skulls. She blew an inch of ancient dust off the object.

"What in Hell is that?" the doctor gasped.

It appeared to be a metal casing with a flat crystal mounted on one side. This crystal resembled a display screen about two inches square and the object fitted into her hand much like a small sleek cell phone. Three crystal "buttons" aligned the artifact just below the "screen."

"What could it be?" she breathed awestruck. "It looks modern."

"Hand it here," Hirham said indignantly shoving the skull at Helen and snatching the artefact from her.

She shot him glare look as he touched one of the crystal buttons. A low hum emanated from the object and the square crystal "screen" began to glow with a soft blue light.

Hirham and Helen exchanged worried glances. The Doctor quickly set the object on the ground and backed away. Despite her curiosity, Helen also took a few steps back.

A tiny shaft of red light shot about six inches above the device. The beam began to pulsate and rotate rapidly until it took on a strobe effect, then it split and began taking the form of random lines.

Helen and Hirham stood fixated on the image. It resolved into a spinning three-dimensional globe of the Earth hanging above the object on the floor. A small blue light blinked over what appeared their location just outside of Machu Pichu.

"Jesus Hirham," Helen looked up at him a huge smile growing on her face," we have just found the proverbial 747 in ancient Egypt here."

"Hell 747 my ass!" he scoffed," This is the freaking Space Shuttle! And you and I will go down in history as the scientists who discovered it!"

They grabbed one another and embraced in a joyous hug. Suddenly, the device beeped in ominous low tones, a split-second apart. The two archaeologists exchanged worried glances and backed away.

"I don't like the sound of this," Helen said as the tone began to crescendo into a shrill shriek that threatened to shatter her eardrums. The frequency and volume increased and she noticed the crystal skulls had begun to glow with a searing light. She felt the heat flow from the skulls across the giant chamber. The place lit up, burning like a hot poker at their eyes.

The heavy chamber door slammed shut sending chunks of the stone ceiling slamming to the floor knocking them to the ground. Hot air rushed in, burning the inside of their mouths and filling their lungs in unbearable pain. The moisture within their bodies seemed to be sucked out in a moment of excruciating agony. Neither scientist could do or say anything as their bodies shriveled in the intense heat.

Moments later their bones were indistinguishable from the other ancient bones that lay about the tomb.

Outside, the mountainside peak collapsed sending an avalanche of jungle foliage and soil over the entranceway choking the valley below in a huge cloud of dust.

Later that day, Dr. Hirham would get his wish. Their names would go down in history as a tiny blurb on the major newswires. Most periodicals never even printed the story. After all, there was more important news this day. A new strain of the flu virus was discovered in China, and ten people died of it this very day.

FREEDOM FLIGHT

Johngy yanked the wheel, and barely missed the huge hover transport as he pushed his car ever higher. He grappled the steering wheel as his foot danced back and forth between his brake pedal and accelerator. He pushed down hard and dove between two taxis only to deploy the rear vector engines to avoid running into the back of an Axon Tour Bus. He was thrown forward and hit his head hard on the upper control console.

"Damn traffic!" He cursed rubbing the growing lump on his forehead. He pulled his hand back and swore again as warm crimson stained his twitching fingers.

Johngy tried to pull around the bus but lines of speeding hover vehicles whooshed past on all sides and Jonngy got the disorientating impression that he was moving backwards within a speeding tunnel.

He let out a heavy sigh, shoved his hand into his jacket pocket and reached for his meditation balls. His hand closed around their smooth metal and reverently he pulled them out. Johngy felt the vibration of the micro components inside fire to life, powered by the warmth of his hand. Immediately the electrical impulses began running soothingly up his arm. He tilted his seat back and relaxed as the microcomputer within the balls began communicating with his brain, triggering the release of endorphins.

He idly looked over and saw from the digital readout on his dash. He was running twenty minutes late - third time this week. His boss would really let him have it this time. He might even terminate his employment.

Johngy shoved the steel meditation balls back into his pocket, tightened the seat restraint across his body and gripped the wheel. He gazed into his rearview monitor screens but saw no opening within the gridlock of speeding metal that raged around him. He reached up and engaged the moon roof button, squinted through the brightness as he peered out of the glass portal.

Lightning reactions gleaned from countless hours trapped on the skyway enabled him to instantly lurch into the small opening as soon as it appeared. His piloting instincts kicked in and suddenly Johngy had moved up three levels dodging in and out of the heavy traffic. Another tight space appeared above him. Johngy rammed the rear engine throttle forward and slammed the accelerator to the floor while pulling back on the steering wheel all in the same motion.

The sudden bone-jarring burst of speed caused the sky to tilt sickeningly one way and then the other. A moment later and he was speeding above the packed sky-lanes below. Johngy felt an exhilaration he had never experienced as adrenaline pulsed through his veins. As he observed the clear sky above him, his mind focused on a surpising revelation.

His whole life he had been imprisoned within a society that blindly raced this way and that, shackled to an anxiety filled life, contained in tightly scheduled order, never deviating over time. Johngy realized he had forgotten his own identity. He realized his spirit had been broken. The world had integrated him into a fabric that was not indigenous to his nature. In the grand scheme of things, his life had absolutely no bearing on the universe. It was all meaningless.

Johngy scanned the clear skies overhead and without a second thought, wrenched back on the stick, hit the accelerator and bounded into the emptiness above him.

"Warning!" His ears were filled with the inhuman computerized voice of the Earth Enforcement Protocol over his car speakers, "Exceeding the altitude limit is strictly forbidden!"

Johngy felt giddy, and his heart burst with exhilaration. He ignored the warning and climbed even higher, reveling in this unfamiliar sensation as his spirit took flight on something he had never set eyes upon in his entire existence. Open space. It engulfed him and the sense of freedom swallowed him up sending his soul into joyous rapture.

"Citizen!" He was cruelly yanked out of his revelry by EEP's harsh voice assaulting his ears once again, "You have prohibited altitude limits and are hereby ordered to return to the skyway level."

A smile crossed Johngy's face as he stared defiantly at the blue horizon. Below, the choked skyway was now a haze of swarming flies covering the surface of the world. "Let see what this baby can do!" he shouted and yanked back on the wheel, pulling away from the earth and shoving the car into a bone-jarring burst of speed.

"WOOHOOOO!"

His head became woozy from lack of oxygen but he pushed the vehicle to it's limits. His extremities tingled and Johngy wondered if it was excitement or lack of air. All that mattered was the elation of being free. He was actually flying for the first time, his life set free from the inhibitions of society.

"This is you final warning!" EEP's metallic voice grated on his ears, "Immediate compliance is demanded! Return to skyway limits at once or be dealt with harshly!"

"Alright then!" Johngy shouted angrily and leveled out his car putting it in hover mode just below a wispy, icy cirrocumulus cloud. "Come get me!"

He stared at the world far below awaiting the swift penalty promised by World Protocol. Minutes ticked by and his head swooned as he realized there was to be no retribution for his act. The EEP's threats were hollow. A society kept in line by fear, threatened with fatal penalties for violation of authority. This protocol was pounded into every Citizen's head from the day they were incubated. The penalty for defiance was death.

"Does Death have no wings?" He asked with a wry smile that suddenly turned to a scowl of terror as an alarm cut the air, "Warning! Low Fuel!"

Suddenly his car plummeted. He felt the weightlessness and saw the ground rapidly rising up to meet him. Despite his impending doom, Johngy felt elated. Ironically his disobedience would end in death, but to Johngy it was not a penalty at all, but salvation. He would end up paying the ultimate price but a brief glimpse of freedom had been worth it. He would soon be free of the shackles that had imprisoned him within the hell that was 'society.'

As he zoomed towards to the ground and oxygen infused his brain, the dreamlike quality of his thoughts coalesced into focus once again. His mind cleared and he remembered that his car had an emergency chute. He reached for the 'deploy chute' button and spied something unexpected through his window. Apparently several citizens had witnessed his ascent and saw there was no penalty for his discretion. Countless cars now hovered over the skyway limit headed heavenward.

Johngy knew he had only precious seconds left, but his finger hovered over the emergency button and a smile spread across his face. He pulled his hand away and instead began flashing his landing lights.

"Citizens," his last words filtered over the car speakers of all within transmission range, "Let the Freedom Flight begin!"

Johngy's salvation was realized three seconds later culminating in a brilliant exploding fireball as his hover car plummeted into the roof of the sector headquarters building of the Earth Enforcement Protocol Department.

THE COIN

Ben idly rubbed the worn silver coin in his wrinkled hand and held it close to his thick lenses as he studied the ladies bust adorning the front of the piece. The word "Liberty" was barely legible across the top of the coin. Ben had rubbed it so many times over the years. At the bottom the coins date was similarly worn - 1795. All that could be deciphered on the back were the words "The United States of America," and an obscure image that vaguely resembling plant fronds with a bird in their midst.

Ben remembered the day he found the coin. He was just a small boy of seven. Their neighbor's farmhouse had burned down and he and George McMurphy, were exploring the burned husk of the home.

He remembered how lucky he felt and the prickle in his stomach when he uncovered the treasure. The old silver dollar felt warm on that brisk morning as if he had just pulled it from the house fire. The farm had burned down two weeks previous.

Fifteen years ago, someone offered Ben six thousand dollars for the coin, but he would never part with it. It was his good luck charm, and had brought him countless good fortune through the years. He remembered how irate the coin collector was when he refused his offer. The man offered five hundred dollars more and became nasty when Ben refused again.

He disliked the fat coin collector and felt little remorse when the man tore off in his car and collided with the tractor trailer right before Ben's eyes. As he watched the firemen pull the obese mangled body from the wreckage he recalled rubbing the coin and thinking how fortunate he had not sold it. It probably would have been Ben himself they were pulling out of that wreckage.

He was brought out of his revelry as a taxi pulled up in his driveway. Ben's childhood friend, George McMurphy, climbed from the back seat lugging an old tattered briefcase.

Even though they were the same age Ben noticed how much older his friend looked as he gave a tired smile and wave before paying the driver. George climbed the steps of the front porch with arthritic knees. Ben shoved the coin in his pocket and walked over to his guest to help him up the last two steps.

"George, my old friend," he patted him on the back as George lowered himself into the rocking chair by the front door, "what brings you to Idaho from your busy life in the big city?"

George took a few moments to catch his breath. His expression was serious - obviously set for business.

"Your 'lucky' coin Ben." The answer came in a gray tone as if mention of the silver dollar left a bad taste in his mouth.

"Not this malarky again?" Ben shoved his hand in his pocket and closed his fist around the coin, "when are you going to give this up? The coin is not cursed. It has brought me nothing but good fortune."

"Good fortune? Name one time."

Ben sighed and pulled a pained expression. He took the coin out of his pocket and rubbed it. His friend jerked back as if Ben was holding a gun rather than a simple coin. Ben thought a moment.

"Margaret." He said proudly. "I remember in high school I was so in love with her."

"She was a cheerleader," George stated flatly, "she was in love with Cappy Montigue, the quarterback of the football team. You should never have had a chance with her."

"I remember one night," Ben said staring at the coin hypnotically, "I was in my room pining for her. I wished with all my heart she was mine." He paused and looked into the eyes of his old friend before he continued. An odd smile crossed his face as he spoke again.

"The coin seemed to give off some kind of energy that night. It seemed to glow in my hand as I wished that Margaret was mine." His smile widened as he stared off into space remembering the past, "The next day, when I got off the bus she bumped into me. We were in love from that day on."

"Don't you remember what happened to her boyfriend the night before you met her?"

Ben returned a confused look and shook his head.

"He took a blow to the head during football practice," George said putting his briefcase across his knees. "Died instantly."

He opened up the case and thumbed through some papers until he found a tattered newspaper article. He handed it over to Ben with trembling fingers.

TALENTED YOUTH DIES IN FOOTBALL PRACTICE ACCIDENT

Ben scanned the headline with a bemused expression.

"Don't you think it odd," George asked, "that Margaret had no clue that her boyfriend, the love of her high school life, died the night before she ran into your arms?"

Ben looked back dumbfounded.

"And what about Charles Carlton?" George asked, "does that name ring any bells?"

Ben handed the tattered football clipping back to his old friend shaking his head no. George handed over another newspaper article the paper yellowed with age. Ben read the headline.

HIGH SCHOOL YOUTH DROWNS IN LOCAL LAKE.

"I don't remember him," he said.

"Ben, the population of this town is so small, we knew everyone in high school. Here are two students that died and you cannot recall them. Don't you find that odd?"

Ben studied the face on the page and shook his head. "I don't remember him George."

"He met Margaret during our junior year. She almost broke up with you to go out with him. She agreed to go to the Spring Dance with him."

"She went with me." Ben responded idly rubbing the silver dollar between his index and forefinger, "I wished for it the week before the dance after she said she was thinking of going with someone else. That's where we kissed for the first time."

"This article," George pointed out, "was from the Herald the week before the dance."

"This proves nothing," Ben shrugged angrily, "you're jealous because you didn't find the coin yourself. I was the fortunate one."

134

George threw his hands in the air, "Charles Carlton was captain of the swim team and an ALLSTATE swimmer! How in the world do you suppose he could have drowned?"

Ben abruptly stood and walked over to the edge of the porch, rested his free hand on the rail while rubbing the coin in the other as he stared across the recently plowed field. "I don't want to hear anymore of this," he said over his shoulder, "I won't give it up. You cannot take it from me."

"Remember when Joseph Steele beat you up our senior year," George continued, fishing out yet another ancient newspaper article, "he took the coin from you. Do you remember what happened to him?"

"I don't know who you're talking about," Ben turned on his heel and leveled his gaze at his old friend, "I think you're making all this up."

"How in God's name could you forget about Joseph Steele, the class bully?" George asked, holding out the newspaper clipping for Ben to read, "He tormented us for four years!"

Ben walked over and snatched the paper from his friends trembling hand.

Once again he read another headline.

TEEN MAULED BY ESCAPED CIRCUS BEAR

"Don't tell me you don't recall that," George said.

Ben shook his head. He looked at the date at the top of the page. "I lost the coin around that day that's all I remember."

"And how did you get it back?"

Ben shrugged. "It was on my night stand when I woke up the next day."

George gingerly pulled himself up from the rocker and walked over to his old friend placing a hand on his shoulder. "Can you not see," he said, "that anyone who has tried to get between you and that God damned coin has ended up in the town's obituary?"

"That's not true," Ben mumbled.

"And what about the one you DO remember," George asked sympathetically, "Margaret? Remember when she tried to convince you to sell the coin."

A pained look crossed Ben's face and he bit his lip in anger. "How dare you go there!" he shouted and jerked away from George's hand. His eyes filled with tears at the memory of his wife.

"She told me," George explained carefully, "that before the brain tumor took her life, she believed it was the coin that was preventing her from giving you a child."

"Shut up!" Ben said shoving his old friend and sending him crashing to the boards, "I will never give it up! It is... precious to me!"

George painfully propped himself up on one elbow. "Listen to yourself Ben," George said rubbing a freshly bleeding gash on the back of his head, "you are obsessed."   He slowly got on his knees and crawled over to the rocker, pulled himself to his feet and staggered almost losing his balance. "Can't you see I'm here to save you?"

Ben held the coin up to his face and studied it.

George took a few steps closer and held out his hand. "Give it to me Ben."

Ben's gaze moved from the coin and focused on his friend. That odd smile grew across his lips and George felt the queasy feeling of dread growing in the pit of his stomach.

"No." Ben answered as George's heart suddenly burst in excruciating pain squeezing the breath out of his lungs.

****

The next morning Ben woke and began his morning routine. He walked to the mailbox and grabbed the newspaper. Upon returning he poured a cup of coffee and sat at the kitchen table and unfolded the paper.

He read the headline on the front page.

HOMETOWN BUSINESS SUCCESS RETURNS HOME AND DIES OF HEART ATTACK.

He read the persons name. "George McMurphy," he said to himself. He thought back to the past. "Maybe from the football team?" He thought back to his time as team captain of the HS Varsity team and pulled the coin from his pocket. "God I hope it wasn't one of the poor souls I bullied back in high school," he said to himself idly rubbing the coin. The name meant nothing to him.

He sipped his coffee and looked out onto the front yard from the kitchen window. At the bottom of the steps to the front porch he spied a tattered briefcase lying on its side. Ben went out and retrieved it, brought it back indoors where he dumped it on the kitchen table. He opened up the case and discovered a dusty leather bound book. The title read:

RARE AMERICAN COINS

"Wow it must be my lucky day," Ben said opening the book reading the copyright date on the inside page.

©1795

He sipped his coffee and flicked through the book, marveling at the pictures of rare coins on the faded pages. There was something odd about the description beneath each coin that Ben did not seem to notice. Printed in faded ink were the names and contact details of every owner of every coin.

PEN TO PAPER

As you read these words consider the ink from which they are printed. If you printed this from your desktop the ink is most likely made up of carbon black, a heavy varnish and an agent which reduced its drying time.

If jotted by an ink pen then the words you are reading are made up of petroleum naphtha, resins and coal-tar solvents. Words scribed by scholars at the dawn of the Enlightened Age would most likely have been made up of a combination of juices, indigo, pokeberries, cochineal and/or sepia.

Then consider the paper upon which the ink is printed. It began as wood chip broken down by steam and chemicals into cellulose fibers that were dried out, heated and then pressed into the surface from which you are reading right now.

For centuries this process has been refined and perfected with ever evolving skill. So, now you see the pinnacle of paper and ink technology before you. The culmination of centuries of sweat, hard work and craftsmanship finds you the reader at this moment ready to be inspired.

Romantic isn't it? Inspired? Of course not.

What you see upon the whiteness of pressed wood pulp is the embodiment of somebody's soul. The author's soul. The cellulose fibers and petroleum naphtha release the adventure, joy and sorrow within the readers mind, painting a picture with far more colors than the black and white that exist on this page, only limited by the capacity of the author who contemplated the words.

This very moment, as you read, is but a snapshot of thought, feeling and imagination imprinted from the author's mind to yours, an intimate connection between two people that provides an insight into the inner workings of another mind. That is what makes reading, both romantic and inspiring, the connection between isolated souls, a yearning to see life from another less jaded perspective.

A good author takes you to places you have never seen through beautiful descriptions, allowing you to escape from the daily bondage of life's problems. A great author can push into your dreams and enhance their essence.

A writer is one whose soul can speak out over generations unhindered by the bounds of time and space to inspire one whose great, great grandfather was yet to be born. The great ones have already taken us to Mars, Jupiter and places beyond before our technology had even allowed us to reach distant galaxies.

What advances in science and technology would exist if it were not first dreamt of by an author? Would the human race have even been inspired enough to dare leave the gravity of Mother Earth's bosom? Would there be objects made by our own hands screaming through space well beyond the bounds of our own solar system?

These endeavors were made possible because writers such as Isaac Asimov and Arthur C. Clark gave such ventures validity by showing us romance, adventure and inspiration beyond our own world.

Writing is the language of the human soul. It just turns out some of us are more fluent than others. Now, as I put down the vessel of resins and coal-tar solvents that is my pen, I must go dream for I have been inspired by one that was able to move my soul before wood chips were steamed and chemically altered into paper or even before my distant relatives were born.

Sleep will come easy tonight.

Tomorrow, another story will be written.

Good night.

THE GIFT

I focused my eyes stubbornly through the bifocals at the snapshot in my trembling hands. The photo was one of those Christmas cards made at the department store mall. A familiar girl with golden hair and innocent smile sat upon 'store Santa's' lap. My vision finally cleared enough for me to read the elegant cursive script and I realized who the child was.

Merry Christmas 2006 from the Daners family.

As I studied the young girls face, the fog of seventy two years lifted just enough for me to peer back to the winter of 1934. That fateful Christmas season that would signal the tragic end of the cherished friendship I shared with Nelly. This little girl would have been Nelly's great niece had she still been alive.

I closed my eyes and breathed deeply from the tube that fed oxygen through my nose. The air rattled in my deteriorated lungs and the brain that had been ravaged by Alzheimer's and dulled with narcotics desperately clung to the memory of my childhood friend.

I reeled from the dizziness that robbed my ageing body of balance, sending me sprawling over my oxygen canister and cart. The last sound my hearing aid registered before it popped out of my ear was the ghastly crack of my skull against the metal foot post of my bed. Then blackness.

When I came to I was being awakened by my old Nanny Shirley, only she was not old. She was just as I had remembered her from my youth. I quickly realized that my mind was functioning normally, devoid of debilitating disease and mind numbing drugs. It rapidly processed the visual stimulation and I deduced that I was back in my old house on Lady's Island. I was reliving the very day that memory had shocked my eighty year old brain causing my swan dive to unconsciousness. This was the day Nelly and I would see Santa for the first time and she would make her Christmas wish for the gift. The cursed thing would not only cost us our friendship, but would eventually take Nelly's sanity, and then her life...

It was December 14th and my parents were away in Albany, New York. My father worked for the railroad and they were unveiling a new passenger train which meant my parents would not be home for Christmas that year. Our chauffeur, Mr. Widdings, and Nanny Shirley were taking me into Beaufort to Winter's Department store on Boundary Street to cheer me up.

As we left, I saw tears in Nelly's eyes walking beside the stream that separated our land from her family's. The dreary December sky had opened up and a steady drizzle soaked the countryside. My heart cried out for my best friend as I saw her wet curls clinging to her misery laden face, so I instructed Mr. Widdings to stop and I invited her along. After a forlorn look over her shoulder back towards her house she wiped a tear from her cheek and hopped into the back of the sedan seating herself next to me.

"Is it your mom and dad again?" I asked after an uncomfortable pause.

"Yes Danny," she said, her voice raw from crying, "my mom cannot have another child so they are taking it out on each other."

"Well we're on our way to Winter Brothers," I said, patting her lightly upon the knee, "I shall buy you a gift to cheer your spirits."

She grabbed my hand and flashed a sad smile. I knew her life was hard. Her parents had lost much of their fortune in the great crash and they would have to leave their land in the country very soon. They were desperately trying to find some happiness to cling to. It weighed heavy on me that Nelly could possibly spend Christmas without a home.

"Oh, Children do not fret," Nanny Shirley's Gullah accent floated to our melancholy ears, "I have a surprise for you wee ones that may cheer yalls up."

Nelly and I exchanged a brief glance and I was delighted to see the hint of a smile creeping back to her pouting lips.

"We're going to have a very special visit!" Nanny Shirley's white teeth gleamed in a huge grin from her dark face, "with Santa!"

Despite the weather the drive to Santa's cottage at the end of Lands End road was enjoyable. Nanny Shirley did her best to steer the conversation away from dark matters and entertained us with jovial stories of her youthful exploits growing up on the outer islands.

As we started down the dirt road to the cottage that was tucked far away from the main road I began feeling an unexplained uneasiness. We passed under moss draped ancient oaks that seemed to guard the fringes of Santa's land from the curious eyes of the rest of the islands residents. Then, as we got closer I thought It may as well have been the north pole for the marsh lands surrounding the cottage seem to stingily conceal dark secrets from passers-by. The whole place had an otherworldly feel until we passed the property's perimeters fence, then it was as if we had stepped from winter into springtime.

Azaleas of every color burst from the bushes surrounding the house. Even the clouds above the tall trees opened up to allow the sun to beam down upon the old cottages thatched roof as birds sung merrily from every corner of the yard. We pulled up to the front door. An old man fitting the description of Christopher Cringle idly puffed on a corn cob pipe and widdled away at on old piece of wood with a worn makeshift knife.

"Santa!" Nelly shouted excitedly and leapt from the car as soon as it came to a stop. I, on the other hand, felt a peculiar resignation as the old man joyfully welcomed us into his comfortable cottage. My darkened mood briefly brightened upon seeing how joyful Nelly was.

We sat in the cozy living room and basked in a cheerful fire as we roasted marsh mellows and drank hot chocolate from over sized mugs. The whole time 'Santa' spoke I could not help the feeling there was something odd and overly cheery about this person and his humble abode. By late afternoon I was feeling quite unnerved.

Upon bookshelves and on the mantel of the huge fireplace countless dolls presided over our party dressed in every possible configuration of clothing of the era one could imagine. Upon several occasions during our stay I had the suspicious feeling that their frozen faces were staring at us. I tried to remain joyous but the longer we spent within the cottage the more jumpy I became.

When the time came to present our Christmas wishes to Santa my fear overwhelmed me and I just had to get out of there. I fled the cottage as if the devil himself were upon my heel, and sat sobbing in the back of the sedan as the others finished their visit with the Lady's Island Santa. As Nelly climbed into the back seat of the car I was dismayed to find she held one of the ghastly dolls lovingly clutched in her bosom. As we pulled away from the cottage Nelly exuberantly waved at the Santa as he waved and grinned back. My eyes met the old man's as we passed and I was quite sure I saw a fiery evilness behind his shiny spectacles.

"You really mustn't be so dramatic Danny," Nelly said with a haughty tone and then in a tiny voice spoke to her doll, "it is not very becoming of someone of his stature in society is it Dusty?"

I looked disbelievingly at my friend as she quietly played with her new doll. I found myself looking out of the window at the passing countryside for the rest of the journey home doing everything I could to avoid setting eyes on Nelly's new gift. I was positive it was making faces at me.

The next few days I saw very little of Nelly. When I did see her I went out of my way to avoid her for she was forever in possession of the dreadful doll. She took it everywhere.

A week later my concern for my best friend prompted me to call on her. Doll or no doll I missed her dearly and I was becoming worried for I had not heard a word.

The house was eerily quiet as I approached and rang the bell. I thought it odd that Capers, the family dog was not barking, and was about to resign myself to the possibility that the family was not in. Suddenly the knob turned and the door opened slightly. Through the crack I saw a single eye peering from the darkness.

"Yes," Mrs. Danford's voice meekly addressed me as if she did not recognize me, "what do you want?"

"I came to visit with Nelly mam," I politely responded.

The door slammed with a suddenness that caused me to jump. I stood awkwardly not sure what to do. I stepped off the porch and heard chains sliding across the backside of the wooden door through heavy metal clasps. The door creaked slowly open and within the framed darkness Mrs. Danford's pale form stood ghost-like in stark contrast to the blackness behind her. She looked cautiously over her shoulder and then rushed down the five steps and grabbed me up by the arms shaking my small frame.

"You must convince her to burn that doll!" She whispered in my ear, her puffy blood shot eyes round with fear, "I find that infernal thing at my bedside every night, just staring at me. I have locked it away and still, it finds its way to the foot of my bed every night. Two evenings ago I woke in the middle of the night to find it sitting upon my face. I am sure it was trying to suffocate me!"

Fear sent goose flesh up my arms over the skin of my scalp as the crazed woman urgently whispered her accounts of the past week.

Tears streamed down her wrinkled face. "Things have gone missing and then turned up broken. When I confront Nelly she claims Dusty did it!"

I tried to console the woman. "I'll do my best to help Mrs. Danford. Where is your husband?"

"I don't know!" She slumped to her knees upon the gravel driveway and sobbed. She held onto me until I thought she would squeeze the life from my body. "Please help," she cried into my flannel shirt. "That doll is from Hell I just know it!"

I yanked myself from her grasp and backed away. She collapsed onto the drive and curled up into the foetal position quietly sobbing. Every fibre of my being told me to flee but my love for my dear friend charged my courage and stoked the fires within my soul melting away the icy fear that had momentarily paralyzed my body.

Stealthily I walked up the stone steps, through the open door and the dank smell of decay immediately met my nostrils. It took a moment for my eyes to adjust to the darkness. I lingered in the foyer until I felt safe to venture into the house without blindly bumping into furniture and other obstacles veiled within the inky blackness. The cold air rivaled the winter outside and highlighted my breath in frosty plumes of mist as I made my way through the entrance hall.

I stepped gingerly into the front room. All that could be heard were the whirling gears and ticking of the grandfather clock that stood stoically in the front hall. I had sat upon the plush and comfortable furniture that graced the Danford living room on countless occasions but the carefree playtime spent there with Nelly reading stories and frolicking in front of the gray stone fireplace seemed as vague as a mostly forgotten dream. My eyes darted from one end of the harsh dark room to the other. The warm reds and browns were replaced with sharp grays and blacks as if all the warmth that used to permeate this once happy home was completely sapped from its once vivacious personality.

Suddenly a shuffling from behind a door just off the main room encroached upon the heavy silence and sent a shaft of bitter cold fear into the pit of my stomach. I slowly approached and, without taking an eye from the closet door I reached out and grabbed a poker from the stone hearth. I reached out and grasped the handle readying the heavy iron weapon for a deadly blow upon whatever evil awaited me on the other side.

I yanked on the door and threw my hands to my face as Rodda the family cat sprang from the clutter and clawed at my face

144

before landing on all fours behind me. I whirled around with the poker held like a battle sword as the cat hissed bared its teeth. I noticed the animal's face was gouged open and one eye stared blindly with puss filled paleness. I breathed a sigh of relief as the creature turned and scurried fearfully out the front door.

Fear sent adrenaline pumping through my arms and legs, numbing my extremities and quickening my breath. A dull ache burned in my temples. The fear was unlike anything I had ever experienced in my short lifetime.

Suddenly I heard footsteps above me, and my brain focused on the task of helping my best friend. I climbed the stairs with poker ready to strike. As I reached the top step the smell of death caused me to stop in mid pace as I promptly regurgitated my breakfast upon the second story hallway floor. I had found Capers the family dog. What was left of the pet was barely identifiable as a canine. From its chest down was a mangled mass of shredded skin and broken bone leaking bodily fluids upon the floor. Bits of bloody flesh clung to the hallway walls and ceiling and matted clumps of red soaked fur littered the ornate carpet. Claw marks were scratched on the wall and into the hardwood floor at the carpets edge indicating the pet met with a violent end.

To my horror, as I stepped over the creature its battered head snapped at me. The poor animal was still alive, left half mutilated to die there on the floor. I reluctantly did what any compassionate boy of twelve years of age would do, and put the pet out of it's misery by bashing its head in with the blunt end of the poker. I vomited what was left in my stomach and silently sobbed as I poked at Caper's remains to make sure he was dead.

It was then that I heard whispering from behind the door at the end of the hall. I slowly made my way to the double oak doors noticing two holes had been blasted into each one. As I got closer I realized the voice belonged to Mr. Danford. I cautiously pushed the damaged doors open to the study to find the man crouched behind an oak desk. In one hand he held his hunting riffle and the other a copy of the Holy Bible.

"...though I walk in the valley of the shadow of death..."

His face was pale and ghostly and his eyes were perfect round circles of fear staring straight past me into the hallway beyond.

"Mr. Danford?" I said slowly crouching and lightly dropping the poker on the floor. I stood and took a few deliberate steps forward with my hands in front of me disarmingly, "are you okay?"

He stopped his prayer and his eyes fixed for a mere moment on mine.

"Please make it stop staring at me." He mumbled and my heart dropped as once again the mumbling mans gaze fixed on the hall way behind me. He raised his gun and pulled the trigger. All that was heard was an empty click as I dropped to the ground nearly wetting my pants. I reached for my weapon but the fire poker was no longer at my feet. Upon hearing tiny pattering footfalls I turned just in time to catch a glimpse of a small figure opening a door down the hall slamming it shut behind.

I jumped as a single shot rang out and I spun round to see Mr. Danford's dead body slump to the floor, half of the man's head splattered upon the wood cabinet behind him. From a place deep down inside a resolve I never knew I possessed enabled my mind rational thought within the chaos of the moment as I quickly crossed the study floor and carefully tore the gun from Nelly's Dad's still warm hand.

Crossing the hall I threw open the door and barged in, gun drawn. It was Nelly's room. She rocked in a small white rocking chair humming to herself as she idly stroked the feathers of the family's dead pet parrot. Nelly seemed oblivious to the birds blood covering her white cotton dress as her eyes slowly looked up into mine.

"Danny," she smiled her mouth filled with crimson, "have you come to play with us?"

Suddenly sharp heavy pain exploded on the back of my head. I fell to the floor and the last thing my fading eyes saw was the doll that was Nelly's Christmas gift standing over me, fire poker grasped within its small hand.

I woke hours later within my own home with Nanny Shirley stroking my hair and placing a hot washcloth upon my forehead. She explained the Beaufort Constable had arrived just in time after Mrs. Danford had raised the alarm.

"I just can't understand it," Nanny Shirley cried, "Nelly was always such a sweet little girl, how could she have done this?"

I sat up and saw a pale and shaken Mrs. Danford sitting at our kitchen table and with a stern look and shake of her head understanding passed between us without a spoken word.

The next day I read the newspaper article with a heavy heart. The paper explained that Nelly had gone insane and killed her father and the family pets. As tears welled within my eyes I could barely read the unimpassionate words before me.

'Police arrived just in time as the insane twelve year old girl held a pistol to young neighbor Danny Sullivan's head, whom she had just clubbed with an iron fire poker. Before she could take Sullivan's life police Constable Charlie McEntire intervened. When investigators asked her why she had committed the brutal murders the little girl responded while clutching her doll, 'Dusty did it."

Nelly was taken away to the mental hospital and spent two tortured years within its walls until she finally took her own life hanging herself with a noose she had made from her own braided hair. Her mother moved to Charleston and met a wealthy banker, Henry Daners, and married. She had two beautiful daughters and would eventually move back to Beaufort. We would remain friends until she died in the Seventies.

I visited Nelly shortly after her incarceration in the hospital only to find her within her room stroking Dusty's hair and humming to the evil doll. During my visit she did not utter a word as I tried to convince her to let me take the doll and destroy it. When I tried to forcibly take the damn thing she bit a chunk out of my hand and spit my own blood at me, a crazed look upon her face.

As I got up to leave the room my dearest friend finally spoke to me, my own blood dripping from the corner of her mouth.

"Dusty just told me he has cursed you."

The wound upon my hand took an unusual time to heal. The following Christmas, after I collapsed while visiting Nelly's mother in Charleston, I found out my heart was diseased. Though the prognosis was I only had days to live I somehow defied medical knowledge of the time and lived on. Each year I found my body was being ravaged by another disease, yet still I lived on cursed to be the walking dead. I had become a medical enigma and my family squandered their fortune trying to cure my endless ailments, so I came under the care of the state of South Carolina and now reside in a government run nursing home for the poor.

I came too in my bed, after hitting my head, fighting the urge to choke on the uncomfortable plastic tube running down my throat as I looked over to see a ventilator breathing for me, pumping oxygen into my shriveled lungs.

"Pull the plug?" The nurse asked into the phone, "are you saying the old bastard is finally going to die?"

The unfeeling words did not bother me. My heart filled with joy upon realizing that Dusty's curse would finally be lifted. As power to the ventilator was cut and the last breath of this world was exhaled from my chest, I floated above my body ready to let go. As consciousness faded I turned my head to see the Christmas card sitting upon the table next to my nursing home bed.

As Dusty had resided over my tortured and diseased existence with horror so did he over my death. My dying eyes focused on Nelly's would be great neice as she sat upon the mall department store Santa's lap. Within her arms was lovingly clutched the very gift that was presented to Nelly herself on that fateful day back in 1934.

Dusty.

UPON A MOONLESS NIGHT

He pressed his back against the wall and readied himself under cover of the moonless night. The changing of the guard would afford the easiest route into the castle. The hilt of his sword felt comfortable in his hand, ready to do what it was made to do. Kill. He slid cautiously along the wall until he came to the edge of the portcullis. The heavy gate stood open.

Bathed in the light of two burning torches he made out a pair of guards, the glow reflecting off of their armor. He reached into his belt and grabbed one of several throwing knives and sprang into action. Five seconds later the first guard lay writhing on the ground choking blood, the knife having found its mark while he was driving home his sword in the other man's gut.

Good, no alarm was raised. He scanned the courtyard assessing his next course of action. Another guard approached from the darkness and he concealed himself behind a large haystack.

The soldier spied one of his dead comrades lying in the circle of torchlight and went to draw his weapon. The assassin was on him before the soldier's sword was halfway out of its scabbard. With one deft motion the soldier's neck was broken before he could mutter a sound.

The assassin crept along the wall and came to a set of stone steps. He took the stairway until he reached a landing and a doorway framed by two more torches. The door creaked open, and another guard emerged. The assassin charged and rammed the man's head against the wall. The soldier groaned and his helmet hit the ground with a metallic clank. Stealth was now pointless. The assassin ran the man through with a quick thrust of his short sword. As he yanked the weapon free he heard shouts from the corridor beyond the doorway.

He readied his sword as the first three soldiers materialized into the torchlight and a swordfight ensued. The assassin had been tutored well and made quick work of the first onslaught, but the alarm had been sounded and others were roused from their slumber.

He forged ahead through the corridor and encountered five more guards in the next room. He engaged the first two and bested them with ease. Then he grabbed a mace from one of the slain men and turned to defend himself against the other three.

He crossed the mace and sword blocking the attack of the first advance. Then cold steal bit home through his back and shoved white hot fire into his abdomen. His knees buckled and his vision became tinged with a blood red haze before he collapsed onto the stone floor.

"Dammit," Chris cursed as he read the message on the screen, "I just can't get past this level!"

QUIT OR CONTINUE?

"Hey dude," his friend called from the kitchen, "ya wanna another beer?"

"Derkon the assassin requires more ale!" Chris bellowed as he hit the continue button.

He pressed his back against the wall and readied himself under cover of the moonless night. The changing of the guard would afford the easiest route into the castle....

PURIFICATION

He had cracked just three days before. That was when this gruelling work started and Greg had barely slept since. He told himself the weekend was almost over and he would sleep once he returned to the normal work routine on Monday. He hated three-day weekends.

This one was the worst yet. The constant assault of 'you knows' and 'likes' pounded his ears like anti-aircraft fire. This war on the English language in America was being lost on the front lines. Television and the entertainment industry as a whole had corrupted the country's youth to the point he needed an interpreter to understand the newer generation.

"So," he asked her with a forced smile, "are you interested?"

"Totally!" she said, pausing her relentless gum smacking. "You, like remind me of my dad, you know. You are so, like, smart and stuff."

Greg grimaced and clenched his fist.

The girl smiled and spat her gum into her hand, looked around the room to make sure no one was looking, and then pressed it to the underside of the table. She reached into her purse, grabbed three pieces more and crammed them into her mouth.

"So, like, do you wanna go to your place or mine?"

"Mine," he said nervously.

"Cool, because you know, I still like live with my parents."

"Of course you do," Greg mumbled under his breath. He paid the tab, got out of his seat and led her out of the bar.

The murder on the language continued during the drive back to his house. The grating upon his nerves intensified with every sentence she uttered. He was relieved when they finally pulled up on his street.

"Like, you live here?" The young girl asked with dropped jaw almost spilling her gum, "like, this is totally awesome!"

Ten minutes later as Greg choked the life out of her young body he stared into the gaping mouth set in a silent scream of terror. He smiled to himself. One more violator down.

He would set things right. If he had to, he would spend every weekend for the rest of his life purifying the English language one enemy at a time.

The next day Greg was preparing for his morning class when Dean Richards entered the room with a young blond lady.

"Professor Silva," The Dean introduced Greg to the young lady, "this is Mairi Edwards. She is a transfer from a New England community college." The Dean faced the young lady, "This is Professor Greg Silva, your new English Professor."

"I am, like so happy to meet you!" she said with a short snorting laugh, "transferring to a new school you know is like so hard and stuff. I am excited to be here."

"And we, my dear, are so excited to have you," Greg courtly shook her hand breathing a heavy sigh.

CAPTAIN'S LOG

Lady and I were caught up in the hurricane five days ago. We tried to make it back to port but the storm blew us of course and drew us further away. GPS was knocked out, along with the radio. We eventually beached here and became stranded. Real Giligan's Island stuff.

Right now, I would give anything for the Professor's know how. He would probably repair the radio with a coconut and have us out of here in a jiffy. Speaking of coconuts, that is why I am writing this all down. To keep from going coconuts. Lady is the only company I have and though she can bark in several canine languages, she speaks no human at all.

At least I am not alone.

Day 6

Provisions are shot. Last of the fresh water was used earlier. No problems though. Lady and I went exploring a bit further today and found a stream flowing from the higher grounds. Fresh water, so we are in luck there. Managed a few small fish after rigging a crude net. They tasted like crap though and even after they were cooked over the camp fire, Lady would not even smell them. I have seen no sign of human life but wildlife is abundant. Mostly small creatures so far. I hope we are not sharing this island with any dangerous carnivores. I have ol' Lady here to protect me so, no worries.

Day 7

Lady and I spent most of the day hiking up into higher grounds following the stream. We managed a few more fish and Lady even chased down a small furry looking thing. It tasted much better than the fish after the fire heated her up. But it just made me realize how much

I miss a good old fashioned USDA graded piece of steak. My mouth is watering as I write.

I do not think the meat set well with Lady though. She spent most of the night growling and keeping me up. That is why I write so late into the night. It is very peaceful here. If there were a strip mall or two it might even be liveable. Still no sign of rescue. I think tomorrow I will start gathering wood for a new signal fire. That is if Lady will let me get some sleep.

Day 8

Lady seemed to be spooked all day. I think from lack of sleep, but they say dogs have a sixth sense about danger, so I kept a wary eye.

Almost made it to the crest of what I have dubbed "little mountain." Saw more of the other side of the island as we got higher. Still no sign of human life, but the other side seems to have a small lagoon. Nice place for a beach house.

I do have reservations about the large carnivore I mentioned earlier. We found one of those little furry creatures Lady caught the other day and it had been tore apart pretty badly. I shudder imagining the size of the claws that could have done that kind of damage. Tomorrow I think I may sharpen some sticks or gather some rocks for some protection.

Lady and I did not get much sleep this night. I do not know what time it is but it must be well after midnight and she has finally settled down. She growled and barked throughout the night. I heard rustling on the edge of the jungle, and I really wish we had not lost our ol' flare gun at sea. As I write, I am relieved the sun is just starting to come up.

Day 9

I managed a few hours sleep but when I woke up I found Lady had gone. I spent most of the morning retracing our path from yesterday but found no sign of her. The loneliness is unbearable and I find myself jumping at every little sound the jungle makes. I certainly hope she is okay. I want to call out to her but I fear I am not alone. An uneasiness grows in my stomach and I feel I am being watched. I used to feel fear like this during dark nights when I was a kid, telling scary tales with my friends. I never imagined I would be feeling as frightened in broad daylight.

This place is definitely not the place for a strip mall, or beach house.

Day 10

Being without, and worrying about, Lady kept me up most of last night. I did not eat at all yesterday and as the sun went down I swore I heard Lady's yelps from the heights of Little mountain. Despite my state of mind, exhaustion took me late last night. Sometime in the wee hours I awoke after my campfire died down. I heard rustling on the edge of the jungle and for an instant I hoped it was Lady. I rolled over and spied two red glowing eyes staring back at me from the jungles edge. I have never been scared enough to shit my pants until last night.

I do not know how long I laid there on my stomach just holding their gaze. The fire completely died out and the cold ocean breeze made me shiver, but I did not break from those staring red eyes. I wanted to make a run for it, but I had no where to flee to, so I just stared. They seemed to glow as if fueled by an inner light, and I knew without a doubt they were evil.

The stalemate was beginning to drive me insane. I had sharpened several sticks earlier and I knew they lay nearby. I decided to creep over, shimmying on my stomach, to grab one. As I inched along the sand, the eyes followed me. I was ready to lunge for my weapon anticipating the beast to pounce at any moment. As I got close enough desperation allowed me to grab my spear and jump to my feet in one single motion. That was all the time it took for the eyes to disappear.

The sun came up an hour ago and I write this with trembling hands hoping it is semi legible. I fear this may be my own obituary so I am going to stow it away inside the remains of the boat just in case I do not make it back. For now, I am arming myself as best as I can and I am going to find some answers. Hopefully I will find Lady in the process.

To my family I send all my love.

For now I may be walking into the valley of death. Just in this case, it is a little mountain.

Christopher A. Mairi.

WISHING WELL

PART ONE

During my early teens I was sent to spend a summer on my uncle's farm in upstate New York along with my brother and sister. Mom and Dad were having a rough time and, even though they were trying to work things out, I was the only one old enough to understand this would be their last summer together.

My Uncle was getting old, so there wasn't really any farming going on at his old place. My Aunt Gertrude died eight years ago, and although Uncle Ralph was always a bit crazy, he had now become a full fledged kook since her death. It was hard getting away from his rambling stories about space aliens, dragons and cavemen. He was adamant about having seen all of them with his own "flesh and blood" eyes.

Once Uncle had gone to sleep after a long summer day, and believe me, to a thirteen year old, these days seemed to last an eternity my siblings and I would play Dungeons and Dragons. Well, we didn't have any dice, or modules, so basically it was me telling my brother and sister medieval stories and allowing them to role play with their imaginations.

Once a week, Uncle Ralph would go into town for supplies and we would go out exploring the farm. Our overly cautious parents had instructed our uncle not to let us out of his sight, so we found ourselves eagerly anticipating the weekly break from the old Kooks ramblings.

By the third week, Steve, Jennifer and I were getting extremely antsy when the weekly hallowed 'uncle free day' finally arrived.

"Now don't you kids wander too far," he warned us as he climbed into the ancient rusted Ford he called a car. He motioned me over. "Lee, you are in charge so watch 'em close."

We watched with giddy anticipation as the car turned around all too slowly in the dirt drive. He stopped in front of the three of us and rolled down his grimy window. "Don't forget, stay out of the woods on the west end of the cow pasture. If I hear tell of you young-ins goin' down there, I promise you, there will be trouble!" As he spoke the last phrase he shook his fist threateningly before slamming his car into drive and tearing off down the drive leaving us in a cloud of choking dust.

"Well, that was a bit ominous," my brother Steve exclaimed.

"What are we going to do Lee?" My little sister asked tugging on my sleeve and looking up into my face with mischievous blue eyes. I looked down into those eyes and muttered the answer I knew all too well she was hoping to hear.

"We're going to explore," I said with a wide grin for I knew we were all thinking the same thing, "we're going to the woods on the west end of the cow pasture of course!"

My brother and sister high-fived one another as I put the ear plugs of my iPod in. As we began to make our way across the cow pasture, I tuned out to the sounds of Bowling for Soup, while my brother and sister gleefully tossed dried out cow patties at one another.

Little did we know our boring summer on Uncle Ralph's farm was about to get much more exciting...

PART TWO

Mischief calls to idle-handed young children much louder than it does to adults and teenagers whose imaginations have been dulled through the rigors of living in the cruel world. That is why I was not surprised that my brother and sister were able to pick up on its siren song just five minutes after we had passed into the western woods. I remembered Uncle's warning but the guilt quickly burned away and I knew mischief was about to be had.

When we arrived at the edge of the clearing a menacing hush had befallen the woods. I experienced this eerie effect, because, just a few moments before, my iPod inexplicably quit, even though I had a full charge. The air about the trees was still, devoid of buzzing insects and chirping birds, as if nature was waiting the next move of three unremarkable curious kids.

Being close through our shared experience of a broken family, the three of us were pretty in tune with each others feelings. There was a unanimous griping fear as we involuntarily held our breaths. After a few uncomfortable moments of inaction Steve boldly strode into the clearing puffing his chest out with false bravado. Jennifer tried to reach out and grab his arm, but judging from the paleness of her face, she seemed too afraid to take a step forward.

The thoughts and feelings of that day have faded somewhat in my memory, but I can still remember that first step into the clearing as if it had just happened this morning. I did not want to falter for I knew how scared my sister was so I did not linger but a second behind Steve. It was as if I had to push past a wall of compressed air. Passing through this "invisible wall" I had to stifle a chill for the temperature inside was much cooler than it was 'outside.' I experienced a certain anxiety as if we had just sprung a booby trap, but I put on a brave face for my younger siblings.

The clearing was a perfect circle of bare earth defiantly refusing any plant life to encroach upon its center. Steve paused up ahead and we waited for Jennifer to take her first nervous step through the clearings perimeter. The strain on her face was evident as she pushed her way through. Even now, ten years later, I can vividly remember it was hard to breathe the heavy air that touched our nostrils with an unpleasant scent of mold and decay. It was hard to keep our breakfasts down within the churning confines of our stomachs.

At the center of the clearing was an old well. The rocks that formed the walls were worn by countless years of passing time. One side of the well had crumbled and the rotten wood housing for the water bucket leaned to one side defying gravity against a final, fatal fall. A frayed rope disappeared over the side and plunged into the dark depths below.

"Hold on a sec," I grabbed my brother's arm as he reached out to touch the bucket's crank apparatus. "I really think we should leave this place."

"What's the matter," Steve put his hands on his hips and jutted out his lower lip, "is my BIG brother a BIG baby!?!"

"Shut up butthole!" I shouted and lightly punched his arm.

"OOHHHH," Jennifer crooned, "those are beautiful."

We looked over as Jennifer skipped merrily over to a patch of pastel flowers growing a few feet away. My brother and I exchanged a confused glance for we knew just ten seconds earlier there were no flowers there. The two of us watched in stunned horror as Jennifer plucked one of the flowers and sucked in its sweet smelling nectar through her nostrils. We both half expected her to keel over dead from poisonous toxins, but to our relief all she did was sneeze.

Steve and I joined my sister's side. She smiled and handed each of us a flower, charging our sense of smell with a head swooning sweetness. Jennifer merrily hummed a tune oblivious to the fear she had been feeling just moments ago.

"I was just thinking of Mom," she said, tears touching her eyes, "We used to go and pick flowers from her garden each morning after you two went to school. Then we would sit in the kitchen and she would read me stories."

The three of us stared at the flowers, locked within private memories of our absent mother. Suddenly there was a commotion from the tree line on the far side of the clearing. Even though it was just the rustling of trees and bushes, the sudden emergence of sound from the stillness was amplified within our young minds. There was someone or something heading in our direction.

I ushered the other two ahead of me and we made a dash for the side of the clearing where we had entered. The heart pounding race for the woods shot adrenaline into my muscles and, before I knew it, I had Jennifer tucked under one arm while shoving Steve through the "wall" with the other. My over stimulated mind had our pursuers right on our heels.

As we raced into the woods I stole a quick glance back at the well and the opposite side of the clearing behind. Later, after our silent trek back to the farmhouse, my fright wore off and my mind concentrated more clearly. It was only then that I realized something odd. I closed my eyes and drew up the last frame of thought I had of the clearing.

The well. It looked in pristine shape. No crumbling walls, no rotten wood and no dilapidated crank housing.

My consternation grew when I recharged my iPod. Right before I put the other two to bed, I popped my earphones in. Instead of hearing music my ears were met with a chorus of whispering voices, the kind of background drone you might hear in a room full of people. My blood chilled as I strained to make out what they were saying, but to no avail. The voices were too hushed to reveal their secrets.

The day's events left me jittery and insecure. Uncle Ralph would be home soon, so I went around and checked all the doors and windows to make sure they were locked. As I checked the kitchen window I peered across the cow pasture into the western woods. The floodlights from the house highlighted four pairs of red eyes staring back at me. The skin on my arms and neck erupted in goose pimples and I felt the skin crawl over my skull as I reached over and turned out the floodlights. My paranoid mind kept a vigilant watch on the western woods, as I anticipated the return of my uncle.

I could not wait to leave this place.

PART THREE

The wind blew tree branches against the old farm house windows, but within my adolescent mind the scraping sounds mutated into the scratching of evil deformed claws. The sounds grated my already shredded nerves and then I heard the unmistakable clunk of Uncle Ralph's old rusted Ford.

My soul lifted and found a melody in the car's mechanical music for it signaled the end of my lonely vigil. The car sputtered to a stop and I heard the creaky car door open and slam angrily shut. I burst onto the porch but my heart sank at the sight before me.

My Uncle stood in front of his car quietly staring out into the yard towards the cow pasture, illuminated by the car's feeble headlights. He turned to me with a look that struck down my revelry with a single blow. Within his eyes I saw a glimpse of the fire my Uncle's soul possessed when he was a younger man.

I stopped so suddenly I almost left my shoes in the dusty old driveway behind me.

"I told you kids not to go out there!" he spat, "do you realize how long it took me to get that damn thing that far away from my house?" As he spoke he stepped aside and waved his hand towards the crumbling well sitting under the old oak tree that separated the side yard from the cow pasture.

My jaw dropped as my eyes moved over the old stonework. A tight circle of dead grass surrounded its base and I noticed that within its perimeter, pieces of bark had flaked off the old oak to reveal swathes of maggot infested wood underneath. Cobwebs on the underside of the structure atop the well were lit from underneath in a dull greenish glow. The webs moved in and out as a breeze emanated from the shaft in beats of whispering ghostly breathing. Instantly I felt as if the well was not a structure at all, but a living entity.

My Uncle crossed the void between us in three huge strides. He leaned over me and looked deep into my eyes with fire in his, I felt my soul bare to his gaze. Rough hands grasped my upper arms with surprising strength, igniting a burning pulse within all of my extremities. I braced for the inevitable pounding I was about to receive and hardened my stare against the angry boiling rage.

I was shocked when his anger softened and I saw an unfamiliar nurturing look of concern on my uncle's face. To my relief his vice like grip eased and he stood up rubbing his chin.

"I--I-- I am s--sorry Uncle," I stammered, "I h--had no i--idea."

He held up a hand to silence me. "Inside boy," he said in quick staccato syllables, "IT can hear you."

As we stepped through the door the old man turned and locked the dead bolt putting his ear to the inside of the door listening for sounds on the other side.

"Uncle--"

"SHHHH!" he said, holding up his hand.

I tried not to move as my heart raced with a terror. I could not fathom an explanation grounded in physical reality. This was a glimpse of the unexplained, of the unseen powers that tie us to the universe. Powers that we could never hope to wrap our collective feeble minds around.

When my Uncle turned, I was struck by how young he suddenly looked - as if twenty years had melted from his face in an instant. A youthful enthusiasm had assumed control of his personality and an air of confidence took over his manner. This was not the same man who had left the farmhouse earlier.

"Son," he said in measured tones placing a warm hand upon my shoulder, "do not be too hard on yourself. It is not your fault. This was inevitable, so maybe it is best it has happened now."

I felt something within me snap and I lost my composure. This was a lot for a thirteen year old boy to deal with. My body heaved and I broke down crying.

"Now stop that!" Uncle Ralph demanded grabbing my upper arms tightly. "Look at me! Do not give it anymore than you already have."

He loosened his grip and reached inside his jacket for a handkerchief which he handed to me.

"Now pull yourself together and get some sleep." He turned me towards the stairs, "don't worry, you will be safe tonight. This old farmhouse, she is strong, and I do not intend letting my guard down for an instant."

I obediently climbed the steps to my room. When I reached the top, I snuck a peak behind me as my Uncle pulled a toy cap gun out of the kitchen drawer along with two boxes of rolled cap "ammunition."

I checked on my siblings finding them resting peacefully within the room they shared across from mine. As I opened the door to my room I fearfully scanned every inch from the lighted hallway. I was half expecting to find red eyes glaring at me from underneath the bed or from the dark confines within the closet.

I hid under the blanket and reached up to turn out the bedside lamp in order to diffuse the dark shadowy apparitions playing upon my mind. Beneath the lamp, resting upon the nightstand I was surprised to see a beat up leather bound bible that was not there before. On the cover, barely legible, Aunt Gertrude's name was stamped into the leather in flaking gold ink.

A dark pall enveloped the room and the light bulb dimmed. A brooding feeling touched my soul and a chill ran down the length of my body. I knew instantly that I was feeling the same presence that I had earlier at the well.

Suddenly, the bible opened and the pages fluttered until a page from the book of Revelations was displayed before my eyes. With Aunt Gertrude's pink pen the passage "and the dead shall rise from the ground," was highlighted and then underlined in red ink. The words seemed to take on a silvery glow until the popping sound of a cap gun could be faintly heard from down stairs. The entity was gone and, as if I had just taken a sleeping pill, I collapsed into a fitful dream laden sleep.

PART FOUR

My eyes fluttered open and stubbornly focused on a pair of muddy boots standing in the doorway of my room. As my vision slewed upwards my groggy brain awoke from the depths of the strange dream from the night before. It took a second to process the information as the sight of my Aunt Gertrude fired across my synapses. Time slowed to a crawl, and one second seemed an eternity.

The heart pounded slowly as my mind focused on the gory details before me. What used to be a pink cotton dress hung, tattered and soiled, from her wasted body. Maggots and worms wriggled and danced inside the gaping holes within her dry skin. Brittle bones poked through dead flesh and dusty fabric as her crow-like fingers curled around the handle of a rusted pitchfork. Then my eyes rested on the face.

I had seen pictures of my beautiful Aunt Gertrude in my mother's photo album. If it were not for the cracked pearl rimmed eye glasses that precariously balanced on the dried cartilage on the bridge of what used to be her nose, I might not have even recognized the walking corpse before me. Patches of mud-caked hair sprouted from her skull like some kind of crazed troll doll and bugs I gnawed on the stumps of flesh where her ears once resided.

Her brow furrowed to reveal her skull beneath the broken flesh and her eyeless sockets seemed to impossibly focus on me. The skin around her mouth cracked as her dry lips parted exposing her rotten yellow teeth.

"The dead shall rise from the ground." The hoarse voice came to my ears and I bolted upright. My body was soaked in sweat and I let out a shrill scream.

There within the doorway, with a surprised look upon her face, stood Jennifer frozen in mid stride. I turned to see my bedside table empty behind me.

"You scream like a girl," my sister said with a distracted tone. Then her face lit up, "you gotta come see!"

I shook the cobwebs from my head and stepped to the floor, realizing I was still dressed in my clothes from yesterday. I pulled on my shoes and my sister grabbed my hand and excitedly pulled me towards the staircase.

"You have to be quiet because Uncle is napping on the front porch."

Immediately last night's details popped into my head and I feared the worst. Leaving Jennifer behind, I bounded down the steps almost missing the last few and spilling onto the hardwood floor. I flew past my brother leaving him with a dumbfounded look and a glass of spilled orange juice on the floor.

I burst onto the porch expecting to find him dead, murdered by some evil creature but to my relief my startled uncle awoke and pointed the cap gun at my head.

"You better put that thing away," I said putting my hands up in a disarming manner, "or you are liable to kill someone."

My Uncle blinked and lowered the toy pistol, a tired look upon his face. He stood and looked over towards where the old oak recently stood. I followed his gaze and saw the great tree had fallen at some point during the evening. Huge branches that had towered above now lay bent and broken on the dusty driveway.

I looked at the unassuming well sitting several yards away. The "dead zone" around it had grown. Where the dried grass was last night only barren dirt existed now. The stump of the oak tree still lay within the circle, what was left of it had rotted away into a pile of moldy sawdust. Peppering the circle I saw several carcasses of dead birds in various stages of decay.

"You kids get back inside!" My Uncle yelled behind him through the open screen door. I saw my brother and sister's sheepish faces as they withdrew fearfully towards the back of the house.

"Uncle Ralph, what is it doing?" I asked him.

"Feeding."

"Feeding? What are we going to do?"

My Uncle sat back down in his rocking chair and scratched the stubble upon his chin thoughtfully.

"I want you to take my car-"

"But Uncle, I'm only thirteen!"

He stared at me without a word, until I sighed and settled down, then he handed me a scrap of paper. "You're going to take my car into town and go to Henson's Hardware. Here is a list I made out last night, just tell them to put it on my tab. It's important we get to it while it is still weak. When you get there ask to see Sheriff Tanner or the Professor. Tell them you are my nephew, and to come quick. They will know what it is about."

"But-"

"Boy," My Uncle's thundering voice hit my face like a fist, "get your head out of your ass and listen to me!"

I bit my lower lip and choked back salty tears, but I did not drop my gaze.

"This is serious," he continued, "and you are going to have to do your part or people are going to get hurt, do you understand me?"

I nodded.

"Good. Get to town as fast as you can, get those supplies and then gather the Sheriff and the Professor. We need to cut the head off of this thing before it gains strength."

He tossed me the car keys. I was so scared at that moment that I surprised myself when I caught them.

"I'll stay here and keep your brother and sister safe."

"Won't they be safer in town?"

"It will be after them before anyone else. Their imaginations are stronger, because they are so young. If you were to take them IT would make you bring them back here. Besides, it would probably make you kill me. The only reason that hasn't happened yet is because it is still weak."

"Uncle, I would never-"

"Son, you do not know what this thing is capable of. You just do what you are told and we just may get through this with all of us alive. Now go! You've wasted enough time already."

"But Uncle Ralph, I can't drive!"

"Learn as you go!" He shouted as he headed back towards the house. " And Lee, whatever you do, for God's sakes. DO NOT WISH FOR ANYTHING! That only feeds its strength!"

PART FIVE

As I climbed behind the wheel of Uncle Ralph's Ford the eager engine fired up after I shoved the key in. I thanked fortune that the car was not a stick shift, and shoved it into drive. The car launched down the drive throwing a cloud of dust towards the well as if in an effort to mask our escape.

My knuckles were white as I hung onto the wheel that jerked back and forth with a will of its own. It was as if the vehicle itself had made this escape many times before and knew from experience how to flee this foe. But it was obvious our enemy was not going to make our escape easy.

Before we cleared the fallen oak, I was startled as a giant limb suddenly slammed down before us sending a shower of broken twigs raining down upon the dusty windshield. Without hesitation, I slammed the car into reverse while turning the wheel into the tree. The back bumper shoved at the old oak as I slammed it into drive and deftly rounded the huge limb. I spied the lumbering bough within the rear view mirror as it lifted itself high into the air again, preparing for another striking blow. I stomped onto the accelerator as hard as I could, and the fire of ancient pistons responded gallantly pounding away in uneven beats of impossible speed.

I breathed a sigh of relief as I looked into the rear view seeing the old oak dragging itself with broken limbs in a vein effort of pursuit. As scared and worried as I was I could not help an nervous chuckle as quick breaths and adrenaline still charged my excitement. I marveled at how me and the car seemed to work in effortless concert facilitating our escape. My mood settled into sullen thoughts of concern for my brother and sister, as I made the two hour journey along the rural roads of Jefferson County.

Blackenbush, New York was a small town that had managed to escape the relentless march of technology. This was a place that did not even show up on some maps. I could not help but think of the paintings by Norman Rockwell we had studied in elementary school as I cruised down the main street looking for the hardware store.

The town was built around an old mill that was rumored to have been a mint building back in the late 1800's before the Civil War. A small canal fed into the center of town and supplied the old building's paddle wheel with constant motion. Besides the Mill, the sleepy town consisted of a handful of buildings huddled around the crossroads of two rural highways. These included a post office, a sheriff's office, two pubs, a general store and the hardware store all nestled in a small valley within the foothills of the Adirondack Mountains.

I pulled up outside Henson's Hardware store and bolted from the car to find the store locked up and no sign indicating their opening hours. There was no one in the street so I banged on the front door.

"Hey," an old bum shouted from the alleyway next to the store, "Can't a guy get some sleep around here?"

As I watched the bum cuddle with his half empty bottle of Jack Daniels, I heard the door lock turn and the kind face of an elderly woman stepped aside and waved me in. She ushered me over to the counter and introduced herself as Matty Jordan.

"You must be Ralph Murkick's nephew."

"Why yes, how did you guess?"

She pointed through the window towards the rusted car.

"Oh, of course." I handed over the list to Ms. Jordan, "Uncle needed these items. I also need to fetch the Sheriff and the Professor."

She read over the list and the smile bled from her face. When she spoke her tone had changed from pleasantness to business.

She read the list aloud. "Twelve car batteries, five pairs of rubber gloves, six metal noodle strainers and seven hundred marbles. Sounds like you are about to perform a reverse polarization."

"Excuse me ma'am?" A reverse what?"

"I will have to go next door and get a few of these items at the grocers." She smoothed her apron and called towards the stairs behind me. "Karen could you come down please?"

Matty came around the counter and placed her hand upon my shoulder. There was a forlorn look upon her face as she opened her mouth to say something, but then thought better of it. She patted my shoulder and smiled sadly. "I'll fetch both the Professor and the Sheriff. Don't worry, I'll be back in a jif."

She left me standing alone and frightened. I scanned the store until my eyes rested on the bulletin board behind the counter. I read the headlines of several newspaper articles pinned to the worn cork.

SMALL TOWN IN UPSTATE CENTER OF UFO HOTSPOT

BIGFOOT SPOTTED IN JEFFERSON COUNTY

BLACKENBUSH, PARANORMAL CAPITOL OF THE WORLD?

Most of the articles read like a line up for a season of the X-Files. The last article seemed out of place from the others.

LOCAL STORE OWNERS DIE AFTER LONG BATTLE WITH RARE CANCER

"They were my parents." I jumped as the words were spoke at my left shoulder. I turned and saw a girl of around my age. As I looked upon her face the pale gauntness could not keep her attractive features from shining through. Sad tender green eyes stared at me from amongst laugh lines cut deep within her skin. Even within her obvious mournfulness, I found her beautiful.

"Sorry," she said as she moved behind the counter, "I did not mean to startle you."

I cursed myself as I was too dumbfounded to respond.

"My Aunt mentioned you were about to perform a reverse polarization." She began reading over the list upon the counter, "my parents helped out with the last polarization, eight years ago."

Part Six

Karen Henson and I were the same age, but the battle her parents had fought with their disease had bled away her youth. As I looked into her sad green eyes I found myself awash in her sorrow as if her soul, through some unseen conduit of communication, touched mine. I shamefully looked away from her gaze as guilt quickly replaced the sadness.

"Don't feel bad for me," she said placing a pale hand over mine, "they are now at peace and no longer in pain."

I looked back into her beautiful face trying to think of something to say, but all I could manage was a sympathetic smile.

"Besides," Karen gently squeezed my hand sending warm blood rushing to my cheeks, "it is I who feels bad for you for what you are about to face."

Outside the store excited voices could be heard coming up the walkway.

"Take this," she whispered pressing a large green marble into my hand, "when the time comes, you'll know what to do."

She leaned over the counter and lightly kissed my cheek. My sullen mood momentarily lifted as the rush of teenage hormones rushed through my veins. She stepped from behind the counter and started gathering items from the list.

Matty came through the door followed by the tall form of Sherif Tanner.

"Gertrude and Ralph Murkick's nephew," his baritone voice boomed as he shook my hand firmly, "sorry we couldn't meet under 'happier' circumstances."

My head spun trying to process too much information as fear grappled with confusion and embarrassing adolescent lust. "Can someone tell me what the Hell is going on?"

Three stunned faces stared back at me. My face that was just seconds ago shaded by puberty driven hormones was now crimson as the three townsfolk exchanged glances.

"Where is the Professor?" Matty asked. "He is best qualified to explain."

A short uncomfortable silence was broken by the sound of the door bell. The disheveled hobo walked through the door while taking a long pull from his booze bottle. He wiped his lips with his dirty shirt sleeve. "So I guess the blasted thing is back from the dead then?"

Sheriff Tanner turned to the vagrant. ""Professor, can you please bring the young lad up to speed?"

Call it over-stimulation, or shear exhaustion, but at that moment it was as if my brain short circuited and I promptly passed out. When I came to, I heard mumbling voices accompanied by a sharp snapping sound like a coin being dropped into a tin can. I sat up and slowly rubbed my head trying to focus my bleary eyes in the direction of the commotion. In later years I would come to familiarized myself well with the state my young body was currently experiencing. Sharp, mind-numbing headache coupled with burning eyes and dry mouth. Hangover.

The group had gathered around a table and were busily grabbing up marbles one at a time. Each would mumble a few words and then quickly toss the marble into a metal noodle strainer placed before them.

"Ah, Lee," Matty exclaimed, "pull up a chair and grab a box of marbles."

"What, may I ask," scratching my head, "are y'all doing?"

"Preparing the Reverse Polarization," the Sheriff responded.

"Right. So what are the marbles for?"

"They're wishes!" The Professor said impatiently, "Now get your ass down here and help us get these strainers loaded. That damn thing is out there getting stronger by the minute!"

"Oh Professor," Karen butted in, "do lighten up on the boy." She smiled and patted the empty chair beside her. A friendly smile touched her tired face, "come sit next to me Lee."

I returned a sheepish smile one of my own. As I passed behind the Professor's chair he grumbled and shot me a contemptuous stare from beneath his bushy grey eyebrows. I noticed Karen's eyes holding my own and did what every red blooded thirteen year old American kid would do; I screwed up my face and stuck my tongue out at the old boozer. Luckily, he had closed his eyes and was mumbling of his next wish. I felt pleased with myself as a giggle escaped Karen's lips and I sat down beside her.

She slid a box of marbles towards me and lightly squeezed my knee under the table as she leaned over and whispered into my ear. Shyness caused me to almost jump in my seat as the sweet sound of her voice tickled the small hairs within my ear canal and sent every hair on my body standing on end.

"You must make every wish as sincere as you can, or it will not work."

I nodded awkwardly drunk within my sudden feeling of ecstasy, only half hearing the words.

The rest of the afternoon I willed time to pass by as slowly as possible sitting in that chair beside Karen. The urgency to get back to my family being held captive by the evil well did not return until we loaded the last of the supplies into the trunk of my Uncle's car. I tried to slide into the driver's seat but surrendered the keys reluctantly to the Sheriff as he flashed me a wan smile.

"Why aren't we taking a police car?"

"Because old Bessy here is the only thing it produced worth a damn," he responded patting his hand on the cars rusted top, "and she is used to helping us out of these tight spots."

Somehow it did not come to me as a surprise that the old car had originated from the well. I could picture my Uncle wishing for the car, all shiny and new, within his youthful past.

I was rudely sent to the back seat after the Professor decided to ride shotgun. He turned and looked back at me, pointing a stubborn finger in the air. "Now don't go falling for the Henson girl boy, she only has about three months to live."

My heart sank as we drove off. I looked through the back window and felt the tears welling in my eyes as I waved at her sadly as she waved back from behind the hardware stores front window.

TO BE CONTINUED…

FATAL FLING

Sonya felt a twinge of jealousy as she thought about her best friend Helen and the handsome man she was out with that night. The microwave beeped and interrupted her thoughts. She opened the door and reveled in the smell, pulled out the package and burned her thumb on the hot bag of popcorn. She cursed out loud.

"Helen is out with Mr. Right," she said to her cat Whiskers as she sat upon her couch, "and I'm stuck here with you watching reruns."

Her cat nuzzled up to her and began happily purring away.

As she flipped on the TV and dug into the bag of popcorn, she thought back to the day the handsome man was brought into their ward at Aspen Memorial last week. She and Helen were immediately intrigued by the dark stranger with the strong chin. They began playing a guessing game with each other that first night, while he lay unconscious in his bed.

"He is a professional skier," Sonya guessed with little imagination, for his injuries were attained on the slopes, "practicing for the next Xgames on the most dangerous course."

"No," Helen countered, "he is a world renowned doctor who was on vacation and had a bad fall after challenging himself on the remote side of the mountain."

That first night her and her best friend played this game for hours, free of guilt because the man's injuries were not life threatening. Each of them had even confided a fantasy or two with one another for he was extremely good looking with a flawless physique. As she thought back to that night she knew they were both smitten like giddy high school girls ripe with puberty.

The green monster reeled its ugly head and she tried to concentrate on the movie that was playing on the television to distract her from her jealousy. A couple kissed on a sunset soaked beach.

"Helen is so lucky," Sonya said out loud absently stroking Whiskers behind the ears.

Her thoughts turned to the next shift the following day when the man finally came to. She and Helen were both in the room, quite on purpose, when his eyes fluttered opened and saw both women standing over him staring hungrily. She recalled how embarrassed they both were as he groggily asked for a glass of water.

"Now Helen and he are out drinking together," she said frustratingly jumping up from her couch sending Whiskers to the hard wood floor. The cat flashed an annoyed look at her and with raised tail, sauntered down the hall towards the back of the house.

She walked over to the window and stared out onto the Helen's dark house across the street. The thought of watching them come home later caused a wave of nausea that made the mouthful of popcorn she crunched on taste like ash.

She felt a flash of guilt for the dark feelings she was having about her best friend. Helen was the pretty one; she had always been the lucky one. Sonya should be happy for her. But as hard as she told herself this she could not convince herself of it.

"I do not even know why I let her borrow my cell," she said a tear coming to her eye. Sonya then mockingly repeated what she had said to her friend aloud to the empty room, "call me as soon as you get a chance and let me know how it is going."

She threw herself back down on the couch and grabbed her big throw pillow hugging it tightly to her breast.

Sonya's mind was back at the hospital that second night. She again felt the frustration upon discovering the good looking stranger had amnesia. No name, no profession, no identification.

'Helen wins again,' she thought to herself as she realized their guessing game that first night had no winner.

She grabbed her television remote and idly began flipping channels until she came to a news channel displaying a composite sketch of a man. Her mind slowly grasped onto the strong chin and dark features in the drawing. Her hearing decided to catch up a moment later...

"The man, known as the 'Montana Mangler'," the newscasters voice devoid of emotion came to Sonya's ears, "has killed seven women to date. He eluded Colorado police somewhere west of Aspen last week and has not been seen since. He escaped pursuit when his car went off road near a popular ski resort on Ajax Mountain. If you have any information on the whereabouts of this man, call authorities immediately. He is to be considered very dangerous, especially to professional women matching his previous victim's description."

Sonya raced to her phone and frantically began dialing numbers overwhelmed with fear for her best friend. The seven women flashed briefly in turn upon the television screen. Each could have been sisters with Helen. She fumbled with the buttons on the phone taking her several tries because in her state she had trouble remembering her own cell.

"Busy signal!?!" she spat in disgust. "Damn cell phones!"

She slammed the phone down on the cradle in frustration after trying the number two more times.

"911." She said aloud reaching for the phone again when she heard a car pull up outside of her house. She ran to the window and saw Helen's car in her drive. Her heart sank as she saw the tall dark handsome stranger open the driver's side door and get out of the car.

She turned, fear driving her to rummage through her kitchen drawer and grab her biggest cooking knife. She ran toward the front door, almost tripping over Whiskers who had come to investigate. When the front doorbell rang she threw open the door and stared wide eyed at the surprised man the knife poised before her.

"Helen wanted to-" He was cut short as Sonya lunged forward with the knife and plunged it deep into his chest. He stood wobbling a moment as his question trailed off as the life left his body, "if you wanted to come along..."

His body hit the ground with a hard thud. Through the open front door Sonya heard the newscasters emotionless voice float on the air.

"This just in Ladies and Gentleman, the Montana Mangler has just been apprehended."

Sonya dropped to her knees dropping the bloodied knife beside her. She looked disbelieving up into the eyes of her former best friend as Helen stood over her and screamed. The last thing she remembered before passing out was her cat Whiskers rubbing up against her leg....

THE ANOMOLY

Daemond would be called alien by many, but the truth of the matter was he was just as much part of the human race as your local government official or mailman. In fact, Daemond had contributed on countless occasions more than any human in history had to the culture of our race inspiring it to revelation and revolution. These achievements were never credited to him directly, but were penned into history under several pseudo names he himself had fancied on said given occasions.

While human civilization exhaustedly sprinted along around him Daemond lived amongst it unchanging over the eons. He had moved from place to place upon the planet always a student of human society, psychology, physiology and culture. But as ever changing as these beings were, he was the only constant within the world, forever cursed to go on living barricaded from experiencing life as a human himself.

Friends and lovers would enrich his life fleetingly before aging and dying before his eyes. These treasured souls would always take a piece of him into the afterlife upon their passing and he often wondered each time how much of his own soul was left to give. His wounded heart would cause him to disappear and isolate himself, but loneliness and boredom always prevailed yearning for companionship and purpose, thrusting him back into the human world.

Purpose. Daemond had given up long ago on figuring out what his was. Sometimes he thought himself a god, other times a devil, but he discovered after countless years of disguising his true nature, he had a good soul. He felt for the humans around him and envied their isolated minds and the capacity they had to feel so many colorful emotions. For coupled with his curse of immortality was his ability to read minds and feel others emotions.

This was exactly why the individual that stood before him now mystified him so. He studied her long raven hair as the ocean breeze commanded it into elegant waves as if it were made of the salty sea itself. Daemond studied her beautiful delicate features honed from the most delightful olive he had seen nowhere upon this Earth. Then he lost himself within her elegant green eyes as he tried to peer into the soul that lay beyond and within. It was as if he had been hypnotized and his spirit felt a cautioning tinge of fear. He could not read nary a thought or emotion.

"Who are you?" He asked confused, but intrigued.

"I am yours." Came her simple reply as a smile crept across her face.

"I do not understand."

"You do not know what you are?" She replied a crease furrowing her brow, "Or why you are here?"

He shook his head a blankness setting his face. He tried with all his might to read her mind but all he got back in return was silence.

She reached out a delicate hand and lightly grasped him on the arm and leveled her gaze at him.

"It seems you have been a bad boy," she said playfully and he felt his heart quicken its pace responding to her soft touch.

"I do not understand?"

"Daemond," her voice was heard within his head as a burning sensation flared on his skin under her hand, "you have been the anomaly within the experiment on this planet and I was made for you."

Fear gripped him as he felt the molecules within the flesh on his arm begin to chemically alter. He tried to jerk his arm back but he could not break her strong grip. Once again he heard her within his mind.

"You have poisoned this world organism and altered its evolution tainting the results so I have been created by the B Cell to neutralize your influence."

Daemond watched in horror as she stepped closer and her body began to painfully meld with his. Everywhere her skin touched his a burning flame seared his flesh. He tried to scream but his throat choked on boiling blood. His eyes stared about wildly as he lost his balance and fell to the sand. Suddenly swarms of birds and stinging insects descended from the skies and several varieties of slimy bug life erupted from the beach around him. Every nerve within his body cried out in anguish as the creatures slowly devoured flesh, organ and bone.

Suddenly, the bonds that had tied his soul to this world weakened and his spirit broke free never to return to Earth again, but to forever fly with the souls he had encountered during his stay.

Instead of feeling different and alien, he was now the same as they were for the first time ever...

BRAIN TRUST

Gary Gilmore was winding down in his dressing room after shooting his latest episode of his popular political science show. His life had taken on such a hectic pace these past five years he found these fleeting moments to allow him reflection few and far between.

His show, GG on the World Scene, had jumped from its small audience base and the small cable network that had incubated it into the national spotlight. A popular major news magazine show picked it up as a segment piece looking to boost sagging ratings. From its new address on the television dial it captivated audiences and not only boosted the magazines ratings, but spun off into a weekly show of its own.

Gary's charisma had become his curse. Now, even the country's political leaders had begun to pressure him to run in the upcoming presidential election. His views opposing the current president's agenda had made him very influential within the American public. Now it seemed an upcoming campaign was inevitable.

He sighed and thought of his wife. She had taken it all with the pride and bravado befitting of a future first lady of the United States of America. Now as he dialed the house number on his cell phone he regretted that he had to let her down once again. She took it with her normal good-natured humor.

"We will have time," she joked, "in ten years after your upcoming run and two terms as President."

After hanging up the phone he dispelled his guilt by turning his attention to the reason he had to cancel his evening plans with his wife. He thought back to the odd conversation just before he went on camera earlier that day.

"Come alone and incognito," his childhood friend had whispered over the phone, "no cameras, and for god sakes, no lights."

He laid out his white dress shirt and tie on the dressing room couch and fished out the black t-shirt and jeans from his closet. He reveled in how comfortable the apparel felt for it seemed the last five years he was never without coat and tie. He pulled the baseball cap close down to his eyes and looked at his reflection in the mirror.

"Ole GG," he said to himself, "I wouldn't want to run into you in a dark alley."

There was a soft wrap at his door and his assistant, Mairi, spoke from the other side, "Sir, they are ready for you in post production."

"Mare," he said opening the door motioning her to come inside, "I need your car. I want you to take the back service entrance and take the limo to my house. That should distract the media and give me plenty of time to make my escape."

His assistant stared back at him as if he were an oncoming train. Her mouth worked up and down but not a sound came out.

"Fun isn't it?" he asked with a disarming smile, "real cloak and dagger kind of stuff."

"W-what," Mairi stuttered, "do you want me t-to do once I g-get to your house?"

"Check out the dumbfounded looks on the medias face when you get out of the Limo." He cracked the door and looked out into the hall then turned back, "and enjoy the wonderful dinner my wife prepared for me and tell her I love her."

Gary slipped out the door and into the night leaving his confused assistance behind.

He drove up I-95 through Maryland and into Pennsylvania. To pass the time he thought about Dr. Mark Jordan, his childhood friend. The guy was the most intelligent person he had ever known, until his brush with death.

Mark had ranted that during his near death experience an angel had visited him and given him special sight. Shortly after, he disappeared and Gary only heard occasional stories about his whereabouts and activities. These stories got progressively more bizarre with the passing of time and most involved the evaporation of his friend's family fortune.

As he pulled into the small park that was the predetermined meeting place he felt excitement as his heart picked up its pace. Gary's headlights shone upon the only other car within the parking lot and a dull fear began to burn within his stomach.

"What if Mark," he asked himself, "has gone 'serial killer' insane?"

As he got closer he saw a tall figure leaning against the back of the car wearing a wide brimmed hat. The man looked down at the ground hiding his face, but as Gary approached he looked up into the advancing headlights. The crazy glint within Mark's eye was unmistakable and Gary tightened his grip upon his steering wheel with his growing anxiety.

He entertained the notion of turning his car around and gunning it as fast as he could back to Washington, DC. Then, Marks lips parted in a warm smile and the fear washed away as the dirt of years of mudslinging were washed away revealing the boyish face of his old best friend. Gary put his car in park and, after nervously looking around, stepped from the vehicle with little notion of what lay just ahead.

Part Two

The two men sat within Mark's parked car and quickly raced through the pleasantries eager to get down to business. Both men's appearances were haggard by the stress of unseen, but vastly different, circumstances within each of their busy lives. Gary was about to find out the weight he was carrying on his shoulders was much less than the load burdening his childhood friend.

"Gary," Mark began after a short uncomfortable silence, "I appreciate you driving all this way without knowing exactly what this is about, but you will see this matter is of the utmost importance."

"I would not have come if it were not for the urgency of our earlier conversation," Gary said with a practice smile that had made him the darling of the media, "besides; I needed a diverting break from the pressures of being society's number one poster boy."

"I apologize for what I am about to do in advance, but what I have to tell you is going to change your life."

Gary's skeptical mood caused him to squirm in his seat as he braced himself for what lunacy his old friend was about to spout at him.

"When Benjamin opened--"

"Benjamin?" Mark was cut off by the question and a scalding look, "if this is about the 'angel' that visited you I want you to stop right now. I did not come all this way for a lesson on religious beliefs."

"I assure you my old friend," the other man held up a palm outward, "this has nothing to do with religion and everything to do with the well-being of our species and our world."

Gary turned to open his door and exit the car.

"Just give me two more minutes," Mark pleaded, "and after, if you want to go I wish you God's speed."

Gary paused a moment after opening the door. The chorus of chirping crickets from the coolness outside played on the air beckoning him to flee the car with his values unharmed and fully intact. He stole a glance over his shoulder and saw the desperate look on his childhood friend's face.

"Please Gary, just two minutes of open mindedness is all I ask."

Gary's shoulder slumped in defeat and he pulled the door to closing the world off outside of the car. He sighed and turned a non-approving eye on Mark.

"Have you ever heard of Rods?" Dr. Mark Jordan pressed onward after regaining his composure.

"You mean like within one's eye?" came a confused response.

Mark shook his head, "No, these are also more popularly known as Skyfish or Solar Entities."

"I have heard of them," Gary responded with a nervous chuckle, "UFO enthusiasts swear they are alien probes." Gary opened his mouth to make more admonishing remarks but paused upon spying the serious look on his friends face.

"Your, UFO enthusiasts, are not too far off my old friend."

"That is it Dr. Jordan!" Gary opened the car door and leapt out, "it is like they all told me, you are absolutely bone-fide coo-cu! I cannot believe I actually came all this way to listen to this crap!"

Gary stomped angrily towards his own car when Mark shouted a response that froze him in his tracks.

"I captured one!"

As a journalist and curiosity dictated he investigate this challenge further. So, for the second time this night, he gave in and turned upon his heel to face his friend.

"If this is a trick to get me to stay longer..."

"I wish with all my being that were not the case," Mark said, his voice shaking, "then this would all just be some kind of horrible nightmare. But I am about to show you, God or no God, this is a cruel hearted reality."

Gary stood a moment pounding a fist against his leg in contemplation. He wanted to give this no more attention but the proof of physical evidence was just too enticing.

"Show me."

A look of relief crossed over Dr. Jordan's face and for the first time since his near death experience, a smile spread across his face. Triumphantly, he would no longer have to endure this great burden alone any longer. The time he had been foretold by Benjamin was now at hand. He breathed a long sigh as he opened up his trunk and retrieved a tattered old briefcase.

"I still think you are crazy." Gary said walking up to his old friend's side.

"Every one does," he responded handling the case as if it had priceless fine china within, "it was the only way I could have found out this information and work under their radar."

"Exactly what are you about to show me?" Gary nervously asked as they opened the doors once again to Mark's vehicle.

Mark's stoic gaze shot stinging icicles of seriousness across the car's roof at Gary.

"Their radar."

"Now Gary," Dr. Jordan began, "I have spent the majority of my adult life and, nearly all of my family fortune, obtaining this information."

Mark opened the briefcase he balanced on his knees. Within, black foam padding with several cut-outs formed the inside space of the case. Within one of the foam compartments there was what appeared to be a cell phone. This he removed and handed it over to Gary.

"What ever you do," he said reverently, "do not misplace this. This will be the most important device in your life from here on out."

"A cell phone?" Gary asked with a smirk.

"NOT, a cell phone Gary." Mark admonished him as he would an eight year old, "I need you to listen. I have very little time to explain and you HAVE to take this seriously! So please Gary, I implore you. Listen."

Gary frowned and nodded.

"This 'cell phone' device is a microcomputer. Within this device there is a vast database filled with the information I have spent decades acquiring. It is also the vaccine to what you are about to see."

Next Mark pulled out a metal case like one would keep a pair of spectacles within and handed it over to Gary.

"When Benjamin opened my eyes," Mark's tone softened, "it took me years to come to terms with what I was seeing. It dawned on me later why I had been given this gift of sight."

"Open the case," he ordered.

Gary opened the glass case to find it empty.
"Is this some kind of--"

Mark him cut him off with a stern look. "Turn on your 'cell phone'."

Gary did so and suddenly within the case a ghostly apparition of a pair of glasses appeared. The news show host stared at them with a slack jaw.

"God is on our side Gary," Mark said passionately, "and our eyes are being opened up to the enemy."

Mark dialed a button on the dash of the car and around them the tint of the windows went completely black blotting out the halogen parking lot light streaming in from outside.
The only light within the car's interior emanated from the glowing pair of glasses.

"How?" Gary murmured the question his eyes fixed on specs.

"Just put them on my old friend and let there be light."

He did so reluctantly and at first, as his eyes adjusted, all was a bright blur. Then the interior of the car slowly came into focus as if it were mid day. Beyond the windows all he saw was darkness.

"How do they work?"

"All will be explained my friend," Mark said pulling out the final item from his briefcase, "but now I want you to 'see' for the first time what we are up against."

He handed over a small but heavy black card box case to Gary.

"Slide the top off."

Gary did so and within there was a thick glass cube. Within this squirmed a glowing alien looking creature writhing to escape its glass bondage. Its body was about ten inches long and cylindrical covered in fine hair-like filaments that glowed brightly at their tips.

"What in Hell is it?" He asked astonished.

"This is a sensing cell," Mark explained. Upon seeing the dumbfounded expression on his companion's face he continued on as patiently as he could.

"I have come to discover that our entire planet is under some sort of surveillance and these little guys are the equivalent to alien radar."

"They are machines?"

"Yes and no." Mark answered and began a practice lecture he had rehearsed within his mind for the past several years.

"They are a living entity that exists only partially within our dimension. They serve a purpose to analyze and keep track of our planet's progress."

"...keep track, planet's progress..." Gary repeated the words as if he had no understanding of their meaning.

"They travel on light waves and light particles. The 'hairs' on their bodies enable them to grab onto the waves and control their speed, direction and attitude. As long as there is no light, they cannot propel themselves or power their bodies. The only reason this one moves is because it is given just enough power to by the stasis cube it is contained within. It took me most of my life to finally catch this one. From it I reversed engineered the glasses and the microcomputer you now possess."

Gary could not find the words to respond. A fear gnawed at his soul as his mind grasped at this new knowledge. He felt his whole belief and support system shudder as his grasp on reality loosened and his head began to spin.

"Open your eyes to the world," Mark said as he dialed the knob on the dash and let the light from the outside in. The inside of the car was suddenly filled with the little creatures flying effortlessly through glass, metal and upholstery on their shear momentum.

Gary could not help the reaction trying to swat them from the air.

"Gary, I believe our planet is being cultivated for something," Mark continued on ignoring the swarming entities, "like humanity would grow something in a Petrie dish our every move is checked and controlled by the program around us. It acts and reacts to steer our evolution towards some final purpose."

"Why are you telling me all this?" Gary asked.

"Because I have served my purpose Gary," Mark said with a smile, "now I have passed the baton onto you my old friend. It is time you serve yours."

Gary noticed that the small creatures were collecting all over his old friend's body. Through their gathering mass he could barely see Mark's face. He reached up to remove the glasses.

"NO!" Mark exclaimed, "NEVER take those off, NEVER! The glasses not only allow you to see them, but counteract their signal so you remain invisible to them."

"Why do you not protect yourself then?" He responded seeing more of the creatures gathering upon him like iron shaving being drawn to a magnets surface.

"To prove my last theory." He explained. "I have studied the system a long time Gary. I believe it works a lot like our own immune system. I have just infected the system and have just become a threat. If I am correct I suggest you get the hell as far away from me as fast as you can."

Gary felt the air about them was charged with electricity. He could smell ozone within the air and he felt the small hairs on his arms and the back of his neck begin to stand on end.

"Gary," Mark said putting a hand on his shoulder, "remember one thing. God is on our side, that makes us dangerous. Now GO!"

Dr. Jordan shoved Gary hard with his shoulder pinning him against the passenger door. Gary reached the handle and pulled spilling himself onto the hard asphalt of the parking lot outside the vehicle. He turned over onto his back and looked into the sky above. Thousands of the sensing cells had gathered above in a massive swirling vortex. Angry clouds whipped up a powerful wind surrounding the car.

Gary got to his feet and stumbled towards his own vehicle. He jumped in and as he slammed it in reverse he saw several bright bolts of lightning strike Mark's car which exploded in a brilliant fire ball.

His instinct for survival climbed into overdrive as they sped away from his past and into an uncertain future.

THE WIZARD WAR

Part One

Devon snagged a corner table at the Dragon Inn and waited for his opportunity. He watched the barkeep clear empty glasses from the tables. He knew this was no ordinary man. The bartender was a member of a secret society aligned against the wizards, and had received an important package just moments ago. Devon had been informed the package contained an ancient artifact that held enough magic to turn the tide of the war. He shivered at the thought. He could not allow the artifact to fall into enemy hands, or worse, into the hands of the Regent. Devon's assignment was to steal the package and deliver it to his master at the guild. Only then could there be lasting peace, at least the wizards would use the artifact for good.

He remembered a time when the world was less populated, and wizards had plenty of magic at their disposal. These legendary wizards were extremely powerful and Devon wished he had lived in that time. Now the world was overpopulated and magic was called on too often and by too many. It had become a scarce commodity.

Suddenly, a scuffle broke out between two men on the other side of the bar. The ruckus spread like a plague across the crowded room. Devon knew his chance was soon to come. He saw the bartender grab one of the brawlers – a man wearing a brown cloak. The hood fell away and Devon recognized Jarrod, one of the Regent's assassins. Jarrod plunged a dagger into the bartender's back, and the man fell to his knees.

Devon stared in horror.

The fight must have been started deliberately to create a diversion - Jarrod was after the package. Devon had to move quickly, or the prize would slip through his fingers.

Jarrod snatched his cloak from the barkeep's desperate grasp, reached into his belt and grabbed a small vial of liquid. With a smile, he threw it to the floor. The glass shattered, and a cloud of smoke rose into the air. The fighting subsided as men choked and rubbed their eyes in the stinging smoke.

But Devon was unaffected. He saw clearly using his 'spellsight.' He rushed towards the stunned barkeep as chaos raged around him. The acrid smell of smoke filled his nostrils but did not distract him from his goal.

The bartender's wife came out from behind the bar and knelt at her husband's side. She grabbed the hilt of the knife embedded in his back and wrenched it free.

"Get the bastard!" The barkeep said with a gasp of pain-wracked breath.

"Yes my love," She answered, grasping her meat cleaver and bolting for the door.

"At last," Devon murmured.

The bartender writhed in pain, blood pooling around him. Devon knelt down beside the squirming man knowing he had to move quickly. There would be other Regent agents waiting for this very same moment.

"Lunarium," he whispered the spell into the man's ear.

The bartender's sleepy head hit the floor with a soft thud.

Devon reached inside the man's jacket and extracted the brown paper package, stood up, and headed out through the kitchen as pandemonium reigned throughout the room. He exited through the back door, reveling at the feel of the brown paper package in his hand, still warm after being inside the inner pocket of the bartender's jacket. But his revelry was cut short when something heavy struck his head. Unconsciousness drew a veil over his eyes as he watched Jarrod pluck the package from his fingers.

"How could I have been so foolish," he thought and passed out on the cold cobbled alleyway behind the inn.

Part Two

As Devon came to, the sun's light was painting the tops of the trees red. The morning light created a haze as it shone through wispy fog that hung close to the rain drenched ground. He sat up and his head exploded in pain causing his eyesight to dim momentarily. His damp clothes clung to his body and at first he forgot where he was. He looked around the rain soaked alleyway and the night before immediately rushed back into his mind.

He cursed out loud.

The package was gone.

The war was lost.

Because of the weak supply of magic, Devon realized his protection spell had failed last night as he exited the inn. In the wrong hands, the artifact would make the magic situation much worse. Once the relic sucked power from the existing magic, all wizards on the 'good' side would become virtually powerless.

"Ah, there you are Devon." Jerik's voice bounced off the wet walls of the dank alley, "I've been looking for you everywhere." Jerik extended a hand and helped Devon to his feet.

Devon thanked him.

"Tell me you got the package." Jerik said, a pleading look on his face.

Devon looked down at his feet as the blood rushed to his face.

"Damn the gods!" Jerik cursed.

"Twas Jarrod that got me." Devon answered defensively, "I thought you were watching out for me."

"I was," Jerik responded, rubbing his bruised chin, "who do you think kept that weasel from nicking the package before you got it? The little bugger got away from me."

"Well, if Jarrod has still got the package, he will be heading to the Heron's inn to collect his money from the Captain. We need to get there before the little weasel does."

"Let us not tary then," Jerik replied, "we are being followed."

Devon looked into Jerik's face and the man gave him a wink.

"Our little red headed friend?" Devon asked.

"Yep."

Devon and Jerik made their way hastily through the village streets. They knew that if Jarrod handed the artifact over to the Captain, all wizard and magic folk alike would have to bend to the will of the Regent. The Regent would disband the wizard orders and send them into exile, or worse... destroy them altogether. Saybon, the Regent, had once been tutored in the Orders but had failed the trials. As a result, he was expelled and harbored a great hatred for the Orders. Saybon especially hated Devon and Jerik – the three of them had been tutored in the same group. Once, they had been best of friends – that was a long time ago. Now they were aligned on opposite sides, and Devon and Jerik had become the main object of the Regents ire.

The two men reached the top of the hill where the Heron Inn was located. They rounded a corner and ran straight into Jarrod, knocking him flat to the cobblestones. The assassin had been admiring the package in his gloved fingers before the collision occurred. He lost his grip on the parcel and it went skidding across the wet stone into an alley shrouded in shadow.

Jarrod rose slowly to his feet and the three men stared at one another for a brief moment. The silence was dispelled by high pitched laughter. A young woman with strawberry blond hair and a sprinkle of freckles across her nose emerged from the gloom with her sword drawn and the package in her hands.

"Looks like you lose boys," She said backing away.

The stared at her, dumbfounded as she stepped back and bumped into the armor-clad body of the Captain. She turned to look up into the eyes of the towering soldier and smiled weakly at him.

"I'll take that," the Captain bellowed ripping the package from her grasp and shoving her to the ground.

Captain Moncrede studied the brown paper package intently. "Magic," he muttered. He knew what was within the package. He knew how important it was to the cause of the war. It would mean victory. Now he pondered to himself, for which side?

"Sir, what shall we do with the prisoners?" one of his soldiers asked.

"Huh?" The Captain grunted, his yes still fixed on the package.

"What shall we do with them?"

The Captain glanced up at the awkward collection of souls before him. He knew what to do the two cloaked ones. "Send those two to the dungeon. The Regent has plans for them."

Devon and Jerik exchanged a nervous look.

"As for the other two…" The Captain scratched his beard without taking his eye off the package. "Execute them."

Devon was dragged away amid spluttering protests and curses. The strawberry red head did not make a sound as the soldiers grabbed her and marched her up the street.

Part Three

Captain Moncrede took the package upstairs to his room at the Inn. He set it on the table and unbuckled his sword. He now possessed the power to win this war, but who would he help? He loathed Saybon, the Regent. He had served the tyrant for years without promotion. He should be a general by now. Without him, Saybon would have nothing, not even control over the lands surrounding this very village.

Saybon had also begun strengthening his army with thieves....and now this, a stolen artifact. Saybon had resorted to thievery himself. To the Captain, theft was dishonorable. But then so was the offer he had received just two days ago from the enemy, and to Captain Moncrede, treason was even worse than thievery. He decided to let events unfold for a few more days before he made his final decision.

Devon and Jerik sat miserably in their cell inside the castle keep. It was cold and wet and the sickening smell of mold stuck in their noses. They tried to use magic to release the iron shackles clamped on their wrists, but their efforts proved futile. A 'ward' spell had already been cast on the iron by their captors, a powerful spell that thwarted their own attempts of magic.

After an hour of exhausted silence, Jarik tried to make conversation. "Tell me Devon," he said, "the package. I know what it means to the side that possesses it, but what does it contain?"

Devon stared into space before answering with a heavy sigh. "Ancient and wondrous magic Jerick. Very powerful and very dangerous."

"But why have I been kept in the dark about this? I'm on the same side – why has no one spoken of it before today?"

A look of sadness drew heavy lines upon Devon's face. "To know about the artifact is a heavy burden. Are you sure you want me to tell you?"

"Yes," Jerik responded, swallowing a lump in his throat.

"Okay, but I warned you. The object within is called the Nureaytumea, a relic discovered by the Svorsomes, an ancient sect of wizards that we know little about. It was said they drew power from the Nureaytumea to keep their lands safe and their settlements hidden for eons. The power of the Nureaytumea was so great they simply erased themselves from the face of the Earth. In recent times the Svorsome's numbers have dwindled and the remaining wizards of the sect have become weak. One of their number left a century ago and settled in a village south of here where he let tales of the Nureaytumea slip into the world.

"The stories were considered myth until our friend the Regent took upon himself to send assassins to the Svorsome's homeland and kill the remaining wizards that guarded the ancient artifact."

"How do you know so much about it?" Jerik asked.

"I was sent to the village to find the stray Svorsome when my superior discovered what the Regent was up to."

"Why is the Nureaytumea so dangerous? Is it true the Wizards could use it to win the war?"

Devon pondered a moment and then answered carefully. "The Nureaytumea draws on the very soul of the planet, the magic deep within the core that brings us night and day. The one who possesses the Nureaytumea would control the very elements of the world. It is unspeakable power." A dark shadow crossed his face as he paused. "Also, if the right incantations are used, the one using the Nureaytumea can....Unmake," Devon choked on the word, "any living being he sees unworthy."

Captain Moncrede tore away the plain brown paper revealing an obsidian box within.

Devon continued. "Our only hope lies within the spells that keep the box magically locked."

The Captain curiously studied his distorted and grotesque reflection on the black surface as he heard the whispering voice repeat over and over in his head, "Noxerea, procurium."

"If you were to unlock the package," Devon spat the words out as if they tasted sour, "they would have untold power."

Captain Moncrede shook his head as if to silence the whispering voice.

"Repeat.....Noxerea procurium." Against his will he mouthed the words and as their echo died away the box split open.

"They would have the power of the gods...." Devon's voice trailed off.

Captain Moncrede reached inside the obsidian box and a grin parted his lips as his hands closed around the Nureaytumea.

"Or the power of the demons." Jerik responded as understanding took an icy grip upon his soul. "Gods help us."

Part Four

The Captain pulled the Nureaytumea from the box, astonished to see a black scaled snake suddenly in his grasp. The snake's eyes were like two black obsidian globes, the creature's tongue flickered across the Captain's wrist as the black diamond shaped head swayed back and forth. The creature had the Captain mesmerized as it slowly coiled itself around his forearm. Moncrede wanted to shake the thing loose but he was paralyzed. The snake's head lowered and the Captain watched in horror as two black fangs plunged into his exposed wrist. Black venom darkened his blood vessels and a stinging fire crawled up his arm. He felt magical power flow with the venom and suddenly his senses sharpened. He felt a surge of strength as the fire reached the base of his skull and he looked at his reflection in the obsidian box. He saw the whites of his eyes and the irises dissolved into black and an overwhelming presence filled his mind.

"Thank you Captain Moncrede." The voice whispered within his head as the human soul that was the Captain drifted away, leaving only his knowledge and memory. These were now the possession of the serpent.

The snake around his wrist solidified into a black metal gauntlet.

"Guard!"

The young soldier standing outside pushed the door open and peered in. "Yes Captain Moncrede?"

"Call for the Regent, tell him to come and claim his prize."

Moncrede studied his new face on the smoothness of the empty black box. An evil grin crossed his weathered face as the young guard closed the door and scurried down the hall. Moncrede ran his fingers over the ridges of the snake. "We are Nureaytumea..." he whispered.

The guard retuned twenty minutes later and knocked at the door. "Sir?"

"Come," Nureaytumea ordered.

The door creaked open. "Sir, the Regent has-" The guard was cut short as Saybon pushed his way past sending the door crashing against the wall showering loose stucco to the wooden floor.

"Where is it Captain?" The Regent demanded, striding into the room with arrogant confidence.

Nureaytumea smiled as he gazed at his reflection in the mirror. He slowly turned to face the Regent without getting up from his chair.

"You will stand and address me Captain!" Saybon ordered, distain dripping like venom from each word. The Regent was astounded when his statement was met by booming laughter. Saybon faltered as he noticed the two black mirrored eyes that stared back at him from underneath the Captains brow.

"It is you who will kneel before Nureaytumea." The Captain's voice echoed off the walls with hollow resonance. "You will give me your allegiance."

The Regent straightened and looked down his nose at the wizened soldier standing next to him. "What is the meaning of this?"

Nureaytumea raised his gauntlet clad hand and slowly stood up.

Saybon felt an overwhelming force pushing down upon his shoulders and he found himself kneeling before the Captain against his will. He tried to voice his dissent but his tongue had suddenly become swollen and he was unable to speak.

Nureaytumea closed his obsidian eyes and began chanting in an ancient language as he approached the Regent. Saybon watched in horror as Nureaytumea raised his hand and grabbed the thread of the Regent's being, before slowly unraveling the fabric of his existence.

Within the space of three breaths the Regent ceased to exist.... His memory was erased from the minds of anyone who had ever come in contact with him. His reign had ended as his badge of office hit the Inn floor with a metallic thud.

Nureaytumea turned to the young guard. "Rally the Garrison Commanders now."

Part Five

Devon and Jerik heard the guards descending the stairs outside of the dungeon.

"I want to do the shorter one on the rack!" One said to the other as they reached the cell door fumbling with the keys, "I want to see if I can make him taller than the other one."

The other guard chuckled as they opened the rusty door.

"Hello boys," the first guard said with a cheerful smile, "we are to be your torturers for the day."

They ushered the two prisoners outside into the corridor. As they passed through the doorway Devon felt the ward spells drop away. Now they could use their magic. Jerik was on the first guard in a flash. The guard went for his sword with his free hand while struggling to grasp at the chain that Jarik had looped around his neck with the other.

Devon already a spell prepared and wasted no time in putting the other guard down. Moments later both men stood over their unconscious would-be torturers and released their shackles.

Devon rubbed his bleeding wrists. "Good thing the Regent is too cheap to hire smart soldiers," he said.

Jerik grimaced as he stooped and snatched the dungeon keys from the guard's belt. "Something doesn't feel right," he said. "That was just too easy."

"Haven't you ever heard of good ol' fashioned luck?"

Jerik's brow furrowed. "In my experience, there is no such thing as luck my friend." He picked up the guard's sword and leapt over the prostrate men. As he landed he looked up at the stone staircase and into the eyes of a young scribe dressed in a tattered grey cloak. The boy stared back, wide eyed with fear.

"Boy," Jerik held up a warning hand, realizing the young one was about to shout out the alarm, "You don't want to do that!"

The boy turned and quickly made his way back up the steps.

Jerik cursed and bounded up the stairs in pursuit.

Devon stood dumbfounded, amazed at the speed at which Jerik reached the first landing before disappearing around the blind corner. Devon was about to chase after his friend but Jerik suddenly reappeared. "Run!" he shouted bounding down the steps.

"What the Hell-" Devon's words were cut off as a trio of vicious dogs rounded the corner, frothing mouths full of sharp teeth and eyes that glowed red.

Hell hounds.

Devon turned on his heal and jumped over the two waking guards. "Good luck boys!" he said over his shoulder as the men sat up and rubbed their heads. Bleary expressions turned to shock as the hounds leapt from the staircase and pounced upon them.

Devon heard the blood curdling screams behind him. He ran hard and tried to think of a spell to facilitate an escape but he couldn't focus. One of the dogs was right on his heals. These animals were aided by dark magic and were too strong to fight by hand, only magic could stop them. But Devon was too panicked to think of a spell. He rounded the next corner, slammed into the wall and fell to the floor, a sprawl of arms and legs. Devon rolled over and gazed into the red glowing eyes of the evil hound springing through the air.

"This is it." The words flashed through his mind.

"Suspendious!" A woman's voice cut through the dank air.

Devon stared up as the animal stopped in mid-air just inches above his face. A spindle of drool dripped from the dog's gaping mouth and ran down the side of Devon's cheek.

"What..." he stared at the evil visage suspended above him, heard the dog whimper as strong hands grabbed him and slid him from beneath the surprised animal.

"Look who I ran into!" Jerik said, pulling him to his feet.

Devon turned to look into the red haired freckled face of his savior. "What....how?" He stammered.

"It's good to see you too!" She said with a wide grin, "We can sort out all the details later. Right now we need to get the Hell out of here!"

Devon heard the other two dogs barking as he looked behind him at the suspended third hound.

"Devon," he heard Jeriks voice from the end of the corridor, "are you coming?"

"No such thing as luck my ass!" Devon scoffed as he ran after his comrade.

Part Six

Devon made his way through the labyrinth of dungeon corridors and thought about all the people who had spent their final moments in this dark underworld. His gaze flashed across the recesses of the dank cells momentarily lingering on old shackled bones. The putrid smell of death and decay was everywhere. His eyes fixed on the strawberry blonde hair of the woman leading the way. Her sword glowed bright with magic light. The luminescence lit up her face and hair, and Devon thought how much her face lightened his heart even in this dark place.

She was a vision...an angel.

"Lone." He repeated the name within his mind and realized he had been in love with her for quite some time. He recalled when they were kids; Saybon would tease him about being in love with her. Devon always denied it. Now as he studied her, he embraced those feelings and his heart ached to be with her.

Suddenly they were plunged into darkness. The three of them stopped and listened.

"What happened?" Devon said quietly.

Jerik answered in a solemn tone. "It appears the magic in here has been drawn to the point of depletion."

"Damn the gods," Devon cursed, "The Nureaytumea!"

"What's the Nureaytumea?" Lone asked.

"The relic we were fighting over, you know, the brown package that landed us here. You tried to steal it, remember?" He turned to Jerik. "Can you believe this woman? Would you like to remind her what was in that parcel?"

The sword within Lone's grasp sputtered back to life, but the light was feeble this time. Devon saw the confused look upon Jerik's face as if he was struggling to recall what they had been talking about earlier.

"Remember Saybon?" Devon said.

"Who?" Jerik and Lone asked in unison.

"What do you mean, who? The Regent, of course." Devon stared dumbfounded at his companions.

Jerik shrugged. "There is no Regent. That's why this village has become the center of the power vacuum."

Devon looked at his friend's confused expression in the magic light and understanding took root in his mind. The spell he had mentioned earlier, had been performed – the spell to 'unmake.' The Nureaytumea must have been unleashed and its power had been used on the Regent. Devon wondered who was now wielding its command.

"Neither of you remembers our childhood friend, Saybon?" Devon asked in dismay.

Jerik and Lone shook their heads. Devon could not understand why he remembered and yet his friends did not? "Come on guys. We need to get out of here and find a certain Svoresome." Even as the last words trailed off Devon was having trouble remembering what Saybon looked like.

"What's a Svoresome?" His two companions asked once again in unison.

Devon wondered just how much longer he would know himself. "I'll explain on the way."

Part Seven

Devon, Jerik, and Lone found an exit through a drainage tunnel and after a brief struggle with an ancient iron grate, found themselves outside of the walls of the keep. The town was a frenzy of activity. Frightened villagers were being herded through the muddy streets by grim-faced soldiers. The three wizards carefully made their way through the town using the alleyways for cover. An hour later they arrived at the village gate.

Lone used an invisibility shield to get them to the other side unseen. She found it difficult to maintain the spell for more than a few moments, but just enough to go unnoticed by the guards.

They found cover just off the main road, within a circle of trees. "We must get as far away from here as possible, and quick," Devon said.

"No, I must stay," Jerik said solemnly. He glanced at Lone and then dropped his eyes, "I have unfinished business. I will find out what the hell is going on."

"Very well my friend," Devon said, and patted him on the shoulder.

Lone embraced Jerik and sent a hot rush of blood to his face as she kissed his cheek.

Devon and Lone remained hunkered behind the trees as Jerik traipsed back to the road. When he had finally vanished out of sight, Lone asked Devon where they were headed.

"South," Devon replied with a sigh. He pulled his cloak tight around him. "The journey will be perilous but I fear things are more dangerous here close to the Nureaytumea."

They followed the main route away from the village and Devon's thoughts turned to the Regent, the Nureaytumea's apparent victim. He wondered why he remembered at all, even though it had become a mere wisp of a memory.

Saybon.

He struggled to recall the name, but refused to let it go. He knew he was in danger of losing all memories of the man and in turn might forget why he was making this journey. It was all a delicate house of cards waiting to be forgotten and the paradox was giving him a headache.

"And who is it we are going to see?" Lone asked studying the far off look on Devon's face.

"To find a Svorvesome called..." he struggled to pull the name from his rapidly dimming memory. He snatched it before it slipped completely into the darkness. "Favreau."

Five days walking found them at the edge of a tree shrouded village, hidden from the road by a ridge of thick foliage. As they neared the timber wall of the village, the gate creaked open and out walked an ancient looking fellow dressed in a white cloak. He approached the two companions and waved at Devon.

"It is good to see you my old friend," The elder said, "I was hoping you could hold on long enough to afford me a visit before I slipped from your memory altogether."

"Favreau?" Devon asked, although he did not recognize the Svorvesome's face.

"At least you remember my name. You seem stronger than I anticipated. This is good news."

"How is it I can still remember when no one else can recall the world before the Nureaytumea?"

"Ah my boy," the old man put a hand on Devon's shoulder, "that is a very good question. Which leads me to ask a question of my own." The old man's lips parted in a sly smile and his gaze turned to Lone. "Who is this beautiful fiery apparition?"

Lone blushed and looked down at her feet.

Favreau turned and beckoned them through the village gate. "Are you coming my boy?" He said with a warm smile, "Or would you care to join the Reichtling as dinner."

Back at the Village of the Keep

Captain Hauk huddled in the corner of the dank basement, drenched in sweat after his mad dash from the scene of battle. He and twelve loyal men had decided not to become one of the Moncrede's "subjects" and tried to resist. Captain Hauk felt good about his chances for 'General' Moncrede had sent all his battle hardened soldiers to the western front. That meant Hauk and his men only had to fight the village folk. He had been a soldier for thirty two years but he had never seen anything like the scene he had witnessed today. His men put up a meager ten minute fight against the locals. Now all that was left of his number was himself.

The people were possessed. They took out veteran warriors with twenty years battle experience like they were pupils on their first day of weapon training. Hauk saw a seventy year old farmer with a pitchfork take out his best swordsman in seconds.

Impossible.

His breath caught in his throat as a rustling sound emerged outside the cellar door. He froze, straining to remain silent. He heard the clink of armor.

"Captain Hauk?" The familiar voice of one of his guards. Hauk waited a moment before answering. Maybe he was not alone after all. He cursed himself for being such a coward, gathered himself up and opened the door.

Before him, Sealic one of his younger guards stood to attention.

"Report Sealic!" The Captain ordered.

"I managed to escape sir," The soldier answered staring straight ahead, "I followed you here."

Something about Sealic's manner struck Captain Hauk as strange. He took a step closer to study the boys face in the light and Sealic immediately held up his closed fist.

"I was told to give this to you."

The Captain froze as he noticed the boy's eyes - dark reflecting globes that stared back at him. The same dark eyes the General Mecrede's subjects possessed. The boy opened his fist and coiled within his hand was a small black snake.

"General Moncrede requires your services."

"No!" Captain Hauk cried throwing his arms up as the snake lunged at him. The creature landed on Hauk's armored shoulder. He tried vainly to swat it away and watched in terror as the snake burrowed into the shiny metal of his shoulder guard. He felt the serpent against his naked shoulder making its way up the back of his neck.

He fixed his eyes on the guard before him.

"Damn you to the underworld!"

The soldier returned an evil grin.

Hauk felt two needle-like stabs in the back of his neck and felt the icy venom spread quickly through his veins. His vision sharpened and the darkness within the basement seemed to light up. All fear, all emotion, all independent thought dried up as he became one with the collective conscience of the Nureaytumea.

Part Eight

Devon and Lone followed Favreau through the quaint village to old man's humble home.

It was built amongst the huge limbs of an ancient oak tree that grew on the side of a grassy hill. Devon were amazed how agile the old man was as he watched him ascend the rope ladder to the tree-home with the dexterity of a teenager.

Once inside, Devon and Lone took seats around a huge oak table in the centre of the room. Favreau offered them sweetbread and raspberry tea. Then, as the old man stoked the fire, Devon noticed his expression turn grave. Favreau gazed back and spoke in an ominous tone. "In the five days since you left town things have grown much worse."

The two wizards said nothing as Favreau turned and whipped away the cloth that shrouded a large obsidian ball resting on a wooden stand in the center of the table. Devon noted that the wood beneath the ball seemed to have turned to glass mirroring the black obsidian reflection.

"The Mother Dragon's Eye," Favreau said. He reached out and took the two wizards by the hands. They made a circle around the "Eye." The old man's eyes rolled back into his head and he tensed up as if gripped in a seizure. Devon and Lone tried to pull away but Favreau had an icy grasp.

The walls blurred and a blast of air whirl pooled around the room. Suddenly they were transported back to the cobbled streets of the town. Everything was quiet, the streets deserted. Then marching around the corner in perfect lines came the towns people. Lone made a move to step back but found herself paralyzed.

"Do not worry child," Favreau said, and squeezed her hand, "we are not really here."

She flinched as the nearest column marched just inches from her face. She knew these people. She had grown up with them, they were her friends.

Only, they were not. Each person stared from obsidian eyes devoid of human life. She saw her sister, Amanda, marching past, and dangling from the back of her neck was a small black snake.

A flash of light and they were back at the tree home.

Favreau quickly covered the Mother Dragon's Eye. "Moncrede is no longer human, "the old man sighed. "He is now Nureaytumea. He has amassed a huge army of mindless slaves to push through this region and take over the country."

Devon and Lone stared back in horror, the scene of mindless villagers marching in unison still fresh in their minds.

"Can they be saved?" Lone asked.

"Now that is exactly why you're here isn't it?" Favreau said cracking a warm smile.

Part Nine

The knight sped across the plain towards the castle gates at reckless speed. His mind raced with what he was to tell his King. How was he going to explain that an enemy they had managed to keep in check for three decades had suddenly routed his entire army within three hours?

His heart caught in his throat as he flashed back to that final battle. He could still feel the chill in his bones from the freak snow storm that fell with a vengeance upon the battlefield. Snow was not due to this part of the world for three months and they had been caught unprepared. It was as if the storm had a mind of its own.

Not that it would have made any difference. General Moncrede's forces seemed unaffected by the deluge of blustery weather. They fought like banshees and with single-minded precision. In all his years the knight had never seen a battle so well orchestrated. It was a military masterpiece.

His horse galloped across the drawbridge and through the huge open gate at breakneck speed. "Close the gates and the portcullis!" He yelled at the guards over his shoulder, "The enemy approaches!"

His horse slipped on the wet cobblestone road as he crossed the bailey and began the ascent up to the great hall. As he reached the bottom of the great stone steps he reigned in his horse and leapt to the ground in one deft move. He was halfway up the steps when the stable boy finally grabbed the reigns of his exhausted animal.

The knight flew past the two guards at the front door who saluted him with the due respect his rank demanded. He crossed the outer foyer and tore off his cloak, throwing it unceremoniously to the marble floor as he ran down the aisle to the base of dais. There, he knelt before the King's throne, eyes cast down at the marble floor.

"Rise, General Frazelle." The King's voice rumbled off the walls. "Report the reason for your informal manner."

"Yes my liege." General Frazelle rose and took a breath before relaying his news, "I am afraid we have been routed my Lord."

"What the heavens do you mean?"

"Moncrede has broken our lines and now marches to the castle! The war is at our gates!"

"My dear General," the King answered calmly. "A new and glorious era is about to begin for I have just made a deal that has just ended the war and has ensured a lasting peace."

"I-I do not u-understand," Frazelle stammered.

"Let me present to you," the King said motioning with a raised arm, "your new commanding field General."

General Frazelle followed the sweep of the King's arm to see General Moncrede step from the shadows of the Great Hall.

Frazelle reached for his dagger. He would be damned if he was going to serve under the hated enemy. As he grasped the hilt he convulsed in disgust, feeling his hand close around several small black scaled snakes that were crawling up his armor. The last thing he heard with his free mind was the combined laughter of the King and Moncrede, evilly echoing throughout the space of the Great Hall.

Somewhere in the eastern forest...

Jerik hesitated at the cave entrance. He knew the counter spell to the wards and quickly recited them before stepping into the darkness. He made his way down the tunnel using his spellsight but had to stop several times to unravel more wizard wards until he came to a great wooden door. He whispered a few words and the door silently slid open. Within the ante chamber billions of insects swarmed forming a slithering undulating wall. He stepped forward and the sea of bugs parted creating passage to an inner door. The door swung inward and he stepped inside.

There upon a dark throne sat a hulking figured cloaked in black, flanked by two guards wearing black armor. Jerik approached and bowed as low as he could to the sandy floor. Suddenly an unseen force threw him back onto the ground, bloodying his nose.

"You have failed me!" The booming voice thundered off the cave walls. The cloaked figure waved his arm and the chamber door swung open. Jerik curled into a ball and covered his head in his hands as a cloud of insects swarmed into the room and began biting and stinging him. Pain seared his flesh from head to toe. The Dark One called off the assault seconds later, but to Jerik it felt like an eternity.

"I give you one more chance," The cloaked one shouted, "now go. Bring it back to me or suffer the consequences."

Jerik jumped to his feet, and felt his body swelling all over as the insect venom took effect. He bowed, and ran from the room as fast as his aching legs would carry him.

Part Ten

Lone had fallen asleep some time ago but Devon and Favreau sat in front of the fire long into the night, engaged in heavy conversation.

"I feel like a failure," Devon said, "I had the Nureaytumea in my hands and let it slip away."

"Devon my boy," Favreau flashed one of his warm smiles, "magic is like everything else in this world, it follows nature's rules."

Devon shrugged wondering where the old man was going. Favreau reached out and put his hand on Devon's shoulder.

"Let me explain. Just as the day and night have balance, so does magic. Sometimes, with the season, the day is longer than night. But the balance always shifts the other way to compensate. There is a constant ebb and flow to this balance. We find ourselves on the opposite side of the year where the night is longer than the day."

"I still don't see-"

"Forgive an old man his ancient mannerisms," Favreau held up a hand palm outward with a smile, "I will eventually come to my point."

"Sorry," Devon answered with a nervous laugh. Favreau had a way of making him feel at ease even in such a bleak hour.

"We are in magic winter." Favreau stated flatly as he got up and walked over to an old chest next to the hearth. He opened the lid and rummaged inside pulling out something wrapped in a stained cloth. "The Nureaytumea's power is magic's night," he continued, "and right now its rule eclipses the day. This happens every few hundred years. The Nureaytumea escapes the Svoresomes because, to put it simply, it wants to. It also escaped you because....it wanted to. But the natural balance of magic dictates there must be a counter balance to the evil power of the Nureaytumea."

Favreau handed the wrapped object to Devon. Confused, Devon carefully unwrapped the cloth revealing a metal gauntlet with a feather pattern engraved on the shiny surface.

"It is called the Nuytumean in Svoresome tongue," Favreau explained, "this is magic's counterbalance to the Nureaytumea. And now it comes to you."

"What?" Devon jumped from his seat, "what are you saying?"

"That you, my boy, are here because the Nuytumean called you here."

"I don't understand..."

"You are the only one who can use its power."

"Me?" Devon asked in disbelief, "Why me? I don't want to use its power. I...I don't even know what its power is!"

"Son, you are the chosen one." Favreau answered. "That's why the Nureaytumea does not have the hold over you that it does everyone else. That is why you remembered when everyone else forgot. That is why you are here."

"I don't understand. Why don't you use its power?" Devon asked shoving the gauntlet at Favreau.

"Because I cannot. The Nuytumean would possess me just as the Nureaytumea has done with Captain Moncrede."

Devon frowned, "I don't want this!"

"You are the only one who can use it Devon because you are the only one who cannot be possessed by it."

"You're talking crazy old man," Devon shouted, awakening a sleeping Lone in the next room, "Why does it have to be me?"

"Because you are the only one in the world, who was not born human, but born of magic."

Lone finally awoke and entered the room with a stretch and a yawn. Favreau sat her down and relayed the same story he had told Devon. She sat open mouthed as she listened intently. When Favreau finished speaking, she said, "So who created these artifacts – where do they come from?"

"That is a long story," Favreau said with a sigh. He cracked one of his warm smiles, "but a good one. Well done my fiery angel!" He walked over to the old oak table and pulled the shroud from the Mother Dragon's Eye. A moment later the reflection of the globe changed and all light in the room was sucked into a black hole.

Devon and Lone squirmed nervously as the room disappeared and a gray haze grew around the Eye.

"It all began Eons ago," Favreau said. The gray haze around them swirled and a scene of green fields and odd looking trees materialized. "The Svoresome were amongst the youngest species on the planet and yet we learned civility. At first, there were no towns or villages, just roving bands of savages. Human savages. They fought and squabbled for dominance over the harsh conditions nature threw at them.

"It was then that one of the Lesser Gods, Nuyrea, took pity and adopted our race to take under his wing. He changed to human form and came down to the Earth. He civilized us, taught us how to use tools and build houses. In return, we worshiped him. But as with magic there is a dangerous duality within all of us. We all have two sides, a good side and a sinister side.

"Nuyrea was not immune to this. Once he began to receive praise and admiration, his darker side responded. Conceit and vanity took root and consumed him. He became convinced he could better his place amongst the Gods feeding off the praise he was receiving from us.

"The Greater Gods became angered and decided to put an end to this upstart's reign on the planet. Each of the twelve Gods gave some of their power to create a magical creature that had enough strength to destroy Nuyrea. Hence, the first dragon, Mother Dragon, was born."

Lone and Devon gasped at the pictures that scrolled before them. The Mother Dragon was a hideous apparition.

"But Nuyrea discovered the plan from another lesser God - his lover, Uratay. In response, Nuyrea drew from the power of the planet. In those ancient times this power was immense as it was raw and untouched. When the huge Dragon lumbered down from the sky the clash of magic was terrible and lasted twenty days and nights.

"The Gods underestimated Nuyrea's influence and did not count on Uratay's help for she too fought alongside her lover. So the Greater Gods sent down their combined magic with the intention of destroying all three beings locked in battle.

"When the smoke finaly cleared and the chaos faded all that was found was Nuyrea's two gauntlets, and the Mother Dragon's two black obsidian eyes. The Gods celebrated their victory, although it would take them all a thousand years to regain their magic.

"During that time, darkness ruled the planet. This is the time the Svoresomes were born. They discovered the artifacts of the magical battle and hid them from the eyes of the Greater Gods. But, upon studying them they realized that Nuyrea had not been destroyed. His soul had been split in two and was banished. Everything good and just, was banished into the feather gauntlet - the Nuytumean, everything bad merged into the Nuyreatumea."

Favreau covered the Eye and the room was thrust back into mid-afternoon light.

Lone and Devon squinted against the brightness trying to shake off the disorientation they now felt from the Eye's affects.

"Favreau?" Devon asked rubbing his aching head.

"Yes my boy?"

"What happened to Uratay and the Mother Dragon? Did they die, or do their souls live on as Nuyrea's does?"

"I am tired," the Svoresome answered bluntly, "I must go and rest now."

As the old man left the room Lone and Devon shared a baffled look.

Part Twelve

Jerik stumbled through the Eastern Forest, and stopped to vomit for the umpteenth time. The venom sickened his body and clouded his thoughts. Visions played within his mind, thousands of eyes stared from the trees around him. His legs became weak and shaky, but he wanted to get far away from his dark master before he stopped to rest. He pushed his body until it failed him and he collapsed in a trembling heap beneath an ancient oak.

Jerik wretched one more time and leaned back against the rotting tree, thankful its bark was soft against his aching back. His head throbbed in time with his beating heart, tiny rhythmic explosions of fiery pain. The full moon was so brilliant he had to squint, causing a shooting pain to gnaw at his temples. He shivered against the cold night and hugged his tired arms tightly around his torso.

Jerik felt something crawl down his cheek. He tried to swat the insect away but his body was paralyzed with exhaustion. He turned his head slightly and saw termites seeping from the bark of the tree like liquid being squeezed from a bloated sponge. Ants and other insects oozed from the ground and began blanketing his body. He braced himself for another stinging attack, but it did not come. Instead, his body warmed beneath the ghastly quilt of writhing bugs. Jerik's mind released the fear as a pleasant tiredness quashed his dark thoughts into dreamless sleep. He felt himself smile under the moonlit sky.

Lone awoke in bed and bolted upright, her body covered in sweat. She lay back down and pulled the covers to her chest, shivering against an imagined chill. She looked over at the fireplace and another shiver ran down her spine. For the rest of the night, she tossed and turned, feeling billions of crawling legs all over her body. Every so often she threw the covers aside expecting to find herself covered in bugs but there was nothing..

Jerik awoke in a panic, realizing he could not move. He was wrapped tightly inside some type of membrane and his entire body was immersed in a thick liquid. He tried not to breathe for fear of drowning in the fluid, and pushed his arms and legs against the restraining cocoon but to no avail. Eventually his lungs urged him to take a breath. His mouth opened up and the thick warm salty liquid filled his lungs. Warm fluid spread through his veins but death did not take him. The sickness and exhaustion that had wracked his body seemed a distant memory. Strength returned to his limbs and he pushed against the membrane. This time it gave way easily. Jerik emerged from the cocoon and walked into the dark forest. The liquid clung to his naked body and glistened against the moonlight. He looked to the ground and saw his clothing tattered and strewn across the clearing under the mangled oak.

Jerik's spell sight allowed him to see into the shadows around him, this he was used to. What surprised him was the keenness of his other senses. He smelled the thick decaying scent of the tree before him and heard thousands of tiny creatures scurrying in the underbrush several yards away. He looked at the ground and sensed the chemical trails used by the miniscule ants. Then he caught the putrid scent and hushed whispers of the pack of Reichtlings that were slowly closing in around him. The half human, half beasts, were notorious for their coordinated and stealthy attacks on unsuspecting travelers in this forest.

Jerik flexed his muscles and noticed they felt powerful. He looked around for his sword but did not see it. As the first Reichtling stepped into the clearing Jerik surprised himself as he leapt forward and quickly pounced on the creature. Instinct drove him to bite into the creatures neck and at this moment Jerik noticed his new set of fanged teeth. Blood sprayed from the Reichtling's severed artery. The taste was intoxicating and sent Jerik into a dreamlike state as the rest of the pack entered the clearing with malicious gaping grins.

The next ten minutes Jerik killed without thought. Pure instinct drove him and he methodically killed a dozen Reichtling with minimal exertion. He fed on the remains late into the night with nary a human thought.

Part Thirteen

Devon saw himself in the mountains looking down into a mist shrouded valley. He suffered a twinge of vertigo, yet the beauty of it touched his soul. He felt a warm tender hand within his and turned to see a stunning raven haired woman at his side. The beauty of the mountains paled compared to hers. Her hair flowed in the breeze but never touched her face. That beautiful face. Glowing as if lit from within. Her eyes were the blue of a cloudless winter day, her skin as pale as the snow. Within her eyes he saw love returned. But there was something else. Warning. If eyes are the window to the soul hers was preoccupied with worry.

As the sun dipped on the horizon, Devon noticed the fiery orb had what looked like a huge bite taken out of it. The sun had caught up with the moon in their race for this day's horizon. The two watched the eclipse happen just as the sun touched the lip of the earth, exploding in a brilliant ring of fire around the dark moon at its center.

Magic crackled in the air and the woman pointed towards the heavens. Devon saw a huge lumbering beast break through the wispy clouds high above.

The brilliant eclipse fire shone off the creature's scales as the beast slowly descended on huge leathery wings. Its mouth gaped and unleashed a roar that shook the mountain beneath them causing them both to stumble. A huge fissure opened up upon a second roar that threatened to separate the two. The woman levitated over the hole and once again stood beside Devon.

They both drew their jewel encrusted swords. Devon marveled at the size of the weapon and how light his felt within his hands. He felt magic flowing through his body the likes he had never imagined before. This was the magic that used to exist in days of old. The magic that made the ancient Wizards legendary. The magic he craved to control. But he felt an unfamiliar underlying arrogance and pride. There was no time to understand this for the creature above rained down a sheet of white hot fire. The two met the downpour with their combined power in a cold shield of domed ice.

The beast hit the ground with an almighty thud that toppled trees and triggered avalanches throughout the mountain range.

Devon stared through the ice shield into the dark black orbs of Mother Dragon, and abruptly he awoke from the dream. It took him a few moments to fight the disorientation and realize he was back in his bed at Favreau's village. He still felt the magic coursing through his body and stared down to see the silver feathered gauntlet adorning his right wrist.

"How did you get here?" He said to the Nuytumean as if it could respond, "the old man locked you away in the old chest by the fireplace."

But the fireplace in his room was dark. He jumped out of bed and padded over to the dark opening not realizing the cold did not bother his naked feet. Devon squatted down on his haunches and saw that the fire was frozen in flame shaped icicles.

His head spun and he felt almost drunk with the white magic that flowed through his body. He pointed at the fire ice sculpture and it leapt back to life, splashing the room once again with warmth and light.

There was a soft knock on the door. Devon answered it to find Lone shivering in the cold hallway.

"Can I-I- come i-in?" She asked through chattering teeth.

"Of course." He took her hand and led her over to the bed where they sat down facing the fire.

Devon felt odd when Lone looked at him. He studied the outline of her body beneath the silk gown but he did not feel lust. Even as his eyes studied her curves and the material straining to hold her breasts within their silky bondage, he did not feel the familiar animalistic instinct. Instead, to his confusion, he felt love for her. He studied her soft red hair in the fire light and longed to run his fingers through it.

"I could not sleep," she said dreamily. Devon felt a twinge of excitement as she pulled back the gown to show him the roundness of one of her breasts. His excitement turned to horror as he saw a red rawness and bleeding insect bites.

"What happened?" He asked confused kneeling beside her and studying her mangled skin.

"I'm not sure," she replied, and for the first time since childhood Devon witnessed her fallibility as she began sobbing. "The attack was unseen, I suppose some sort of dark magic."

"We should show Favreau," He said moving towards the door but then paused. He looked down at the Nuytumean and turned back to Lone. He knelt beside her once again looking into her tear filled eyes, which widened upon seeing the gauntlet.

"How-"

"Shhhhh." Devon put a finger to her lips to silence her.

He gently opened up her gown and slid it from her shoulders revealing her battered skin. He began caressing her naked shoulders with a light touch and to both their amazement, the skin that was massaged returned to its former soft beauty. The itching and pain dried up as the two were suddenly overwhelmed and caught up in the moment. He massaged lower and Lone kissed him passionately. Her moist lips energized his body. Pain and irritation was taken over by ecstasy and they made love for the rest of the evening.

As sunlight touched the morning with a soft glow Devon held Lone naked within his arms. She absently stroked the metal gauntlet upon his arm basking in the afterglow of their intimacy.

"I thought Favreau had locked this away?" She said looking into Devon's eyes with a playful grin. "You think the night would have ended the same way if I had gone to him instead of you?"

They looked at each other and laughed.

The door to Devon's room burst open.

"Come on my boy-" The old man made his entrance and stopped mid-sentence upon the scene before him his face blushing red. "Ah, I see the Nuytumean found its way to you last night… amongst others." The last words were said out of the corner of the old man's mouth. "Come young ones," Favreau smiled, "get dressed, I have breakfast prepared. We must make haste for there is much to do this day." Then with a smile and a wink he said, "I hope you did not wear yourselves out last evening."

Part Fourteen

Jerik sat on a high limb overlooking the small village listening to the symphony of the woods around him. He closed his eyes and heard the rush of the river two miles away, a monotonous melody providing the background for the countless other voices of the forest. In the foreground, and even in this very tree, birds took the lead merrily chirping away at each other. Jerik admired their frantic energy. He heard scratching - a great black bear sharpening his claws on a tree two hundred yards away. Jerik admired the bears great strength and hunting skill.

Then, there were the insects. Their song was always there, clear and loud within his mind. A great pulsing beat like a giant heartbeat delivering communication throughout the whole Eastern Woods. It was like a sixth sense. He used it like he would sight, able to see a threat, or a meal, at a distance his eyes would fail him.

"I am one of them," the part of him that was still human thought as he let out a long slow breath.

Jerik had never felt so inhuman. Instinct ruled his actions, without barely a human thought and he felt a freedom he had never experienced before. That was, until the suffocating presence of his master thrust itself within his mind for the second time this day. Immediately he focused on the task at hand.

"That is the one," the baritone voice instructed.

Jerik's eyes focused on a child of about eight summers old playing in a field with her friends. Jerik's mind flashed on his original task to obtain the Nureaytumea and he wondered why his master wanted to trifle with a small child.

"Concentrate!" A sudden sharp pain exploded within his head as if his brain were being throttled within his skull. "This is the task at hand! I want you to bring her to me. Now."

With lighting reflexes Jerik launched himself from the high branch and was immediately airborne. He had just discovered this new ability to fly the day before while hunting a giant hawk through the tree tops near the raging river. He had grabbed a rotten branch that gave way and suddenly he was falling toward the rapids when he felt the wings expand behind him in a moment of desperation. He remembered that exhilarating first glide on the cool air above the river as he scooped up the child from the field and headed back to the Eastern Woods.

After putting some distance between him and the village he landed by an ancient elm. As he rested in the tree's shadow he realized this young one had not let out a single peep since her abduction. He looked over and studied the girl with detached interest. Blue eyes stared back at him without emotion.

"I do not scare you little one?" He asked, his own voice sounding strange to his ears.

"You are not a monster." She responded in a soft voice. "The one you take me to, he is."

Jerik crouched next to her. She did not flinch as he grabbed her chin and pulled her face close to his own. He saw no fear in her eyes. "You knew I was coming?" he said.

"I have dreamt of it for several nights," she responded grabbing his wrist and gently pulled his hand from her face. "The dark one's face has haunted my dreams next to yours."

Jerik shrugged his shoulders. "You are not at all what you appear to be."

"Neither are you Jerik," she said, "then again, none of us are what we truly appear to be."

"How do you know my name?"

A smile crossed her face. ""I told you. I have dreamt about you for over two weeks now. I know you and your two companions as well as I know my village neighbor."

"You are a Seer?"

"Yes. That is what the village elders call me." She gently touched his hand "My friends call me, Tika."

The little girl had an intellect and demeanor well beyond her years. Jerik could see why his Dark Master had an interest in this young one. She had already proved she was a powerful Seer.

"You want me to call you Tika," Jerik asked jumping to his feet and turning from her, "even though I take you to your doom?"

"I can see your heart bugman," she answered in a kind tone, "though your mind is in turmoil, your heart remains pure and just."

"You are a fool!" Jerik answered in anger, "you do not know what my Master is capable of."

"No, Jerik," she said softly, letting a nervous look slip, "I have seen your Master's true form, and it is you who fail to grasp the graveness of your situation. You must not cross the Dark One, bugman. You must take me to him as quickly as possible."

Jerik admired her bravery but was left confused as he grabbed her and took to the skies. He found himself, despite his intentions, developing a liking for this young blue eyed girl. He dreaded the time when his master would undoubtedly cause her pain, or even worse, her death.

Part Fifteen

The imposing figure that was once Moncrede stood at the crest of the hill surveying the battlefield below. The floor of the valley was littered with the enemy casualties as far as the eye could see. The setting sun shone upon the mass of corpses and their weapons that still dripped with blood. He could not distinguish between red stains of blood and the rusty glares of twilight sun meeting his black glassy eyes as he climbed upon his dark horse.

An evil grin crossed the wizened face as he descended the slope into the graveyard. Moncrede breathed in the smell of fresh blood and burning flesh. He felt a surge of excitement at the thought that another kingdom had fallen at his feet. He did not have the power left to convert any more humans into his forces.

He closed his eyes and communed with his massive collective of soldiers and minions.

"Who is burning the dead?"

Immediately through the eyes of his soldiers a scene materialized within his mind. Enemy captives had started a funeral pyre on the western flank so they could dispose of their fatalities. Moncrede turned his horse west and rode as hard as he could toward the setting sun with a blazing red fire burning in his dark eyes.

"Favereau," Devon asked as they made their way through the village, "what did you mean when you said I was born of magic?"

The Svoresome shot a glance at the gauntlet upon Devon's arm. "I see the Nuytumean destroyed my little memory spell easily enough."

"I feel its magic and you were right Favreau, I feel no threat of possession from the raw energy. But I fear I will not be able to contain its massive power."

"That is why I am here my boy," the old man smiled warmly, "to teach you the skills you need to control the Nuytumean's magic."

"But do we have enough time? The Nuytumean has shown me that the Nureaytumea controls all the lands to the north. Moncrede is just a week's march from here."

"Relax Devon," the old man said, placing a reassuring hand on his shoulder, "Moncrede and the power of the Nureaytumea have an unseen detour ahead of them. We will have the time required to train you properly."

The Svoresome reached inside his cloak and retrieved the old stained cloth the Nuytumean was originally wrapped in.

"You must remove the gauntlet," he said handing the tattered piece of materialto Devon, "as the enemy approaches they will be drawn to its magic and our position will be revealed."

Devon took off the glove, placed it in the cloth and reluctantly handed the parcel to Favereau, feeling the power suddenly drain out of his body.

"You still have not answered my question," Devon said with a smirk.

"All in good time my boy." Favereau smiled and shoved the wrapped gauntlet into his cloak.

"But what about the training?"

"There are more important things to concentrate on at the moment," Favereau said with a wink and motioned with a nod towards a merchant cart under the shade of a nearby oak tree.

Devon saw Lone bargaining with an old lady over a pair of leather boots. He looked back at the old man with a confused look. "How can that be more important than our impending doom?"

An indignant look crossed Favereau's wrinkled face. "Never underestimate the power of a woman!" He promptly disappeared in a puff of white smoke leaving Devon slack jawed staring into empty space.

Jerik landed several yards from the cave entrance and softly set Tika down on the forest floor. She smiled up at him with gratitude. He felt an ache within his chest as he knew this was probably the last time he would lay eyes upon her.

During their short flight to the heart of the Eastern Woods they had chatted and he discovered they were kindred souls, despite the fact he was no longer human. He could not face seeing her torn apart by his dark master.

"Tika," he tried to grab her arm before she walked towards the cave entrance, "let me fly you out of here."

Suddenly his skull exploded with pain as the Dark One's presence thrust inside his mind. Jerik dropped to his knees holding his head within his hands trying to endure the intense torture.

The small girl touched him upon the shoulder and suddenly the pain was gone. Confused, he looked up into her delicate face. She smiled at him and the blueness of her eyes seemed to intensify.

"Our paths part here. You are to wait." She turned to go. "Never give up hope bugman," she said without looking back.

As Jerik watched her disappear inside the cave, he felt a tear roll down his face.

Part Sixteen

Jerik waited outside the cave as instructed. He thought of the girl and tried to swallow the lump in his throat as another tear slid down his face. He guessed Tika was enduring some kind of torture at the hands of his Dark Master. It would be better if she were already dead. He looked down at his arm and rubbed his hand across the coarse, once human skin. In recent days his body had undergone more changes. At night, while resting, his pores secreted a thick liquid. Upon awakening Jerik found the liquid dry, white and hard upon his flesh.

Tika had put an absurd thought in his head during their time together. She had told him his bones were leaking and that he was developing an exoskeleton.

"Bugman." He repeated Tika's childish nickname for him and could not help a smile.

He felt a tingle on the back of his neck. His heightened senses told him there was someone exiting the cave. Jerik silently slid behind the thick trunk of a nearby tree. His heart raced in fearful anticipation of his Master'spresence.

Instead Tika's small form materialized from the shadows. She was followed by one of his evil Master's huge knights. In the black armor clad soldier's arms was what appeared as the Dark Master's lifeless body.

Jerik's heart leapt with sudden joy. Had this little one bested the evil being that held him captive for these last three years? He stepped from hiding and Tika stopped in front of Jerik. He looked down upon her small face and her blue eyes met his gaze calmly. A small half smile parted her lips.

"Tika, how-"

"Jerik!" She said with a dark expression furrowing her brow, "get the hell out the way."

Jerik stepped aside slack jawed.

"Guard," she ordered, "nail that body to this tree. I want all to see in the Eastern Wood that the Dark Master is dead!"

As the soldier obediently carried out his order Tika turned to the befuddled Jerik.

"Bugman!" She ordered as if spitting venom, "we fly north to the Nureaytumea."

The funeral pyre lit up the post dawn sky in a brilliant rouge glare. A red glow touched the low lying clouds that were just beginning to roll in behind Moncrede and his approaching horse. As he dismounted the clouds thickened overhead.

Moncrede surveyed the scene until his black obsidian eyes came to rest on the knot of enemy survivors tossing bodies onto the blaze. They were being directed by a young captain who barked out orders above the roaring fire.

The General strode over to the young captain and a loud clap of thunder boomed causing the soldiers to stop their grueling task. As Moncrede marched up to the group a bolt of lightning shot from the clouds and knocked everyone but Moncrede and the opposing captain to the ground.

"What is the meaning of this?" Moncrede barked at the enemy captain.

The soldier stood to attention and raised a proud chin toward the evil General as another clap of thunder rocked the ground beneath them.

"Battlefield etiquette sir," the man answered dutifully, "the vanquished shall be allowed to dispose of their dead at the end of a battle."

Rain began pouring down and the fire hissed amid the deluge. Black smoke enveloped the clearing. The smell of charred human flesh hung heavy in the air and the rain caused the smell to almost stick to the skin.

"The only etiquette that applies here," Mondcrede said unsheathing his sword, "is the Nureaytumea's etiquette!"

The General ran his sword through the captain's breastplate and through the man's heart. The Nureaytumea flared in the darkness and though the captain's heart was pierced he did not die.

"I want everyone to see the price of defiance," Moncrede said to the bulging eyed captain. "I want the rotting stench of your decaying men to be a beacon to all who would oppose me!"

Moncrede lifted the man off the ground with his sword. The captain groaned in agony as one of Moncrede's troops brought a pike over. Without straining a muscle Moncrede neatly impaled the man upon the stick. The stricken captain could barely breathe. The evil General climbed the pile of the former funeral pyre. With little effort he plunged the pike deep into the crest of the mound of dead as the rain suddenly stopped.

"And if there is any confusion in the matter," Moncrede said standing back and looking up into the bleeding eyes of the captain, "you are to tell them personally."

Part Seventeen

Devon stood atop a mountain and looked down upon the darkness far below him. On the eastern horizon a sliver of the moon rose from a pool of blood-like haze signaling the sun was not far behind his celestial partner. Devon took in the dark landscape far below in a long sweeping gaze before pausing on the opposite horizon of the sleeping world. Two lights danced across the black valley towards the impending dawn. As they made their way closer he noticed one was a white pin prick of light shining with the brilliance of a hundred stars. The other was a floating orb that was a smudge of greenish glow, reminding Devon of moonlit fog on the moors.

As they moved in and out of one another they were drawn together by an unseen attraction. But, another equally unseen force kept them from touching. The two lights passed in front of Devon and he sensed a familiarity radiating from the bright one and immediately realized this was the Nuytumean. His heart lurched as a loneliness caused by the hindrance of a joining filled every fiber of his being. The Nuytumean was incomplete and longed for this union with such soulful yearning that it galvanized his emotions and sent a torrent of tears running down his cheeks.

Then, the second orb passed before him and its sickly light touched his skin. Devon felt a dull ache as it yanked at the bonds holding his soul to his physical body trying to draw on his life's energy. He felt a brooding evil that sent shots of ice to the center of his heart. His mind flashed back to the memory of a childhood friend who had died of the plague before his eyes. The same dull green of this boy's face when drawing his dying breath reflected in the orb's light. The Nureaytumea. He was relieved when its touch passed beyond him.

The two orbs danced toward the brightening horizon and a new feeling pressed down upon Devon, as if the heaviness of thousands of years pressed upon his frail skin. The air grew thick and he found it hard to breathe as the decaying stench of passing time filled his nostrils. Realization dawned. The Nureaytumea and the Nuytumean had performed this dance for eons never allowed to rejoin into the wholeness they once were.

Devon watched them move toward a rising sun that briefly poured crimson light into the cold valley before it passed behind the lagging moon. As the two celestial lovers met as one so did the two dancing orbs, celebrating their respective reunions in a great solar eclipse that brought day and night together, awakening the world below.

Devon felt a presence behind him and turned to see a raven haired beauty placing a loving hand upon his shoulder.

"Now," she smiled looking into his face lovingly with crystal blue eyes, "we can be together again."

The clouds of dream parted and before his blinking eyes the raven haired goddess was replaced by the wizened old face of Favereau. Devon closed his eyes and tried to picture her beauty once more but the old man shook the image away and brought him rudely awake.

"C'mon my boy," He said with uncharacteristic urgency, "it is time to start training."

He heard Lone stirring beside him in the bed and reached over to wake her.

"Shhh," Favereau whispered, "leave her be. Today just you and I train."

Devon yawned and threw off the covers as Favereau shoved a bundle of clean clothes into his hands.

The old man placed a hand gently upon his shoulder, "she will need her rest now that you have left her with child."

Jerik flew high above the canopy of trees, but even at this height he could sense the disturbance within the insect population below. He smelled death and decay through the hive mind of the insect community but some evil magic kept the bugs from instinctively descending upon the dead.

They passed over a swathe of churned earth and the bodies of the fallen began filling their view. Jerik felt Tika squirm within his grasp.

"Over there," she shouted above the rushing of the wind, "on the horizon."

Jerik followed her gaze and saw the sun rise from behind a mound of slain soldiers. Atop this gruesome pile, one soldier was skewered upon a long pike pointing skyward like a beacon.

"Land!" Tika ordered.

Jerik set down upon the dew covered mud with a soft thud. The smell of the dead embraced them as if beckoning them towards the crest of the rotting mound.

"Magic," Tika said with a scowl, "the Nureaytumea has grown powerful more quickly than I expected."

The sound of retching prompted the two to look up. The soldier on the pike shifted and coughed sending a spray of blood upon them.

"P-pl-please," the man begged through lips bubbling with crimson, "k-ki-kill m-me." His breath came in raspy gulps. "M-mon-crede" the soldier spluttered," M-mon-crede!"

Tika bent down and rummaged among the dead bodies for a sword. She prized a broadsword from a dead soldier's fingers and with surprising agility leapt through the air and with one skillful swing neatly severed the captain's head from his shoulders. It fell amongst the charred corpses and rolled to a stop at the base of the deadfall.

"P-pl-please," the dismembered head still spoke.

"Much more powerul than expected," Tika said scratching her chin thoughtfully.

"M-mon-crede" the head screamed through bubbling blood.

"Shut the HELL up!" She yelled and with a powerful kick she sent the head into the underbrush at the edge of the clearing. "Birdman, let's fly!"

Jerik obediently scooped the little girl up and in one move launched skyward. As he soared into the air, he could still hear the unfortunate captain painfully shrieking from the underbrush. "We fly to Moncrede Master?" He asked.

"No," Tika shouted, "we go North first. We will need help to take the Nureaytumea from Moncrede."

"Where to then?"

"Petriputrid Peak."

Part Eighteen

"I said I need someone strong with magic!" Moncrede screamed at the village elder, his hand wrapped firmly around the man's throat.

The elder cringed, more out of fear than as reaction to having smelled the decay on the General's breath. He looked down at the young man he had just pointed out as the village Mage. A pang of guilt touched his heart as his eyes ran over the broken and bleeding mass that was once the young man's body. Rage sparked a fire deep within his soul and he tensed against the Nureaytumea's grasp. The elder spat in Mocrede's face.

Mecrede's cold stare intensified and an evil grin spread across his face. He squeezed harder, relishing the guttural chocking sounds coming from the old man's throat. Finally, a merciful snap of the spine, a spray of blood from the elder's lips, and the village leader was dead. Moncrede threw the old man down, disgust and rage screwing his face up into a horrid mask.

"You bastard!" A dark haired young woman in flowing grey robes shouted from the crowd.

"Nayla, don't!" One of the villagers tried to hold her back, but the woman broke free and raced to the dead elder lying at the General's feet. She fell to her knees and embraced the corpse, her body racked with heavy sobs.

The General reached down and grabbed a hand full of the woman's raven hair. "And what do we have here?" A nervous shift and hushed murmur rippled through the crowd, but all knew to challenge the General was suicide. He pulled her up and noticed the magic amulet fall from beneath her tunic. He reached out and yanked it from her neck.

The amulet glowed with a soft bluish light as it dangled from the Nureaytumea's fist. "A Mage?"

"I will never help you. You killed my Grandfather!"

Moncrede leaned in close and putrid breath burned at the young woman's nostrils. Bile rose into her throat and vomit burst forth splashing Mecrede's cheek. Nayla braced herself for the impending blow as a gauntlet clad fist raised before her ready to throw a punch. But instead an odd look suddenly crossed the evil man's face. He let go of her and she looked on in horror as the flesh on his face and the exposed part of his arm began tearing open. Blood soaked the dirt under Moncrede's feet.

Nalya tried to step back but found she was paralyzed. The gauntlet on the General's arm changed. It manifested into a black scaled snake swaying back and forth in a slow hypnotic dance just inches from her face. She cringed as the serpent slithered onto her neck and under her tunic, It crawled down her left arm and wrapped itself around her wrist.

A scream escaped Nalya's lips as she felt the two needle-like piercing pricks accompanied by the fiery rush of venom in her veins.

"Now that's more like it!" She exclaimed wiping the vomit from her chin. She stared through her new glassy obsidian eyes at the convulsing body of Moncrede. As the snake solidified into metal around her wrist, the General's body, devoid of life and soul, hit the ground with a dull thud. All the knowledge that was his was now hers. A deafening silence fell over the scene as she raised a gauntlet clad arm to the darkening sky and rain began showering the village.

Writhing upon the ground within the pooling puddles, countless small black scaled snakes swarmed the dumbfounded villagers. Every man, woman, and child was infected, and added to the Nureaytumea's growing army.

"We are Nureaytumea!" Nalya shouted. A gale howled through the village and the assembled mass of soldiers and villagers fell into line and marched out with the wind at their backs.

"She is pregnant?" Devon shouted in disbelief, "but how?"

"My dear boy," Favereau chuckled, "I am here to instruct you how to wield the power of the Nuytumean, not to explain the facts of life."

Devon noticed a couple of women giggling and whispering as they walked past. He looked around embarrassed at the odd stares, and immediately lowered his voice. "I thought I was 'unable,'" he said.

"No young one," the old man patted him on the shoulder, "just unwilling."

"I don't understand."

"You will my boy. We begin our training at the Temple of Knowledge," The Svoresome pointed towards a mountain peak across the valley. They walked a few steps towards the village gate before Favereau stopped and scratched his bearded chin. He turned on his heel scanning the opposite horizon. "Or was it that mountain?"

Part Nineteen

Jerik did not know if the overwhelming dread he felt was from losing Tika to his Dark Master or from the fact they were headed to PetraPutrid Peak. Since he had met the girl his human side had grappled with the insect hive mind for control over his soul. For the first time in days his mind was alive with coherent thought instead of the bug-like instincts that had ruled his recent actions. He felt like his former human self again.

He mourned the loss of the sweet little girl. The loathing he felt for his Dark Master was beginning to overtake the fear that had kept him obedient. The 'bugman' felt renewed confidence and he considered dropping his small passenger from this great height. But he knew this was futile for the Dark One possessed magic to prevent such a fall from ending His life. Jerik decided to wait for an opportunity to catch the Dark Master unaware. he would make him pay for taking Tika's body and soul.

Jerik turned his mind to their destination. Petra Peak was taught to all potential Mages during the First Year within the Order. It was rumored to be a great source of power but most who had ventured there lusting to harness its energy never returned. In his grandfather's time people and animals from the outlying regions began disappearing in the middle of the night and dark tales of a great evil within the mountain began circulating throughout the land. By the time his father was born a foul odor had begun emanating from the area which prompted the population to flee and change the mountain's name to PetraPutrid Peak.

"There!" Tika shouted above the rushing wind, shaking Jerik out of his daydream. He looked to the horizon to see the jagged snow covered mountain thrust upward from a flat plain and pierce through dark angry storm clouds. Bone shattering thunder claps sent banks of powdery snow avalanching down the mountainside. His father had dubbed this phenomenon as, "thunder snow."

Lightning made the clouds of snow glow in a permanent bluish haze. Jerik found its dangerous beauty awe inspiring.

"Get above the clouds!" Tika ordered.

Jerik climbed into the churning mass. For several minutes they endured the bone chilling hell of pelting hail and icy darkness until merciful sunlight from above lit the air around them. They broke through the clouds and were hit with surprising warmth. Jerik's momentum carried him through this thin barrier of warmth breaking into the icy air above. He hovered for a moment or two but found it impossible to fight the turbulent winds that seemed to rage from the peak before them.

"Set down over there!" Tika's command was faintly heard through the howling tumult as she pointed towards a cloud close by.

"On top of the clouds?" Jerik responded in disbelief, "have you absolutely lost your mind?"

"Just do it Bugman!"

He reluctantly lowered his passenger as instructed and was amazed when the billowy surface did not give way. Jerik looked around in astonishment. Above him within reach of his fingertips, the racing wind howled above an unseen barrier, but, where they stood, the atmosphere was calm and comfortable. The Bugman was thankful for the respite for they had been flying nearly all day long without rest.

"C'mon Jerik," Tika's voice resonated with an eerie echo, "we must walk from here."

Jerik shook his head in awe, "Powerful magic indeed, this is fantastic."

The Peak rose out of the clouds before them like a giant black finger pointing skyward. From its crest a plume of black smoke was ripped by high altitude currents in all directions. This created a thin veil-like canopy that hung over the mountain for miles.

"It's the ideal place to hide from the Gods' prying eyes." The Dark Master explained. Such evil sounded strange spoken from the mouth of a little girl.

"Why?" Jerik asked, "what is being concealed from them?"

A great roar from high above answered the Bugman's question. Three huge black dragons descended in slow lazy circles towards them.

A smirk played on the little girl lips and a devious glint fired in her small blue eyes.

"My army," He replied with Tika's soft sweet voice.

Lone awoke to find Devon had gone. Her senses focused and she got the nagging feeling she was being watched. She shrugged it off and spent the morning polishing her armor and preparing her weaponry for the upcoming battle.

As the morning fog burned away outside, and the sun rose high into the sky, the feeling of paranoia intensified. Lone decided to leave the tree home and go into the center of the village in the hope that having people around her would be of some comfort. The opposite turned out to be the case. As she entered the main square she noticed a heavy silence blanketed the entire parish. She paced down the main street and was greeted by blank stares from the locals.

She nervously looked over her shoulder as the shuffling of dozens of feet was the only noise that met her ears. "What is going on here?" She turned on her heel and faced the growing mob. Her heart sank as the mass of people marched forward in complete silence. She turned and ran intending to double back to the tree house, but upon reaching the first alleyway, she was met by more villagers blocking her path. They had formed barriers across each alleyway she came to. Lone wished she had worn her weapons and armor as she realized the village population was methodically corralling her towards the main gate.

"Devon, Favereau!" She screamed in desperation hoping the men were within earshot.

The villagers jostled her through the open gates.

"Why are you doing this?" She screamed out.

The throng silently stared at her without emotion. The gates swung closed leaving her stranded outside. She fell to her knees feeling unexplained weakness throughout her whole body.

From somewhere high above she heard a high pitch screech followed moments later by the painful grasp of sharp talons ripping into the soft flesh of her shoulders. Her head spun as she felt herself being whisked away, high into the air, at bone jarring speed. She looked down to see the village's rooftops rapidly falling away before slipping into unconsciousness.

Part Twenty

The two men had been climbing the rocky mountain for hours. Devon wished the village was still in sight. The young mage's mind kept going back to the statement Favereau had made about Lone. Pregnat? It just couldn't be possible. His mind dismissed it as the ramblings of a crazy elderly mind.

Devon's exhaustion was beginning to overtake him physically and had tainted his already sour mood. He looked upward and several yards ahead Favereau agilely made his way up the steep path barely breaking a sweat.

"How much further!?!" Devon shouted contemptuously.

"Almost there my boy," The old man responded, deftly leaping atop a giant bolder. Her turned and thrust a hand toward Devon. "C'mon slowpoke, I can see the summit from here."

Devon growled and struggled the last few feet before reaching the offered hand. With surprising strength the old man hauled him up. Devon fell to his knees and let himself fall back against a gnarled tree trunk, gasping for breath. Both men stared upward toward the end of the path cresting the mountain a few hundred feet above them.

"See my boy," Favereau said, bending down and patting Devon on the shoulder, "almost there."

The old man bounded gleefully ahead leaving Devon far behind and still gasping for breath. The young man felt a sudden tingle at the edge of his soul. At first he could not identify it but soon it revealed itself as a nagging hatred directed at the old man.

"Sorry my boy."

Devon was startled as Favereau suddenly appeared at his side.

"I-I , um," the young mage stuttered pointing towards the mountain peak, "didn't I j-just see you up there?"

The old man held out the soiled cloth containing the Nuytumean. A shiver ran through the young mage and his mouth watered as he remembered the artifact's pure power coursing through his veins. He reached out and grabbed the gauntlet.

"Put it on my friend," Favereau's playful demeanor was replaced with an ominous seriousness, "the Nureaytumea nears and is attempting to poison your mind."

"How close? Do we have time to train?"

Favereau shook his head motioning towards the end of the path, "slow down young one. All your questions will be answered when we reach the top."

Devon quickly donned the Nuytumean and his body tensed as the immense power flowed into him melting away his exhaustion and soreness within a single breath. His head momentarily swooned as he fell into step behind the old man and easily made the top of the mountain with little effort.

Devon took in the awe-inspiring view about him sending his soul into flight with overwhelming joy. A sudden gust of wind blew across the peak knocking Devon painfully onto his backside.

"You must learn to control the power boy," Favereau stood over him his eyes gleaming with a bluish glow, "just because you were born to wield its power does not mean you cannot be possessed by it."

Devon looked up into the face of the old man standing above him and was confused as faint wisps of memories untold years old played upon his mind. He felt an ancient connection to the Svoresome as if their souls had been inexorably tied to one another in some odd kinship since time long forgotten.

"Now seize it," the old man said forcibly, "and focus it. Concentrate on harnessing and controlling it."

To be continued....

A TASTE OF MORIAVARATU

Betrayal

Valden sat across the table from the sobbing woman. He sensed her fear and a smile crossed his face. The room was dark. He had been sitting across from her for over an hour, reveling in the hatred she must be feeling towards him.

He slowly got up and pulled the cord on the bulb that hung from the ceiling. A shaft of harsh light shone directly onto his captive as he ripped away her blindfold.

A sob escaped as she looked around the room. The light was so bright she could not see him in the shadows.   "Who are you?" She asked her voice raw from her earlier screaming. Last thing she had remembered she was eating lunch on the avenue in the warm afternoon summer sun and now she was in this cold underground hell. The musty smell within the room had made her lose her lunch an hour before.

"You're going to kill me aren't you?" She cried.

A pause. She heard the shuffling of feet.

Eventually, he said, "I just need someone to talk to."

"Why me? " She looked up, straining to see his face through the glare.

He looked at her straight long raven hair falling around her shoulders shining in the light, her beautiful dark complexion and tear filled brown eyes that pleaded for her very life. "Because you look like someone who was once close to me," he said anger creeping into his voice. "Someone, who is now very far away."

"I am not her!" She yelled shrinking back in her chair. Her body racked with heavy sobs.

"Shhhh…" He stepped into the light and revealed his face.

"David Valdstar?" She gasped.

"The one and only." He spread his arms wide, palms upward lifting his head and closing his eyes basking in the light.

She stared at the strange image before her. 'He looks almost angelic,' she thought forgetting her current situation.

He leveled his gaze at her blue eyes glinting in the harsh light.

Before she had a chance to blink he was on top of her. She strained at the chains that bound her hands. He moved in close and whispered in her ear.

"I will never forgive you for what you did to me Nan." His voice dripped with contempt." I won't rest until I know you have died a painful and slow death!"

"I am not Nan!!!" The woman screamed. "Let me go!"

"You betrayed me!" A far away look crossed his face and he stared blankly at his captive.

"Please don't kill me," she cried.

Valden snapped out of his trance and smiled.

The woman turned her head and stared back at him from under her brow, fear building in her heart. There was something in his eyes that made her feel more unsettled as he approached and knelt in front of her. He leaned in and gently kissed her cheek.

"Please let me go," she said as his face backed away from hers. Valden smiled and she noticed two fanged teeth in his smile that weren't there before.

"Oh, I am going to my dear," he said in mock tenderness, "I am going to set you free from your pathetic earthbound life."

He moved back into the shadows and she heard metallic scraping against the wall. He re-emerged with a long metal lance.

"Remember this Nan? This is the very lance that you pierced my body with."

"I am not Nan!" She screamed.

He balanced the weight of the lance in his right hand and with the other ripped open his shirt revealing a wound in his left shoulder. Blood and puss oozed from the torn open flesh.

"You missed my heart," Valden said as a tear rolled down his cheek, "but you damaged it just the same."

He spun the lance in his right hand and grabbed onto her with the other. A split second later he stabbed the lance through the middle of the woman's heart. He moved in close to her seeing the woman's dying thoughts as he watched the life slowly drain from her eyes.

"But I am not Nan..." her mouth formed the words but not a sound escaped her lips.

He leaned in and kissed the dead woman on the cheek.

Valden stared at her lifeless body, her eyes fixed in a stare glinting from the light from above.

"How angelic you look," Valden laughed and turned on his heals and exited the room.

RATS and FIREFLIES

LATE TWENTY FIRST CENTURY....

Agent Danny T. Norris crept up to the electrified fence surrounding the Pahvali military facility outside Esfahan, Iran. His mission - to rewire a warhead and detonate the building. He had to make it appear as an accident. He knew the inside of the building like the back of his hand; he had studied the blueprints for months. He had been sent as a last resort, a desperate attempt to force Iran to give up its nuclear weapons program. This situation had been escalating since the early twenty first century. The Iranian government had been playing a dangerous cat and mouse game with the UN and the US Government.

North Korea's nuclear program ended disastrously twenty years before when the country's power hungry leader launched a nuclear warhead at Japan. Millions were killed and millions more in North Korea when Japan retaliated with three of its own nuclear missiles. The environmental impact was equally devastating. Great swathes of land in both countries were uninhabitable for thousands of years.

The US responded by starting a covert taskforce nicknamed "dark dagger." The taskforce's objective was to cause a "mishap" to any country who insisted on starting a nuclear weapons program. The idea being if the country experienced an "accident" and the loss to its own people it would in turn, through internal political and public persuasion, lose its will to have such weaponry.

So now here he was the first active agent of this taskforce ready to carry out its objective. He knew after his nights work there would be over a million people dead including, if things did not go as planned, himself. That was a risk he was willing to take if it would save several million more if not the planet.

This was a very unstable part of the world and the stakes were much higher here then they were in the Far East. Who knows what would happen if there was a nuclear warhead unleashed in this part of the world. He knew it was his responsibility to keep that from happening.

He took a deep breath and gathered his resolve, pulled a silver spray canister from his belt and a small tube of blue liquid from his breast pocket. He carefully set the silver spray canister on the ground for he did not want these chemicals to prematurely mix. He shook up the small vile of blue liquid and waited until it started to glow in the desert night, picked up the canister and turned it over.

There was a small hole in the bottom of the container made for the glass vile of liquid to be inserted. He slid the application end of the vile into the hole and watched the glowing blue liquid drain into the canister. He would only have about forty five seconds to dispense all the liquid before it would explode inside the container. As the last drop drained into the bottle he pulled the empty glass vile out and dropped it to the ground. He turned the canister up and sprayed the mixture onto the electrified fence in an arc big enough to accommodate him crawling through. He sprayed the bottle empty and sat back and watched the chemical reaction he saw so many times in training take place.

The arc he had just sprayed began to spark and the chain link began glowing red. He watched as the metal disintegrated before his eyes. The chain link the lay within the arc folded over and landed with a quiet thud on the ground before him no longer electrified. He knew he could not touch the intact fence.

He carefully dragged the orphaned piece of fence towards him. Now there was a hole big enough for him to crawl through. He could still see sparks flying off of the jagged pieces of fence around the perimeter of the hole.

He heard no sirens or alert horns so he knew the first stage of the mission was complete. He had not tripped the alarm and he could safely breech the fence.

He peeked at his watch and noted the time.

1:13AM Iranian time. He was ahead of schedule. He then pressed a button on the side of the watch that recorded the exact GPS coordinates of his position so he could find the breech in the fence on his was back.

"Now for the fun part." he quietly whispered to himself.

He quickly grabbed the metal spray canister and glass vile and put them into opposite pockets of his pants. He lay on his stomach and crawled through the hole careful not to touch any of the jagged edges of fence and frying himself.

He knew he had a long crawl in front of him. He had to craw through desert brush for three hundred yards until he made the first building. He knew he had to crawl it slow once he got close so he would not alert the sentry guards to his presence. Thank goodness there was a stiff breeze blowing down the mountainside behind him. He could afford quicker movement since the brush would be moving vigorously in that breeze.

At 2:33AM he was peering through his night binoculars at the entrance on the outer building. He knew there was minimal security on this night because it was Ramadan. The shift change just occurred and he knew the habits of the night guards well enough to know that the late shift would not be around for another fifteen minutes or so.

He still had to get past the camera and the motion sensor. He pulled another vile from his belt. This one was different from the first in that it had a cork on one end and instead of liquid it contained a small metal ball looking a lot like a large BB.

He pressed another button on his watch until the watch screen read "firefly". He then pressed his index finger on a small ball on the front of the watch that was disguised as a screw. He held up the glass tube. The 'BB' split in half and unfolded. The outer part of the small ball began vibrating like an insects wings.

'God Bless nanotechnology,' he thought to himself as he uncorked the tube.

Using the watch-screw like a joystick he guided the firefly out of the tube. The watch screen blinked to life with a firefly eye view. With a skill that only years of training could provide he steered the firefly to land above the entranceway of the building just by using the watches tiny screen and joystick. He pressed the joystick down on the watch until the word "menu" popped up on the lower left-hand corner of the image that was being transmitted by the firefly. He then scrolled down to scan/record and chose the option. After being prompted for "time of recording" he chose five minutes. He just hoped the guards didn't show up within the chosen time frame.

The firefly found the frequency the camera operated on and began recording the image footage. After five minutes it would automatically play back the footage in transmit mode. All anyone would see in the control room was the recorded footage until agent Norris switched modes.

Five minutes later his watch flashed at him indicating the recording was done and firefly was now in transmit mode.

'Good.' he thought to himself, 'still no guards.'

He pulled what appeared as an ink pen from his other breast pocket and what looked like an American express gold card out of his back pocket. He gave the pen a twist until the ballpoint extended outward. On the other end of the pen a small red light blinked to life indicating the device was working.

Only he knew that this device was jamming the motion sensors. Anyone else would only suspect a ballpoint pen. He stood up and quickly closed the distance to the entranceway. There was a key card slot above the door handle in which he slid the American express card. The American express logo suddenly glowed red. Danny waited for it to change to green before he tried the doorknob. Tripping the alarm now would result in assured capture, the last thing he wanted.

Then he suddenly heard voices from around the corner. The guards were returning to their post at the door.

"Come on, come on," he said under his breath urgently.

The cards logo still appeared red.

The voices grew closer.

Danny's heart began to pound and he felt sweat beading upon his brow.

The voices were just around the corner now and he had just seconds until being discovered when the card's express logo turned green. He quickly turned the knob and pulled on the door. Nothing happened.

"Damn," he cursed quietly as the guards were so close now he could hear their footfalls.

'Push,' he thought to himself. The door swung inward. He hastily stepped inside and closed the door quickly and quietly behind him. Agent Norris suddenly realized he was holding his breath and exhaled a long breath and slowly slid down the wall into a sitting position.

His heart was still pounding inside his chest when he suddenly realized the guards always checked in with the control room by saluting the camera.

"Shit!" the agent fumbled with his watch and switched the firefly into "dormant" mode just as the first guard looked up and saluted the camera on the other side of the heavy steel door.

The guard in the control room nonchalantly dismissed the sudden jump of the camera and appearance of the guard on his monitors view as a technical glitch and went back to reading his magazine.

Agent Norris sat on the tiled floor gathering himself for the next phase. All the reconnaissance they had done and he cursed himself for not knowing which way the doors opened. He looked at his watch and noted the time. 2:45AM.

"Still ahead of schedule," he said softly and allowed himself a few moments to rest and let his heartbeat slow before moving on.

Five minutes later he was headed down the hall to his first target destination. A small broom closet. Within the closet he found the technician's gold colored jumpsuit that was hidden right where it was supposed to be. He found the hardhat and goggles above the ceiling tiles, so far the inside man was batting a thousand. One more thing - the laminated identification card. He looked around the broom closet.

Bleach, where is the bleach?

He scanned the shelves. He knew he would not get much further without that ID card. Then he spied the squat white bottle with the word bleach written in Arabic across its front. He picked up the bottle and turned it upside down and screwed the bottom off. There concealed inside was what he was looking for. The full access ID card.

"Bingo." he whispered and quickly changed clothing.

He checked his watch once again. 2:58AM. He was still way ahead of schedule. Danny put his ear to the door making sure there was no one present on the other side. He turned the knob and exited the closet. He reached inside the jumpsuit to make sure he still had the leather pouch the detonation device was encased in. He breathed a sigh of relief and made his way purposefully down the hall trying to look as inconspicuous as possible.

He knew his course through the labyrinth of corridors he had to take and he made his way with haste. He wanted limited contact.

He came to a set of thick double steal doors reinforced by huge steal bands. Across the center metal band large Arabic letters read "central weapons facility." There was a guard on each side standing at eternal attention. As he approached one guard stepped forward and grabbed the id that was clipped to the pocket of the jumpsuit without saying a word. He brought it over to a desk nearby and ran an ultraviolet light over it. He nodded and handed it over to the other guard who ran it through what resembled a credit card swiping machine that was mounted on the wall above the desk. He nervously watched this whole process wondering if he was going to have to make a pointless break down the hallway wench he came.

He felt the sweat beading upon his brow and running down his back. His stomach tightened and he felt fear building in the pit of his stomach. He was about to give up hope and he clinched his fists getting ready for a futile fight. He knew there were several cameras trained on him at this very moment. The inside informant must have been not as good as he was lead to believe.

Just as he convinced himself he was going to lunge for the closest guard and go out fighting there were two short staccato beeps that broke the tense silence. The second guard walked over and handed the card back to him.

"Good evening Dr. Norris," he said in well spoken English surprising the agent, "we have been expecting you. Your credentials check out. Your level of clearance is confirmed."

"Umm. Thank you," agent Norris said clipping the card back onto his pocket.

"Protocol dictates that you check in on the hour," the guard said in stern tone, "you must not break protocol. Do you understand Doctor?"

"Yes," Norris said managing to sound pretty calm, "clearly."

"Very well sir," the guard responded, "areas that are a radiation risk are clearly marked. Make sure you suit up in a radiation suit in decontamination once you pass through this door."

"I know the procedure well enough," he said to the guard "enough with these delays. I have important work to do."

"Of course sir," the guard fumbled a bit taken back by the indignant tone, "my apologies sir."

He gave a curt bow and signaled the other guard to open the door.

The second guard went over to a keypad and punched in a long code and ran his card through a slot on the side of the key interface.

Giant gears could be heard turning inside the door and several snaps as giant tumblers retracted inside the door. They slowly swung open on over-sized hinges. Agent Norris nodded to the guards and passed between the large doors. It appears their inside man was really worth the money they were paying him.

He checked his watch. 3:12AM. He was well ahead of schedule.

As the door closed behind him he breathed a sigh of relief. He knew in this restricted area he would not have to contend with anybody else until he had to make his way out.

Twenty-five minutes later he was suited up in a radiation suit and he was in the corridor right outside the room that stored the warheads.

Another steal banded door clearly marked with the "Danger Risk of Radiation Contamination" warning sign. He went up to the keypad beside the door and slid his id card in. He then pressed the button marked intercom.

"Yes Doctor," speakers cracked with the guard's voice.

"Just checking in," he responded, "I am about to commence my diagnostics procedure. It will probably take about an hour and a half."

"Gotcha Doctor," the guards voice came back, "we will go ahead and sign you in."

The sound of giant gears grinding drowned out the guards last words as the giant door slowly swung inward.

Agent Norris made his way into the room. He knew this room very well for they had recreated it back in the states at the Dark Daggers training facility. He had trained so hard once he stepped into the short corridor that lead to the large room beyond he knew exactly where he would be invisible to the surveillance cameras covering the area.

He walked five feet into the corridor and abruptly stepped to the left hand wall of the corridor where he knew he could not be seen. He reached into his radiation suit and pulled out the black leather pouch that held the implements of his mission. Danny pulled out a small metal box and pulled up the small antennae on its top. He reached up to the top of the corridor wall and mounted the box at the point where the wall met the ceiling. The box had a magnetic backing and easily stuck to the metal wall of the room.

The agent then activated the device by pressing a small green button on its face. He waited a second until he was sure the device was transmitting.

He had spent hours recording footage of himself performing his 'diagnostic procedure' in the mock-up of this room back in the states. He knew the device transmitted that footage to all the cameras within the room and he was now safe to moon the cameras if he felt like it. All the guards in the control room would see would be the recorded footage transmitted by the little black box.

Agent Norris made his way into the room. He allowed his eyes a moment to adjust to the red lighting of the room and then made his way to the predetermined warhead that was in the back of the room. There were twelve warheads neatly lined up in the room. Yellow and black caution lines marked defined rows on the concrete floor. He could not help feeling a bit nervous knowing how much uranium sat in this room. He knew that the warheads were not active and could not explode but that did not calm his nerves one bit.

He pulled out the leather pouch and pulled out his tools and got to work. First he pulled out a battery-powered screwdriver cleverly disguised as a fountain pen and removed the faceplate of the nuclear warhead before him. Once the faceplate was off he had to unscrew the plate to the inner access panel.

He knew if the warhead was not in this secured facility that he would need an access code to do this, but the digital screen mounted inside the warhead read "inactive."

He made quick work of the inside faceplate and uncovered the computer interface that granted him access to the hard drive within the warhead. He pulled out what appeared to be a razor thin cell phone and opened it up.

He quickly punched in a number and watched the display waiting for it to read "device ready."

The screen read "acquiring satellite signal" for about forty-five seconds before flashing the words he awaited.

The 'phone' briefly vibrated and the word "device ready" flashed on the display. He then slid the device into a groove on the front of the computer interface. It slid neatly into the groove and he made sure the contacts on the bottom of the phone made contact with warhead computer.

The display changed and flashed "CODE ACCEPTED. WARHEAD ACTIVATED."

'Our inside guy pays off again' he thought to himself.

Large numbers appeared on the warheads computer interface screen and began counting down. He now had six hours until detonation. And one hour to sit here in this room and wait.

He looked at his watch and sighed as he slouched down on the floor.

The past few days had been a flurry of activity and this was the first time he had time to catch his breath. He tried not to think about the millions that were about to die and concentrated on the billions that would be saved. He was convinced this was for the best.

"Pssst." He heard from his left in the corner of the room.

He was instantly on his feet and standing in a defensive posture as he wheeled around. There standing ten feet away was their 'inside guy.'

"Doctor Armond?" he said with a sigh of relief, "I did not hear you come in."

"I have been here the whole time." He said blandly. "I have something to show you that you might find interesting."

"What about the guards?" Agent Norris asked, "I have prerecorded footage transmitting to the cameras, wont they be suspicious you are not on their monitors?"

"Its okay," Dr. Armond said with a sly smile, " they do not even know I am in here."

"How is that possible?" Norris asked in disbelief. "This whole facility is under surveillance."

"Not the WHOLE facility Agent Norris," he responded, "that is what I want to show you."

"I don't understand." he said a bit befuddled. "This is highly irregular."

"I understand you do not trust me Agent," he answered, "but has not my help proven my intent to help your mission succeed assurance enough I have your best interests at heart here?"

There was a long pause. Agent Norris knew he had time to waste but

this was a breech of protocol, and that was never good for a missions success.

"This information would be very useful for your government agent." The

Doctor said assuredly.

Something in Agent Norris' mind told him he could trust this man. So against his better judgment he decided to humor the Doctor.

"Alright sir," he said with a sigh," show me what you must but I must have your word it will not jeopardize this mission."

"You have my word agent," the Doctor said, "and after you see what I have to show you will know it is important you know this information."

The Doctor led him around the warheads and to the other side of the room. There he stood for a moment in front of the steal wall. He was mumbling something when suddenly the outline of a door appeared. There was the sharp sound of metal on metal and the door seemed to recess inward into the wall itself and then it slid to the side with a "woosh" sound.

"How did you do that?" Agent Norris asked in awe.

"There are many secrets this facility holds," the Doctor answered nonchalantly. "You will soon know one of its darkest."

This last was in an ominous tone that made the agent feel a little uneasy. They passed through the doorway and traveled down a series of iron-grated corridors that were suspended in midair within the darkness of the inner belly of the facility.

Beyond the grated corridors Agent Norris caught glimpses of heavy machinery and ductwork for, what he assumed, was the ventilation system. They seemed to be within a service corridor used to inspect the inner workings of the facility's network of sustaining mechanized systems.

The agent began to feel as if he was being watched.

"No need to worry," the doctor said as if he knew what Norris was thinking, "there are no cameras and no workers within this area of the facility. We are completely alone."

His words echoed eerily back from the darkness around them coming back to the agents ears in ghostly tones.

Despite the encouraging words from the doctor he still felt as though there were eyes watching their every movement. He suddenly wished he had refused the doctors wish and stayed back in the warhead storage room.

"You will see this will be worth it," the doctor said reassuringly, once again as if you knew exactly what the agent was thinking.

"I hope you are right," he replied in a very shaky voice," this could compromise the mission."

He nervously checked his watch.

"You still have plenty of time agent," the doctor said as they cam up to a what appeared as a metal hatch, much like you would see on a submarine. The doctor gave the wheel in the center of the door a turn and yanked the door to. There were grinding of hinges and the door slowly swung open. From inside a red glow splashed over the two men and the steel grated corridor around them.

"Mind your head," the doctor warned as he stepped inside. Agent Norris followed dipping his head to allow for the low clearance of the hatchway.

The corridor ran for another twenty feet ending in another hatchway.

"IDENTIFY YOURSELF," a metallic voice blurted out at them. The agent was a bit surprised it was in English.

"Dr. Armond and guest," answered the doctor.

"GOOD DAY DOCTOR," came the automated response, "YOU ARE CLEARED."

He reached the next door and the wheel turned by itself and the hatch swung open.

Agent Norris was confused as he caught his first glimpse of what lay within the room. On both sides of the narrow corridor large glass tubes lined the walls for as far as Dan could see. The corridor stretched out of site. What appalled the agent was what was inside the glass tubes. Human bodies. As they stepped into the room the agent studied these encapsulated bodies closer.

Upon this closer inspection the agent was left with the impression some of these people were still alive. Some of the bodies were obviously dead and in different states of decay.

"What is all this?" Dan asked turning to the doctor. He then looked back at the grotesque display before him. He noticed there were men, women and children of several different races. And that was just what

he could surmise by what was in eyeshot. There were several levels of these tubes stacked atop of one another reaching into the darkness above them. He could only imagine how high the ceiling was. The corridor ahead of them stretched out of sight as well. 'How many bodies?' he thought to himself.

"By last count," Dr. Armond answered his unspoken question," over twenty-two thousand."

He could not take his eyes off the scene before him. He went from face to face. Then, to his astonishment, he realized that there was a display at the base of each tube that had readout of the vital statistics of the occupants within. He was aghast to see some of these people were still alive.

"Oh my god," He breathed, "Dr. Armond what is this all about? Where are these people from? What are they here for?"

" I am afraid they have been lab mice," Dr. Armond responded," for a virus my government has been working on. A selective virus that only attacks certain people by the make up of their genes. They have been perfecting it for years and now they have succeeded in a version they are satisfied with."

"The perfect biological weapon," Dan breathed walking up to one of the tubes and studying the face of the young girl within. She appeared to be Caucasian, about twelve years old. This girl could be his daughter.

"What kind of..." he choked up. He was not used to being in touch with his emotions. He was taught to disengage his feelings. But seeing the face of this young girl before him put him in touch with something inside. The emptiness he felt for not having a family. The emptiness of putting ones career and government before ones self and replacing love for another with obligation of duty.

He studied the soft features before his eyes and he felt tears welling in his eyes. Suddenly the young girls eyEs sprung open and he fell back in sudden shock gripped with a fear.

"Holy mother of god!" he screamed, "we have to help her!"

Dr. Armond stepped in front of agent Norris.

"It is too late," he said blankly, "besides, If you are to help her would you not help the others?"

Dr. Armond waved his hand and Dan could see several of the other subjects had awoken and were banging on the insides of their glass coffins with clinched fists. No sound could be heard for the only thing the glass would allow escape were their tortured images.

"We have to do something." He looked up into the Doctors cold eyes pleadingly.

"We have already," answered the doctor nonchalantly. "In about five in

a half hours they will be put out of their misery."

"I don't understand," Agent Norris said in disbelief, " I thought you wanted to help. "

"I have helped," the Doctor said coldly, "I am getting rid of the evidence. And thanks to you and your government, you have presented a timely and cost effective solution."

"You bastard!!" Agent Norris screamed out. "what about all of your own people who are going to be killed? Do you care nothing for them?"

"My people?" Dr. Armond grabbed the agent's arm with surprising strength. Agent Norris felt his watchband dig into his skin. He felt warm blood trickle down his arm. "You know nothing of MY PEOPLE.

These poor pathetic souls mean nothing to me."

The doctor began to laugh. A low maniacal laughter that made Agent Norris shiver.

"I bid you farewell agent," he said and turned on his heal to leave the room.

Agent Norris felt a swelling of hatred building up in the very core of his being and he stood body pumping with adrenaline. He rushed at the retreating figure of the doctor with all the strength he could muster.

With surprising agility the doctor turned and knocked him to the steal grated floor in one quick motion. He was pinned to the floor not being able to move a muscle.

"Relax," the doctor smiled an evil grin, "you are way ahead of schedule."

Dr. Armond was up and stepping through the first hatchway.

Agent Norris gathered up what strength he had left to give chase. He was on his feet and through the first hatchway in the space of a singe breath. Dr. Armond had paused by the outer hatch.

"Computer," Dr. Armond called out, "this man is an intruder. Would you please contain him."

From above a glass wall slammed down separating the agent from doctor.

Behind Danny heard the other hatchway slam shut. He was trapped.

On the other side of the glass he saw the doctor slowly turn. He walked up to the other side of the glass and stuck his nose real close. Dan could see the frost from his breath. Dan raced back and let a fist fly. His hand exploded in pain as he dropped to his knees grasping his wounded appendage.

He looked up to see the doctor laughing. He leaned close to the glass and with his breath he made a large swath of frosted area. With his finger he traced out a message: LITTLE LAB MOUSE, YOUR

MAZE ENDS HERE.

He turned laughing as he exited the last hatchway.

The despair Dan felt was beyond measure. He knew this mission would be looked on as a success with the unfortunate casualty being himself. He now knew exactly how much of a failure it was. If there was a way he could get a message out to his superiors. Or even better, stop the countdown and expose the conspiracy.

Wait a sec. Firefly!

He was ready to activate the firefly but his heart sank as he looked at his watch. When Doctor Armond grabbed his wrist he effectively crushed watch and in turn, his last hope.

He slumped into a ball of despair and defeat. He knew he had a cyanide capsule he could swallow to make it a quick and painless death. But he chose to forego the capsule and meet his demise at the same time the people that he failed on the other side of this bulkhead met theirs. He crawled over to the hatchway and rested his head on the doors wheel.

He pictured the young girl on the other side of the door a mere twenty feet away and waited for the next five hours to pass. He knew at the end of this day he would be considered a hero back home, but right now he felt nothing more than a fool.

SUMMER SOLSTICE

The Professor found himself in a field just after dark. The western horizon was still ablaze with the sun's final effort to push back the veil of the darkness of night. There was a slight chill in the air but that did not faze him one bit, which was a bit odd. He would usually run for his sweater at the slightest nip in the air.

He made his way through the field and glanced over his shoulder to see nine others following him. His brief glimpse of the faces behind him brought no recognition, but he felt they were familiar companions.

Up ahead he saw torches lighting up the unmistakable forms of huge monolithic stones. He recognized it right away. This was Stonehenge.

Within the stones a throng of white robed figures chanted and danced. There was a festival like feeling in the air as he heard rhythmic drum beating reach him.

He found, once again, it was a bit odd that it was as if he was not really hearing the beating drums, but it was if he were feeling them. He felt a loathing hatred he did not understand. Druids. The word itself made his stomach turn. He marched up to the outer circle of stones.

"What are you doing here?" He heard himself ask with seething hatred in his oddly unfamiliar voice.

"We are celebrating the Summer Solstice," one of the white cloaked figures said with a great smile, "we are here to welcome the dawn."

The others behind him caught up and fanned out on either side of him. The professor found he felt superior to everyone around him. The robed men before him might as well have been cattle. This confidence was unfamiliar to the professor, he felt almost 'godlike.' He was uncomfortable with the conceit, but regardless, this self-love permeated every pore of his being unsettling him.

"All of you," he ordered, "leave at once."

"It is our right brother," the druid replied with kind patience in his voice, "if you would like to be initiated into the ranks as a novice then please grab a robe and follow me."

"A novice?" He heard himself laugh sounding very evil to his ears. "I tell you what hippie, why not gather your people and leave at once."

"It is our rite to be here," the man replied disturbed, impatience creeping into his voice, "our ancestors built this place. We have celebrated the Summer Solstice every year since it was erected."

He felt laughter welling up inside. It came bursting forward in an evil chuckle. Hatred filled him up and he looked from underneath his brow as to stare pillars of fire blasting forth from his eyes.

"I built this place!" He shouted his voice full of contempt," You are trespassing and I suggest all of you leave now or there is going to be.......trouble."

The dancing and merriment suddenly stopped. The drumbeats fell silent and several of the men in robes made their way towards the strangers.

The professor felt his body tingle and he felt the surge of adrenaline course through his veins. He was not scared at all even though the druids outnumbered them fifty to one. He knew even though they were peaceful they would still try to jump them. After all-they were human.

"I am going to have to ask you to leave," the druid said after looking to his left and then to his right realizing he had reinforcements, "this is a peaceful celebration and you are disrupting our festival."

He heard his evil laughter echo off the stone monoliths.

"Festival," the loathing obvious in his tone. He raised his arms out to his sides with palms skyward and an ominous grin parted his lips, "your gods are here before you now. Kneel and give us penance!"

"Screw you wanker!!" One of the other druids shouted with a heavy English accent.

"Tisk tisk," he replied shaking his finger before him, "for your subordinance you must repent."

"Hey man," the first druid said, "you are crazy! You just need to turn around and leave at once."

"That is no way to talk to one of your gods," he said the evil grin spreading his lips once again," you must now offer me a sacrifice."

"Fuck off!!" The cloaked figure shouted and flipped him his middle finger.

"Very well then," he replied, "if you want to play...LETS PLAY!"

In the blink of an eye the professor pounced on the first druid and sunk his teeth deep into the man's neck. He tasted the sweet blood and felt it running down the back of his throat and felt the immediate rush of unbelievable energy coarse through his body.

A second later he pounced with catlike reflexes on the next man within site ripping his neck open with sharp finger nails and latching on with his mouth gulping down warm blood. He threw the body to the ground and looked around at the carnage around him.

White cloaked figures ran about everywhere their clothes stained in blood. Terror filled their eyes their screams filled the night air. He saw his companions methodically working their way through the crowd drinking their fill.

"What do you think of your gods now!?!" He shouted into the English night.

THE EMPORER'S PLAYROOM

Early 15th Century...

Uslum waited outside the Chinese border for the overseer that was assigned to him by the emperor. The time and place had been prearranged and he did not like to be kept waiting.

His whole life he was considered an important man and this impromptu lateness angered him, a man who had never been made to wait.

He realized that is why his majesty had chosen him to be the envoy to his country because he was so important. He was sure that the fact that his father happened to be Chinese helped the decision as well. This was to be an honor, but all Uslum felt was contempt.

He had a business to run after all, and this was just an inconvenience. The king told him he was to show nothing but the utmost respect the whole time he was here, why was he not given this same courtesy? This was an outrage.

Why was it they needed the Chinese anyway? Oh yes, what was it his majesty had said," they were powerful where we are weak and to earn trade status with the Chinese would mean to be protected by the Chinese. That is their way Uslum. We are in danger of being over run by barbarians on all sides, for our country to have a chance to survive we have to befriend the Chinese."

Resentment is all he felt. He resented he was chosen for this task, he resented that he was a thousand miles from home and the merchant business he loved.

That brought him to the reason he resented this task the most, the Ming Dynasty was very distrustful of merchants. They were considered the lowest of Chinese society next to eunuchs.

Right now he wished his emperor did not trust him so much, he could be back at home in Ayutthaya enjoying this mid summers day in the comfort of his own home. Instead he was waiting on the side of a mud-laden road far from the comfort of his vast estate.

There around the corner a convoy of wagons slowly made their way towards the border. The black and red flags of the emperor Wang Wei Wu fluttering in the breeze.

"Wang Wei Wu," Uslum said under his breath, "I wonder how many of the rumors are true."

"You mean that he can read minds?" Asked his bodyguard Bemna.

"Or, that he has the strength of a ten men?" scoffed Uslum. "I have also heard he he is a thousand years old!"

"I wonder if you can see in the dark?" Bemna's great chest heaved under his leather breastplate as he chuckled.

The overseers cart pulled up beside them. Two Chinese guards came up to Uslum and his bodyguard cautiously. One of the guards unrolled a scroll he had been carrying under his arm. He unrolled the scroll and with a quick bow of his head he began to read, "Uslum Sunan, you are hereby invited into the presence of the emperor Wang Wei wu and are granted passage through his great empire safely to the imperial city."

Uslum gave a short bow and stepped forward.

"I am sorry sir," the other guard stepped in front of him, "you will not be permitted to carry any weapons within our borders."

Uslum nervously eyed the two guards.

"Not to worry sir," the first guard said quickly, "the armies of the Emperor will ensure your safety while you enjoy the hospitality of China."

"Very well," Uslum said with a sigh handing over his sword, "I respect your wishes and hand over my arms."

Bemna began to unbuckle his sword when the first guard turned to Uslum.

"I am sorry sir your bodyguard will not be permitted entry into China," the guard said and turned to Bemna looking up into the cool stern eyes of the hulking bodyguard, "the invitation is for the envoy of Siam only. No one is to accompany the envoy; you are now under our protection."

Bemna strode forward and stood toe to toe with the Chinese guard towering over the man by a foot and a half. The Chinese guard stood his ground not wavering as Bemna let out a low growl.

The unsheathing of a metal sword broke the tense stare as the other

Chinese guard had circled around and now stood behind the two Siamese men sword drawn and ready to pounce at the first sign of trouble.

"Settle down Bemna," Uslum put an arm across the man's giant chest," you take the horses back to our King and tell them Emperor Wang Wei Wu will soon have his gift from Siam."

"Yes Uslum," Bemna huffed and gave a short bow, "It will be done."

Bemna turned on his heel and pushed his way past the second Chinese

guard, sword still drawn, almost knocking him to the ground.

The guards motioned Uslum across the border and he stepped into the land his father had called home.

The two soldiers led him to one of the carriages and opened the door. Each bowed and motioned Uslum to go inside. He climbed the three steps into the compartment inside. The guards closed the door behind him and Uslum stood, crouched over, without moving for a moment allowing his eyes to adjust to the darkness within. It was almost pitch dark. Black thick curtains hung over the windows allowing only a small amount of daylight within the carriage.

He could smell the perfume of some kind of incense that hung in the air the smoke burning his eyes.

"Welcome envoy," came a snakelike voice from with the darkness, "Allow me to be the first to welcome you to Chinese soil."

A sudden flash of light and an odd shaped face jumped forth from the darkness. The strange looking man lit a lantern on a table and motioned for Uslum to sit upon silk pillows laid out on the floor of the carriage.

He gave a short bow and lowered himself onto the pillows.

"And who do I have the honor of meeting?" He said holding the strangers gaze. "And thanking for the welcome to your country."

Pale thin lips cracked into a wry smile, "So proper, so respectful."

The voice hissed and once again he thought how snakelike was his voice.

"Civil men," he answered with a half smile, "should always show respect and properness to one's host. It is what separates us from the savage barbarians."

The stranger just stared at him for a moment. His eyes seemed to burn through to Uslum's very soul. He began to feel very uneasy under the scrutiny of the stare of those dark eyes. This man was playing with him. He saw the man's expression slightly change.

"Excuse my rudeness," the man hissed, "I am Feing Dong Fu, your overseer for this tribute mission."

"I am honored." Uslum replied with as much respect he could muster and

a curt bow of his head. "Siam is in Chinas debt for the invitation."

Uslum did not like the Chinese Tribute System. He did not think any ruler should have so much power over another country.

The way the system worked was first the emperor realized he wanted something from the country and he would "invite" them to China. That country would then send an envoy to represent them before the Emperor on what was called a "tribute mission."

The envoy would be made to wait just over a month before he was permitted to see the emperor.

In that time China would show each envoy opulence they had never experienced before. They were not allowed to roam the Imperial City, they were held "political captive" within the emperors palace. In that time the envoy was always accompanied by an overseer and was shown the best China had to offer. A show of extravagance. The envoy was required to offer a gift to the emperor while prostrate in a kowtow bow and request his country be allowed to trade with China. The emperor, under the assumption he is the center of the universe, would agree or disagree to allow the envoys country trade with China. The emperor even decided what would be traded and for what.

The arrogance sickened Uslum to the core.

"You do not approve of the way China does business do you?" Uslum was jolted from his revelry by the Overseers blunt question. His contempt must have been visible on his face.

"Um, oh no." he tried to recover and repair the damage his emotions obviously had just caused. "I deeply respect the politics of China."

"You seek protection do you not?" the pale skinned man sneered.

"My country is weak at this time," Uslum said his eyes dropping to the

floor, "we have many threats and we would be honored to become one of the protected ones of Mother China."

"I know how you feel about the way we do things Uslum," the strange looking man said so softly that Uslum had to lean forward and strain to hear, "you will soon see how powerful our emperor is and you will know that the Chinese way is the only way."

Uslum bit his tongue. He wanted to lash out at this pompous rude remark but he knew it would not serve his country's interests to derail this political visit before it even got started. He was really beginning to dislike this Feing Dong Fu, and he did not look forward to having to spend a month with the man.

"You don't have to like me," the pale skinned mans icy stare was really becoming unnerving to Uslum," truth be known I don't like you or your country."

Uslum had become very uncomfortable and he was beginning to think that maybe this man was the man who could read minds and not the emperor after all.

"Then I feel this shall be a very long trip for both of us." Uslum said, " truth be known I really did not want to come on this trip. But out of respect for my King I came."

"And now you regret that decision don't you envoy?" The contempt in the Overseers voice was palpable. "Your king must owe you a favor or perhaps you are an old friend and you are being rewarded?"

"I feel Mr. Fu," Uslum said with a sigh, "that you have made it apparent that this trip is going to be anything but pleasant so I look at this mission as more torture than reward."

"Just remember those words later," the overseer said with a very evil looking smile on his face, "When it is reported back to your king your contempt for China has cost Siam political isolation from the most powerful nation on the planet."

He clinched his fist until he felt his fingernails bite into his flesh. He felt beads of sweat building on his forehead and he clinched his teeth so hard they began to grind on one another. It was all he could do to keep himself from spitting out obscenities at this poor excuse for a human being.

Uslum stared into the sunken and cold eyes of Feing Dong Fu determined he was going to win this staring match. He would be defiant and not blink before his adversary. He felt a trickle of blood run down his hand as his eyes began to sting with the pain of drying out. His adversary seemed to be unaffected as shrill laughter escaped his lips. Uslum could not hold the stare any longer and dropped his eyes to the floor just in time to see the droplet of blood from his hand silently fall and splatter on the carriage floor.

"Well Uslum," Feing Dong Fu chuckled, "I certainly admire your spirit."

The overseer thrust a bony hand toward Uslum gesturing for a handshake. Uslum did not know what to think. The handshake was more of a Western tradition and frowned upon in the Orient. He only knew of the tradition because of his position trading with Europe and England.

Even though he hadn't known this person very long this seemed out of character for this man. He eyed the outstretched hand suspiciously and, after a sigh, reluctantly reached out and shook the outstretched hand.

The Siamese envoy was taken back at how cold to the touch the strangers was. As he withdrew his hand he had noticed, with a little embarrassment, he had left a streak of blood across the man's pale bony hand.

"Not to worry," the pale man said looking at the crimson stain on his hand," I am accustomed at having blood on my hands."

Uslum noticed a brief glint in the man's eyes as the last words came out in a final hiss.

Suddenly the carriage lurched forward and Uslum was thrown to the floor with the sudden jolt. Their trip to Beijing had begun.

As he scrambled up into a crouched position, he thought he glimpsed his odd companion lick the blood off his hand.

"Does your hand need attention?" Feing poorly faked a concerned tone, "you appear to be injured."

"I am okay," Uslum shook his head, "I am fine."

"Very well then," Feing said with a wry smile," Uslum Sunam, let us see if the gods favor you and yours on this mission."

After a very long carriage journey and several of hours of odd banter they finally passed through the walls of Beijing.

Exquisite granite and statue work towered over the plains and city below. Uslum was in awe at the craftsmanship in the architecture. He had never seen anything of its like.

The streets were wide and very organized. Even the alleyways off the main street were wide and clean. He began to get the impression of a giant chessboard. Every street either ran north and south or east and west. Everything seemed well planned out and gave an impression of security and organization.

"You have not seen anything yet," Feing said with obvious pride, "wait till you see the Tar-tar district. It is the shining achievement of Chinas superior intellect in city planning."

Uslum's stomach began to turn at the man's conceit.

"Many of the buildings there were standing when Kublai Khan ruled China from this great city."

Uslum glanced over and saw a far off look on the Chinese mans face. It was as if he was focused on something far beyond the horizon.

The carriage passed through another gate and Uslum looked up to the top of the wall. Guard towers, much like the ones on the Great Wall itself, stood atop the wall every twenty-five yards or so.

The Siamese envoy began to realize that this city was indeed very well thought out. It was also very well defended. The city was a series of walled-in sections that were built around the Forbidden City in the center. The 'Forbidden city' itself was a complex of buildings and city squares that housed the Emperor and the high Literati that ran the Chinese government.

Not very many people were allowed inside that final gate.

Thus it had become known as the 'Forbidden City.' The Meridian wall was about one hundred and twenty feet tall and had four watchtowers on each corner that towered high above the wall itself. They passed through the great Meridian Gate accompanied by the ringing of bells and the banging of drums.

"Those bells ring for you," Feing hissed," they signal your arrival to the great palace."

"I am speechless," Uslum gulped as he turned to look out the carriage window as they passed beneath the final arch of the Meridian Gate and into the huge square the lay beyond.

They passed over a small bridge that spanned an inner mote into the largest city square Uslum had ever seen, and he had visited several foreign cities during his life, this one impressed him beyond compare.

At the other end of this square lay another gate, the Gate of Supreme Harmony. Guards lined both sides of the lane that ran down the center of the square, each carrying a banner displaying the colors of the emperor.

Despite the hatred he had for the man that sat before him, he could empathize with the man's pride in this city. This truly was a spectacle to behold.

"Impressive isn't it?" Feing said with a wry smile. "Some that come to this city never leave it, as they are captivated and awed by its beauty."

"It truly does inspire one so." Uslum replied still awestruck by the scale of what lay before him. "My heart still lies with my hometown of Ayutthaya. I doubt there is any city that can steal my heart from her embrace."

"We shall see," Feing said lips curled over discolored teeth. "Many have said those words never to see their homeland again."

Something in this man's tone left Uslum feeling uneasy and the next several moments were spent in silence until the carriage came to a stop and he was escorted to the most magnificent room he had ever stepped foot in. But the opulence was wasted on him because the feeling of insecurity would not allow him to feel impressed.

His thoughts stayed focused on Feing Dong Fu, and he had the feeling the man was deliberately toying with him. He had come to the conclusion that this man was more black hearted than anyone he had ever met and he was glad to be away from those piercing eyes, even though it was only for an hour or so. He only hoped the emperor was nothing like Feing.

Suddenly Uslum was awash with homesickness. He just wanted to go home.

A couple of hours later Uslum was awaken with a loud knock at his door. He barely remembered falling asleep after lying down on the lavish bed in his room. Now his heart beat with the shock of being suddenly jolted awake. For a moment he was paralyzed and struggled to get his body to respond and sit up. He tried to catch his breath and managed to finally sit up.

"Come in," he said weakly.

The door swung open and in walked the most beautiful woman he had ever laid eyes on. Long dark hair flowed behind her hanging down to the small of her back. Her straight hair framed a pale beautiful face with soft pouting lips and round rosy cheeks. She walked up to Uslum and with a short curt bow her blue eyes looked up into his and with a smile she said in a small shy voice,

"The emperor would like to see you," she waved a hand towards the door," if you will please follow me."

Uslum slowly stood and followed the young woman toward the door. He was completely captivated by her beauty. He studied her body intently as she seemed to glide toward the door with incredible grace.

'She is the perfect picture of beauty,' he thought to himself.

"What is your n-name?" He stuttered

"My name is not important," she said softly," what is important is that the Emperor would like to see you now."

"I thought it would be sometime before I met the emperor," he said a bit confused, "I don't understand."

"Apparently the emperor has taken a special interest in you," she answered him, "there are two other envoys here in the palace as we speak and both have been here for three weeks each. The Emperor has shown no interest in seeing them at all."

She looked over her shoulder and gave him a smile that mad Uslum feel as if his heart would melt. "It seems my emperor shows you favor he has only shown one time before."

Uslum did not understand why the Emperor would have had any special interest in him for he was just a mere merchant. That to the Chinese meant he was a second-class citizen.

She looked over her shoulder once again and saw that he was confused.

"Not to worry envoy," she said playfully, "I heard that, the one time this happened before, the guy was made very wealthy and powerful by my Emperor."

A smile slowly spread across his face. It was not at the mention he might be made wealthy, but at the playful tone she had taken with him. Suddenly his heart felt as though it was about to beat out of his chest.

She slowed her pace and allowed him to walk even with her. Then she reached out and grabbed his hand for a moment and gave it a squeeze. He felt a tingling sensation throughout his whole body and all the homesickness he had felt earlier left him in a rush of blood that made his cheeks blush.

The rest of the walk to the emperor's throne room was spent in relative silence. Uslum walked through great halls of beauty with exquisite statues made completely of jade, tapestries of unrivaled quality, artwork painted by the greatest artist of the time, but the only beauty that moved him was the one with whom he walked with now. He wanted this moment to last forever.

But, as life always does just as he had this last thought they arrived at their destination. They stood before double doors that were about eighteen feet high made of Red wood. Two guards stood posted outside staring straight ahead into space.

"I must go in and announce your arrival," she said to him, "stay here until called for."

One of the guards opened the door for her and she disappeared inside.

A few minutes later she re-emerged and came over and gently she grabbed his hand.

"The emperor will see you now." She said softly, "Remember to show respect and don't do anything to insult his highness. He does not react well to disrespect."

She leaned in and gave him a light kiss on the cheek.

"Ehemm!" Came the sound of one clearing ones throat from across the corridor.

She quickly pulled away and straightened up. They both looked over to see Feing Dong Fu emerge from the shadows on the other side of the hall.

"I must go," she said fearfully. And began to make her away across the hall. Uslum paused and watched her gracefully glide away. About halfway across she turned smiled and said, "Uslum. It's Meeka."

"Excuse me," He said somewhat confused.

"My name," she smiled, "that is what the ones close to me call me."

"Slave girl!!" Feing's voice shattered the moment from across the corridor.

She gave a quick bow and smile to Uslum and turned on her heel and raced across the hall towards Feing. Uslum looked at Feing and saw those cold steely eyes staring at him.

'Does this man even have a soul,' he thought to himself.

Meeka reached the other side and Feing put an arm around her shoulder and pulled her close never breaking his gaze with Uslum.

He whispered something in her ear and ran his tongue over his lips. A devious grin curled over his stained teeth.

Meeka's eyes dropped to the floor and Feing escorted her into the darkness. Uslum watched as those eyes, never looking away, fade into the darkness. Anger welled up inside him and he realized he was really beginning to develop a strong hatred for this man.

"The emperor awaits," one of the guards said.

"Oh yes," he quickly snapped out of his last thought," sorry."

He straightened up and walked through the double doors and into the throne room of Wang Wei Wu.

The room beyond was enormous with vaulted ceilings fifty feet high and polished black and red marble floors. The marble floor also had magnificent tile work in the image of a red dragon in the center of the room. Statues of impeccable detail lined the walls on all sides of the room. He saw statues of deities, men, dragons, familiar creatures and creatures that looked very foreign to him. One close to the throne was very strange to him depicting some deity-like creature holding a skull in one hand and a flame in the other. It seemed like there were statues of every creature imaginable, and some imagined.

On the opposite side of the room there was a platform on which the Emperors throne sat. In front of the platform stood four guards that rivaled the size of his bodyguard Bemna. They stood alert and very well armed.

The throne itself was as exquisite as everything else in the room. It appeared to be made entirely of gold and the arms and legs were encrusted with jewels in a rainbow of colors. The high back of the throne had more high polished gemstones making arranged to make the image of the ever-present red dragon.

The value of this throne alone probably rivaled the treasuries of some of the world's countries.

Atop the throne sat one of the most powerful, and ruthless, emperor

China had ever seen. This man killed people for sport and could take over any country in the orient on a whim. He was the most powerful man in the East and not to be trifled with. So powerful in fact those countries around China feared him above all, and began not long ago to hold him in a supernatural light. It was said that he could even read minds.

A tinge of fear washed over Uslum as he thought this last thought. What if Wang Wu was listening to his thoughts at this very moment?

'Nonsense,' he thought to himself, 'an intelligent man would never fall folly to such ideas.'

"An intelligent man," the Emperors booming voice suddenly came to his ears, "would know to bow to ones superior when in his presence."

Uslum froze in his tracks. The four guards drew their swords in perfect unison.

He fearfully bent over at the waist and bowed his head as close to the floor that he could get it. He couldn't help but feel he was offering his neck to these burly guards that stood at the ready before him. He averted his eyes, staring at the floor, as the thought that maybe this man could read minds flashed in his head.

"A thousand pardons your majesty," Uslum said, "I was momentarily captivated by the beauty of your throne room your highness."

"Or was it the beauty of our women?" came the Emperor's reply accompanied by booming laughter.

There was the sound of sheathing swords and the guards joined in the revelry adding their own laughter to the echoes of the Emperors'.

"Rise son of Siam," the emperor said, "China welcomes you!"

The emperor's sandaled feet appeared before Uslums kowtowed eyes. He reluctantly raised his eyes to the emperors smiling face.

He couldn't help the thought that this man could not be the infamous dark hearted ruler of China he had heard so many dark stories about. This man seems to have a almost "jolly" disposition about him. The eyes were warm and the face kind. He felt very confused.

"I don't understand sir," Uslum stuttered.

"It means you can stand up straight son," the Emperor laughed," the formalities are over. Now go back to your room and get some rest for tonight we feast."

The emperor walked him back to the double doors.

"Your highness? Uslum asked.

"Yes Uslum." Wang Wei Wu answered," you may speak freely."

"I was just wondering, why have you taken a special interest in me?"

"Uslum," the Emperor laid a hand on his shoulder," you can say that you are the right type of person that I have in mind for something special."

Uslum just stared at the emperor with a dumbfound look on his face.

"It will all come clear later tonight Uslum, in the meantime go back toyour room and get some rest. Tonight is a big night. And it is all for you!"

As the double doors opened before him he held his breath hoping to see

Meeka there to escort him back to the room. Instead there stood Feing with a evil grin on his face.

"Nice to see you again Mr. Siam," Feing hissed.

The trek back to the room was uncomfortable as expected. He wanted to ask about Meeka but he did not want to let Feing know he cared about her. He did not think that would help her out much with this man, so he chose to keep quiet.

Later that night there was someone else at the door, no Meeka. Another woman, just as beautiful, but not Meeka. The servant girl escorted him to the banquet hall without a word. The banquet hall of the Imperial Court was huge.

A huge throng of people mingled and socialized under its cathedral ceiling. There was every type of food imaginable to man prepared and laid out on giant tables. The smells of food mingled with the smells of incense hanging heavy in the atmosphere of the room. As he stepped inside the doorway he immediately felt the effects of the smoky perfumes that hung in the air. His head began to swim and his vision slightly blurred. A guard came up to him and said he was to escort Uslum to sit at the place of honor at the right hand of the Emperor.

As he was sat down Uslum was beginning to feel detached from his physical body. Time seemed to speed up and everything flew by him in a blur of food, drink and revelry. He seemed to be sitting off to the side watching the night go by as if he were just some interested bystander.

He tried to look for Meeka, but it was in vain. She was not there.

But neither was Feing. That was one bit of news he had no problem dealing with.

The night wore on and whether it be from drunkenness or exhaustion, heads began to hang low and the guests slowly began making their way back to their rooms or homes from winch they came.

Uslum soon became aware that it was down to the emperor, himself and a small contingent of guards left in the huge room.

"Uslum," the emperor said in a concerned voice, "are you okay."

It was then that Uslum noticed that when the emperor spoke his voice seemed to have a strange resonance, the words seemed to not only reach his ears, but his mind in the same instance.

He shook his head as if to try to shake the absorb thought out of his mind. This had to be an effect of the incense he told himself and tried to pull himself together.

"I am just a bit tired." Uslum managed to blurt out. He felt really disoriented and drunk.

"What did you think of your party?'" the emperor asked him.

"Excuse me sir," Uslum replied, confused. "MY party? I don't understand."

"Come with me," the emperor replied, "I have something to show you and

I am going to make you an offer you won't be able to refuse."

The emperor motioned Uslum to follow and he got up and blindly followed him out of the banquet hall of the Imperial Court.

He followed the emperor down several corridors until they came back to the throne room. They walked up to the strange looking statue he had noticed earlier that day. The emperor stood before the creature and bowed his head while he raised a hand pointing his ring and index finger at the strange statue.

He said something in a strange language that sounded alien to Uslum. With

a wave of his hand the statue slid to one side revealing a passageway behind.

"This way," the emperor motioned him to follow.

They made their way down the narrow corridor, which sloped downward for several hundred feet. There were torches every twenty feet or so lighting their way. They came to a spiral staircase leading down even further beneath the Imperial Palace.

They descended the staircase, which led them to another narrow corridor. This passage way ran for fifty feet opening up into a vast room beyond.

Uslum just followed in silence not knowing what to say or what to expect. He had no idea why he was here.

"Your confusion will end soon Uslum." The emperor said. "You soon will understand why you are here."

They passed out of the passageway into a well-lit room beyond. Uslum had to allow his eyes to adjust to the brightness after passing through the darkness of the narrow passageway.

Light poured from above provided by globes that hung from the ceiling suspended by thick chains. The globes lit the room so brightly it was as if it were midday outside.

But Uslum was only impressed briefly in the rooms light fixtures as he quickly scanned the room and took in what the room held.

He was appalled at what he saw and suddenly realized he was in a torture room.

"What do you think?" the emperor smiled.

"I-um, I don't know what to-to say." Uslum stammered. He looked around the room and saw horrific machines made to break bones and break spirits. "Why am I h-here?"

"I want to give you the honor of being one of the first persons to see my new invention." The emperor said as a smile crept

across his face.

Uslum began feeling an intense foreboding. He feared that he was going to do more then 'see' this new invention of the Emperor. By the looks of the other devices that were in this room he did not think it would be too pleasant of an experience.

"Out of due respect," Uslum weakly replied, " I would just as soon this never happened and just return to Siam and tell my king anything you want me to."

With catlike reflexes the emperor was suddenly on him, pressing a hand over Uslum's mouth at the same time pinning him up against a stone column. Uslum hit the column with such force it knocked the wind from his lungs. The Emperor had incredible strength and struggle as he may Uslum just could not break free.

The emperor moved in close staring right into Uslum's eyes. He was so close that Uslum could make out the patterns in the Emperor's irises. Even as his mind raced trying to plan an escape he could not help but to marvel at how blue the emperor's eyes were. The emperor moved his mouth to Uslum's ear and whispered so quietly Uslum could barely hear the words.

"I want to hear you beg for your life."

The Chinese ruler backed away with those catlike reflexes so fast all Uslum saw was a blur.

Uslum immediately crumpled to the floor gasping for air.

Suddenly he felt the emperor's fist hit him on the back of the head and he was facedown on the stone floor.

"Now that is how someone SHOULD bow down before me." The Emperor placed a sandaled foot on the back of his head and pushed his face hard onto the stone floor.

"Now beg Son of Siam."

Uslum rolled to one side up onto his knees. He looked up into the eyes of the most powerful man in the known world and spat at the man's feet.

"Never!" he shouted defiantly.

The emperor began to laugh and Uslum started to see this man was as evil as his laugh was.

He attempted to bolt for the spiral staircase corridor but his way was blocked. The emperor was just too quick.

"Where are you going son of Siam" the emperor toyed with Uslum," this party is in your honor."

The emperor roughly turned him around and shoved him forward toward the opposite end of the room. Uslum stumbled and almost fell from being pushed so hard. They traversed the room to a heavy wooden door on the other side. As they approach the door slowly swung open and there stood Feing.

"Is everything prepared for our guest of honor?" the Emperor asked

Feing.

"All is ready highness," Feing hissed. "Our lady friend has just about done."

"Excellent." The emperor grabbed Uslum by the arm and shoved him across the room. On the other side of the room there stood a metal statue about seven and a half feet high. It had the face of a woman and what appeared to be two halves of a door that apparently opened outward. He noticed an opening on one side and near the bottom of the statue.

A huge clay bowl sat upon the floor just underneath filled with what looked like blood.

The Siamese man noticed there was still some dripping from the opening into the bowl.

Uslum turned and defiantly stared the emperor in the eyes without saying a word.

"How do you like my new invention?" the Emperor walked up close to Uslum. The Siamese envoy just stared straight ahead and did not say a word. "Uslum," the emperor said, a smug look upon his face, "I am sad to say you will not be the first to test the device out even though I had intended that honor to be yours."

"But you did do us the honor of choosing the first person to test it out on." Feing hissed at Uslum. Immediately his heart sank for he knew exactly who Feing was talking about. Feing reached up above the split door on the "statue" and grabbed a small knob and pulled back a small sliding door revealing a small window.

Uslum peered inside and his fears were confirmed. All he could see were the eyes but that is all he needed to see to know that this was Meeka.

"You bastards!!!" he shouted and banged on the statue fists clinched tightly. He noticed to his horror recognition in Meekas eyes and came to the realization she was still alive. Upon seeing his face there was a brief look of relief in her eyes and then they glazed over as the life left her body before his very eyes.

Rage welled up inside him as he turned to face the two Chinese men.

But, Feing suddenly had his arms behind his back and bound his hands tightly. He struggled against the bonds to no avail.

He had never felt so much like killing someone so badly as he did at this very moment.

"You are nothing but barbarians!!" Uslum shouted his voice filled with his inner rage.

"Correction," the Emperor smiled while going over to the statue and opening one of the doors, "We were barbarians, now we are Chinese noblemen."

The Emperor opened the other door and there was an audible ripping sound as spikes that were attached to the inner side of the door freed themselves from Meeka's lifeless body dripping with her blood.

Uslum winched with imagined pain. Meek's body still stood upright in the back of the morbid statue. Even in death her beauty was stunning.

"Beautiful is it not?" The emperor reverently said. "You see the spikes in the back of the 'statue' and the spikes connected to the door are hollow. When the person is placed inside the spikes in the back hold them in place as the doors are closed thus placing spikes into the front of the body holding them completely still."

"You heartless bastard!!!" Uslum shouted, his voice hoarse and racked with pain. He watched as the emperor roughly grabbed Meeka's body and unceremoniously yanked it free of the spikes and threw her to the floor. He broke down into a fit of soft sobbing.

"You see the spikes drain the blood from the person slowly," the Emperor continued on ignoring the interruption." So the beauty of this machine is that you don't die right away. This way there is plenty of time to interrogate the subject without much effort from the torturer to keep applying the pain. Not only does the individual feel excruciating pain the whole time but, claustrophobia as well. And all of this in pitch black-darkness."

"It is absolute genius," Wang Wei Wu bowed.

"I hope you both die horrible deaths." Uslum spat out in between sobs.

"The only horrible death you will see today," Feing said with an evil grin," is your own Son of Siam."

Feing reach out and grabbed him by the shoulders with incredible strength.

"Mind your head!" He effortlessly tossed Uslum's one hundred and eighty five pound frame into the 'statue' as if he was tossing a child's ragdoll. Uslum hit the back of the device with a thud as simultaneously he felt several explosions of searing pain from his shoulders down to his buttocks. He tried to move but he could not budge an inch and every time he winced it aggravated the pain. The Emperor's form filled the opening of the metal statue.

"It would be incredibly helpful," he said with a wink of a blue eye,

"If while you were in there to think of a good name for my new invention."

Uslum tried to reply but one of the spikes had pierced one of his lungs and he could not draw in enough breath to speak.

"I love leaving them speechless!" the emperor laughed and slammed the half door down onto Uslum's body.

He could not even scream as the spikes slammed into his body with searing hot pain. Then the other door came crashing down one second later. He heard the emperor voice from the other side of the metal door barely audible. "Sweet dreams son of Siam."

Everything was quiet. All he heard was the blood rushing in his head. The pain was unbearable and every time he tried to move the tearing spikes made it even worse. All his mind could grasp was the pain. But one stray thought kept crossing his mind through the agony.

'Why me? What did I do to deserve this fate?'

The sliding door slid open and the emperor's face was framed in the opening.

"I told you before," the emperor held up a crystal glass that looked as if it was filled with blood. "You were the right type." With the last comment the little door slammed shut on Uslum and his existence.

Emperor Wang Wei Wu and his Imperial advisor Feing Dong Fu went missing from the Forbidden City a few days later. There was very little remorse shown by the members of the Imperial Court.

It seems that the emperor and his advisor were not well liked by the ruling party in China. The Literati, the scholar class that ran the government, immediately began rewriting the recent history of the unpopular Emperor.

The Literati, being educated in the Confucius beliefs, knew that in time the memory of the dark emperor would fade like a bad winter into a thawing springtime.

Wang Wei Wu had no immediate airs so the Literati put one his distant relatives in power.

The dark stigma the Emperor left on the court was immediately dispelled by the new Ming Dynasty ruler. An age of enlightenment soon followed and the dark Emperor was just a wisp of memory and rumor just a short twenty years later.

History would completely forget the Emperor thirty years later after a broken and elderly Bemna passed on after a vain lifelong search for the emperor who had killed his charge, Uslum. A few short weeks after Bemna had returned to the capitol city of Siam he received a visitor. A cloaked figure showed up banging on his door late one evening delivering a package.

No clue was given to the origin of the package and the stranger disappeared into the night as if he were a ghost. Bemna had left the package alone for several hours unsure as whether he should open it or not. After the entire night passed without any sleep his curiosity finally got the better of him.

He opened the package early the next morning. Inside he found a piece of parchment neatly rolled up and tied with a ribbon. He untied the parchment and carefully unrolled the paper.

Neatly written on the paper was a message addressed to him:

YOUR SERVICES AS BODYGUARD TO USLUM SUNAN ARE NO LONGER NEEDED.

ENCLOSED YOU WILL FIND A TOKEN OF OUR APPRECIATION

OF A JOB WELL DONE.

COMPLIMENTS OF WANG WEI FU, EMPEROR OF CHINA.

Inside the box was an abject wrapped in fine silk. He carefully picked up the object and unwrapped it.

To his horror it was a dismembered finger. What horrified him even further was what was on the finger. A fine piece of Siamese jewelry. A gold ring with the family crest he had seen a thousand times before and knew so well.

This ring was Uslum's, he could only assume the finger belonged to him as well.

"Uslum," he shouted raising a fist toward the sky," I won't rest until Wang Wei Wu dies! This I swear to you!"

Thirty years later the last words he would utter would be an apology to his old employer and friend.

"I have spent my life chasing shadows, I am sorry I have failed you old friend..."

www.ingramcontent.com/pod-product-compliance
Lightning Source LLC
Chambersburg PA
CBHW020615260626
47157CB00003B/1020